The Seduction of the Crimson Rose

'Willig's series gets better with each addition, and her latest is filled with swashbuckling fun, romance, and intrigue'
Booklist

'There is wit, laughter, secrets, lies, grand schemes, and of course all those lovable spies. Don't miss this next instalment of this awesome series by an author who has a talent of keeping her readers glued to the book until the end'
A Romance Review

The Temptation of the Night Jasmine

'Willig spins another sultry spy tale . . . an elegant and grandly entertaining book'
Publishers Weekly

'Witty, smart, carefully detailed, and highly entertaining, Willig's latest novel is an inventive, addictive novel'
Romantic Times

'The characters, romance, history, action and adventure, and most of all the wonderful writing, makes *The Temptation of the Night Jasmine* a superior and definite page-turning reading experience'
Romance Readers Connection

The Mischief of the Mistletoe

'Forget all the Austen updates and clones – Willig is writing the best Regency-era fiction today'
Booklist

'A light-hearted and sweet holiday romance . . . A shift of focus away from espionage and toward Jane Austen makes for a fun, fresh instalment in a successful series'
Kirkus Reviews

'Delightful . . . an exciting story'
Publishers Weekly

A native of New York City, LAUREN WILLIG has been writing romances ever since she got her hands on her first romance novel at the age of six. Like Eloise Kelly, Lauren is the proud possessor of an unfinished Harvard History department dissertation, and spent a year poring over old documents at the British Library before abandoning the academic life for the more lucrative world of law. Once Lauren received her JD magna cum laude from Harvard Law School, she practised as a litigation associate at a large New York firm, but decided that book deadlines and doc review didn't mix and departed the law for a new adventure in full-time writerdom.

www.laurenwillig.com

a&b

The Temptation of the Night Jasmine

LAUREN WILLIG

First published in Great Britain in 2011 by
Allison & Busby Limited
13 Charlotte Mews
London, W1T 4EJ
www.allisonandbusby.com

A CIP catalogue record for this book is available from
the British Library.

First published in the US in 2010.
Published by arrangement with Dutton,
a member of Penguin Group (USA) Inc.

10 9 8 7 6 5 4 3 2 1

ISBN 978-0-7490-0878-9

Typeset in 11/15pt Adobe Garamond Pro by
Allison & Busby Ltd.

The paper used for this Allison & Busby publication
has been produced from trees that have been legally sourced
from well-managed and credibly certified forests.

Printed and bound in the UK by
CPI Bookmarque, Croydon, CR0 4TD

To Abby Vietor
For more reasons than will fit on this page

Prologue

January 2004
Selwick Hall, Sussex

'Not there,' said Colin.

'Huh?' I looked up from slinging my bag onto the guest room bed to see my very recent boyfriend hovering in the doorway, looking as sheepish as a strapping, six-foot-tall Englishman can contrive to look.

'That is, unless you would prefer this room,' he said, developing a sudden interest in the floorboards. 'I had hoped you might stay, um, down the hall, with me, but if you would rather have your own room . . .'

'Oh!' If the floor had been less stubbornly corporeal, I would have sunk through it. 'I just – ooops. Autopilot,' I exclaimed, scooping up my bag with more haste than grace.

Having stayed in that room on my last visit to Selwick Hall, B.D. (before dating), I had automatically retraced my route without giving any consideration to the thought that sleeping arrangements might have changed since then.

I grimaced in what I hoped was a suitably penitent fashion. 'I didn't mean – well, you know.'

It's amazing how many land mines there can be in the first

month of a relationship. Goodness only knows we had had more than our fair share of land mines, rocket fusillades, and artillery batteries in the short period in which we had known each other. And I'm not just referring to romantic sparks.

'I was afraid it was my snoring put you off,' he said with a slight smile, one of those comments that's clearly meant to be a joke but doesn't quite make it.

'No, just your habit of stealing all the covers,' I said, deadpan.

To be honest, I didn't really know whether he snored or not. As for the cover stealing, I just took it on faith. In the month in which we had been dating, there hadn't been as much occasion as I would have liked to find out. He lived in Sussex; I was based in London. My basement flat was the size of a postage stamp, with a sloping bathroom ceiling designed to brain anyone over five and a half feet; he stayed in the flat of his ageing great-aunt when he came to town. While Mrs Selwick-Alderly wasn't exactly anyone's idea of an Edwardian chaperone, I wasn't going to risk being caught sneaking out of Colin's room at two in the morning, like a guilty teenager. I hadn't even been that sort of teenager when I was a teenager.

Our week together in Sussex killed two birds with one stone. One, I got my hands on Colin. Two, I got my hands on his archives.

And by archives, I do mean archives. That was how Colin and I had met, a very long three months ago, on the ides of November.

At that point, I had been in England since August and had learnt three crucial things in that intervening time: (1) if you need to get anywhere, the tube will break down; (2) the reason so many British women have short hair is because their shampoo comes in tiny bottles; and (3) if no one has ever tackled a dissertation topic before, there's probably a reason why.

It was that third item that was the real clincher. I had been so smugly proud of the topic I had chosen as a G3 (that's third-year grad student in Harvard lingo). My colleagues were all working on riveting projects like 'The Construction of Gender Identity in Franco's Spain'; '"Mine Golde Doth Yscape Mee": The Household Accounts of James I'; or, my personal favourite, 'Turnip Mania: The Impact of the Turnip on the English Economy, 1066 – 1215.' Let them have their turnips! My topic was exciting; it was sexy; it involved men in knee breeches. What wasn't there to love about 'Aristocratic Espionage During the Wars with France: 1789 – 1815'?

I had overlooked one crucial fact: Spies do not leave records. If they did, they wouldn't be in business long.

The spy I most wanted to track down, the one spy who had never been unmasked by French agents or American historians, had been in business for a very long time, from 1803 all the way through to Waterloo. No one knew who the Pink Carnation really was – because the Pink Carnation had been at great pains to keep it that way. I wore tracks through the lobby of the Public Records Office at Kew; I froze the reference computers in the Manuscripts Room of the British Library; I nearly got locked into the Bodleian. By November, my laptop was beginning to look more than a little bit battered, as was I.

Fortunately, I had one last card to play.

Not only had Lord Richard Selwick, aka the Purple Gentian, bequeathed a hearty pile of documents to his descendants, their owner, an elegant lady of a certain age, kindly extended to me the right to read them. However, as all readers of fairy tales know, any good treasure trove comes with a dragon. In place of scales, my dragon wore a green Barbour jacket. Instead of a hoard of gold, he considered it his personal duty to guard the cache of family manuscripts. From me.

Have I mentioned that he was a decidedly attractive dragon? When he wasn't breathing fire at me, that was.

Let's just say he came around in time. As Shakespeare so sagely said, all's well that ends well. Not only had I found more material than I could have ever hoped for my dissertation, I had acquired a boyfriend in the process. It was like a buy-one-get-one-free sale. On Manolos.

It was, in a word, the utter end in happily ever afters.

The only problem with happily ever after is the ever after bit. Don't get me wrong, I was happy. And, as far as I could tell, Colin was, too. At least, in the limited time in which we had been together.

Therein lay the rub. A mere two weeks after our first official date, Christmas had flung us our separate ways. My tickets back to New York had been booked and paid for well before there was any whiff of a relationship on the scene. As for Colin, he spent Christmas Day in London with his great-aunt and sister and New Year's in Italy with his mother, all of which made phone calls more than a little bit complicated. Every time I called him, there was invariably someone in the background pulling Christmas crackers (his great-aunt) or jabbering in Italian (his mother, who apparently liked to pretend she wasn't actually English anymore). Every time he rang me, there were my parents, conspicuously pretending not to listen, and my little sister, Jillian, squealing, 'Oooh! Is it the boy?'

Might I add that Jillian is nineteen and at Yale?

Jillian likes to say that she's mature enough to be immature. My parents call it something else entirely, and did so very loudly,

12

contributing to the din as I pressed my cell phone to my ear and tried to sneak off to my bedroom unseen.

Anyway, between our families, we seldom managed more than a few moments on the phone unmolested. By the time I had returned to London, in early January, Colin had gone off on some sort of business trip to foreign climes. To be honest, I wasn't quite sure what his business was. At this stage in the game, it seemed a little tacky to ask. I'd been dating him (even if we hadn't been in the same country for most of it) for nearly a month and a half. Shouldn't I know by now what he did? On the other hand, it was too soon in the relationship to demand to know where he'd been. I was damned if I did and damned if I didn't.

I consoled myself with the thought that it was probably something farm related. From the few comments Colin had made, I got the impression that most of his time these days was involved in trying to make Selwick Hall and its surrounding lands self-supporting, recruiting tenant farmers to do whatever tenant farmers do. Since my knowledge of agriculture is limited to the fact that milk comes from cows, and cows say 'moo' (thank you, Fisher-Price), I didn't have much to contribute on that topic.

Considering that Colin used to be an I-banker or, as he would put it, 'something in the City,' I was surprised that he did. But, then, he had been raised in the country, so perhaps some of it came from pure osmosis. I had been raised in Manhattan. The only thing I had osmosed was how to hail a cab.

'Don't worry,' Colin said as he led the way back down the hall. 'I've stocked up on extra blankets.'

'Women feel the cold more than men,' I said loftily. 'Besides, our clothing is skimpier than yours.'

'Amen to that,' said Colin, with an appreciative squeeze of my shoulders. Not that there was much skin to be squeezed through my layers of shirt, sweater, and quilted Barbour jacket. But I appreciated the thought. That was certainly one way of turning up the thermostat. 'And here we are.'

It was certainly a much larger room than mine – I mean, than the room I had stayed in last time. There were windows on two sides, by which I cleverly deduced we must be in one of the wings rather than in the central block of the house.

The first thing I noticed, naturally, was the bed. It was a big old four-poster, practically high enough to require stairs, prosaically covered with a very modern blue duvet, clearly Colin's contribution. What is it about men that makes them always go for either deep blue or fire engine red for their bed coverings?

Aside from the duvet, and the small change and various personal possessions littering most available surfaces, the bedroom must have been decorated in the late nineteenth century and not overhauled since. Curtains in a William Morris print of twining golden flowers on a crimson background hung from the windows, faded to a pink and beige by continual exposure to the sun. The paper on the walls was the obverse, red flowers on a golden background. It was hard to tell whether the draperies and wallpaper were the original or a reproduction. If they were reproductions, they were very old ones.

'It's the pimpernel print,' said Colin, seeing me looking at the wall.

Huh? Was that like the Poe Shadow or the Da Vinci Code?

'The wallpaper,' Colin said patiently. 'It's Morris's pimpernel print. A bit of an inside family joke, that,' he added.

'Oh!' Wiping off my village idiot expression, I laughed a

little too heartily. 'Of course! Didn't he have any pink carnation paper?' I asked archly, in a belated bid to make up for my sluggishness.

'Too obvious,' said Colin. 'And too feminine.'

'I don't know,' I said, ostentatiously taking in the room, with its heavy, masculine furniture, and incongruous navy blue duvet. 'You could do with a bit of pink in here.'

'I'll settle for one redhead,' said Colin, suiting actions to words.

There are some positives about the early stages of a relationship. I figured I'd better take advantage of it while it lasted, before we descended into the 'who used the last toilet paper roll?' stage of the relationship. If we lasted that long. But I wasn't going to think about such things now. Instead, I happily wound my arms around his neck and concentrated on convincing him that one redhead was a necessary accessory to any room.

After an indeterminate amount of time, we broke apart, smiling foolishly at each other, as one does.

'Right,' said Colin, in that way men do when they're trying to look like they're in control of the situation but haven't the least idea of what they meant to say. I couldn't help feeling a little bit smug. If they can remember their own names, you're doing something wrong. 'Um, right. Make yourself at home.'

I grinned. 'I thought I was.'

'You might want to take off your coat,' Colin suggested mildly. 'And unpack your things.'

'Oh, those.' Things seemed vastly immaterial at the moment. And I didn't like to tell him that taking off my coat seemed a tad too adventurous, given the climate. No, I'm not referring to any fear (or hope) that Colin would commence bodice ripping once the protective armour of my Barbour was removed. I meant the literal climate. It had to be about forty degrees in the house. With deep trepidation, I remembered reading biographies of the Mitfords – or was it someone else? – in which everyone seemed to spend childhoods in English country houses covered with chilblains.

That was one of those little things we'd have to work on. I am a child of central heating. I may have grown up in a cold climate, but I preferred to keep it on the outside and me on the inside, next to a toasty radiator.

But it was still early days, so when Colin reached for my coat, I meekly let him remove it, rather than squealing and clutching desperately at it. I was very glad I had layered on that extra sweater.

I watched indulgently and made suitably admiring noises as he displayed the amenities of his room, including the drawer he had cleaned out for me, presumably by dint of shoving everything that had previously been in it to the back of the wardrobe. There was a phone on the bedside table, email access down the hall in his study, hangers in the wardrobe, and a fine collection of dust bunnies under the bed. He didn't mention those last, but I found them nonetheless. I assessed them with a connoisseur's eye. If one could make a fortune by breeding dust bunnies, I would be endowing chairs at universities.

While Colin checked his cell phone messages, I grabbed a handful of lingerie in two fists and hastily stuffed it into the drawer he had opened for me. I had packed for all contingencies, i.e., a silk slip nightie and a heavy flannel one. Given the temperature in the house, I had a feeling I would be using the flannel.

A door on one side of the room led to an en suite bathroom, confirming my impression that this must be the master suite.

Did Colin's mother really dislike Sussex enough that she had relinquished all claim to residence? All I knew was that she lived in Italy, with a second husband. Colin tended not to talk about his family much. I'd managed to gather that his father had died of cancer a few years back and his mother had decamped to Italy. It was, however, unclear whether the decamping had occurred before or after.

There was no sign that a woman had ever inhabited this room. The furniture was all heavy, dark wood, and the wardrobe and drawers would never have begun to accommodate the accumulated clothing of two people rather than one.

Wiggling my vanity case out of my overnight bag, I padded through to the bathroom, which looked like something out of a *Jeeves and Wooster* episode, only without Wooster's rubber ducky. It was one of those bathrooms that had clearly begun life as something else – a dressing room, perhaps, or a small sitting room. White wainscoting ran all along the walls, which were papered above with yet another Morris print, peeling from the effects of continued steam over time. There was even a rug on the floor, a faded Persian marred and snagged from years of use, with the odd blob of what might have been toothpaste or shaving cream ground into the warp. Hey, it sure beat my Kmart bath mat.

The only concessions to modernity were the modern shower head that had been installed above the tub and the electrical outlets that I was relieved to see had been stuck in at bizarre intervals along the walls. Even the toilet was the old sort, with a wooden case affixed high on the wall with a chain dangling from it.

I efficiently unloaded the necessities of life from my bag. Shampoo and conditioner on the side of the tub (like most men, Colin only had the two-in-one dandruff stuff), glasses and contact lens case on the vanity, toothbrush in the toothbrush holder.

There was something scarily domestic about the way our toothbrushes nestled together in the toothbrush holder, his contact lens solution jostling for space next to my contact lens solution on the vanity.

He wore contacts. I hadn't realised that. There was a lot I didn't know yet, for all the casual assumption of intimacy created by our twin toothbrushes.

Back in the bedroom, Colin was still listening to his voice mail messages. Whatever it was clearly did not please him; his eyebrows had drawn together and there was a twin furrow between them.

He clicked the phone off when he saw me (ah, those early days of relationship), although he still looked abstracted. 'Tea?' he asked. 'Or library?'

'Library,' I said decidedly.

'Do you remember where it is?'

On a scale of one to ten? I gave that about a three. I was pretty sure that it was on the same floor we were on, which narrowed the search down a bit, but I didn't mind opening and closing doors until I found the library. To be honest, I was more than a little curious about Colin's house. If I wanted to pretend I was being a good little historian, I would claim it was because it was the same house owned by the Purple Gentian, the house in which he had plotted and schemed, the house from which he had run – with his wife – his spy school. But, as Colin had told me on a previous visit, the house had been entirely gutted and remodelled in the late nineteenth century, the same time all the Morris prints and Burne-Jones tiles and heavy dark wood panelling had been put in. The only bits that remained intact from the early nineteenth century were the façade, the gardens, and the long drawing room that spanned the entire width of the main block on the garden side.

My desire to prowl around the house had far more to do with the man who occupied it now. It was the same sort of impulse that drives you, early in a relationship, to go through the entirety of the other person's CD collection, as if some deep insight into his character could be gleaned from the fact that he once bought this or that CD. I wanted to see where he lived, how he lived, where he spent his time.

So instead of saying, 'Point me in the right direction,' I smiled confidently and said, 'I should be able to figure it out.'

Colin's hand closed protectively around his mobile. 'You don't mind if I abandon you for a bit? I have some work that needs to be sorted.'

'No problem at all.' In fact, it worked very well for me – even though I was dying to ask him what work exactly he had. Cows, perhaps. Or sheep. Or something left over from his City days. Or just catching up on email, which goodness only knows can be work enough after a long trip without Internet access.

'Brilliant,' Colin said, and flashed me a smile that almost made me want to reconsider this whole going our separate ways for the afternoon thing.

But the archives were calling me. With one last, lingering kiss (yes, we were still at the stage where we kissed hello and goodbye on moving between rooms), I set out down the hallway toward the library.

'Eloise?'

Ah, clearly he could not bear to allow me out of his arms for more than a moment.

'Yes?' I called back, bosom heaving as best it could under a bra, a polo shirt, and a lambswool sweater.

Colin's lips were twitching, and not, I regret to add, with uncontrollable desire. He pointed at the other hallway, the one I had failed to take. 'The library is that way.'

I threw him a little salute. 'Aye-aye, Captain!'

God only knows why I do these things; sometimes my hands and mouth move of their own volition, without any input from my brain. Making a smart about-face, I scurried down the other hallway.

'Just keep on going,' Colin called after me. 'The library is in the East Wing.'

It was very sweet of him to assume that I had any notion where east was. The keep-going bit was more helpful. After a long and arduous journey past many closed doors and a broad hallway that gave onto the central stair, I hit what I presumed must be the East Wing. My presumption was based largely on the fact that the hall stopped going.

As soon as I opened the door, I was back in familiar territory, surrounded by the comfortable smell of old paper and decaying bindings, cracked leather chairs, and musty draperies. It smelt like most libraries I had known (with the exception of certain branches of the New York Public Library, which smell more like disinfectant and eau de bum). Row upon row of crumbling books soared two stories into the air, bisected by an iron balcony that ran along all sides of the room, reached by a twisty iron staircase with tiny pie-shaped steps. Grey January light seeped through the long windows that looked to the north and east, the sort of winter light that obscures more than it illuminates.

Groping along the wall, I found a light switch. After a brief resistance, it finally consented to flip, and a massive two-tiered chandelier hanging from the centre of the ceiling flickered into light. Some of the bulbs never bothered to go on, others blinked twice and then winked out, but there were still enough to cast a reasonable amount of light down over the warm blue carpet with its pattern of red flecks. I do love old libraries, and this was the real deal, a late-nineteenth-century Gothic fantasy complete with a baronial stone fireplace, tenanted with books that had been acquired, read, and loved over the course of more than a century. There was everything from early editions of Dickens, with broken spines and scribbles in the margins, to piles of paperbacks with the lurid covers so common in the seventies. Colin's father had obviously had a taste for spy thrillers.

A veteran after one prior visit, I strode straight to the bookshelves at the back of the room, crouching in front of what looked like mere wainscoting to the uninitiated eye. I expertly twisted the hidden handle, and there it was – a pile of old James Bond novels? That was not what I had been looking for. Scuttling sideways like a crab, I tried the next panel over, and there they were: big old folios with handwritten labels and piles of acid-free boxes bound with twine, with legends like 'Household Acc'ts: 1880 – 1895' in faded type on the labels glued to the sides.

I wasn't interested in the household accounts of the late nineteenth century, or even, although it was more tempting, the diaries of a Victorian daughter of the house. It wasn't my field. Stacking aside the document boxes, I went for the folios in the back, where the older documents were stored.

Someone, a very long time ago, perhaps even that same Victorian young lady, had taken her ancestors' old letters and pasted them into folio volumes. I bypassed 'Correspondence of Lady Henrietta Selwick: March – November 1803' (I had read that volume before) and reached for the one behind it. A slanting hand had written 'Corresp. Lady H'tta, Christmas 1803 – Easter 1804.'

Bingo.

From my recent researches in the Vaughn collection, I knew that the Pink Carnation had gone off to France in October or November of 1803, for unspecified purposes. I needed those purposes specified. What was the Pink Carnation doing in Paris in late 1803? And with whom?

If anyone would know, it would be the Carnation's cousin-by-marriage, Lady Henrietta Selwick. The two had concocted an ingenious code, based on ordinary terms one might expect to see in the innocent letters of two young ladies, things like 'beaux,' and 'Venetian breakfasts,' and 'routs,' all with highly unladylike secret meanings.

Settling back on my heels, I propped the volume open in my lap, flipping over the heavy pages with their double burden of letters glued to either side.

There were faded annotations in the margins and heavy strokes of the same pen crossing out whatever the Victorian compiler felt unsuitable for the eyes of posterity. Fortunately, the ink used by the would-be censor wasn't nearly as good as that of the original authors. It had faded to a pale brown that did little to obscure the darker letters beneath. Although it did say some very interesting things about what later generations considered improper while the Georgians did not. It always fascinated me how much more open mores were in the eighteenth and very early nineteenth century than in the period that came immediately after.

All that was well and good, but there was one thing missing: the Pink Carnation. Not one of the letters in the folio had been written in her distinctive hand. I recognised some from Henrietta's husband, Miles (I had got to know his sloppy handwriting, full of blotches and cross-outs, pretty well the last time I was at Selwick Hall), but most were closely written in a small and swirly script, punctuated by large chunks of dialogue. Had one of Henrietta's friends been playing at novelist? Amused by the notion, I flipped to the back of a letter to check the signature.

Of course. It was Lady Charlotte Lansdowne, Henrietta's best friend and bookworm extraordinaire. Cute, but not necessarily what I was looking for. I could flip through it later, just for fun.

I was reaching for the next folio in the pile, hoping it might prove more useful, when a word on the open page caught my eye. Well, really, it was two words, applied in conjunction. 'king' and 'mad.'

King George had gone mad again in 1804, hadn't he? It was my time period; I was supposed to know these things. Of course he had. And a huge worry it had been to the Prime Minister and his Cabinet, as well as to the queen and his daughters. It had entirely thrown off the conduct of the war with France.

But what had Charlotte and Henrietta to do with the king's madness? And, yet, from the page I was looking at, they certainly had. It was all very curious.

Hmm. Settling back down, I regarded the folio with new interest. I was at Selwick Hall for a whole week, after all, I reminded myself. I had plenty of time to take the odd detour in my research. Besides, I liked Charlotte. Her handwriting was extremely legible. That makes a huge difference to a researcher.

Abandoning any pretence at searching for other materials,

I struggled to my feet with my prize and plumped down in a comfortably sagging armchair next to a gooseneck lamp, wrestling the folio open to the first letter.

Girdings House
Christmas Eve, 1803

My dearest Henrietta,

Isn't Christmas Eve two of the loveliest words in the language? The holly and the ivy have been gathered, and mistletoe hangs from every place we could find to hang it. Turnip Fitzhugh already has a scratched face — not from the ladies resisting his importunities (he hasn't made any, except to Penelope, who finds it a great joke rather than otherwise), but because he can never seem to remember to duck when he walks under the low-hanging bits. But the greenery isn't all we brought in tonight. If I tell you who has come to Girdings, I have no doubt you will think I write in jest. But it is true, darling Henrietta, even if I have to pinch myself to believe it . . .

24

Chapter One

Lady Charlotte Lansdowne's knight in shining armour finally appeared on a cold Christmas Eve. Not only was he three years late (an appearance on the eve of her first Season would have been much appreciated), but he appeared to have mislaid his armour somewhere. Instead of a silver breastplate, he was wrapped in a dark military cloak, the collar pulled up high against his chin. His steed was grey rather than white, dappled with dun where trotting on winter-wet roads had flung up patches of mud.

Charlotte noticed none of that. With the torchlight blazing off his uncovered head reflecting a seeming helmet of molten gold, he looked just like Sir William Lansdowne, the long-dead Dovedale who had fought so bravely at the Battle of Agincourt. At least, he looked just like what the seventeenth-century painter who had composed the murals along the Grand Staircase had imagined Sir William Lansdowne looked like.

As the visitor reined in his horse, Charlotte could hear the bugles cry in her head, the clatter of steel against steel as armoured knights clashed, horses slipping and falling in the churned mess of mud and blood. She could see Sir William rise in his stirrups as the French bore down upon him, the Lansdowne pennant whipping bravely behind him as he cried, 'A moi! A Lansdowne!'

Charlotte staggered forwards as something bumped into her from behind.

It wasn't a French cavalry charge.

'Really, Charlotte,' demanded the aggrieved voice of her friend Penelope. 'Do you intend to go out or just stand there all day?'

Without waiting for an answer, Penelope edged around her onto the vast swathe of marble that fronted the entrance to Girdings House, the principal residence of the Dukes of Dovedale. The basket Penelope was carrying for the purpose of collecting Christmas greenery scraped against Charlotte's hip.

'Oh, visitors,' said Penelope without interest. 'Shall we go?'

'Mm-hmm,' agreed Charlotte absently, without the slightest idea of what she was agreeing to.

The man in front of the house rose in his stirrups, but instead of shouting archaic battle cries, he took the far more mundane route of swinging off his horse and tossing the reins to a servant. He wore no spurs to jangle as he landed, just a pair of muddy boots that had not seen the ministrations of a valet for some time. Behind him, his friend did likewise.

'Do you know them?'

It took her a moment to realise that Penelope had spoken. Considering the question, Charlotte shook her head. 'I don't think so.'

Given her tendency to go off into daydreams during introductions, she couldn't be entirely sure, but she thought she would have recognised this man. His wasn't the sort of face one forgot.

It didn't affect Penelope in the same way. But, then, Penelope had always been remarkably hardheaded when it came to the opposite sex, perhaps because they were anything but hardheaded when it came to her.

Shrugging, Penelope said, 'Well, your grandmother will know. They must be more of the Eligibles.'

The Eligibles was Penelope's careless catchall for the men Charlotte's grandmother had invited to spend the Christmas season at Girdings. All were young – well, except for Lord Grimmlesby-Thorpe, who was closer to fifty than thirty, even if he did paint his cheeks and pad his pantaloons to provide the illusion of youth. All had the prospect of titles in their future. And all were in want of a dowry.

It was, in fact, all a bit like a fairy tale, with all the princes in the land invited to vie for her hand. Or it might have been, if the group hadn't tended more towards toads than princes.

Tearing her eyes away from her knight without armour, Charlotte looked thoughtfully at her friend. 'I don't think they can be. Grandmama only invited ten, and they've all arrived.'

Penelope regarded the newcomers with somewhat more interest than she had shown before. Her face took on a speculative expression that Charlotte recognised all too well. She had last seen it right before Penelope had 'borrowed' Percy Ponsonby's perch phaeton and driven it straight into the Serpentine. The Serpentine had been an accident. The borrowing had not.

'Perhaps these are *in*eligibles, then. Let's introduce ourselves, shall we?'

'Pen!' Charlotte grabbed at the edge of her cloak, but it was too late. Penelope was already descending the stairs, hips and basket swinging.

Since there was no way of stopping Penelope short of flinging herself at her and toppling them both down the stairs, Charlotte did what she always did. She followed along behind.

Pen paused two steps from the bottom, using the added height for good effect. With the torchlight flaming off her hair, she looked more like a Druid priestess than a minor baronet's daughter. 'Good evening, gentlemen,' she called across the divide. 'What brings you this far from Bethlehem?'

The darker one, the one whom Charlotte hadn't noticed, made a flourishing obeisance. 'Following your star, fair lady. Is there any room at the inn?'

Men said things like that to Penelope.

They did not, however, generally look right past Penelope, furrow their brow, and stare at Charlotte. They most certainly did not ignore Penelope altogether, take two steps forwards, hold out a hand, and say, 'Charlotte?'

And, yet, that was precisely what Charlotte's knight without armour did.

'Charlotte?' he asked again, with a bemused smile. 'It *is* Cousin Charlotte, isn't it?'

'Cousin' wasn't quite the endearment she had been hoping for.

'Cousin?' Charlotte echoed. Although her grandmother claimed kinship with any number of peers and minor princes, the Dovedale family tree had run thin for successive generations. There were very few with any real right to call her by that name. 'Cousin *Robert*?'

His eyes, brilliantly blue in his sun-browned face, crinkled at the corners as he smiled down at her. 'None other,' said the long-absent Duke of Dovedale.

'Oh,' said Charlotte stupidly. What on earth did one say to someone who had disappeared well over a decade ago? 'Hello?'

Somehow, that didn't seem quite adequate, either.

'Hello,' her cousin said back, as though it seemed perfectly adequate to him.

'Cousin?' echoed Penelope, who didn't like to be left out. 'I wasn't aware you had any.'

The connection was so tenuous as to make the term more a courtesy than an actuality. The Dovedale family tree had been a sparse one over the past few generations, sending the title scrambling back over branches and shimmying down collateral lines until it reached Robert, at the outermost fringe of the ducal canopy. Robert was, if Charlotte recalled the intricacies of her family tree correctly, the great-grandson of her great-grandfather's half brother, having been the progeny of her great-great-grandfather's much younger second wife. Her grandmother had been furious at the quirk of fate that had sent the title spiralling towards an all but unrelated branch, with a claim more tenuous than that of the Tudors to the Plantagenet throne, but formalities were formalities and courtesies were courtesies, so cousins they were, as long as they bore the Lansdowne name.

Charlotte looked from her cousin to Penelope and quickly back again, just to make sure he was still really there. He was. It seemed utterly impossible, but there he was, after – how many years had it been? Closer to twelve than ten.

She had been nine, a silent child in a silent house, still in mourning for her mother, watching helplessly as her father lay dying in state in the great ducal bedchamber, a wax figure on a field of crimson and gold. Terrified of the sharp-tongued grandmother who had snatched her up like the witch out of one of the tales her mother used to tell her, shivering with loneliness in the great marble halls of Girdings, Charlotte had been numb with grief and confusion.

And then Cousin Robert had appeared.

He had must have been fifteen, but to Charlotte, he had seemed impossibly grown-up, as tall and golden as the illustration of Sir Gawain in her favourite storybook. She had shrunk shyly out of the way (she had got used to staying out of the way by then, after nine months at Girdings), a book clasped in front of her like a shield, but her big, handsome cousin had hunkered down on one knee and said, in just that way, 'Hello, Cousin Charlotte. You are Cousin Charlotte, aren't you?' and Charlotte had lost her nine-year-old heart.

He didn't look the same. He was still considerably taller than she was – that much hadn't changed – but his face was thinner, and there were lines in it that hadn't been there before. The healthy, red-cheeked English complexion she remembered had been burnt brown by harsher suns than theirs. That same sun had bleached his dark blond hair, which had once been nearly the same shade as hers, with streaks of pale gilt.

But when he smiled, he was unmistakably the same man. The very stone of Girdings seemed to glow with it.

'Yes,' Charlotte said as a dizzy smile spread itself across her face. 'This is my cousin.'

'I wish my cousins greeted me like that,' groused the dark-haired man, his eyes still on Penelope, who didn't pay him any notice at all.

'Happy Christmas, Cousin Charlotte,' her cousin said, her hand still held lightly in his. It felt quite comfortable there.

Giving her hand a brief squeeze, he relinquished it. Charlotte could feel the ghost of the pressure straight through her glove.

'But—' Charlotte shook her head to clear it. 'Not that I'm not very happy to see you, but aren't you meant to be in India?'

'I was in India,' said her cousin blandly. 'I came back.'

'One does,' put in his friend, with such a droll expression that Charlotte would have smiled back had all her attention not been fixed so entirely on her cousin, who was leaning towards her with one elbow propped against a booted knee.

'I take it you didn't get my letter.'

'Letter? No, we received no letter.' As witty repartee went, that wasn't much better, but at least it was a full sentence.

The duke exchanged an amused look with his friend. 'I have no doubt it will arrive eight months from now, having travelled on a very slow boat by way of Jamaica, Greenland, and the Outer Hebrides.'

'Don't tell me you've been to the Outer Hebrides,' drawled Penelope.

'No, just India,' said the newly returned duke, as though it were the merest jaunt.

India! The very name thrilled Charlotte straight down to her bootlaces. She imagined elephants draped in crimson and gold, bearing dusky princes with rubies the size of pigeons' eggs in their turbans. A thousand questions clamoured for the asking. Was it all as exotic as it seemed? Had he ridden an elephant? Did the men there really keep multiple wives? Why had he come back? And why couldn't he have come back on a day when she wasn't wearing an ancient cloak with her nose dripping from the cold?

It wasn't that Charlotte hadn't known he would come back

someday. He was the Duke of Dovedale. He had estates and tenants and all sorts of responsibilities that were supposed to be his, even if her grandmother had blithely appropriated them all years ago, as though the existence of a legitimate claimant were nothing more than a troublesome technicality. It was just that in Charlotte's daydreams, his return had usually occurred at the height of summer, in a choice corner of the gardens. She was also usually a foot taller and stunningly beautiful, too, neither of which seemed to have occurred in the past ten minutes.

Charlotte looked hopelessly at the barren stretch of ground, the empty stairs, the thick smoke from the torchères that smudged seamlessly into the early December dusk. This was no fit welcome for anyone, much less for the return of the duke after a decade abroad. There should have been fanfare and trumpets, servants in livery, and Grandmama there to greet him with her own peculiar brand of regal condescension. There was something shameful about so shabby a welcome.

'Had we known you were coming, we would have made proper provision to welcome you home.'

Her cousin's eyes flickered upwards, over the vast and imposing façade of Girdings. 'Lined the servants up and all that?'

'Something like that,' Charlotte acknowledged, feeling very small on the broad stairs with the vast stone bulk of the house towering behind her. 'Grandmama does like the grand feudal gesture.'

'I think I prefer this,' said Robert, in a way that made the sentiment into a nice little compliment to her. 'I can do without the banners and trumpets.'

'Although a blazing fire would be nice,' added his friend

plaintively, rubbing his gloved hands together. 'A flagon of ale, a few plump—'

'*Tommy*.'

'—pheasants,' finished Tommy, with a wounded expression. 'We've been travelling since dawn,' he added for the ladies' benefit.

'And by dawn, he means noon,' corrected Robert. 'Cousin Charlotte, may I present my comrade in arms and thorn in my flesh, First Lieutenant Thomas Fluellen, late of His Majesty's Seventy-fourth Foot.'

Lieutenant Fluellen bowed with a fluid grace spoilt only slightly by the broad grin he gave her in rising. 'Many thanks for your kind hospitality, Lady Charlotte.'

'It's really Cousin Robert's house, so it's he you have to thank.'

'I'd rather thank you,' said Lieutenant Fluellen winningly, but his eyes snuck past her to Penelope as he said it.

'Behave yourself, Tommy. It's been a very long time since he's been in the company of gentlewomen,' Robert explained in an aside to Charlotte.

'I would never have guessed,' said Charlotte staunchly. 'I think he's doing quite well.'

She was rewarded with a beaming smile. 'My five sisters will be more than delighted to hear that. They all took it in turn to beat some manners into me.'

'And all the sense out,' finished Robert, banging his hands against his upper arms to warm them. His breath left a fine mist in the air.

'Won't you come inside?' said Charlotte belatedly, gesturing towards the doors. The doors obligingly swung open, spilling out light and warmth. The servants at Girdings were impeccably trained. Charlotte looked guiltily from Lieutenant Fluellen's red nose to her cousin's faintly blue lips. 'I don't know about the ale, but there's plenty of hot, spiced wine to be had, and a very warm fire besides.'

No one needed to be asked twice. The gentlemen trooped gratefully into the entrance hall, where a fire crackled in one of the two great hearths. The other lay empty, waiting for the Yule log, which would be ceremonially dragged in later that evening. The dowager duchess kept to the old traditions at Girdings. The holly, the ivy, and the Yule log were always brought in on Christmas Eve and not a moment sooner.

Robert looked ruefully at the red ribbons Charlotte had tied around the carved balusters on the stairs. 'We hadn't meant to intrude on Christmas Eve.'

'Can you really intrude on your own house?' asked Charlotte.

'Is it?' Robert said. His eyes roamed along the high ceiling with its panorama of inquisitive gods and goddesses, leaning out of Olympus to rest their elbows on the gilded frame. His gaze made the circuit of the hall, passing over the vibrant murals depicting the noble lineage of the House of Dovedale, from the mythical Sir Guillaume de Lansdowne receiving his spurs from William the Conqueror on the field of Hastings, past Charlotte's favourite hero of Agincourt, all the way up to the first Duke of Dovedale himself, boosting a rakish-looking Charles II into an oak tree near Worcester as perplexed Parliamentarian troops peered about nearby. 'I keep forgetting.'

'It is a bit overwhelming, isn't it?' Charlotte automatically reached out to touch his arm and then thought better of it. Letting her hand fall to her side, she tilted her head back to stare at the familiar figure of Sir William Lansdowne, who really did look remarkably like Robert, if he had been wearing gauntlets and breastplate and waving a bloodied sword. 'I felt that way, too, initially.'

'I remember,' Robert said, looking not at the murals but at her. And then: 'I was sorry to hear about your father.'

Charlotte bit down hard on her lower lip, willing away a sudden prickle of tears. It was ridiculous to turn into a watering pot over something that had happened so very long ago. Eleven years ago, to be precise. By the time her father died, Robert had been five months gone from Girdings, far away across the sea.

'It was a very long time ago,' Charlotte said honestly.

'Even so.'

Lieutenant Fluellen looked curiously from one to the other, his brown eyes as bright and inquisitive as a squirrel's. Fortunately, Charlotte was spared explanations by the intrusion of a rumbling noise, which became steadily louder.

Both Penelope and Charlotte, who recognised it instantly for what it was, stepped back out of the way as the noise resolved itself into the synchronized rhythm of four pairs of feet. The four sets of feet belonged to four bewigged and powdered footmen, who bore on their shoulders a litter covered with enough gold leaf to beggar Cleopatra. On a thronelike chair in the centre of the litter, draped in purple silk fringed with gold, perched none other than the Dowager Duchess of Dovedale, the woman who had launched a thousand ships – as their crews rowed for their lives in the opposite direction. She inspired horses to rear, jaded roués to blanch beneath their rouge, and young fops to jump out of ballroom windows. And she enjoyed every moment of it.

The skimpy dresses in vogue had struck the dowager duchess as dangerously republican. The dowager preferred the fashions of her youth, so she had never stopped wearing them. In honour of Christmas Eve, she was garbed in a gown of rich green brocade glittering with gold thread. Her hair had been piled into a coiffure reminiscent of the work of agitated spiders, crowned with a jaunty sprig of mistletoe.

As the duchess rapped her fabled cane against the side of the litter, her four bearers came to a practiced halt.

'Good evening, Grandmama,' said Charlotte primly. 'You do remember Cousin Robert—'

'Of course, I remember him! I may have lost my looks, but I still have my wits. So, you've come home at last, have you? Took you long enough.'

'Had I known I would receive such a gracious welcome, I would have come sooner.'

'Hogwash,' the duchess snorted. She gestured imperiously with her cane. 'Don't stand there gawking! Help me out of this thing!'

The footmen stood, impassive, holding their gilded poles, as Lieutenant Fluellen rushed into attendance.

'Wouldn't a wheeled chair have sufficed?' enquired the prodigal duke blandly.

The dowager paused with her hand on Lieutenant Fluellen's arm, one leg extended over the side. 'And break my neck on the stairs? You only wish, my boy! I used to have these lot' – she waved a dismissive hand at the footmen – 'carrying me around, but I didn't want them to get too familiar. Gave them ideas above their station.'

Robert's mind boggled at the notion of the blank-faced footmen being stirred to uncontrollable passion by the dowager's wrinkled face and grasshopper arms.

Tommy simply looked stunned, although that could, in

part, have been because the dowager had landed on his foot in passing.

'Ah, these old legs aren't what they once were,' mused the dowager, wiggling a red-heeled shoe. 'In my day I could out-dance half the men in London. Outrun them, too.' She emitted a short bark of laughter. 'Except when I wanted to be caught, that is. Those were the days.' She shook her cane in the face of a practically paralytic Tommy. 'Who's this young sprig and what is he doing in my hall?'

Robert very nobly refrained from pointing out that it was, in fact, his hall. 'May I present Tommy Fluellen, late of His Majesty's service?'

'Welsh?' demanded the duchess.

'With the leek to prove it,' Tommy replied cheerfully.

The dowager regarded him thoughtfully. 'There was a Welsh princess married into the family in the twelfth century. Angharad, they called her. I doubt you are related.'

The dowager duchess turned her gimlet gaze on the duke, for an inspection that went from his bare head straight down to the mud on the toes of his boots.

'You do have the Lansdowne look about you,' she admitted grudgingly. 'At least you would, if you weren't burnt brown as a savage. What were you thinking, boy?'

'Not of my complexion.'

'Hmph. That's clear enough. Still, you look more of a Lansdowne than Charlotte.' The dowager jerked her head in Charlotte's direction by way of acknowledgment. '*She* favours her mother's people.'

Charlotte was well aware of that. She had heard it often enough over the years she had lived under her grandmother's care. The dowager duchess had never forgiven Charlotte's father, the future Duke of Dovedale, for running off with a humble vicar's daughter.

It hadn't mattered one whit to the duchess that the vicar had been the grandson of an earl or that Charlotte's mother had been undeniably a gentleman's daughter. The duchess had had her heart set on a grand match for her only son, the sort of match that could be counted in guineas and acres and influence in Parliament.

They had been happy, though, even in exile. Or perhaps they were happy because they were in exile. When she tried very hard, Charlotte could remember a golden age before she had come to Girdings, when she and her father and mother had lived together in a little house in Surrey, a quaint little two-storied house with dormer windows and ivy growing over the walls and a stone sundial in the garden that professed only to count the happy hours.

The duchess had never forgiven them for being happy, either.

Ignoring the duchess, Robert bent his head towards Charlotte. 'I regret I never had the honour of meeting your mother.'

'*She* was not a Lansdowne,' the duchess sniffed.

Robert cocked an eyebrow at the duchess. 'If everyone were a Lansdowne, where would be the distinction in being one?'

'Impertinence!' The duchess's cane cracked against the tiles like one of Jove's thunderbolts. 'I like that in a man.'

Her cousin caught her eye, making a face of such mock desperation that Charlotte had to bite her lip to keep from smiling. His friend simply looked mesmerised.

'You'll have the ducal chambers, of course,' said the duchess. 'Don't look so frightened, boy! You shan't find me through the connecting door.'

'I wouldn't want to dispossess you.'

'I occupy the *queen's* chambers.' Having established her proper position, somewhere just to the right of Elizabeth I, the duchess waved a dismissive hand. 'These gels will introduce you to the rest of the party. You may find some acquaintances from India among them. Not a one worth knowing in the lot of them.'

She snapped her fingers, and the pole-bearers dutifully sank to their knees.

'You!' she barked, and four different potential yous stood to attention all at once. 'Yes, you! The one with the leek!'

Lieutenant Fluellen snapped into parade-ground pose.

'Well?' the duchess demanded, batting arthritic eyelashes. 'Don't you know to help a lady into her litter?'

'It would be my honour?' ventured Lieutenant Fluellen.

The duchess favoured him with a smile as her pole-bearers struggled to their feet. 'Correct answer. You may keep your head. For now.'

And with that, she swept off, her bearers' feet beating a staccato tattoo against the marble floor.

'Good Lord,' breathed Lieutenant Fluellen. It wasn't a prayer.

'Grandmama seems to have taken a fancy to you.'

'A fancy?' echoed Lieutenant Fluellen incredulously. 'I'd hate to see her take against someone.'

'Oh, no,' Charlotte hastened to reassure him. 'Grandmama generally just ignores people she doesn't like. She doesn't believe in wasting her energy on them.' She caught Robert's eyes on her again, too shrewd for comfort, and hastened to change the subject. 'Do you have any baggage?'

'Our bags are in Dovedale village. We thought it better not to presume upon our welcome.'

There it was again, the past, jabbing at them. Charlotte lowered her eyes. 'I'm sorry if Grandmama was . . . unkind, all those years ago. She—'

'She had every right to be,' her cousin interrupted flatly. 'She was remarkably well behaved under the circumstances.'

Lieutenant Fluellen looked from one to the other with undisguised curiosity. 'I feel as though I'm missing something.'

'Most of your wits,' countered Robert amiably.

'I packed them in my other case. Which, by the way, is still at the Rusty Dove in Dovedale village.' He turned to Charlotte. 'What *is* a rusty dove?'

It was too clumsy a change of subject not to be deliberate. Charlotte liked him tremendously for it.

'It's my guess that rusty is a corruption of "russet,"' she explained earnestly. 'The first Duke of Dovedale had red hair, you see. Hence the Russet Dove, in compliment to the duke.'

Lieutenant Fluellen looked critically at his friend. 'If they named a tavern for Rob, it would have to be the Muddy Dove. Did you leave any dirt on the road between here and Dovedale, Rob?'

'An adage about pots and kettles comes to mind.' The duke turned his attention back to Charlotte with an alacrity that would have been flattering if she hadn't had the impression that his thoughts were a million miles away. Or perhaps only several thousand miles away, across the seas in India. 'The duchess mentioned visitors from India?'

'Only one,' Charlotte said apologetically, wishing she could offer him more. 'Lord Frederick Staines.' Something in Robert's expression prompted her to add, 'Do you know him?'

'Only by reputation,' said Robert smoothly. 'But I look

forward to knowing him better. We old India hands tend to band together.'

Penelope swung her basket in the direction of the door. 'Lord Frederick and the rest of the party should be outside already, cutting holly and mistletoe. If you join us, you can meet him.'

'Although I imagine you'd probably prefer to stay by a hot fire at this point,' Charlotte put in, with a glance at her cousin's chapped cheeks. Much as she wished he would join them, it would be cruel to drag him back out into the cold. It was silly to imagine that if she let him out of her sight, he would disappear again, like a cavalier in a daydream, riding back off into the haze of her imagination.

Or, as he had twelve years ago, packing and stealing away without a word to any of them at all.

'Rather,' agreed Lieutenant Fluellen wholeheartedly. 'A hot fire, a hot fire, my kingdom for a hot fire.'

He looked like he might have expatiated on that theme, but the duke preempted him by strolling deliberately towards the door. Glancing back over his shoulder, the duke winked at Charlotte in a way that made her stomach flutter like five and twenty blackbirds baked in a pie.

'Come, Tommy,' he said easily. 'Where's your seasonal spirit? How often does one have the chance to participate in a proper country Christmas?'

Lieutenant Fluellen held out both hands palms up, in the traditional gesture of surrender. 'How could one refuse?'

Chapter Two

There were many emotions Robert Lansdowne, fifth Duke of Dovedale, might have experienced upon returning to his ancestral home. Elation. Triumph. Fear. Mostly, he just felt cold.

Charlotte was right: He was longing for a hot fire. Preferably a dozen of them all at once. After a decade overseas, he had nearly forgotten the merciless chill of an English winter. Robert thought back to all those soldiers he had known in India who had spent half their time mooning over memories of England, saying fatuous things like, 'Oh, to see a good English winter.' Madmen, the lot of them. He had lost the ability to feel his feet somewhere just west of King's Lynn. Since he was upright, he assumed they were still attached to his legs, but he wouldn't have been willing to vouch to their presence in any court of law. As to the rest of him . . . well, it didn't bear thinking about. At this point, fire and brimstone were beginning to sound more like a promise than a threat. The Devil could have his soul for the price of a hot water bottle.

Yet here he was, turning his back on the promise of whatever warmth might be available in this frosty and unpleasant land, and going voluntarily out into that cold night. It was only just past five, but the early winter dusk had already fallen, turning the ground of Girdings House dark as night. The great parkland stretched before them like the uncharted seas of a medieval explorer's map, the topiary rearing from the landscape like sea serpents along the way. The torches placed at intervals along the uneven paths served more to cast shadows than to illuminate, making two of every shrub and tree.

Ahead of him, his cousin bobbed around, peeking over her shoulder. Wisps of blond hair had escaped from her hood, sparkling like angel dust in the light of the torches interspersed along the path. At the sight of him there behind her, she looked – pleased. As though she had actually meant those words of welcome. They did say time healed all wounds. But then, people said a lot of bloody silly things. Didn't she realise that she wasn't supposed to be happy to see him?

Robert decided it probably wasn't in his own best interest to remind her of that.

He sent a warm smile her way, undoubtedly a wasted gesture given the uncertainty of the lighting and the fact that her friend was already claiming her attention with a hand on her arm and a whispered comment that made his cousin laugh and shake her hooded head.

Little Charlotte. Who would have thought it? She was still very much Little Charlotte, Robert thought with a slight smile, for all that she must be turned twenty. The top of her bright red hood came up just to her taller friend's ear, and she walked with a bouncing step that was nearly a skip. He remembered her as she had been, a whimsical, wide-eyed little thing with rumpled blond curls that no one ever bothered to brush and a disconcertingly adult way of speaking.

He hadn't thought to find her back at Girdings. To be honest, he hadn't thought about her at all. Cultivating family ties hadn't been high on his list of objectives in returning to Girdings. Coming back to Girdings had been no more than a necessary evil, a means to an end.

Next to him, Tommy sunk his chin as deeply into his collar as it would go, which made him look like a disgruntled turtle. 'Feather beds,' he muttered. 'Mulled wine. A fire. Remind me why we're here again?'

It required only one word. 'Staines.'

'Oh. Right.' Tommy sunk his head even deeper into his collar. 'If he has any sense, he won't be out here, either.'

'Sense isn't something he's known for.'

Tommy wrinkled his brow, the only bit of him still visible over his collar. 'Who's the less sensible – he for being out here, or we for following him?' When Robert didn't answer him, his tone turned serious. Swiping wool out of the way of his mouth, he said very carefully, 'Rob – are you sure this is a good idea?'

Since that wasn't a question Rob wanted to examine too closely, he countered it with one of his own. As he had learnt from Colonel Arbuthnot, a good offensive was always the best approach when one was on weak territory. 'Do you have a better one?'

Tommy looked wistfully back along the alleyway to the great house behind him, the windows ablaze with light. 'This is a nice little place you have here. We could just forget about this whole revenge thing, have some mulled wine, enjoy the holiday . . .'

Robert's spine stiffened beneath layers of wool. 'It's not about revenge. It's about justice.'

'I take it that's a no to the mulled wine, then.'

'Don't you want to see justice served?'

'General Wellesley—'

'—has other things to worry about.' When Robert had tried to voice his suspicions to the general's aides, he had been laughed out of the mess.

But, then, what commander wanted to hear that one of his own officers had betrayed him? In the flush of victory after Assaye, no one had wanted to talk about what might have gone wrong. What was one murdered colonel when the day had been so gloriously won? People die in battle. And if a man died from a shot in the back from his own side, well, that was regrettable but far from unheard of. It was battle. People lunged and mingled and dashed about. It was not always possible to make sure that bullets went where they were supposed to go. That was what they had said, in a patronising tone that suggested that, after a decade in the army, he ought to have known that, too.

Except that this bullet had gone exactly where it was supposed to go – right into Colonel Arbuthnot's back.

For the thousandth time, Robert wandered the torturous paths of might have been. It might have all turned out so differently if only he had paid more attention to the colonel that night, when the colonel had told him that he suspected Arthur Wrothan of selling secrets to the enemy. Robert had been ready enough to believe it. He had never liked Wrothan, with his sly quips, his toadying ways, and that absurd sprig of jasmine he affected, more suited to a London dandy rather than a commissioned officer in His Majesty's army. But Robert had been preoccupied with the day to come, with the battle to be fought. There would be plenty of time to deal with Wrothan later, after the battle; plenty of time to interest the proper authorities and turn the whole bloody mess over to them. It had never occurred to Robert that Wrothan might strike first and strike fatally.

It had never occurred to him – but it ought to have. The scent of jasmine still made his stomach churn with remembered guilt.

That, however, was not something he was going to admit to Tommy. 'If Wrothan did it once, what makes you think he won't betray us again? Who will die next time? Are you willing to take that risk?'

'You make it bloody hard to argue with you,' muttered Tommy from the depths of his collar. 'It's deuced unfair.'

'Maybe that's because I'm right.'

'Or just bloody-minded.'

'That, too,' agreed Robert genially. 'Are you in?'

'I'm here, aren't I?'

'Are you sure it's not just for the feather beds?'

Tommy sunk his chin deeper into his scarf. 'I'll let you know when I see one,' he said dourly.

Robert clapped a friendly hand on his shoulder. 'Good chap. Once this business is done . . .'

And there he stuck. Once Wrothan had been brought to justice, preferably on the point of his sword, he hadn't the foggiest notion what to do next. He had sold his commission before leaving India, selling with it the only life he knew. There was a big blank stretch beyond, terra incognita, as forbidding and faceless as the winter-dark grounds of Girdings House.

If he had any sense, he would take Tommy's perfectly logical suggestion and make his pretended return to Girdings a real one, settle the ducal mantle around his shoulders, and . . . what? He hadn't the foggiest notion of what a duke was supposed to do. He wasn't even sure if dukes wore mantles.

He was a mistake, a fluke, a duke by accident, and when it came down to it, he'd rather face an oncoming Mahratta army. At least he would know what to do with the army.

For a moment, it almost seemed as though his wish had been granted. As they rounded a curve in the path, heading towards a stand of trees, torches flared into view and what had been a low rumble escalated into a full-fledged din.

Man-high torches sent orange flames into the sky, casting a satanic glow over the men disporting themselves about the edge of the forest. If it was an army, it was an unusually well-dressed one. The flames licked lovingly over silver watch fobs and polished boot tops, scintillating off signet rings and diamond stickpins. Charcoal crackled in low, three-legged braziers, emitting heat and plumes of sullen, dark smoke. To add to the confusion, dogs darted barking underfoot, worrying at fallen leaves, snapping at boot tassels, and getting in the way of the liveried servants who circulated among the mob offering steaming glasses balanced on silver trays.

Judging from the raucous tone of the men's voices, the liquid was not tea but something much, much stronger.

'Ah,' Robert said smoothly. 'We seem to have found the rest of the party.'

Tommy eyed the dogs and torches with deep suspicion. 'They look like they're about to hunt down a head of peasant.'

Robert stuck his hands in his pockets and assumed a superior expression. 'Don't be absurd. Peasant is too tough and stringy. Hardly worth the bother.'

He wished he felt quite so sure as he sounded. For all his urbane words, there was something distinctly off-putting about the pampered lordlings prancing along the edge of the forest. The torchlight distended their open jaws and lent a yellow cast to their teeth, making exaggerated caricatures of their features, turning them into something predatory, primal, their faces florid in the flaring light of the torches.

These were the sort of men Arthur Wrothan had collected around him in India, the spoilt, the bored, the wealthy. That was how Wrothan had operated. He had battened on the young aristocrats playing at soldier, winning their loyalty by introducing them to all the vices the Orient had to offer. He had made a very special sort of club out of it, one that operated by invitation only. It was a group Robert had steered well clear of – he had no use for amateur officers dabbling in debauchery and even less for bottom-feeders like Wrothan – but in such a small world, it was impossible not to know of them.

They had tended to travel en masse, Wrothan's lordlings, clattering into the officers' mess in a burst of clanking spurs, gleaming silver buttons, and shouted ribaldries, well-groomed hair as burnished as their buttons, cheeks flushed with drink rather than sun. They reminded Robert of the thoroughbred horses his father used to take him to see race at Newmarket, glossy on the surface, but skittish underneath. In the midst of those animal high spirits, one would invariably find Wrothan, calm and contained, the dark kernel at the centre of the storm.

Lord Frederick Staines had been Wrothan's greatest coup and most devoted acolyte. His selling out of the army at the same time as Wrothan might have been coincidence – but Robert doubted it.

Under pretence of adjusting his collar, Robert scanned the group of men under the trees. Aside from his cousin and her friend, the group consisted almost entirely of men, shrouded in many-caped greatcoats, boots shining as though they had never touched anything so mundane as earth. Between high collars and low hat brims, it was next to impossible to make out individual features. To Robert's prejudiced eyes, they all seemed cast from the same mould: overbred, overdressed, and distinctly overrated.

Robert strolled casually over to Charlotte. 'I take it this is the rest of the house party?'

She had to tip her head back to look at him, bumping her nose on the side of her hood. 'Only those who weren't afraid to brave the cold. The faint of heart decided to stay in and toast by the fire.'

Despite himself, Robert's frozen lips cracked into a smile. 'After all these years, you still speak like a book.'

'That's because she generally has her head buried in one,' put in her friend, with equal parts affection and scorn.

'I like books,' said Charlotte disingenuously. 'They're so much grander than real life.'

'Certainly grander than this lot,' snorted her friend, sounding more like the dowager duchess than the duchess herself, but she ruined the effect by raising a hand and acknowledging the enthusiastic halloos of the gentlemen, several of whom seemed quite delighted to see her. Two men broke off from the group, starting forwards in their direction, one considerably ahead of the other.

The man in the vanguard might, just might, have been Freddy Staines. He was certainly of the same type. His coat possessed enough cloaks to garb a small Indian village and his many watch fobs jangled like a dancing girl's bracelets as he walked. His light brown hair had been brushed into careful disarray before being topped with a high-crowned beaver hat. Rings jostled for precedence on his fingers, a signet ring bumping up against a curiously scratched ruby in an overly ornate setting.

'Miss Deveraux!' he exclaimed, before adding, as an afterthought, 'Lady Charlotte.'

He raised his glass in a toast to the two ladies, sloshing mulled wine over the side in the process. It made a sticky trail through the mud on Robert's boot.

No, decided Robert. It wasn't Staines. This man's skin was too fair ever to have weathered an Indian summer, and the pronounced veins beginning to show along his nose suggested a prolonged course of heavy drinking with the best smuggled brandy London had to offer.

He eyed Robert arrogantly through a slightly grimy quizzing glass. 'And you are?'

'This is Dovedale,' Miss Deveraux said bluntly, before Robert could get a word in edgewise. 'It's his mistletoe you're cutting.'

'Good Gad! You're *Dovedale*?'

If a duke fell in the forest, there was no doubt that the entire *ton* would hear it. The mention of his title commanded universal attention. Conversations stopped. Baskets dropped. Even the dogs ceased barking, except for one spaniel who yipped out of turn before whimpering into silence.

Robert sketched a wave. 'Hullo. Carry on.'

'Makes me feel like I ought to curtsy,' murmured Tommy.

Silencing him with an elbow to the ribs, Rob turned back to the other man. 'Yes, I am Dovedale.' The name felt clumsy on his tongue. 'And you are?'

'Frobisher. Martin Frobisher.' Suddenly the man was all eagerness to please. Letting the quizzing glass fall, he stuck out a gloved hand, noted the sticky splotch of spilt wine that marred the surface, rubbed it hard against his leg, and held it out again. 'I believe our families are distantly connected . . .'

'Through Adam, perhaps,' drawled the man behind him. 'I can't conceive of any connection closer.'

Frobisher's cheeks mottled, but, surprisingly, he refrained from retaliating in kind. With a quick sideways look at the other man, he subsided into obedient silence.

'I don't believe I've had the pleasure,' said Robert neutrally.

The newcomer wafted a languid hand in greeting. 'Sir Francis Medmenham, at your service. Like the rest of these louts, I am passing the holiday season on your largesse.'

With his gleaming boots and large gold signet ring, he made a very unconvincing mendicant. His appearance accomplished that towards which Frobisher only strove, his coat boasting a restrained three capes, his hair brushed into a perfect Titus, and his hat brim tilted just forward enough to provide a rakish air without obscuring his vision.

The name poked at Robert's memory. 'You haven't been in the army, have you?' he asked.

'Me? No. I might sully the shine on my boots. My valet would never forgive me.'

'I wish you would,' grumbled Frobisher. 'Then he might finally defect to me.'

Medmenham looked the other man up and down with chilling disinterest. 'I don't think so.'

Frobisher scowled, but was still.

'It's just that your name sounds familiar,' said Robert.

Medmenham's lips curled in a thin smile. 'You're probably thinking of my illustrious relations – the Dashwoods of Medmenham Abbey.'

'Good God,' said Robert. 'So that's it.'

'What's it?' asked Charlotte innocently.

'Nothing,' said Robert quickly.

At least, nothing his cousin ought to know about. Medmenham Abbey had, in the previous century, been home to a group of devoted debauchees known sometimes as the Order of the Friars of St Francis of Wycombe, sometimes as the Monks of Medmenham – in short, the Hellfire Club. Robert's father, who had tottered drunkenly on the edge of polite society by virtue of his position as son of the second son of a duke, had once been invited to their revels. He enjoyed recalling the occasion in lurid detail while in his cups. There had been strange initiation ceremonies and underground chambers dedicated to mysterious rites, most of which seemed to involve wine and women, generally in that order. As far as Robert could tell, it boiled down to nothing more than wenching with a fringe of the occult.

It was, however, exactly the sort of organisation with which a certain Arthur Wrothan specialized. Wrothan had run his own version of the Hellfire Club back in Seringapatam, pandering to the jaded palates of the officer set. Having firmly turned down his first invitation, Robert hadn't been asked again.

'I have a rather well-known house,' said Sir Francis smoothly. 'An architectural gem of its time.'

'Really?' said Charlotte innocently. 'How nice.'

'Oh, it is rather,' agreed Sir Francis genially. 'We have lovely parties.'

'I'm certainly glad you could join our party,' Robert broke in smoothly, shifting so that he stood between Medmenham and Charlotte. 'Are you passing the entirety of the holiday at Girdings?'

Medmenham observed the new arrangements with quiet

amusement. 'Ten lords a-leaping and all that rot. Sorry – I forgot that it's your rot, now. No offence meant, old chap.'

'None taken,' said Robert, echoing his tone of urbane detachment. Charlotte, he noticed to his relief, had been distracted by the task of extracting her friend from the company of Mr Martin Frobisher. From the practiced way with which Charlotte looped her arm through her friend's and gradually eased her away, he gathered that this was not the first time that particular manoeuvre had been effected. 'You'll have to acquaint me with the other leaping lords. I'm afraid I've been abroad a very long time.'

'Have you been on the Continent?' Medmenham enquired, his eyes roaming idly over the rest of the party. In the shifting light of the torches, Charlotte was shepherding her friend away across the clearing, towards a very large young man in a cravat patterned with pink carnations, who appeared to be attempting to cut down a tree with the blunt side of his saw. 'I hear there are still bits of Italy that are habitable, despite Bonaparte's best efforts.'

'No,' said Robert shortly. 'I was in India.'

'Ah.' Medmenham looked him full in the face. 'You must know Freddy, then. Lord Frederick Staines,' he clarified.

Robert plastered on his best expression of worldly ennui. 'I'm afraid I know him only by reputation.'

'I needn't ask what that is,' said Medmenham, with casual scorn. 'Freddy always was too dim to know which tit to nurse from.'

Robert raised an urbane eyebrow. 'So you're friends, then.'

Medmenham's lips quirked in appreciation. 'Old Freddy has his redeeming points.'

'Such as?'

'A talent for collecting . . . interesting people.' A red ring glinted on Medmenham's gloved hand as he lifted his handkerchief delicately to his nose. It looked, thought Robert, uncommonly like the ring he had noticed on Frobisher's hand as well. 'And a perpetually open purse.'

'A useful person to know.' What had seemed like mere scratches on Frobisher's ring were more deeply etched on Medmenham's. The incised lines took up the entire surface of the stone, curving in a series of overlapping curlicues. When seen right side up, the whole came together as a stylized flower that Robert recognised from thousands of temple carvings. One could scarcely go anywhere in India without seeing the representation of a lotus.

It was not, however, a flower generally favoured for pictorial purposes in England, at least not that he could ever recall. The only recollection he had of the lotus flower prior to India was classical in origin, the island of the Lotus Eaters in Homer's *Odyssey*, where the inhabitants dreamt their days chewing on the opiate leaves of the lotus.

'I shouldn't think you would be wanting for blunt.' Medmenham ran an appraising eye over the huge urns that towered along the roofline of the jutting wings of Girdings. 'How many tenants do you have?'

Robert supposed he must have tenants, but it wasn't an item with which he had acquainted himself. He had made a point of never taking any income from the estates that accident had tossed his way. They were not, as far as he was concerned, really his. But that certainly wasn't something he was going to share with Medmenham.

Instead, he shrugged, like any other bored young man of the world. 'Who keeps count?'

It was obviously the right answer. The lotus ring glinted in another lazy pass through the air. 'Who, indeed. Leave that to the estate agents. That's what they're there for. Why drudge away when there are so many other pleasures to be had?'

'Why, indeed,' echoed Rob as the hazy outlines of a plan began to take shape. It couldn't be coincidence that both Frobisher and Medmenham bore the same ring, or that Staines was reputed to collect 'interesting people.' If one of those interesting people was the man Robert sought . . .

Rob's pulse pounded in his ears as he said, with studied casualness, 'If someone unfamiliar with the land were to wish to know more about such pleasures . . .'

'I believe that might be arranged,' said Medmenham. 'For a price.'

In the torchlight, his eyes gleamed as red as his ring. 'There is always a price.'

Chapter Three

It was Christmas Day, and all throughout the county, Christmas bells were ringing. Robert's head was ringing, too, from too much strong drink the night before.

Charlotte hadn't lied: the duchess did celebrate Christmas in the old style, complete with pipers piping, lords a-leaping, and mummers' plays put on by grizzled locals with accents thick enough to cut up and serve as Christmas pudding. Robert hadn't seen the partridge in the pear tree yet, but he was sure there had to be one somewhere. It was impossible to pass through a doorway without being attacked by dangling bits of mistletoe and roughly hacked pine boughs perched precariously on every plausible surface. The pungent scent made Robert's stomach churn.

Long after the frozen revellers had returned from the woods, long after the Yule log had been ceremoniously dragged in and set alight, the mulled wine continued to flow. The ladies had said their good nights and retired; the duchess had thumped through on her way to her stately – and, one presumed, solitary

– bed; and the younger and more dissolute had kicked back in the aptly named Red Room, dealing cards and knocking back whatever beverage came to hand. By eleven, poor Tommy had been all but horizontal, more out of his chair than in it. By midnight of the dawning of the day of the blessed Saviour's birth, Martin Frobisher was puking out the window. An hour later, Lord Henry Innes passed out in front of the fire and had to be carried out by a pair of blank-faced footmen.

The Duke of Dovedale and Sir Francis Medmenham played cards.

By three in the morning, Robert had won fifty guineas and a tentative invitation to Medmenham. He would have preferred information to the invitation, but Medmenham was damnably tight-lipped about his little club, even after several decanters of port. Carefully calibrated questions elicited only a raised eyebrow and the unhelpful comment that only initiates were privy to the 'inner mysteries.'

Medmenham, thought Robert irritably, was deriving altogether too much enjoyment from stringing him along.

Medmenham and Frobisher hadn't been the only ones wearing the ruby rings with the lotus petals etched on the bezel. There had been the sullen gleam of a red stone on Lord Henry Innes's finger as he collapsed before the fire. When Lord Frederick Staines had lifted his hymnal in church that morning, a red ring burnt on his finger like a little cauldron of condensed hellfire. It had become a morbid sort of game, picking out the rings, wondering who else was part of their secret society – and whether Wrothan lay at the heart of it, or merely a pack of debauched dandies reenacting the greatest hits of Sir Francis Dashwood and the Monks of Medmenham.

Robert rather hoped he could track down Wrothan without

having to go through the mockery of an initiation ceremony into Medmenham's little Hellfire Club. Whatever his father might have enjoyed, he really had very little interest in running around in a robe in a clammy cavern, bare-arsed, while dandies in masks gibbered what they fondly believed to be demonic incantations. There were better ways to spend an evening. Like being slowly flayed over a hot fire.

Tommy was being no help at all. He was too busy gazing longingly at the bright red head of one Miss Penelope Deveraux, as though she personally had taught the torches to burn bright.

He would have to see what he could get out of the other, less guarded members of the club. Lord Henry Innes was a type he recognised, a simple-minded brute with equally predictable appetites for wine and wenches. Not women, wenches. Innes had been quite explicit on that point. As he had explained before sprawling out on the hearth rug, he enjoyed the kind of gel one could get an arm around – none of them squealing milk-and-water young misses for him, although he supposed the mater would make him marry one of them sooner or later, eh, what?

Innes reminded Robert tremendously of his father: an inebriate brawler, and all-around lout. The only thing noble about his father had been his name, and he had done everything possible to debase it. He had died as he had lived: in a brawl in a tavern.

Like his father, Innes had a certain rough charm that was nine-tenths bravado and one-tenth pure thuggishness. Plied with enough strong drink, away from Medmenham's inhibiting presence, Innes would cheerfully tell him anything and everything he knew – presuming he knew anything at all.

As for Frobisher, there was a different kettle of eels, and just as slippery. Given the way Medmenham had quelled him the night before, Robert had no doubt that Medmenham held something over him, even if that something was only the threat of cutting off his access to their exclusive society – but he might be driven into admissions by his own desire to boast. With the right conditions, he might just be egged into bragging about their secret rites and what a very central part he played in them all. But would he know Wrothan?

And then there was Freddy Staines, who might be questioned if only Medmenham would ever leave his side. Staines hadn't been part of the group the night before, having taken to his bed with an attack of la grippe that Robert suspected more aptly translated to the mother of all hangovers. Once he made his appearance on Christmas morning, he had been impossible to pry away from the rest of the pack. The four of them moved in concert, like a pack of dogs. They had gone together from Girdings to the village church, and then from the village church back to Girdings for the duchess's morris dancers, mummers' plays, and other pseudo-medieval flummery. Robert had left them all in the hall, placing wagers on whether St George, as played by the village blacksmith, was going to trip over his own spear.

They placed wagers on everything. So far, he had watched them wager on how many times the vicar would say 'um' in the course of his sermon (thirty-two); whether anyone would slip on that icy patch right in front of the steps (yes, but only because Innes crowded them into it, which was accounted a foul); and how many times Turnip Fitzhugh would walk right into the same sprig of mistletoe before remembering to duck (eight and still counting). When they started wagering on whether the dowager duchess wore drawers, Robert knew he had to get out. While the others were peering interestedly at the duchess's nether regions, he had ducked under that dangling mistletoe, slipped out the door of the hall, and kept right on going. Even a mere two rooms away, the air felt clearer and sweeter, free of the miasma of last night's port that seemed to seep through the pores of their skin like rot.

Or maybe he was the rotten one. If they were rogues, then wasn't he doubly so, for using them?

Grimacing, Robert rubbed his head. Life had been much simpler back in the Regiment, knowing one's task and one's enemy, knowing that one was fighting for the cause of right, and that it was honour to do so. The extermination of a traitor ought to be an honourable goal as well, but the means of it – the spying, the skulking – made him feel unclean.

Robert turned right, walking briskly through an abandoned music room and an anteroom of uncertain utility. The sound of his own strides echoed after him, pursuing him down the row of linked rooms like a phalanx of angry ancestors. At the end of the row, he came to the gallery, a vast rectangle of a room that stretched across a full half of the West Front of the house, the perfect place to stretch one's legs on a cold afternoon.

Afternoon sunlight spilt through the long windows, turning the parquet floor the colour of fresh honey. Silver threads sparkled in the ice blue upholstery, and even his ancestors in their heavy, gilded frames looked less grim than usual in the frank glow of the late afternoon sun.

Robert's steps slowed as he realised that someone else had taken advantage of the sunshine and solitude. Halfway down the long room sat Charlotte, curled in a comfortable ball on a padded bench by the window.

There was a book in her lap, of course, tilted to catch the

sunlight. She had tucked her feet up beneath her, tucking the long skirt of her green wool dress up around her for warmth. She sat with one cheek leaning against the cool of the windowpane, pulling her hair free from its pins so that it stood up unevenly against the window on one side and snaked down on the other. With the sunlight washing over her, she glowed like one of the illuminated capitals on a medieval manuscript, from the gold of her hair to the deep green of her dress and the rich red of the cover of the book in her pale hands.

She didn't look up as he ventured nearer, all her attention bent upon the page in front of her.

Robert tilted his head to try to read the title. '*Evelina?*'

'What?' Glancing wildly up, Charlotte dropped her book and cracked her head against the glass. 'Owwwww.' Robert winced in sympathy.

'I'm sorry,' he said, bending over to retrieve her book. From the look of the binding, it had been in an advanced state of dilapidation even before taking its latest plunge. Robert smoothed out a bent page, closed the cover, and handed it ceremoniously back to her. 'I shouldn't have startled you.'

'That's all right,' said Charlotte, holding out one hand to take the book from him as she pressed the other to the back of her head. 'I was just . . .'

'Elsewhere?' Robert provided for her.

'Very much so.' Charlotte looked tenderly down at her book with the sort of affection usually reserved for well-loved pets and very small children. 'Evelina was just carried off by Sir Clement Willoughby!'

Having no idea who either party was, Robert couldn't tell whether that was a cause for congratulation or condolence. 'Is that good or bad?'

'Very bad,' Charlotte informed him. 'But fear not, she manages to free herself from his vile clutches.'

'I am immensely reassured to hear that.' Robert looked quizzically down at her. 'I gather you've seen this Evelina carried off by Sir What's-His-Name before?'

'Many times,' Charlotte admitted. She regarded the battered binding critically. 'I may need to get a new copy soon.'

Robert rather felt that would be in order.

'Shouldn't you be watching the mummers?' he asked, with mock reproach.

Wriggling her legs out from under her, Charlotte cast about for an excuse. 'I saw them last year.'

'And they're awful,' said Robert drily.

Charlotte grimaced. 'And they're awful. But they do try so hard.'

'It might be less painful if they tried a little less hard.' Robert held out his hand to help her off the window seat, since she seemed to keep getting tangled in her own skirts. 'Having St George battle both Bonaparte and a group of maddened pygmies was certainly a unique concept.'

'It might have been worse,' said Charlotte, shaking out her skirts, which were sadly wrinkled from her sojourn by the window. There was a crease across one cheek where she must have been leaning against the edge of the drape. She looked flushed and comfortable and adorably rumpled. She shoved a stray wisp of her hair back behind her ear, a move that did little to right the rest of her coiffure. 'Last year they had Mr Pitt fighting off the Saracens with a broomstick.'

'I'm sure he's capable of it,' said Robert diplomatically. 'Should there be any Saracens to fight.'

'I believe they're called Ottomans now,' said Charlotte. She tucked her book neatly under her arm. 'I wonder if any of them still think of us as Normans.'

Robert had to confess that it wasn't a problem that had ever presented itself to him before. 'Were we ever?'

'Well . . .' Charlotte bit down on her lower lip as she considered the question. 'Grandmama would like to think so, but I've found no documents going further back than the sixteenth century. All of the stories about the Lansdownes at the Battle of Hastings and Agincourt come from an Elizabethan chronicle that purports to tell the history of the family. I rather doubt that it's entirely accurate.'

She looked at him so expectantly that Robert couldn't quite bring himself to admit that he'd had no idea that they'd had any ancestors anywhere near Agincourt.

'You don't believe it, then?' he heard himself asking, as if he had every idea what she were talking about.

'Doesn't it strike you as more than a little bit suspicious that there aren't any mentions of us at all before the Tudors? The Elizabethans had a lamentable tendency of making up ancestors,' she added confidingly. 'Especially if they hadn't any.'

'Are you saying we're nothing but upstarts?'

'Not exactly upstarts,' Charlotte hedged. 'More . . .'

'Opportunists,' Robert provided. His father must have been a chip off the old block.

'Adventurers,' Charlotte corrected. She rolled the word off her tongue with obvious relish. 'Elizabethan privateers sailing the high seas in search of Spanish gold.'

'In other words, pirates.'

'But very gentlemanly ones.'

'Gentlemanly' wasn't quite the term Robert would have applied to the sort of person who boarded other people's ships, but it seemed cruel to deprive his cousin of her romantic illusions.

'Sir Nicholas Lansdowne was a great favourite of Queen Elizabeth's,' explained Charlotte. 'It's said that when Sir Walter Raleigh threw down his cloak for the queen, Sir Nicholas stepped in, swept her up in his arms, and carried her right over Sir Walter's cloak.'

'Thus keeping his own feet dry?'

'*And* the queen's favour.' Charlotte looked as pleased as though it were she who had trampled on Sir Walter's cloak.

'I'm surprised Sir Walter didn't call him out.'

'Oh, he did him one better. He hired a gang of bravadoes to set upon Sir Nicholas that very night.'

'Don't tell me. Sir Nicholas ran them all through and then sent a mocking note to their master.'

Charlotte shook her head, a mischievous smile plucking at the corners of her lips. 'No. He had too much sense for that. He crawled under a carriage, down a back alley, and took the next available ship to the West Indies.'

Robert regarded her with bemused fascination. 'Where did you learn all this?' He couldn't imagine the duchess blithely telling tales of the peccadilloes of her husband's ancestors; other people's ancestors, yes, but Dovedales, no.

Tilting her head, Charlotte smiled reminiscently. 'My father.'

Robert felt his answering smile freeze on his face.

His cousin didn't seem to notice. She was a thousand miles away, in the golden haze of once upon a time. 'He used to tell me bedtime stories about all the characters lurking in our family tree,' she said fondly. 'We do have some wonderful rogues to our credit. Or discredit, I suppose.'

Discredit was one way of putting it. Every time she said 'our,' he felt the lash of it like a whip on his back. It didn't seem right that he ought to be included in that 'our,' in that family history, when he had stumbled in off the sides, the collateral line of a collateral line, when he bore the title her father had borne so briefly, the title his own father had plotted and schemed and quite possibly murdered to acquire.

'I'm sorry,' he said. 'I'm sorry that I'm here and he's not.'

Charlotte looked up at him in surprise. 'It's not your fault.'

What could he say to that? It had felt like his fault. It still did. He remembered coming with his father to Girdings all those years ago, like vultures hunting out their prey. Only his father hadn't bothered to wait until his prey was decently dead before descending on the carcass.

He had never known whether their arrival had hastened the duke's death. The loud and constant rows between the dowager duchess and his father certainly couldn't have done anything to improve the duke's condition. As to whether his father had done anything else to speed along the duke's demise . . . he would never know for sure.

Charlotte's eyes searched his face. Whatever she saw there made her brow wrinkle with concern. 'I wouldn't want you to think that I don't want you here. I'd rather have you here than neither of you.' She bit her lip in frustration. 'Oh, dear. That came out wrong somehow.'

'No,' said Robert simply. 'It didn't. It came out just right.'

Charlotte didn't seem to notice. She was too busy trying to make him feel better. 'You were so good to me in that awful time,' she said earnestly. 'I missed you terribly when you left.'

She had been very easy to be good to. It had been an undemanding way of assuaging his own conscience, taking the time to pay attention to a neglected little girl six years his junior. If he were being honest with himself, it had been as much to distract himself as her, an excuse for staying out of the way of their brawling elders. At least dancing attendance on her had never been dull; she played elaborate games of make-believe, spinning fanciful stories in which he sometimes participated and sometimes just watched.

Robert smiled at the sudden recollection of one of those fancies. 'Do you still believe in unicorns?'

Charlotte's cheeks flared with colour. 'I can't believe you remember that after all these years!'

He hadn't, until now. 'How could I forget? It's not everyone who goes unicorn hunting with a plate of jam tarts.'

'I thought it might be hungry,' protested Charlotte. 'It seemed like a good idea at the time.'

'It was.' Robert smiled reminiscently. 'Those were excellent tarts.'

'You told me the unicorn had come for them!'

'I didn't want you to be disappointed.'

Charlotte folded her arms across her chest, trapping her book in front of her breasts. 'You mean you liked raspberry tarts.'

'That, too.' Robert grinned down at her, watching as she struggled to keep up her air of mock reproof and failed miserably. He was surprised to hear himself saying, 'Perhaps we should go unicorn hunting again sometime.'

Charlotte beamed at him. 'Only if you leave some of the tarts for me this time.'

'We'll have the kitchen make up a double batch.'

'Triple,' corrected Charlotte. 'We'll want some for the unicorn.'

Looking down at her shining face, her hair glinting like a personal halo in the light of the setting sun, Robert could almost believe she might find her unicorn, somewhere out in the gardens of Girdings House. In the army, overseas, he would have scoffed at the notion that such radical innocence could still exist, even tucked away in the remote corners of an English country house. It was a bit like stumbling upon a unicorn, or some other creature generally believed extinct.

Reaching forward, Robert tucked one of her flyaway curls back behind her ear. 'You look like a lady in a medieval tapestry. All you need is the unicorn at your feet.'

'And one of those big, conical hats,' suggested Charlotte, tilting her head in a way that he remembered from all those years ago. 'I believe those are de rigueur for unicorn-hunting maidens.'

'We'll have to find you one,' said Robert. 'There must be one somewhere in this great pile.'

Clasping his hands behind his back, he glanced around the gallery. Great pile didn't even begin to describe it. The sheer vastness of Girdings House resisted comprehension. Forget conical hats – one could store a whole regiment away in a corner of one wing and never even know they were there.

Robert was startled out of his thoughts by the tentative touch of a hand against his arm.

He looked down to Charlotte regarding him earnestly, her book tucked under one arm.

'I really am glad to have you back. I would never want you to think otherwise. You were all that made that time bearable.'

'The feeling was mutual,' he said soberly. Robert thought of Medmenham and Staines in the other room, of the sour smell of spilt port, and the hideous dark holes being burnt into his soul, and realised with surprise that he hadn't given a thought to any of them the whole time he had been in the gallery. 'It still is.'

Charlotte's face lit with such gratitude that Robert found himself, for once, entirely at a loss. He wanted to tell her that he didn't deserve that kind of approbation, he wanted to tell her that he wasn't worthy of such simple, uncritical affection, but his throat closed around the words.

Instead, he did what he did best. He pasted an easy smile across his face, held out his arm, and said teasingly, 'Shall we see about finding you that hat?'

'Yes, let's,' said his lady with the unicorn, and she walked out with her arm tucked trustingly through his.

Chapter Four

'How goes the Parade of Eligibles?' demanded Lady Henrietta Dorrington, flinging herself into a chair beside Charlotte.

They were in the Gallery of Girdings, where all the furniture had been pushed back against the walls to make room for dancing. Tonight's was only an informal dance, a prelude to the grander festivities that would take place the following day. Some of the local families from the county had been invited. They stood in their own little groups around the edges of the room, the red-faced squires and their fresh-faced daughters looking like the characters in Charlotte's books.

Tomorrow, a larger party would be coming up from London, replacing the locals and augmenting the house party. There would be proper London musicians, champagne flowing down the centre of the table, and hothouse flowers blooming improbably out of immense marble urns. There were rumours that the Prince of Wales himself might make one of the party, rumours that Charlotte suspected her grandmother had put about herself for the sheer fun of watching people scrounging around corners, looking under sofas for misplaced royals.

Henrietta and her husband had only joined the house party that afternoon, just in time for the Twelfth Night celebrations, having spent the bulk of the holiday with Henrietta's family in Kent, engaging in what Henrietta blithely referred to as 'a spot of parental placation.' Charlotte was ridiculously glad to see both of them. She was bursting to discuss the last week with Henrietta, to present everything that had occurred to her more assured friend for dissection and analysis. Not that Charlotte was sure there really was anything there to dissect, short of her own imagination, but it was rather nice to be the one with something to dissect for a change.

'Eligibles?' demanded Miles, following Henrietta into their little corner and tripping over a small gilt chair in the process. 'You mean this lot?'

Charlotte smiled and scooted over, making room for Miles to stand next to Henrietta. Scorning the chair and the equally dainty benches, Miles chose instead to prop his broad shoulders against the pale blue silk of the wall, towering comfortably over his wife and her friends.

Penelope pulled her chair away, too, but not to make room. Penelope made no pretence of her feelings about her best friend's marriage. In anyone else, her attitude would have been called sulking. In Penelope, it was more like a slow smoulder. If looks could char, Miles would have long since gone up in flames.

'They have no charm, no conversation, and most of them have no chins,' put in Penelope caustically. 'Other than that, it's been just scrumptious.'

'They're not the most inspiring collection of humanity,' Charlotte admitted. 'I'm not sure why Grandmama chose them.'

'Because,' said Penelope, 'all the good ones have already been taken. All we're left with are the louts and the lechers. Usually in the same package.'

Miles's ears perked up. 'Do you need any help keeping the lechers at bay?' he asked Charlotte. 'I'm told I loom rather well.'

He looked immensely cheered at the prospect of enlivening his stay at Girdings with a spot of intimidation.

'As much as I appreciate the offer, I don't think it will be the least bit necessary.' Charlotte looked down at her modest gown of silver net over green satin. It had seemed so pretty at the modiste's – and that was just what it was. Not alluring, not seductive, just pretty. She sighed. 'I need a little less go hence and a little more come hither.'

'That depends on whom you're hithering,' declared Henrietta.

Miles crinkled his nose. '*Hithering*?'

Henrietta waved that aside. 'Is there anyone the least bit hitherable in this assemblage of gargoyles?'

Charlotte betrayed herself with a quick glance across the room to the spot where Robert stood, exchanging pleasantries with Sir Francis Medmenham. She hadn't needed to look around the room to ascertain where he was; she just knew, the same way an astronomer knew the position of stars in the firmament. Over the past eight days she had become something of an adept on the subject of Robert. If he had been a university topic, she would qualify for an advanced degree.

Henrietta's hazel eyes narrowed shrewdly. 'So that's the way the land lies.'

'There isn't any land there,' said Charlotte regretfully. 'Not even a very small island.'

'Island?' Miles echoed.

Henrietta understood instantly. 'You don't know that.'

'He calls me *cousin*.'

'Well, you are his cousin,' interjected Miles. 'What is he supposed to call you? Spot?'

Finding himself the recipient of two outraged female glares, Miles backed up, both physically and metaphorically. 'Not that you have any. Spots, that is. It's just a figure of speech.'

'I understand,' said Charlotte generously. She hadn't forgotten all the times Miles had saved her from her usual post by the wall by sacrificing himself for a dance. It had all been at Henrietta's behest, of course, but Charlotte loved both of them all the more for it, Henrietta for ordering and Miles for obeying, and both of them for caring enough for her to try to pretend it was otherwise.

'We need to minimize your cousinly qualities,' mused Henrietta.

'How can you minimize her cousinliness when she is his cousin?' demanded Miles. 'You have many talents, Hen, but I don't think you can go about lopping the limbs off family trees just like that.'

'It's a matter of metaphysical cousindom,' said Henrietta loftily.

Charlotte intervened before Miles could point out that cousindom wasn't a proper word. 'Even if we weren't cousins, it still wouldn't matter. One can't engender warmer feelings where they don't otherwise exist.'

'Rubbish,' said Henrietta, sounding eerily like her mother. 'It's not a matter of engendering warmer feelings, but of directing his attention to them. It's as simple as that.' She tilted her head up at her husband. 'Isn't it, darling?'

Miles winced at the memory. 'Simple isn't quite the word I would have used.'

'Simple-minded, more likely,' muttered Penelope, just a little too loudly.

'They don't call me Clever Pete for nothing,' said Miles cheerfully.

Penelope regarded him balefully. 'They don't call you Clever Pete.'

'I know,' said Miles imperturbably. 'I just like the sound of it.'

Charlotte considered the merits of this. 'Wouldn't you have to be Clever Miles?'

Miles shook his head. 'It just doesn't have quite the right ring to it.'

'There's a reason for that.' Penelope tossed back half of her glass of wine in one long swig.

Charlotte had managed to 'misplace' Penelope's last glass while Penelope was dancing, but Penelope was rapidly making up for lost time. Penelope had always been a bit wild – or, as disapproving chaperones put it, fast – but since Henrietta's marriage, she had thrown herself into the pursuit of her own ruin with single-minded efficiency. Sometimes, Charlotte felt as though she were trying to slow down a runaway carriage by clinging to the boot.

Henrietta leant forward, effectively lodging herself between Penelope and Miles. 'I want to know more about Charlotte's duke.'

'Charlotte doesn't have a duke,' said Charlotte. Since that hadn't come out quite as effectively as it had in her head, she added, 'Well, I *don't*.'

'Don't you?' said Penelope, lounging back in her chair like a dangerous jungle cat. The glass in her hand was quite, quite empty.

'No, I don't,' Charlotte repeated, twitching the gauze overlay of her skirt. 'Just because—'

Colouring, Charlotte broke off.

'Aha!' Henrietta jabbed a finger in the air. 'Just because what?'

Penelope cast her eyes up to the intricate plasterwork on the ceiling, reciting in a monotone monologue, 'Long walks together, domestic interludes at the breakfast table, tête-à-têtes in the library . . .'

'It was hardly a tête-à-tête!' protested Charlotte in a fierce whisper, desperately craning her neck in the fear someone might have heard. 'We simply happened to be alone in the same place at the same time.'

'Same place. Same time. Alone.' Penelope ticked the words off on her fingers. 'How else would you describe a tête-à-tête?'

'Exactly as it sounds. Head-to-head. And ours weren't. They were quite properly on opposite sides of a table.'

'Hmm,' said Penelope.

Miles pushed back his chair with an exaggerated scraping sound.

'Right,' he said, holding up both hands and backing slowly away. 'I know when I'm not needed. I'll be in the card room if anyone wants me.' He dealt Charlotte an avuncular pat on the shoulder. 'Best of luck with your duke, old thing.'

'I don't have a duke,' repeated Charlotte. It sounded less and less convincing each time she said it. It would save her considerable time and energy to embroider the phrase on a sampler and hang it around her neck. 'This is beginning to sound more and more like a game of cards,' she added, to no one in particular.

'Don't be silly,' said Henrietta. 'That would be kings, not dukes, and we don't have any of those here.'

'Just jacks,' put in Penelope, her lip curling as her gaze made the circuit of the men scattered about the room. Neither Charlotte nor Henrietta was under any doubt as to what she meant. The jack was also commonly known as the knave. 'We have plenty of those.'

'Well, Martin Frobisher, surely,' said Henrietta, surveying the assemblage. Charlotte would never forget the memorable occasion where Martin Frobisher had attempted to make an improper suggestion to Henrietta and been rewarded with a sticky stream of ratafia all down the front of his new jacket. He had never tried that again. A least, not with Henrietta. 'And Lord Henry Innes. They're as thick as thieves. And I've heard all sorts of stories about Sir Francis Medmenham, but other than that . . .'

'Don't forget our duke,' added Penelope.

Charlotte didn't like the way Penelope's lip curled as she said it. 'Robert isn't like them.'

'No?'

'No,' said Charlotte vehemently. It was one thing for Penelope to put on worldly airs, but quite another for her to insinuate untruths about someone she barely knew. Penelope didn't know him; she did.

'He hasn't been back in the country long enough to do anything appalling. Has he?' asked Henrietta with interest. 'Unless you heard something about his time in India.'

Penelope nodded in the direction of Sir Francis Medmenham. 'Just look at the company he keeps.'

'What other company is he meant to keep?' argued Charlotte, as much for herself as for Penelope. 'They're the only ones here.'

Penelope just shrugged. It was amazing how much innuendo Penelope could pack into one small shrug.

Charlotte's chin lifted stubbornly. 'I don't see why you need to be so cynical about everyone. Especially about Robert.'

'Dear Charlotte. Dear, *innocent* Charlotte,' said Penelope

condescendingly, 'if you had been out on as many balconies as I have, you would be a cynic, too.'

'Well, who told you to go out on all those balconies?' said Henrietta tartly. 'That's just asking for trouble.'

'But I do it so well.' Stretching sinuously, Penelope rose from her chair. 'Speaking of which, I promised Lord Freddy a dance. You'll have to carry on the duke-hunting without me.'

With a backwards twitch of her reticule in farewell, she turned her back on her friends and began to move away. Henrietta exchanged an alarmed look with Charlotte behind her back.

'Pen?' Henrietta called.

Penelope stopped where she was and angled her head over her shoulder, her very stance a challenge. For all her bravado, she looked very alone and strangely vulnerable as she looked back at Henrietta.

Henrietta forced out a smile. 'No balconies.'

Penelope's habitual mask of indifference clamped down over her features. 'It's too cold for balconies. Alcoves, on the other hand . . .'

'Are an equally bad idea,' finished Henrietta, but Penelope was no longer there to hear her.

'Blast,' said Henrietta.

Charlotte squeezed Henrietta's arm. 'She will come around, you know. In time.'

'I know,' said Henrietta, but she didn't sound as though she meant it, and there was an unhappy expression on her face as she watched Penelope swagger across the ballroom.

Charlotte could feel the mirror of it on her own face. It hurt her to see Penelope hurting so, and to know there was nothing she could do about it. It wasn't as though she could fill Henrietta's place for Penelope. As much as she knew Penelope did care for her, and as fiercely as Penelope would defend her if anyone were ever to threaten her, they had never quite spoken the same language. It was Henrietta to whom Penelope had always turned, Henrietta who knew how to jolly Penelope out of her bad moods, and persuade her out of her more ridiculous schemes. But Henrietta, as Penelope saw it, had chosen Miles over her and that was the end of that.

'It's just that she doesn't like change,' Charlotte tried to explain, knowing how inadequate her efforts were.

Henrietta twisted indignantly in her chair. 'But I *haven't* changed.'

She might not have, but her situation had, and for Penelope, that was much the same thing.

Since there was nothing else Charlotte could say, she did the only thing she could do. She squeezed Henrietta's hand. 'She *will* come around.'

Henrietta made a moue of annoyance indicative of extreme dissatisfaction. Shaking her thick brown hair like a horse swatting off flies, she twisted around in her chair, scanning the ballroom. 'Enough of this. Where's your duke?'

Charlotte's duke (although he would have been very surprised to hear himself referred to as such) was busy trying to look like a bored man of the world.

At least part of that was accurate. He was certainly bored. Standing around ballrooms evaluating the charms of the ladies and criticising other gentlemen's cravats had a very limited appeal. The card room appealed even less. Robert had never really seen the point of wagering one's wages on the turn of a card. Perhaps that was because, for him, they had been wages. He had earned them. These bored young bucks of the *ton*, with their allowances and their constant excursions into what they called 'dun territory,' were a complete mystery to him, as exotic as the elaborate multiarmed goddesses in the Indians' temples.

After ten days of attempting to win their confidence, Robert was developing an extreme allergy to idleness. His enforced inactivity itched like a rash. Give him a river to be crossed, an enemy to be run through, even a ledger to be balanced, something simple and straightforward that one could do and get done, as opposed to this prolonged game of tricking confidences out of the unwary. Tommy had been no help; he was too busy yearning after Miss Deveraux. Without his cousin's company over the past ten days, he probably would have run screaming out into the gardens of Girdings. Only his walks and conversations with Charlotte had provided a modicum of distraction from the distasteful exercise in amateur espionage.

It was, he realised, not unlike the roles they had played twelve years before, when dancing attendance on his shy little cousin had provided a welcome escape from the sordid arguments between their elders.

But they weren't children anymore. And he wasn't the only one to have taken notice of Charlotte.

Next to him, Medmenham trained his quizzing glass on the small figure in silvery green silk. 'The little Lansdowne is in excellent looks tonight.'

Given that Medmenham had assessed all of the women in the room – most of them unfavourably – at some point in the evening, the remark should not have filled Robert with the fervent desire to pluck the quizzing glass out of his hand and stomp it to smithereens under his heel. But, then, none of those other women was his responsibility.

His very innocent, very defenceless responsibility, who

was indeed wearing a very becoming dress.

Her hair had been pulled back from her face in a series of curls that seemed more golden than usual against the silvery green of her dress, making her look like an earthbound Christmas angel. Her cheeks were pink and her eyes bright as she carried on an animated conversation with her recently arrived friend.

As Robert watched, Charlotte's friend said something that made Charlotte look up. Catching his eye, she cast him a slightly sheepish smile and quickly looked away again, her cheeks even pinker than before.

'Yes, she is,' Robert said shortly.

Medmenham's glass remained trained on Charlotte. 'Well dowered, I suppose?'

Robert had no idea. 'Naturally.'

Medmenham let his quizzing glass dangle from one finger. It swung slowly to and fro, light glinting off its surface. 'Excellent,' he said.

Robert forced his hands to unclench, finger by stiff finger. 'I hadn't realised you were in search of a wife, Medmenham.'

From society's standpoint Medmenham was everything that could be desired in a husband. He had five thousand pounds a year, a baronetcy, and at least three properties of which Robert knew: the infamous Medmenham Abbey, a hunting box in Melton Mowbray, and a sugar plantation in the West Indies. He was young, personable, and undeniably clever. Charlotte needed someone clever, or at least someone who could understand her vocabulary, a requirement that ruled out a good three quarters of the *ton*. It wouldn't be a brilliant match for a duke's daughter, but it would be a respectable one.

At least it would be if Medmenham were the least bit respectable. Somehow, Robert just couldn't see marrying off his only cousin to an amateur diabolist, no matter how many sugar plantations he owned.

Being the head of the family was far more complicated than he had realised.

Medmenham regarded him with the casual scorn he reserved for his closer acquaintances. 'You really have been out of the country too long. Why do you think we were all dragged out here? It's not for the rural amusements, that's for certain.' The way Medmenham's glass dipped towards a country-bred squire's daughter made it quite clear just which rural amusements he was referring to. 'The dowager has been trying to market the little Lansdowne for years now.'

'I hadn't realised that's what they were calling it now.'

'We, my dear Dovedale, are men of the world. Why call a spade anything but what it is?'

'Because by another name it might smell sweeter,' countered Robert.

Medmenham pursed his lips, an expression that made him look disconcertingly like Charles II, only without the long wig.

'An interesting point. Our senses are so often led by our expectations. Take the red-haired chit over there.' His glass angled towards Miss Deveraux, who was dancing down the line with Lord Frederick Staines. 'Her features are commonplace enough, but she has flash and flair. We expect beauty from her and therefore we find it.'

Robert didn't, but if Medmenham chose to redirect his attentions to Charlotte's friend, that was perfectly all right with him. From what he'd seen of Miss Deveraux, she could take care of herself. She already had poor Tommy on a very short string, following along after her looking like a whipped dog hoping to be tossed a treat. Personally, Robert didn't see the attraction.

'And then there's the little Lansdowne. When you look at her closely,' said Medmenham, suiting actions to words, 'she's not an unattractive thing. But she lacks elan. And there is that unfortunate grandmother of hers.'

'The duchess comes as part of the deal,' said Robert quickly. If anything could kill passion, it was the thought of the duchess lurking behind the bridal bed.

Medmenham brushed the duchess aside. 'She must be eighty, if she's a day. I give her another five years, at most.'

Robert forced out an incredulous laugh. 'The dowager duchess? She'll outlive us all, and kick the Devil in the shins when he comes to fetch her.' With feigned nonchalance, he raised an eyebrow at his companion. 'Besides, wouldn't marriage rather put a damper on your subterranean bacchanals?'

Medmenham looked at him with genuine surprise. 'I don't see why. Fidelity is too, too crushingly bourgeois.'

If that was the case, then Robert was a bourgeois at heart. His father's amorous adventures had brought him no happiness; only an empty purse, an emptier hearth, and a whopping case of the French pox. 'Infidelity doesn't seem to quite do the range of your activities justice. What does one call philandering on an epic scale?'

Medmenham raised his quizzing glass, turning it slowly in the light so that it winked like the star the wise men followed to Bethlehem. 'Divinity.'

'I'll vouch for that once I've met some of your divinities,' retorted Robert. 'From my experience, fallen women tend to be more earthy than divine.'

'It depends on how one defines the divine. Some of the pagan goddesses were notoriously earthy jades. Venus herself was a tired old tart.'

'Is it Venus you worship, then?' The last time Robert had looked, the attribute of the goddess had been a dove, not a lotus.

Medmenham smiled blandly. 'We are ecumenical in our devotions. And in our appetites.'

Robert bit down on a sharp retort as Medmenham's gaze once again strayed towards Charlotte. To show irritation would be a fatal mistake; Medmenham controlled his followers by probing at their weaknesses.

Instead, Robert assumed an aggrieved expression. 'Damnation. Duty calls. I promised this set to my cousin.'

Medmenham raised one well-groomed eyebrow. 'And you mustn't disappoint her.'

Robert pulled a wry face. 'I mustn't disappoint her grandmother. If the dowager doesn't come after me, her little dog will.'

As he had learnt during his brief stay at Girdings, all the young blades of the *ton* went in mortal terror of the dowager's little yipping dog, which she employed to great effect among their ranks, like a capricious goddess unleashing plagues for her own amusement. It was said her dog could shred a new pair of pantaloons in about three seconds flat.

'If you'll excuse me, Medmenham . . .'

Medmenham's eyes glinted with his usual diabolical amusement as he waved a languid quizzing glass.

'Carry on, old chap, carry on. I'll be here. Waiting my turn.'

Chapter Five

We went to the local pub for dinner. In the interval since my last relationship, I had forgotten that strange alchemy by which moonlight and roses turn into dropped socks and empty takeaway cartons. Not that I was complaining, mind you. I liked takeaway. I also liked pubs. Besides, how much more English could you get than ye olde country pub with ye not so olde local landowner? It was the sort of thing impressionable Anglophiles dream about. Admittedly, when I'd dreamt about it in the past, ye olde landowner had been looking a lot like Colin Firth and had been wearing knee breeches, but I had no complaints to make.

I had had more than my fair share of living in the past that afternoon as I read through Charlotte's letters to Henrietta from Girdings. Henrietta's arrival at Girdings had entailed a predictable gap in the correspondence, but I had been sufficiently caught up in the story by then to dig around in the wainscoting like a research-minded mouse until I found Henrietta's journals.

As Colin manoeuvred the Range Rover along a twisty

country lane, I asked something that had been puzzling me all day: 'How come all of Henrietta's papers are here, instead of at Loring House?'

'Probably,' said Colin, expertly navigating around a rut, 'because that line died out. No male heirs. One of Henrietta's great-granddaughters married back into the Selwick side.' He frowned at the windshield. 'Great-great-granddaughter?'

I did some hasty mental math. If a generation is generally considered to be about thirty-five years . . . 'So that would be your grandmother?'

'Great-grandmother,' he corrected, braking briefly to avoid hitting a wayward rabbit.

'So you're descended from Miles!' I exclaimed delightedly.

Colin was less excited than I was. 'And monkeys, too, if you go back far enough.'

'I could tell *that*,' I said, with an exaggerated eye roll. 'It's just . . . It's a bit like finding out that the characters in one of your favourite books are actually real.'

'Eloise, I hate to tell you this, but they were real. Otherwise I wouldn't be here.'

'I know. But . . .'

It was hard to explain. As a historian, I found myself all too often treating my historical subjects like fictional characters, malleable entities that could be made to do one thing or another, whose motivations could be speculated upon endlessly, and whose missing actions could be reconstructed and approximated based on assessments of prior and later behaviours. It was one of the hazards of working with a fragmentary source base. You had little scraps, like puzzle pieces, and you put them together as best you could. But no matter how faithful you tried to be to the historical record, there would always be that element of guesswork, of imagination, of (if we're being totally honest) fiction.

'They lived and loved and died,' said Colin briskly, competently swinging the car onto a road that was mercifully paved. My posterior thanked him. Dirt roads might be picturesque, but they were hard on the backside. 'They lost money, they died in wars, they suffered broken hearts. It isn't all trumpets and glory.'

'I know, I know.' Although I sincerely doubted that Charlotte was heading for a broken heart. Her romance with the Duke of Dovedale was shaping up as prettily as a novel by Georgette Heyer. I wondered if he would propose on Twelfth Night? True, it was all very fast, but when you know, you know. I had a good feeling about them. So did Henrietta, which is probably why I did. That's another pitfall for the historian, falling prey to the prejudices of our sources. 'I think that's why one sees more happily ever afters in fiction than in biographies. It's not that the two trajectories are necessarily so different, but in fiction you can take the moment when everyone is happy and just clip off the thread of the narrative there, right at that trumpets and glory moment.'

'Even in fiction, isn't it more interesting when you look at the whole picture, with the bad as well as the good?' argued Colin. 'I'd rather know the whole story, even if it ends on a low note.'

'Warts and all?' I said, quoting the famous phrase about Cromwell. 'Perhaps. It may be more interesting. But sometimes it's less satisfying.'

Every now and then, you just need to believe that everything can be frozen in that one moment where everything is going right.

Like right now. Part of me would have given anything to freeze us as we were at that moment, before the blush could wear off the relationship. It might become something better as it went on, if we made it past the intermediary stages where mundanities take the place of philosophical discussions and shaving no longer seems quite such a necessity, but it would never again be what it was then, new and shiny and perfect.

I didn't say that, though. What I did say was, 'Oooh, is that the pub?'

My stomach grumbled, as if seconding my question. 'The very one,' said Colin, swinging around the side of the building.

Twisting in my seat to stare through the back window, I squinted at the sign hanging from a long pole stuck in the ground in proper ye olde pub fashion. It featured a decidedly potbellied deer. Picture Homer Simpson as Bambi's fat old uncle (the one who likes to drink and smoke and refuses to go running with the rest of the herd) and you get the idea. The name of the pub was the Heavy Hart.

'You've got to be kidding me,' I said, pointing at the sign through the car window. 'That can't be the real name.'

'I think the real name was the Hart and Hare.' Colin brought the Range Rover to an expert halt in the anachronistic but very convenient car park that had been laid to one side of the building. 'Something nondescript, at any rate.'

'I like it,' I said. 'Nice little in-joke there. So is this your local watering hole?'

Aside from the name and the beer signs in the window, it was the very image of an Old World pub, a two-storey building of white stucco with a roof that slanted down over chimneys on both sides. White lettering on the bottom of the sign proudly declared, *est. 1682*. A chalkboard stuck beneath the inn sign advertised that Tuesday was Quiz Night. Despite living in London for three months, I'd never actually been to a pub quiz. Perhaps Colin would be up for going on Tuesday.

This, I thought smugly as I climbed out of the Range Rover, was the stuff of which real relationships were made. We wouldn't be one of those couples who had to spend all their time in each other's pockets. No, we could spend the day happily immersed in our own pursuits and then rejoice at coming together again for a pub quiz or a romantic tête-à-tête over bangers and mash. Because nothing says romance quite like a large pile of sausages.

Trip-trapping merrily along in the three-inch stacked loafers that were the closest thing I owned to sensible shoes, I followed Colin in through the suitably battered door of the pub, into a long room with all the dark wood and exposed beams my little heart could desire. And came to an abrupt halt as vague shapes formed into people, and recognisable people, at that.

What I hadn't stopped to consider was that if this was the local watering hole, there would probably be locals in it.

'Sorry,' Colin muttered out of the side of his mouth, pasting on a big, friendly smile. 'I didn't know they'd be here.'

'S'OK,' I whispered back, pasting on a fake smile of my own.

I had met a smattering of the locals at a cocktail party my last time there, back in the days when I was still a tagalong American researcher rather than rehearsing for the role of mistress of the house. For the most part, I had found them incredibly friendly and welcoming.

For the most part.

The exception to that was sitting at a round wooden table

set into the curve of the bow window. She had angled her chair out, to provide the best possible view of a pair of unfairly long legs tucked into a pair of trim tan slacks designed to put one in mind of riding gear without actually being riding gear. She had had a haircut since I'd last seen her; her straight blond hair was now jaw-length, with a curve at the end. In fact, she had *my* haircut.

From the nonplussed expression on her face, I could tell that Joan Plowden-Plugge was about as happy to see me as I was to see her.

If you're wondering how I managed to alienate someone on such short notice, allow me to assure you, quite sincerely, that it wasn't so much me as it was me-with-Colin. Quite simply, Joan would have hated any reasonably nubile female who appeared in public with the man for whom she harboured a decade-long crush that made Petrarch's thing for Laura look like chump change. As you can imagine, I felt much the same way about her. It didn't help that she was fashion-model thin and Revlon-commercial blond to boot.

To add to the fun, the first – and only other – time I had been at Selwick Hall, before we were dating, Colin had employed me as a sort of human shield to keep Joan at bay. Manlike, he hadn't bothered to warn me beforehand, perhaps because he feared I'd refuse to cooperate and throw him right into the lion's jaws. This had not endeared me to Joan.

We stared at each other for a long moment in complete mutual loathing before the silence was broken by the man beside her scraping back his chair.

'Selwick!' exclaimed the vicar with the sort of forced cheerfulness you use when social bombs are going off around you. 'When did you get back?'

'Just this afternoon,' said Colin. It had really been more like late morning, but who was being picky?

'Well, we're glad to have you back,' said Joan's sister Sally, doing her part to counteract the chilling effect of the human icicle sitting next to her.

Sally was what my Dresden doll-size grandmother would call a 'big girl,' tall, big-boned, with a broad forehead, broad cheekbones, and an even broader smile, framed by a profusion of exuberant brown hair. Sally was about twice Joan's width and, to my mind, twice as attractive.

Of course, that might also be because Sally was smiling a genuine smile of welcome while Joan was wearing the sort of expression Cruella de Vil might have bestowed upon a wayward dalmatian. If I were a dog, I would have put my tail between my legs and whimpered.

But I was stronger than that; I was bigger than that. And I had the man. Ha. Take that, Cruella.

I returned her glare with a benign smile.

From the corner of my eye I saw the vicar wink at me. From what I could recall, he didn't have much patience for Joan, either.

'You remember Eloise.' Colin slung a casual arm around my shoulders, adding, just as casually, 'My girlfriend.'

Joan's nose twitched as though she had suddenly smelt something very unpleasant. Sally bounced out of her chair and gave me a warm hug.

'Lovely to see you again,' she said, all but smothering me in her hair. It was part genuine nice person-ness, and part, I suspected, an attempt to give her sister time to compose herself. You may not always adore your siblings, but they are yours.

'Lovely to see you, too,' I sneezed, fighting my way through the mass of Pre-Raphaelite curls.

'I can't say how *utterly* delighted I am to see you back so soon,' said the vicar, kissing me on both cheeks in the Continental style. Since I didn't see the second one coming, he got my nose instead of my other cheek, but he didn't seem to mind.

'Ditto,' I said, rubbing my nose.

'Don't you find it terribly dull after London?' asked Joan, the only one who hadn't bothered to rise, in tones so terrifyingly posh that they couldn't possibly be real. Especially since Sally didn't sound like anything of the kind.

'Not at all,' I said cheerfully. 'There's plenty to occupy me at Selwick Hall.'

'I should think so,' said Sally, with a mischievous glance at Colin.

'It's my ancestors who are the attraction,' he said, in mock woe. 'Not me.'

I shot him a glance to make sure that there wasn't a grain of truth beneath the mockery. It wasn't that long ago that his little sister had emerged from a disastrous relationship with a man who had used her solely to gain access to the family archives. It was part of why Colin had been so beastly when we'd first met; he had seen me as yet another vulture trying to batten off the family history.

It all seemed to be OK, but I leant into him a bit just the same, trusting the pressure of body to body to do more than a hundred reassuring words.

Joan's face closed like a fist. 'Anyone for a drink?' she asked in tones you could have used to cut glass.

'Guinness for me,' said Sally, and I saw her sister wince. 'Eloise?'

I looked to Colin.

'Sit down, Joan,' he said easily. 'I'm buying.'

'I'll come with you,' I said quickly.

'Gin and it?' he said, nodding to the vicar.

The vicar cast his eyes towards heaven. 'If only all my parishioners were like you. Who needs a flower rota?'

'Drinks rota, instead?' I suggested.

'That's heresy around here,' Colin said. 'We hold our flower arrangements sacred.'

'But we also like our gin.' The vicar made little shooing motions at Colin. 'Go on, go on. Fetch.'

'You mean you like gin,' I heard Joan saying as I meandered with Colin over to the bar.

'Oh, we're not going to start all that about gin being the drink of unwed mothers again, are we?' griped the vicar. 'Think of it as a good, imperial drink, the stuff the Raj was built on. That should tickle *your* fancy.'

From the tone of her response, it was clear that Joan was less than tickled.

I poked Colin in the arm. That's one of the best bits of being in a relationship: all the legitimate little touches that let you know that you belong to someone and someone belongs to you. You can't poke just anyone, after all.

I stood on the toes of my boots to whisper in his ear, 'Do you think he's flirting with her?'

Colin made a distinctly sceptical face at me. 'Eloise, half the parish has a pool going on whether he's gay.'

Considering I had wondered the same myself, it wasn't exactly a surprise. 'But if he's not . . .'

Colin was already giving drink orders to the bartender, with whom, like everyone else, he appeared on extremely familiar terms. It seemed that this pub was the local equivalent of Cheers. 'Vodka tonic for you?' he said to me.

'You remembered!' I exclaimed with pleasure. There had been a dreadful Thanksgiving party during which we stood at a bar pretending not to know each other. Well, maybe not so dreadful after all, since he had asked me out at the end of it. It had taken quite some time for me to figure out that I was being asked out, but fortunately my friend Pammy was there to interpret for me and prevent my botching it all too badly.

Colin's ears turned slightly pink. 'It's not exactly the theory of relativity,' he mumbled.

'Still.' Rising on my tiptoes, I brushed a quick kiss against his cheek. 'Thank you.'

Colin smiled down at me in a way that warmed me straight down to my toes. 'You're welcome.'

I would be lying if I said I didn't hope Joan was watching. The kiss on the cheek was, to use a very homely metaphor, a bit like a dog peeing on its territory to ward off other dogs.

Speaking of peeing . . . there was a convenient little hallway just off the end of the bar, with the traditional male and female signs prominently displayed. I took a step back from the bar, hitching my bag higher up on my shoulder in the universal gesture of 'I'm just going to the bathroom.' It's like opening your mouth when you're putting on mascara. Everyone does it without realising it.

'If you'll excuse me for just a moment . . .' I said, nodding towards the bathrooms. 'I'll be right back.'

The bathroom was much cleaner than those I'd been to in city bars, presumably because the clientele knew exactly to whom to complain if it wasn't. There were four stalls all in a row, and the row of sinks and mirror across from them. Going for the stall on the far end, I was just zipping up my pants when I heard a flurry of feet barging through the bathroom door.

'—bring her here,' Joan Plowden-Plugge's voice shrilled through the air like an electric drill.

There was a rustle of hair and a sighing noise that sounded like, 'Oh, Joan.'

I slunk back against the wall of my own stall, desperately hoping that neither of them would notice an extra pair of feet in the last loo. Fortunately, they were too preoccupied with their own conversation to notice me – or if they did see my feet, they didn't recognise them.

I could hear Joan's voice, smug, even through the stall door. 'I wouldn't want to be in her shoes when she finds out what he does.'

'I don't think you could fit into her shoes,' commented Sally casually, and I could hear the bolt of her bathroom stall sliding home.

Joan's stall door banged shut with considerably more force.

As I heard the rustle of a skirt being raised, I realised that this was the ideal time for me to make good my escape, while they were both incapable of exiting to investigate. But I stayed, like a rabbit in a hedgerow, frozen by my own curiosity. And probably just as likely to get mown over by a Range Rover. I didn't think Joan was the sort to brake for fluffy bunnies.

Joan's cut-glass tones sliced straight through three stalls. 'That's not what I meant. I just think it's disgraceful, a grown man who had a perfectly respectable career—' A forceful stream of pee drowned out the rest of her words.

'That's you,' said Sally. 'Not everyone would feel the same way.'

Joan clearly had little patience for relativism.

'I wouldn't want my boyfriend' – the gurgle of the toilet flushing all but extinguished the rest of the sentence, right up until – 'spies.'

Wait. She hadn't really said 'spies,' had she?

Maybe she had said 'sties.' As in pigs. I couldn't see Joan Plowden-Plugge having any truck with livestock that couldn't be ridden.

I tamped down on a betraying giggle at the thought of Joan Plowden-Plugge riding pig-back in her immaculate *Country Life* riding gear.

It did make sense, though, that she would look down on farming. For all her lady of the manor pretensions, everything I had seen of Joan Plowden-Plugge implied that it was the money rather than the land that counted with her. Oh, she wanted the land, too, but only if it came with designer gardens and the latest in fashionable topiary. Someone who did something in the City, eventually ending up on the honours list for dodgy financial favours done to his local MP, would be much more in her style than the gentleman farmer who actually farmed. I was reminded a bit of Hyacinth Bucket from the old comedy *Keeping Up Appearances*, forever pushing her husband, Richard, to be more posh, even though Hyacinth's view of posh was decidedly naff. Did anyone even use the word 'naff' anymore?

As I pulled myself back from that fascinating byway, the other toilet finished hiccuping. '—rather interesting, really,' Sally was saying.

Presumably not sties, then. I doubted even kindhearted Sally could find much to ooh and aah over in a sty. But spies? No. Too silly. I just had spies on the brain, courtesy of my dissertation research. It was one thing to have gentlemen spies running around in the nineteenth century, quite another in the twenty-first.

'If you like that sort of thing,' said Joan pettishly. I heard a rustling sound, like a purse being excavated none too gently.

'I like that shade,' said Sally, in a conciliatory tone.

Oh Lord, they were putting on makeup? I began to wish I had run for it while I still could. Of course, then I would have missed all that about Colin. It had been about Colin, hadn't it? And me.

It seemed like forever that they tarried in personal grooming, Sally drawing a brush through her hair, Joan frowning critically at her own reflection in the mirror, twitching a hair in place here, adding a dab of lipstick there. But then they were gone, and I sagged against the pink-and-white-papered wall, my trousers going loose at the waist as I let out all the breath I'd been holding in a long sigh of pure relief at not having been caught.

As I let myself out of the stall, I grimaced at the thought of what Colin must be thinking. I just hoped he didn't mention to the others that I'd been in the loo. Well, only one way to forestall that. Washing my hands in the sink, I dried them briskly on a paper towel and headed purposefully for the door.

It was time that the Plowden-Plugges and I were better acquainted.

Chapter Six

In her usual spot, on a small gilt chair by the wall, Charlotte could have pinpointed to the second the moment the Duke of Dovedale nodded farewell to Sir Francis Medmenham and set off across the ballroom – directly for her corner.

Charlotte immediately sat up straighter, a move that did not escape the attention of her best friend.

'Hail, the conquering duke approacheth!' exclaimed Henrietta, who didn't need wine to make her dangerous.

'Shhhhh!' hissed Charlotte, making an ineffectual batting motion. 'He might hear you.'

'I,' said Henrietta, enjoying herself altogether too much, 'am not the one your duke is here to see. Or hear.'

Charlotte decided it would be a waste of time and breath to reiterate that she did not, in fact, have a duke. Besides, her – er, *the* duke – was already upon them, looking painfully dashing in the light of the mirror-backed sconces.

He was wearing the same sort of evening kit as everyone else, with a garnet-toned waistcoat adding colour to an otherwise starkly black and white ensemble, but on him, it looked different. It wasn't just that his cravat was simply tied rather than being teased and creased into whatever the latest fantasy of fashion demanded. It wasn't just that his breeches stretched against genuine muscles rather than padding when he walked. Charlotte knew she wasn't supposed to notice such things, but after years of Penelope, one did, and a very nice view it was.

There was something alive and vital about him that made the glittering stretch of the gallery seem small and fusty. He needed a horse beneath him, a spear in his hand, an expanse of muddy battlefield, with trumpeters following along behind to sound out a triumphant peal as he passed.

'Charlotte?' whispered Henrietta. 'Are you all there?'

'No,' admitted Charlotte. 'Do you think it's quite normal that whenever I see Robert, I hear trumpets?'

'I've heard of violins, but . . . trumpets?'

'I know,' sighed Charlotte. 'It's all the fault of Agincourt.'

There was no time for Henrietta to demand that she explain herself; Robert was already upon them, and the trumpets flared to a final, triumphal fanfare in her head.

It was rather odd to reflect that she had known him even before she had known Henrietta, whom she always thought of, in all capital letters, as her best and oldest friend.

Henrietta, however, seemed determined to make Charlotte re-think that designation.

'Hello!' Henrietta popped out of her chair, ignoring protocol with the blithe unconcern of one to the marquisate born. 'You must be Charlotte's duke.'

At the moment, Charlotte didn't want a duke; Charlotte wanted a hole to open in the parquet floor and swallow her up.

'I'm afraid you have the advantage of me,' said Robert,

although he did not, Charlotte noted with guilty pleasure, challenge Henrietta's description of him. Of course, he couldn't very well admit to being a duke but deny being Charlotte's. So there was really very little to read into it, other than the fact that she was behaving like a complete ninny and needed to stop *now*.

'I am Lady Henrietta Sel – um, Dorrington.' Henrietta hadn't quite got into the habit of her married name yet. She smiled winningly. 'Charlotte's oldest and dearest friend.'

'In which case,' said Robert, bowing over her hand, 'I am doubly honoured to make your acquaintance.'

Over his bowed head, Henrietta pushed up her eyebrows as far as they would go and pursed her lips in the general direction of Robert's head. After years of Henrietta's facial expressions, Charlotte was able to correctly translate it as, 'I like this one! Keep him.'

As Robert straightened, Henrietta returned her features to their normal positions, assuming an expression of exaggerated innocence. At any moment now, she was going to start whistling.

'Henrietta and her husband are here for Twelfth Night,' said Charlotte primly.

'Twelfth Night,' agreed Henrietta, her eyes flicking back and forth between Robert and Charlotte. 'It's . . . on the twelfth night.'

'I had hoped to trouble you for a dance,' said Robert to Charlotte. 'But if you're otherwise engaged . . .'

Behind his back, Henrietta made enthusiastic shooing gestures.

Charlotte swallowed a smile. Henrietta was so dear, and so unsubtle.

'I would be delighted,' said Charlotte, placing her hand on his arm. It looked rather nice there. She was very glad she had thought to wear fresh gloves.

It was not until they were lined up with the other couples and the first couple was galloping enthusiastically down the line that Charlotte realised that Robert was only about one quarter there. He said all the right things at the right time. He complimented her dress and twirled her in the appropriate direction and made the requisite snide comment about Turnip Fitzhugh's execrable taste in waistcoats, but he did it all by rote, with a smile that never quite reached his eyes. He also appeared to have developed a twitch that involved frequent glances over his shoulder at the left side of the room.

'Is something wrong?' Charlotte asked as they pranced down the centre of the long row of clapping couples.

'Have you promised anyone the next dance?' he asked abruptly.

'No.'

'Would you mind if we get some air?'

'No, not at all,' said Charlotte, although the air in the gallery seemed perfectly fine to her, and the Fairy Queen was one of her very favourite country dances. Charlotte sank into a curtsy as he bowed. 'It is a little close in here.'

Rising from her curtsy, she saw Robert looking grimly over his shoulder again. 'Close is just the word for it.'

Charlotte looked quizzically at him, but Robert made no offer to explain, and she didn't press him. Whatever reason he might have for suddenly finding the gallery too close, she had no objection to anything that led them together to a quiet corner. One might even call it a tête-à-tête. Penelope certainly would.

Charlotte hastily got her visage under control before a very silly smile could break out.

She was, she realised, being exceedingly silly. She had managed to pass eight days in her cousin's company behaving like a perfectly normal and rational human being – well, no more irrational than usual, at any rate – and there was no reason that being translated from their usual routine onto a dance floor should make her all fluttery and tongue-tied, even if Robert himself was behaving exceedingly oddly. Charlotte would have liked to think it was because he was nobly battling his passion for her, but it seemed far more likely that he was having the usual reaction of the healthy male to being made to mince around in circles in the centre of a ballroom. Henrietta's Miles tended to react in much the same way, and could usually be found fleeing for the card room sometime after the first quadrille.

Either way, she would far rather be not dancing with Robert than dancing with anyone else. For the first time, she began to understand what drove Penelope to seek out secluded balconies – although she still had extreme difficulty understanding why Penelope chose the men she did to accompany her.

'Shall we go that way?' Charlotte suggested, pointing towards the far end of the gallery.

The rooms along the garden front had all been pressed into service for the party, with one salon set up as a supper room, and another as a refuge for gentlemen looking to play cards. But on the far side of the gallery, effectively blocked off behind the musicians, the remaining rooms of the West Wing lay dark and still. It wasn't quite a balcony, but it would be warmer, and just as quiet. Quieter, probably. Penelope had disappeared with Freddy Staines a good quarter of an hour ago.

'Wherever you lead,' Robert said, and then gave the lie to his words by hustling her along beside him at a pace that forced her to take two steps to each of his one.

It wasn't until she stumbled over the long hem of her skirt that Robert noticed she was having trouble keeping up. Righting her with one hand beneath her elbow, he made a penitent face. 'Sorry,' he said, slowing down. 'I didn't mean to rush you.'

'If you really didn't want to dance, you could have just said so,' Charlotte teased.

Robert looked at her blankly.

'Never mind,' said Charlotte. Wherever he was, it wasn't somewhere jokes could follow.

The entrance she sought was blocked by a cunningly hung tapestry featuring a stirring representation of the second Duke of Dovedale welcoming King William III as he stepped off his ship, the *Den Briel*, at Brixham Harbour. Certain tactful licence had been taken with the historical scene, such as adding an extra six inches to the king so that the second duke wouldn't tower over him quite so badly. The Lansdownes did tend to run to height. That was another way in which Charlotte had taken after her mother's family.

Her lack of inches was, however, very convenient for ducking through small doorways. Charlotte gestured Robert through the gap behind the arras, into a curious octagonal room with three-sided windows on either side and delicately carved stone arches that rose to meet around an elaborate rosette in the centre of the ceiling. The fabric swished back into place behind them, sealing them away as effectively as a medieval maiden barricaded into a tower.

They might be only just on the other side of the gallery, but the thick stone walls and heavy fabric made it feel a world away. The only light came from the torches flickering in the grounds outside. Filtered through the thick glass panels of the leaded windows, the light made pretty shadows on the stone benches beneath the windows, like fish beneath the waters of a pond. It was also dramatically cooler, shrouded in thick stone, away from the light and press of bodies in the room beyond.

Away from the ballroom, Robert looked considerably more cheerful. Stopping in the precise middle of the room, he linked his hands together and stretched up towards the ceiling. Tall as he was, his arms didn't come near the centre of the roof.

'Where are we?' he asked, examining his surroundings with interest. 'I don't remember this from my last stay.'

'This is the anteroom to the old chapel,' Charlotte explained, resting one knee on the stone window seat as she leant over to unlatch one of the leaded windows for the promised fresh air. There had been cushions once, but the duchess had ordered them removed, pointing out that penitence ought to be as hard on the bum as it was on the soul. In reality, Charlotte suspected that it was just that her grandmother hadn't wanted to go to the trouble of having them replaced. 'There's a theory that the room was designed this way as an allegory of the Trinity, with each of the three-sided window embrasures representing the Father, the Son, and the Holy Ghost.'

Propping one elbow against a carved niche in the wall, Robert appraised her knowingly. 'But you don't believe it,' he said.

It gave her a warm and cosy feeling to know that he knew her that well already, like hot tea on a rainy day.

'But I don't believe it,' Charlotte admitted. 'I think it's more likely that Vanbrugh just liked the way the curve of the wall looked from the outside. He used a similar technique at

Blenheim. Don't mention that to Grandmama, though. She likes to think that we're unique.'

'You are,' said Robert fondly.

Before Charlotte had time to bask in the compliment properly, he added, in an entirely different tone, 'And so is your grandmother.'

'Every fairy tale needs a witch,' said Charlotte unthinkingly, and then hastily added, 'not that Grandmama is a witch, of course. Just a bit . . .'

'Witchlike?' contributed Robert.

'Set in her ways,' finished Charlotte.

The draught from the window was going right up the back of her neck – there were some disadvantages to upswept coiffures – so she turned to shut the window. Having once tasted freedom, the panel didn't want to close again. Robert's large hand settled over hers, pushing the latch capably back into place.

'The duchess isn't very kind to you,' he said, so close that she could feel his breath warm against the back of her neck.

Maybe upswept hair wasn't such a very bad thing after all.

'She doesn't mean any of it unkindly,' said Charlotte, addressing herself to the windowpanes in the hopes that if she stayed very, very still, he wouldn't move away. The hairs on the back of her neck prickled, but it wasn't an uncomfortable sensation. Every inch of her body felt gloriously alive and aware. She wondered what would happen if she turned around. Would he stay where he was, close enough to kiss?

Charlotte's voice was slightly breathless as she added, 'It's just the way she is. Would you condemn a tiger for biting?'

'I would, actually,' said Robert, stepping back. 'Especially if it lopped off part of my anatomy.'

Turning, Charlotte smiled up at him. 'Grandmama seldom

lops anything. She pokes and prods, but her victims are usually left whole, if slightly bruised.'

'She seems to have taken a fancy to Tommy.'

'She's made him her cane-bearer for the evening. It's really a rather good position to be in. If he's holding it,' Charlotte explained, 'he can't be hit by it.'

'Better him than me,' said Robert feelingly.

'She likes you, too,' said Charlotte, settling herself down on the stone bench. Cold still seeped through the edges of the warped old panes, but with the window closed, the draught was bearable. 'I heard her say at breakfast the other morning that you were a Lansdowne "through and through, by Gad."'

'Is that meant to be a compliment?'

'It's generally better just to take it as one,' said Charlotte comfortably, fluffing her skirts out around her feet.

'Very wise advice,' said her cousin, sitting down next to her.

Against the stone floor, the silver embroidery on her green slippers looked like tiny stars. Charlotte wiggled her toes to make them twinkle. 'Why were you in such a terrible snit just now?' she asked.

'I wasn't—' Robert broke off with a sigh as she looked at him. 'It wasn't a terrible snit.'

'One seldom has small snits,' said Charlotte. 'They'd be barely noticeable as snits and then what would be the point of having them?'

'Shall we call it a snit of medium size and leave it at that?'

Charlotte's lips quirked. 'A snit of average snittiness?'

Robert leant his forehead against the windowpane in an attitude of mock agony. 'I think I'm all snitted out for the moment, thank you very much.'

'You still haven't said what it was that set you off.'

For a moment, Robert seemed like he might be about to demur, but Charlotte pinned him with her very best inquisitive expression.

Pushing up off the bench, Robert strode over to the small, carved face of an angel on the opposite wall.

'It was just something Medmenham said,' he muttered, poking at the pointy end of the angel's wing. 'I may have overreacted.'

Charlotte wondered what Medmenham had said. Robert had shown himself to be fairly unflappable, even during his last visit all those years ago. Not even all the duchess's poking and prodding managed to elicit anything more than a raised eyebrow and a carefully composed riposte. He carried his very own shield along with him, welded to his skin. It was a nicely gilded shield, charmingly crafted and pleasing to the eye, but it was a shield nonetheless. Every now and again a flicker of stronger emotion flared up, but he always caught it and stuffed it back beneath his pleasant façade before she got to see anything interesting.

'Sir Francis does seem to have that effect on people,' she said carefully.

Robert looked up sharply from his angel. 'Has he been bothering you?'

The idea was so absurd that Charlotte couldn't quite suppress a smile. 'Me? Don't be silly.'

'I don't see what's so silly about it,' said Rob stiffly.

'I'm not the sort of girl Francis Medmenham bothers,' said Charlotte simply, as though that were that.

In Charlotte's opinion, that *was* that.

Her cousin felt otherwise.

'If Medmenham asks you to go anywhere with him, don't.' Robert searched Charlotte's face for comprehension and found only polite attention.

What did he expect? Good God, the girl was even prepared to believe the best about the dowager duchess. She would be easy prey for a hardened rake like Medmenham. In Charlotte-land, gentlemen were gentlemen, everyone was exactly what they seemed, and indecent propositions were things that happened to other people.

Robert raised the level of urgency in his voice. 'Don't go anywhere alone with him,' he stressed. '*Anywhere.*'

'You mean somewhere like here?' Charlotte teased.

'You probably shouldn't be alone here with me, either,' said Robert grimly. 'Not with anyone.'

Charlotte looked up at him from under her lashes. 'Are you planning to make improper advances?'

Robert went red straight through to the tips of his ears. 'Certainly not!'

'Well, there you are,' said Charlotte cheerfully, as though that explained everything.

Robert wasn't quite sure how he had managed to lose that argument. 'Someone else might have, though.'

'But that someone else wouldn't be you.'

'You're very trusting.'

'You needn't make it sound like it's a bad thing,' said Charlotte with a laugh. 'Isn't it better to trust people than not?'

'Not always.' There were only a handful of people in his life who had proved themselves worthy of trust. Tommy. Colonel Arbuthnot. Charlotte.

Charlotte raised her chin. She still looked like an angel, but a very stubborn one. 'I believe that people tend to live up or down to your expectations. When you trust them, you give them the opportunity to vindicate that trust.'

'And if they don't? That sounds like a very dangerous

philosophy. You shouldn't trust anyone too far. Including me,' he added repressively.

'Why ever not?'

'I'm a rotten apple.'

A dimple appeared in Charlotte's right cheek. 'You certainly don't look like an apple.'

'A *rotten* apple,' Robert stressed, just in case she might have missed the crucial point. It seemed, somehow, absolutely imperative that she be warned what she was dealing with. The product of taverns and alehouses, drunken mess parties and rough marches. 'Wormy and canker-ridden.'

Charlotte glanced at him sideways. 'If you were really wormy and canker-ridden, you wouldn't be admitting to it.'

Robert grasped at straws. 'Can't one be canker-ridden with a conscience?'

Charlotte shook her head so decisively that strands of her hair tangled in her eyelashes. Robert's hand tingled with the urge to smooth them back. 'It's a contradiction in terms. Cankers have no consciences. Just look at Francis Medmenham.'

'Don't,' Robert said irritably. 'And hopefully he won't look at you, either.'

Charlotte favoured him with one of her disconcertingly level glances. 'If you think so poorly of him, why do you spend so much time with him?'

For a moment, Robert was tempted to confide in her, to tell her the whole sordid story of the colonel's death and Wrothan's disappearance. It would be a relief to have someone else to talk to; Tommy, good and loyal friend though he was, had all but disappeared in Miss Deveraux's train, living for her smiles and moping at her frowns. It made him decidedly less than useful for plotting and planning purposes. Besides, he didn't want Charlotte thinking that he patronised Medmenham for, well, for the obvious reasons, for his connections to gaming hells, opium dens, loose women, and other licentious pleasures. Robert wasn't sure why Charlotte's opinion mattered so much to him, but it did. She was his touchstone, his lodestar, his shining spot of virtue in a dark world, everything that was good and kind and pure.

And sheltered.

If he told her about the colonel – she would understand, that much was for sure. Knowing Charlotte, she would immediately conceive of it as a glorious quest, St George sallying forth to kill the dragon and make the world safe for afternoon tea, sticky toffee pudding, and all the good yeomen of England. Charlotte would want to play, too, not realising that it wasn't a game, but in deadly earnest. He didn't want her anywhere near Wrothan. And even if she stayed clear of Wrothan, what of Sir Francis?

Charlotte was still looking at him, waiting for an answer. Robert shrugged, packing it with as much nonchalance as he could muster.

'Everyone needs a diversion now and again. Medmenham's an amusing fellow.'

That was true as far as it went. Medmenham would be an entertaining companion but for that whiff of brimstone that hovered around him. However, he was certainly not a fit companion for Charlotte. Under any circumstances.

It wasn't so very long ago that unscrupulous men had made a practice of kidnapping heiresses as brides. When he thought what someone like Medmenham might do . . . Robert's hand closed so tightly around the angel's wing that it left a dent in his palm.

Robert forced himself to release his grip. It wasn't as though Medmenham and his friends were going to kidnap Charlotte as a virgin sacrifice for their ridiculous Hellfire Club. At least, he hoped they didn't have virgin sacrifices. And even if they did, they wouldn't dare touch Charlotte. She was too well connected to be lightly trifled with, and by all that was holy, he would make sure that Medmenham and the rest of his crew knew it. No one toyed with the cousin of the Duke of Dovedale.

It was slightly lowering to know that the Dowager Duchess of Dovedale was probably more of a deterrent than he was.

The devil of it was, he probably was overreacting, prey to morbid fancies and all that rot. Feeling that he had already belaboured the point far too much, Robert scuffed his shoes against the worn flagstones of the floor and said, 'Just be wary of Medmenham, that's all.'

Charlotte rose from her perch on the window seat and touched a hand lightly to his arm. Her gloved fingers were tiny and very pale against his sleeve, like a china miniature. 'You're very sweet to look out for me.'

'Sweet?' said Robert, with feigned indignation. 'You'll have me laughed out of my regiment.' The words were already out of his mouth before Robert remembered that he no longer had a regiment. It was an oddly empty feeling, no longer belonging to anything.

'Kind, then,' she said, smiling at him as though he were Lancelot, Sir Galahad, and the rest of the Round Table all wrapped into one.

Robert's hand closed over hers. 'You make it very hard to refuse a compliment.'

Charlotte tilted back her head, tossing a loose curl back over her shoulders. 'I'll just keep throwing adjectives at you until you accept.'

The faint light of the distant torches slanted through the uneven old windowpanes, sending golden flecks dancing along her curls like angels on pins.

Robert leant forwards, his hand tightening on hers. 'I'd better accept then, hadn't I?'

Her lips looked very pink and soft as she smiled up at him, that small, close-lipped smile that was so distinctively Charlotte's. It would only take just a whisper of movement, barely a movement at all, to lean forwards and brush those lips with his, to tangle his hands in that net of golden hair and kiss her until the torches in the garden flickered and died.

What in all the blazes was he thinking?

Dropping her hand, Robert stumbled back a step, bumping into his old friend, the carved angel. The angel's wing jabbed him painfully in the ribs, like an outraged duenna.

Robert clapped a hand to his bruised side. He could swear the bloody stone angel was smirking at him. It served him right. What *had* he – no, he didn't want to go into what he had been thinking. It was best to think about something safe and neutral, something that didn't have anything to do with lips or kissing or other decidedly uncousinly concepts. Like refreshments.

'Would you like some ratafia?' he asked hastily. 'I'll fetch you some ratafia, shall I?'

'I don't think there is any ratafia,' said Charlotte, blinking at him as though he had just gone mad, which, to be fair, he had.

'Lemonade, then,' he said, backing away towards the doorway. 'Everyone likes lemonade.'

'Lemonade would be lovely,' said Charlotte, bemused but game.

Robert offered her his arm, a very stiff arm, held a full six inches away from his body, just in case her guardian angel decided to get feisty again.

'Shall we?' he said. 'Let me take you back to the gallery. It's getting a little chilly in here.'

'Really?' she murmured as she accepted his arm. 'I found it quite warm.'

She didn't know the half of it.

'Lemonade,' gabbled Robert as he all but pushed her back through the arras, into the warmth and light and, most important, people. Lots and lots of people. 'Let's get you that lemonade.'

'That would be lovely,' Charlotte said, and smiled up at him with her big, innocent, pale green eyes.

It was deuced uncomfortable being a canker with a conscience.

Chapter Seven

A s they ducked under the tapestry, the glare of the candlelight hit his eyes like an attack of conscience. After the dim confines of the chapel anteroom, the light of the gallery was blinding, with all the candles in their mirror-backed sconces blazing away, beaming off of the gilding on ceiling and walls and the jewels worn by ladies and gentlemen alike. The sudden glow left spots in front of Robert's eyes, like fireworks on the king's birthday. Wincing, Robert imagined this must be what it would be like on the Judgment Day, with truth winkling out all the dark places in one's soul.

'Hullo!' Lord Frederick Staines hailed him across the room. 'There you are, Dovedale. We've been looking for you.'

'Oh?' Robert deliberately looked anywhere but at Charlotte. It was an entirely unnecessary measure. Staines looked right over Charlotte's head as if he hadn't even noticed her presence at Robert's side. Admittedly, being a good foot shorter than the two men, she was well below Staines's eye level. And Staines wasn't the sort of man to notice anything that didn't immediately touch his own concerns.

Staines's cheeks were flushed with what might have been wine or windburn or both. Judging from the matching colour in Miss Deveraux's cheeks, apparently he had been enjoying the amenities of the balcony, despite the inclemency of the weather.

'Are you coming?' Staines demanded, jerking his head in the direction of the door.

'Where?' Robert asked warily, prepared to politely extricate himself from high-stakes card games and absurd wagers, like betting on how many times Turnip Fitzhugh could hop the length of the gallery on one foot while balancing a glass of port on his head.

'To the tree.'

'I beg your pardon?' Robert might be going mad, but he wasn't quite that mad. King George might occasionally think that he was Noah and lived on an ark, but Robert was fairly sure one didn't go calling on trees at midnight. Or ever.

Staines looked at him as though he suspected Robert might be just a little bit thick. 'To the Epiphany tree.'

Charlotte came to his rescue, stepping in before he could embarrass himself any further. 'It's an old country tradition,' she explained. 'On Epiphany Eve, the gentlemen gather round the biggest tree on the estate – or at least the most convenient big tree – to scare away the evil spirits.'

'How does one go about doing that?'

Lord Henry Innes clapped Rob on the shoulder in passing. 'You shoot them, man. What else?'

Robert eyed the pistol Lord Henry was idly swinging from one finger. He hoped to hell it wasn't primed. 'Does the duchess know you have that in her ballroom?'

'It's your ballroom now, old sport,' said Lord Henry, and went on swinging.

'Brilliant,' muttered Robert. 'Why don't you go along outside and I'll grab up a weapon and be right with you.'

'No need.' Lord Henry produced the twin to the pistol in his hand. He twirled it professionally before handing it over to Robert. It was not, Robert was relieved to see, loaded. At least, not yet.

'Thought you might not have come prepared, having been away and all that.' Some of Robert's surprise must have shown on his face, because Lord Henry added, 'You're one of us now. We take care of our own.'

'Not quite one of you yet,' said Robert guardedly, all too aware of Charlotte at his side.

Lord Henry brushed that aside with a sweep of his pistol. 'Soon enough. Now we just need the rest of the kit for tonight.'

'The rest of the kit?'

Freddy Staines, who had been unabashedly sizing up the ladies as the men talked, popped back into the conversation. An expectant grin spread across his face, all but dislodging his ridiculously high shirt points. 'The cider.'

Charlotte held up her hands. 'I can't tell you anything about the cider, other than that it is also a local tradition.'

'No old stories about it?' Robert teased. 'No local lore?'

'Well . . .' began Charlotte, but Lord Freddy's loud voice overrode hers as though she weren't even there.

'To tell stories, you need to remember them,' said Lord Freddy sagely. 'And you won't after this cider.' Raising his gloved fist in the air, he called out, 'To the tree!'

'To the tree!' echoed raggedly throughout the room.

The cry was seconded as loudly by the local men as it was by the London bucks. From around the room, red-faced squires rousted out muskets that looked like they had last been used during the War of the Spanish Succession and charged towards the ballroom door as though personally on their way to stave off a French advance. Or a horde of maddened trees.

Robert had assumed the locals had been invited as a courtesy to the county set; now he wondered whether they were part of this ceremony of the tree. Yet another thing he didn't know about his own estate. Not for the first time, he heartily wished himself back in India. Among other things, in India, he wouldn't be freezing in the January cold, shooting at a tree.

'Coming, Dovedale?' tossed off Innes over his shoulder. 'It is your tree.'

Medmenham was heading to the exit with the rest, holding an elegant pistol with silver chasing and mother-of-pearl inlay as though he knew exactly what to do with it. Robert looked down at Charlotte's golden head. She didn't seem the least bit alarmed at being surrounded by an inebriated mob of heavily armed men, although whether that was the result of a country upbringing or because her imagination transmuted them all to dashing cavaliers, he wasn't quite sure.

At least if Medmenham was outside shooting at a tree, he wouldn't be inside with Charlotte.

'Sweet dreams, cousin.' Robert squeezed her hand in what he hoped was a cousinly way, adding with all the emphasis he could muster, '*Stay inside.*'

'Of course,' said Charlotte, blinking up at him in complete and happy obliviousness. 'I wouldn't dream of trespassing. It might ruin the ritual.'

'I was thinking more of stray bullets,' Robert lied.

'I believe the general practice is to fire up,' said Charlotte thoughtfully. 'But I've never actually seen it.'

'I wish I could say the same. It's bloo – er, ridiculously cold out there.'

'You've spent too much time in India,' teased Charlotte. 'This is nothing more than a stiff breeze.'

'Dovedale!' hollered Lord Henry.

Robert sighed. 'Duty calls.'

Charlotte flapped a hand at him in farewell. 'Enjoy your tree.'

Robert cast a comic look of disgruntlement over his shoulder as he followed after the other tree-hunters.

'Well!' said Henrietta, grabbing Charlotte by the crook of the arm and dragging her towards the nearest alcove. '*That* was interesting.'

'Define *that*,' said Charlotte breathlessly, trotting along in her friend's wake.

Henrietta dropped her arm and gestured broadly. 'Him. You. *That*.'

She peeked around the corner of the ice blue brocade screening the alcove and, finding it unoccupied, waved at Charlotte to precede her in. Dragging the drape shut behind them, she dropped onto the cushioned bench.

'That look. And you were out of the ballroom together for the longest time. You were together, weren't you?'

'Yes, we were,' admitted Charlotte. A dimple appeared in her left cheek. 'Tête-à-tête, even.'

Henrietta's hazel eyes gleamed. 'Tête-à-tête? Or TÊTE-À-TÊTE tête-à-tête?'

On a sudden impulse, Charlotte reached out and squeezed her friend's hand. 'Oh, Hen, I *am* glad you're here. You don't know how much I've missed you these past few days.'

Henrietta beamed. 'I've missed you, too. But you still haven't answered my question.'

Charlotte considered the question. 'Somewhere in between, I think. I don't believe it was initially intended as a tête-à-tête, but it became . . . somewhat tête-à-tête along the way.'

'And by that, you mean . . . ?'

Charlotte thought back over those few minutes in the chapel anteroom. It was already becoming hazy in memory, filmed with a heavy layer of wishful thinking. 'I wish I knew.'

'Charlotte!'

'There's not terribly much to tell. He was very insistent that I should stay away from Sir Francis Medmenham—'

'Jealous!' crowed Henrietta. 'He's jealous!'

'Or just being protective,' corrected Charlotte, in the interest of fairness. 'Sir Francis's reputation isn't the best. And Robert is the head of the family, no matter how long he's been away. It's his responsibility to look out for me.'

Amazing what a lowering word 'responsibility' could be. Charlotte approved of responsibility in principle, just not as directed towards her.

Henrietta waved that aside. 'Protective, jealous. They're both sides of the same coin. Just ask Miles.' A satisfied smile spread across her face. 'He was delightfully cranky about Lord Vaughn.'

'So was your mother.'

'Not in the same way,' said Henrietta definitely.

Charlotte decided it was better not to go into that one. Lady Uppington, like Henrietta, was a woman of strong opinions and not afraid to voice them. Charlotte wondered what Lady Uppington would think of Robert . . . With an effort, Charlotte wrenched her attention back from that fascinating line of speculation.

'So?' demanded Henrietta. 'What happened after he warned you off of Medmenham?'

'Well . . .' Charlotte bit down on her lower lip. 'We were standing in the chapel anteroom, and I thought, for a moment—'

'Yes?'

The colour rose in Charlotte's cheeks as she fiddled with one of the pearl buttons on her glove. 'I thought for a moment he was going to kiss me. But he didn't,' she added hastily, before Henrietta could say whatever it was she was obviously bursting to say. 'So I must have been imagining things. As I am wont to do.' She sighed.

Sometimes, having an overactive imagination could be a distinct liability. The daydreams were lovely, but it was always so disappointing when they turned out to have no relation to reality. Her debut three years ago had been a case in point.

Henrietta, on the other hand, saw nothing to be disappointed about. She sat bolt upright and jabbed a finger into the air. 'Ah! An almost kiss!'

Charlotte wrinkled her nose at her dearest friend. 'I didn't know there could be an almost about a kiss. It seems like the sort of thing that either happens or it doesn't.'

'Oh, no,' said Henrietta, with the worldly wise air of someone who had been married for a whole six months. 'There's an entire universe of near misses out there, kisses that almost were, but weren't.'

'How very sad,' said Charlotte. 'Can't you just picture it? The Land of Lost Kisses. All the loves that might have been but weren't.'

Henrietta's chin lifted with an expression of pure determination that Charlotte recognised all too well. 'Yours will be. You just need to make almost an actuality.'

* * *

It wasn't as cold as he had feared. That was one of the saving graces with which Robert consoled himself as they tramped across the park towards their designated tree. Like good elves, the ubiquitous staff had been there before them. In their wake, a substantial bonfire burnt a safe distance from the tree line, the leaping flames adding a pagan tang to the evening.

The servants had also left a folding table on which rested two rows of rough brown jugs made of a coarse pottery that contrasted strikingly with the snowy cloth of Irish linen that had been laid across the table. Lord Henry Innes made straight for the table, while two of the locals, clearly men of substance in the local community with preexisting grudges, began quibbling over which oak was meant to be the Epiphany tree.

Robert didn't see how the particular tree mattered; once they started shooting off all those pistols, rifles, muskets, and – heaven help them all, was that a blunderbuss? – any evil spirits who had had the poor judgment to roost anywhere within a two-mile radius were sure to be rousted out and set to flight.

Both men tramped over to him, firearms in hand, and poured out their competing theories. Fortunately, Robert managed to refrain from asking why in the devil they were chewing his ear off. He had nearly forgotten. He was meant to be the duke, and thus expected to settle this sort of dispute. He might not know about trees, but he did know about quarrelling men.

Robert picked a third tree at random.

'This one,' he said as the flames cast grotesque shadows across their expectant faces. 'It's clearly the biggest of the lot.'

'How positively Solomonic,' murmured Medmenham. It didn't sound like a compliment. Strolling to the other side of the tree, he tapped it lightly with one knuckle. 'Crammed full of evil spirits, too, I warrant.'

Robert suspected any evil spirits were outside rather than inside the tree. But since they were holding firearms, it didn't seem like a good time to press the point.

Instead, he said mildly, 'Shall we get on?'

Turnip Fitzhugh warily circled the tree, as though expecting it to engage in a pre-emptive strike. 'I say, are we meant to shoot at the tree or away from it?'

'At it, I should think,' replied Lord Freddy Staines, polishing the stock of his pistol to bring out its pretty sheen. His initials were tooled onto the stock in shiny silver filigree, all extravagant curlicues and improbable flourishes. 'How else are we to kill the evil spirits?'

Fitzhugh nodded as though that made perfect sense to him.

Robert gritted his teeth and resisted the urge to bang someone's head against the tree, preferably Staines's. He had seen Staines's type time and again in the army, pampered aristocrats, confident to the point of obtuseness, who barely knew one end of a gun from the other but had no scruples about sending whole regiments of men far more seasoned than they to their deaths in battle plans so ridiculous that even a five-year-old child could have seen the flaws.

In short, the sort of man who would recommend so idiotic a measure as pointing a bullet at a hard object at point-blank range with a large group of people clustered around. There was a name for that. It was called suicide.

Robert did his best to put it in an idiom they would all understand. 'I'd say shooting at the tree would be a jolly dangerous idea.'

'Why?' demanded Lord Henry Innes, trooping over to join the group, a brown jug in one hand and his pistol in the other. 'It ain't going to shoot back.'

Medmenham rose to Robert's aid. 'Ricochet,' he said succinctly. 'I, for one, have no desire to breathe my last because of a bullet bouncing off a tree.'

'Better than at the hand of a jealous husband, eh?' put in Frobisher, sending an elbow towards Medmenham's ribs.

Medmenham neatly sidestepped, sending Frobisher stumbling sideways into the tree. Given the way Frobisher bounced off, Robert decided that the score was tree: one; men: zero. 'My dear fellow,' he said in a tone of mock censure, 'I do not toy with married women.'

'Safer than the unmarried ones,' retorted Frobisher, brushing bark off his sleeve. 'Right, Staines?'

Staines looked up from his pistol with a smug grin. 'I'd say it depends on which unmarried woman.' It was painfully clear to whom he was referring.

Tommy pushed away from his post by the tree. 'Don't you mean *lady*?'

Staines regarded him coolly, his fashionably high shirt points pushing against his cheekbones. 'I always say exactly what I mean.'

Something crackled in the air that wasn't the bonfire.

Robert stepped neatly between them. 'Isn't it about time we got our revels under way?'

Neither man moved. Robert could hear the puff of their breath in the cold air, the shuffle of feet against the cold ground in the unnatural stillness that preceded a challenge.

But there wasn't going to be one. Not if he could bloody well help it.

Robert seized on the first expedient that came to mind. Assuming his best ducal air, he called out, 'As your *host*, I claim the privilege of the first toast.'

He didn't have a glass to hand, or even a jug, so he made up for it by lifting both hands in what he hoped was a magisterial gesture.

'To Epiphany Eve, a time for revelry' – there was some cheering and lifting of bottles at that, a nervous, too shrill sound – 'reconciliation' – he looked pointedly at Tommy, who looked grimly back at him – 'and revelation.'

Around him, he could hear the popping sound of stoppers being yanked from jugs. 'Epiphany Eve!'

Staines let his pistol drop to his side.

Robert raised his voice to be heard above the others. 'And now – let's drink!'

'I'll drink to that!' one of the locals called out and the group dissolved into a milling mass, separating into small groups, as the men let their weapons fall and dropped onto the frozen ground for a good spot of drinking and masculine companionship. Robert wouldn't have been surprised to learn that the whole ritual was largely an excuse for getting out of the house while the women fussed over preparations for Twelfth Night. Charlotte would probably know, or at least have a theory about it.

No one seemed particularly concerned about frightening away the spirits; they were far more interested in getting at the cider and telling long, boastful stories about their weaponry. Given the amount of cider sloshing into the roots of the tree, any evil spirits were going to be too sloshed by the end of the evening to work any harm. Robert hoped that the same could be said for the humans.

Tommy stalked past, moving in the direction of the house. 'I'll be in my room,' he tossed over his shoulder in passing. He was clearly not in the mood for either revelry or reconciliation. That still left revelation.

Snagging Tommy by the arm, Robert fixed a wide smile to his face. 'I need you to talk to Frobisher,' he said softly, smiling all the while. 'Engage him about their club. Find out whatever you can.'

'Can't you do it?'

'I'm going to tackle Innes.'

Tommy shrugged his shoulders irritably. 'All right. Just don't expect me to cosy up to Staines.'

'Trust me,' said Robert. 'You will immeasurably improve my evening if you both stay as far from each other as possible. And I don't mean forty paces.'

Tommy knew exactly what he meant. 'He deserves it,' he said.

Considering that the lady in question had absconded to a balcony with Staines, the question of her honour was rather debatable. But he knew better than to say that to Tommy, at least not if he didn't want to be facing the other end of his friend's pistol. Tommy tended to fall in love about twice a year, and it was always excruciating while it lasted. Fortunately, it seldom lasted long.

'Fair enough,' Robert said evenly. 'But not now. Not when we need him to find Wrothan. Who knows? We may discover enough to bring your friend down as well.'

The latter argument had its intended effect. Without saying anything else, Tommy turned and made his way towards Frobisher. With any luck, Frobisher would already be foxed enough not to notice that the smile pasted across Tommy's face was decidedly lopsided.

Meanwhile, Robert set off in search of his own quarry. Medmenham might know the most, but of all the group, Innes struck him as the weakest link, blunt, straightforward, a reminder that man wasn't all that far removed from the animals when it came down to it. He was also, unfortunately, the one least likely to be entrusted with information of any use.

'Is that the famous cider?' Robert asked by way of opening gambit, flinging himself down onto the turf beside Lord Henry. Damp immediately began to seep through his breeches. The frozen ground was bloody cold and bloody hard.

Hoisting the jug up in the air, Lord Henry regarded it tenderly. 'The very same. Norfolk's finest.'

Yanking out the cork with his teeth, Lord Henry spat it out onto the ground beside him and took a long pull from the bottle. 'Ah,' he said, shaking his head like a dog after a dousing. 'That's more the thing. Dovedale?'

Robert accepted the jug in a philosophical spirit. It was many years since he had tasted English cider, apples not being exactly a staple of the Indian diet. But it was made out of fermented fruit. How bad could it be?

It was like drinking gunpowder.

Robert took a swig and nearly spat it out again. That had been apples once? He didn't believe it. After just one slug, his ears were ringing as though he'd been standing in the middle of a cannonade.

'Good God, man, what do they put in this brew?'

Innes snagged the bottle back. 'Don't ask, just enjoy.'

'Words to live by.' Robert snatched the bottle back and made a show of drinking deeply, working the muscles of his throat in imitation of a swallow even as he blocked the flow of liquid with his teeth. He knew how to make it look convincing. Hadn't he been trained by his father, after all? The man's main talent, the one of which he had been the most proud, had been his ability to drain any cup of spirits without coming up for air.

The effort wasn't a wasted one.

'Not bad.' Innes's voice was tinged with a connoisseur's appreciation for the concerted consumption of alcohol. 'My turn.'

His exhibition was even more impressive, given the fact that Robert was pretty sure that Innes was actually drinking. His throat muscles worked convulsively as he held the jug tilted over his mouth, some of the amber liquid trickling down along the sides of his face. Putting the jug down with an explosive gasp, he dashed the back of his hand across his mouth.

'You are clearly a master,' said Robert politely.

'It just takes practise.' Innes's voice was a little ragged, so he soothed his throat with another slug of cider.

'Cider-drinking contests at your secret society?' Robert suggested, just to get him talking. 'I'll have to start getting back in practise, then.'

The cider hadn't had time to do its work. Innes tapped his nose. 'Can't expect me to give away the club's secrets till you've been initiated, old man. Strictly against the rules.'

'Whose rules?'

Innes dropped his voice. 'Our avatar.'

'You mean Medmenham?'

'No, no. Medmenham's the fakir.' Innes helped himself to more cider.

'The *what*?' Robert didn't have to feign incredulity. Fakir or faker? It was just the sort of play on words Medmenham would enjoy, promising exotic mysteries to his credulous friends and laughing up his sleeve all the way.

'Some Oriental something-or-other,' said Innes vaguely. 'He used to be the Abbot, back when we still called ourselves the Friars of Medmenham, but then old Francis decided that that was too last season.' Innes hiccuped on the last word. 'Bloody stuff,' he said, regarding the cider fondly.

Leaning on one arm, Robert adopted his best man-to-man voice. 'You strike me as a man of action.'

In fact, Innes struck him as a man of violence, a very different thing. But Innes preened, just as Robert had known he would. He was the sort who had never entered the army, but always wished he had. He did have some sort of position in the king's household, as gentleman usher or gentleman-in-waiting or something of that ilk, a role Robert found entirely incongruous for the blunt-speaking, hard-drinking, horse-hounds-and-wenches Innes. Almost as incongruous as hearing the Eastern terms 'avatar' and 'fakir' issuing out of his chapped lips.

'Do you actually believe all this rubbish about avatars and ancient rites?'

Innes sputtered into the cider jug. 'Hell, no! I'm here for the same reasons you are.'

A deathbed promise to a good and noble man?

'The women,' finished Lord Henry. 'It's too much demmed trouble hunting them down oneself. I don't know where Medmenham finds them, but his lot will do anything. No screeching, no "I've changed my mind." I tell you, they're above rubies.'

It had been a while since Robert had consulted a Bible, but he could have sworn it was the virtuous woman who was above rubies. Lord Henry obviously had a rather different concept of virtue.

'Only the best for our orgies, that's our motto.'

'I imagine it sounds better translated into Latin,' said Robert kindly.

Lord Henry waved the jug, sending cider sloshing in an

126

arc across his own coat. 'Oh, it's all Indian these days.'

It didn't seem worth explaining to him that there wasn't any such language. During his twelve years on the subcontinent, Robert had picked up a smattering of Hindustani and Marathi, just enough to say 'please,' 'thank you,' 'is this really the price?' and 'can you tell me where the Mahratta intend to attack?'

Robert leant back on his elbows, watching as Turnip Fitzhugh executed a mock duel with a tree branch, using another tree branch. 'Really? I didn't realise Medmenham had travelled in India.'

'Francis? No.' Innes was beginning to look vaguely cross-eyed. 'Freddy brought the chap back from India.'

'Chap?'

'The avatar.' Lord Henry tossed aside the empty jug, narrowly missing one of the locals in the process, and reached for another from the little stockpile he had cunningly set up next to his chosen spot on the ground.

'Is he Indian, then?'

'I haven't the foggiest, old chap. Comes masked, you know,' slurred Lord Henry. 'We all do. I say' – Lord Henry's eyes took on a gleam of animal cunning – 'shouldn't be telling you this. Not before the sh-sheremony.'

'Of course,' said Robert smoothly, uncorking the next jug and handing it to him. 'Any idea when that might be?'

If he could find out the date and time, there was always the chance he could spy on their ceremony and assure himself of Wrothan's presence rather than actually going through with the whole rigmarole himself. If he could waylay Wrothan either on the way there or the way back . . . the whole dirty business could be done.

And then?

Rather than the winter-scarred tree, Robert had a hazy image of summer at Dovedale, summer as it had been all those years ago, with the gardens bright with flowers and summer sun gilding the surface of the lake. They had played bowls on the lawn and rowed on the lake and risked the wrath of the gardener making garlands for Charlotte to wear on her unicorn-hunting expeditions. Memory played tricks, though. Instead of a little girl in a black frock, it was a very grown-up Charlotte across from him in the boat on the lake, dabbling her fingers in the water and getting pecked at by an irate swan.

It might not be so very unpleasant staying on at Dovedale if Charlotte were there with him.

Robert viewed the brown jug with something approaching awe. That was certainly powerful stuff to send him woolgathering after just one swallow. Robert set the jug down. Hard.

'When's the next meeting?' he asked, somewhat more brusquely than he had intended.

'Next meeting?' muttered Innes, trying to focus and failing. 'Dunno. Never know.'

'Then how will I know to go?' asked Robert reasonably.

'When Francis wants you to come, you'll know.' Innes upended the jug, following its movement backwards straight onto his back. It was a bit like watching a tree falling. His voice rose hollowly from the ground. 'Trust me, you'll know.'

Chapter Eight

It wasn't until eight the following night that the party reassembled in the Red Room for the opening of the fabled Twelfth Night festivities. The Epiphany tree had obviously put up quite a fight. Against the crimson wall hangings most of the gentlemen looked only a shade less green than the boughs of holly decorating the hall. Except for Robert, who remained perfectly tan without a hint of green.

A portrait of a long-dead duchess leered at him appreciatively from above the mantelpiece. Charlotte could more than understand why.

'Oooh, it's your duke!' hissed Henrietta unnecessarily.

'I knew that,' muttered Charlotte.

A whole troupe of morris dancers jostled for space in Charlotte's stomach. After a whole day of reliving almost kisses, with improvements, Charlotte had had so many conversations with Robert in her head that she was a little fuzzy on what had actually happened and what hadn't.

Henrietta propelled Charlotte directly into Robert's path like a horticulturalist displaying a prized specimen.

'Doesn't she look ravishing?' demanded Henrietta.

Charlotte shot her a quelling glance that had absolutely no quelling effect whatsoever.

'Ravishing is just the word that comes to mind,' said Robert gallantly. 'Good evening, Cousin.'

Charlotte's morris dancers stopped dancing. She couldn't look all that ravishing if he was thinking of her as cousin. Drat. She knew she should have eased her bodice that crucial inch lower. Penelope had always told her that her gowns were cut too modestly, and now she was beginning to see why.

'Happy Twelfth Night!' she said brightly, trying to make up in enthusiasm what she lacked in décolletage. 'Did you have a nice day?'

Robert's lips twisted with amusement as he surveyed the collection of green faces scattered about the drawing room. 'Better than most, I should think.'

'How did you escape the general blight?'

'I struck a deal with the tree spirits. I wouldn't bother them if they wouldn't bother me.'

Charlotte nodded emphatically. 'Very sensible of you.' Henrietta had drifted away, but not quite far enough. She grinned encouragingly at Charlotte from behind a potted plant. Charlotte pointedly turned to the side, blocking Henrietta from her line of vision. If she couldn't see her, she wasn't there. 'I imagine they took some persuading. Tree spirits aren't known for being cooperative.'

'Tree spirits?' demanded Lieutenant Fluellen, appearing at Robert's side. Despite his carefully brushed hair and a festive red flower stuck into his buttonhole, he looked as prickly as a bunch of mistletoe. It didn't take much guessing to determine the cause. Penelope was with Staines again.

'They're spirits—' Charlotte began.

'—who live in trees,' Robert finished obligingly, and smiled down at her.

Life couldn't possibly get any better than this, thought Charlotte. Not for all the towers toppled in Ilium, not for all the knights slain in Camelot.

'We've received our marching orders from the duchess,' announced Tommy, giving his best friend a very odd look. 'You,' he said to Robert, 'are to take in the charming Lady Charlotte—'

'The *ravishing* Lady Charlotte,' Robert corrected with a slight bow in Charlotte's direction that thrilled her down to her very toes. Her neckline was suddenly perfect just as it was. In fact, everything was utterly perfect, even Turnip Fitzhugh's emerald green cravat.

'—while I have the pleasure of the company of Miss Arabella Dempsey.'

Charlotte knew Miss Dempsey only vaguely; she rather suspected the other girl had only been invited because she was even more of a wallflower than Charlotte and thus likely to pose little competition.

'What about Penelope?' asked Charlotte.

'Miss Deveraux,' articulated Tommy, 'will be going into table with Lord Frederick Staines.'

'Oh, dear,' murmured Robert.

Charlotte gave Robert's arm a warning pinch as she made a sympathetic face at Tommy. Being madly, head over heels in love herself, she wanted everyone else to be just as happy as she was. 'I wouldn't refine too much on it. Grandmama enjoys setting the seating for her own personal amusement and it probably amuses her to see Penelope poke fun at Lord Frederick.'

'I would feel far better if that's what I thought she would be doing,' said Tommy gloomily.

'Penelope hasn't the slightest interest in Lord Frederick,' Charlotte said firmly. 'Besides, he has a laugh like a braying donkey.'

'A very *wealthy* braying donkey.'

'You can gild the donkey all you like, but he's still a donkey,' said Charlotte.

'Is that like worshipping a golden calf?' asked Robert blandly.

Charlotte beamed giddily up at him. 'Yes, and you know what happened to *them*.'

'Frogs, toads and assorted pestilences?'

'Hmmm.' Tommy seemed unconvinced. Across the room, Penelope was flirting her fan at Staines in a way that suggested she found him anything but pestilential. 'They still had a jolly good revel before the smiting began.'

'And so shall you. Just wait till the dancing begins after supper and you can sweep Penelope away from Lord Frederick's clutches.'

'Tossed over his saddlebow?' enquired Robert.

Charlotte dimpled. 'Can't you picture the look on Grandmama's face at a horse in the ballroom?'

'Impertinence!' mimicked Tommy, thumping an imaginary cane.

'She'd be expecting you to carry her off, no doubt,' commented Robert.

'I wouldn't dream of it,' said Tommy, so earnestly that they all laughed. 'She'd probably have my head chopped off.'

'I don't think they let you do that anymore,' said Charlotte thoughtfully. 'Chop off heads just like that.'

'Yes, but once my head's off, I won't be there to complain to the authorities, will I?'

'Don't worry, old chap, we'll complain on your behalf,' said Robert offhandedly. 'And we'll build you a smashing funerary monument.'

'Oh, *that's* all right, then,' grumbled Tommy, and took himself off, either to find his appointed dinner companion or to moon after Penelope from another angle. Charlotte suspected the latter. Charlotte wondered if Lieutenant Fluellen knew about the balcony. For his sake, she hoped not.

'Poor man.'

'Why poor Tommy?'

'Because Penelope will never take seriously any man who admires her so obviously.'

'And what about you?'

Charlotte's heart danced a quadrille under her velvet bodice. 'That would depend on who was doing the admiring.'

Robert lifted her hand to his lips. 'Any man with eyes enough to see.'

Despite being the sort of compliment Charlotte had always daydreamed about, the praise had something a little unsatisfying about it, like a piece of hollow, gilded wood, all shimmer on the outside, but no substance within. Charlotte shrugged the feeling aside. She was ungrateful and silly and it was a perfectly lovely compliment.

Robert tucked her hand back into the crook of his arm. 'Shall we go in to supper?' he said prosaically. 'If we don't start the procession soon, your grandmother may take it upon herself to prod us into place.'

'*May?*' said Charlotte, making Robert laugh. 'You really ought to be taking Grandmama in.'

'May I say that I'm delighted to bend etiquette in this instance?'

'I would be more flattered if I thought you desired my company more than you feared Grandmama's stick,' Charlotte said ruefully.

Robert arched an eyebrow. 'Fishing for more compliments?'

'Will I get any?' Charlotte asked hopefully.

Robert patted her gloved hand. 'As many as you like.'

Charlotte wrinkled her nose at him. 'That won't do at all. An overabundance would cheapen their value.'

Robert looked down at her. A curious smile creased the corners of his lips, fond and rueful and wry all at once.

'Nothing could cheapen your value,' he said matter-of-factly.

There was nothing in his voice to have made Charlotte turn pink and look away, but she did. 'Shall we go in to supper?' she said hastily.

'If you'll show me where it is,' joked Robert. 'If you leave the guests to me, I might lead them to the stables by accident.'

'I should hope the smell would be rather different,' said Charlotte, steering him deftly down a long corridor hung with Lansdownes. It was so cold in the passageway that her breath formed little puffs in the air as she spoke. Girdings had been built for show rather than comfort, with fur cloaks rather than short sleeves in mind.

Two by two, their fellow guests fell in behind them as they wound their way from the Red Room to the state dining room. It was, thought Charlotte, a bit like Noah's Ark, only with a great deal more jewellery and fewer elephants. In their pairs, they took their seats at the long, mahogany table beneath a series of lurid murals representing the first duke's triumphs in King William's wars. There was to be an intimate supper for the thirty-odd houseguests, after which would follow a proper ball with town musicians and town guests, gorgeously arrayed, jewelled and feathered, arriving in richly caparisoned coaches that would give the villagers something to talk about until next Twelfth Night.

Charlotte took her seat beside Robert, wondering at the odd arrangement of the table that left the two of them stranded in state at the head, like a medieval lord and lady in an illuminated Book of Hours. Trying to fathom her grandmother's purposes was generally a fruitless task; she might have meant it as a statement about the superiority of the Lansdowne blood, a punishment to Robert by giving him no one but Charlotte to talk to, or a spot of ducal matchmaking.

Charlotte snuck a sideways glance at Robert. She knew which theory she preferred.

The service was *à la française*, with dishes left upon the table for all to serve themselves. Wielding a carving knife, Robert neatly helped her to a serving of roast swan, smoothly transferred oyster patties from a platter to her plate, and manoeuvred the transition of a spoonful of peas without any daring to roll away, making sure her plate was full before taking anything for himself.

Taking up her fork, Charlotte toyed idly with it, watching her dinner companion as he repeated the procedure for his own plate. In profile, with the candles casting shadows across his face, picking out the long lines of his cheekbones, he seemed suddenly very remote, as far away as the flat painted faces of the long-dead Lansdownes on the walls.

She hoped, very much, that he didn't mind being secluded with her at the head of the table. Had she daydreamed their interlude in the chapel anteroom last night? Read too much into simple cousinly kindness?

Charlotte's mouth moved without bothering to consult her brain. 'I missed you in the library today. Not that I expected you, of course.' She stabbed furiously at a pea, which promptly rolled over the edge of her plate and dribbled its way along the tablecloth.

'I wandered down to the estate office.'

He had kept his voice carefully neutral, but Charlotte's heart did a mad little hop, skip, and a jump. 'Really?'

Robert shook his head in wonder, looking younger than she had ever seen him. 'I had never realised quite how . . . involved the estate is. I meant to spend only half an hour. Four hours later, I was still squinting at ledgers, and we hadn't even got past the home farm.'

'It does take a lot of managing,' said Charlotte carefully. 'Even with a good estate agent. And Grandmama is getting on.'

Robert smiled a little ruefully. 'Are you implying I should take on the task?'

Keeping her eyes on her plate, Charlotte picked at a congealing slice of roast swan. Grandmama's culinary extravagances always sounded better in theory than in practice. 'You are the duke.'

'I certainly wouldn't be the first absentee landlord in the history of the realm.' Robert's eyes slid sideways, away from her. 'Girdings will probably fare far better free from my inept ministrations.'

'How do you know they would be inept?'

Robert pushed his chair back restlessly from the table, making the wine rock back and forth in his glass like a ship on an unquiet sea. 'I don't see how they could be anything but. I haven't been trained to this, Charlotte. I haven't been trained to any of this.'

'I imagine the first baron wasn't either,' Charlotte said

thoughtfully. 'The one who fought at Agincourt. He was a soldier, you know. A professional soldier,' she added, just in case he had missed the point. 'A sort of hired mercenary. When King Henry V gave him this land to hold, he probably didn't have any more idea what to do about it than you do.'

'How did he manage?'

'Oh, he had a very clever wife,' said Charlotte without thinking. 'I didn't mean—' she began in confusion, and broke off, covering her hot cheeks with her hands. *That you should marry me?* There was no way that sentence could end well.

'An excellent solution,' agreed Robert, mischief dancing like candlelight in his eyes. 'Are you suggesting I try the same?'

Charlotte bit down hard on a mouthful of swan. 'Not as such,' she said rather indistinctly. 'After all, you do have Grandmama.'

'I am not marrying your grandmother,' said Robert decidedly. 'However clever she may be.'

'To help you manage, I meant,' Charlotte said reprovingly, chasing away the swan with a long draught of wine. The liquid tingled on her palate, making her feel bolder. 'As you know very well.'

Robert shook his head, the light from the chandelier overhead burnishing his dark blond hair. 'I know few things very well.' He peered at her over the rim of his wineglass. 'Will that be a disadvantage in the acquisition of a clever wife?'

'One doesn't acquire wives, one woos them,' said Charlotte decidedly, feeling on rather firmer ground. Wooing was a topic of which she had made extensive study, even if it was entirely in the abstract. 'Preferably with deeds of great daring.'

'Deeds of great daring are increasingly hard to come by in this modern world. They've gone extinct. Like dragons.'

'Next you'll be telling me there are no unicorns.'

'Never that.' They exchanged a gaze warm with shared memories. 'But it is hard to imagine anyone going on a quest anymore. What would there be for them to find?'

Charlotte waved her knife in protest. 'I should think you of all people should know better. What about the more far-off parts of the world? ". . . antres vast and deserts idle, / Rough quarries, rocks and hills whose heads touch heaven . . ."'

Robert looked curiously down at her.

'Faraway lands and glorious places,' translated Charlotte dreamily, abandoning *Othello*.

'And dust and flies and dung.'

'That's not terribly romantic.'

'Neither is the wider world,' Robert said, with an attempt at lightness that didn't succeed at all. Propping his chin on one hand, he regarded her seriously over the plucked bones of the swan. 'I just don't want you to be disappointed. There is far more dust and dung than there are knights in shining armour left in the world.'

'For one good knight in shining armour, might not the kingdom be saved?'

'That depends on how much tarnish there is between the greaves,' said Robert grimly. 'He might be too rusty to do any good at all.'

'Rust is removable,' said Charlotte blithely. 'Just ask the downstairs maids.'

'Unless it eats away to the basic fabric until there's nothing worth saving.'

There was no longer any use pretending that they were speaking in abstracts. A chance phrase from the night before teased at Charlotte's recollection.

'Like a rotten apple?' Charlotte asked, watching him closely.

Robert nodded, his lips twisting with a dark sort of amusement, sickly sweet as fruit rot. 'Exactly like a rotten apple.'

Planting both hands on the table, Charlotte leant forwards. On an impulse she couldn't quite explain even to herself, she asked, 'Why did you leave when you did?'

Robert shot her a quick, startled glance. 'What?'

Charlotte caught his gaze and held it. 'All those years ago. You just disappeared. What happened?'

'I did leave a note. I understood that was the usual procedure.'

Despite herself, Charlotte couldn't help smiling. 'You forgot to leave bedsheets dangling from your window.'

'I certainly wasn't going to risk my life rappelling off linen twenty yards from the ground when there was a perfectly good staircase to be had. I was running away, not committing suicide.'

Charlotte might be amused, but she wasn't diverted. 'Why run away, though? I know Grandmama was being awful to you, but . . .'

Robert stared at the glass in front of him for a very long time. He stared at it for so long that Charlotte was tempted to take a look herself, just in case she was missing something interesting in there.

'It was a long time ago,' he said abruptly. 'It's hard to remember just what I was thinking. Ah, look, there come the cakes.'

'You do know that you're not very adept at changing the subject,' said Charlotte, to Robert's wineglass. 'And you're not a rotten apple. Or a rusty greave.'

'Cake?' said Robert blandly.

Charlotte took the cake. There was no need to punish the pastry just because Robert was being provoking.

In the proper Twelfth Day tradition, Cook had sprinkled coloured sugar over the top so that it glimmered like a dragon's hoard. Charlotte poked experimentally at the centre of her cake. In one of the little cakes was hidden a small gold crown for the Twelfth Night king or queen, in another an equally diminutive jester's staff for the Lord of Misrule. In most households, it would be a bean and a pea, but the dowager duchess had no truck with legumes.

A great shout arose from the other end of the table as Freddy Staines pumped one hand into the air, spraying crumbs across the table and down more than one lady's décolletage. A tiny golden staff glinted in his fist.

'All hail your Lord of Misrule!' he cried, thrusting his arms over his head with an enthusiasm that did serious damage to the high-piled coiffure of the lady on his right.

'Do we bring you your pipe, your bowl, and your fiddlers three?' drawled Medmenham.

'Devil take the fiddlers, bring me wine!' shouted Freddy, getting right into his role. Two footmen hastened to obey, smartly cracking decanters. The misrule was getting nicely under way.

'At least it's not Penelope this year,' began Charlotte, turning back to her dinner companion. 'Last year—'

She broke off as she noticed a blob of dough on her plate that decidedly hadn't been there before. Poking out of one corner was the unmistakable glint of gold. Next to her, Robert's cake bore a suspicious crater in its middle that just happened to be exactly the shape of the piece on her plate.

Charlotte looked hard at Robert.

Robert smiled benignly back.

Charlotte wasn't the least bit fooled. 'Did you just give me your crown?' she demanded.

Robert adopted an air of beatific innocence that wouldn't have deceived a five-year-old. 'It must have been tree spirits.'

Charlotte narrowed her eyes at him. 'Next you'll be telling me it was a unicorn.'

'It went out by the other door.'

Flaking off the remaining cake crumbs with a gallantry worthy of Sir Walter Raleigh, Robert placed the gold crown on her palm and folded her fingers firmly around it.

'No arguments,' he said, squeezing her hand. 'It always belonged to you.'

Releasing her hand, he stood, pushing back his chair so abruptly that it tottered back and forth behind him and had to be quickly rescued by the waiting footman.

'We have a monarch!' he thundered, in the sort of voice that Charlotte imagined must have brought whole regiments to heel. 'Queen Charlotte!'

'I say, does he mean the real one?' demanded Turnip Fitzhugh, craning to see over his shoulder. 'Didn't know she was coming.'

'Oh, do be quiet,' said Penelope, whacking him on the shoulder with her fork. The fact that the fork still had some cake on it was entirely beside the point. 'It's our Charlotte – *that* Charlotte. Over there.'

Robert ignored them both. 'If my Lord of Misrule would provide the crown?'

'With pleasure, Your Majesty.' Essaying a sweeping bow – a little more sweeping than intended due to the amount he had already imbibed – Lord Freddy swept up the gilded circlet on the point of his jester's staff and swaggered down the length of the table. Brandishing the garland in the air for the benefit of the audience, Lord Freddy wafted it about like a gypsy with a tambourine while the others at the table hooted, applauded, and called for a coronation.

While Freddy postured, Robert neatly snagged the crown.

Charlotte had to bite her lip to keep from giggling at Lord Freddy's expression of indignation. Laughing at a subject in distress would be decidedly unqueenly.

'I say!' protested Freddy. 'Highway robbery, by Gad!'

Robert smiled blandly. 'Nothing of the sort. I merely claim my ducal prerogative.'

The wine had already been flowing a little too freely. Someone called out, 'Is that like the droit du seigneur?'

The duchess's cane came down with a loud thump, followed by a yelp of pain.

Charlotte could see Robert's lips twitch, fighting to maintain an expression of due solemnity as he lifted the crown high above her head.

Charlotte bowed her head in a pretence of humility, knowing that if she were to meet his eyes, the laughter welling in her own throat would break out and shatter any pretence of composure. Something snagged on her hair and prickled against her scalp. Cautiously, Charlotte raised her head and felt it slip and catch, pulling painfully at her upswept hair. Like so many of her grandmother's ideas, a crown of gilded mistletoe worked better in theory than actuality.

Moving very carefully, so as not to dislodge her crown, Charlotte rose to her feet to acknowledge the cheers of her subjects.

'Allow me to be the first to felicitate you on your ascension.'

Once again exercising his ducal prerogative, Robert lifted Charlotte's hand to his lips. 'Congratulations, Queen Charlotte. Long may you reign.'

When he bowed in obeisance over her gloved hand, Charlotte felt like a queen. Her spine straightened, her shoulders moved back. She was Gloriana, the Virgin Queen, resplendent in silks and velvets, confounding foreign ambassadors and dazzling the eyes of her courtiers. And Robert? He was Sir Walter Raleigh, promising her new worlds and new kingdoms and strange little brown leaves called tobacco. Or maybe he was Robert Dudley, Earl of Leicester, the queen's Master of the Horse and secret love, ready to whisk her off for a clandestine tryst behind an alcove within yards of the courtiers milling about.

Charlotte thrilled to the romance of it, feeling gloriously imperious and utterly unlike herself.

Facing down the long table, Robert lifted his glass high, commanding the attention of the unruly revellers at table. 'To Her Majesty, our Queen of the Feast – Queen Charlotte.'

Crystal glittered in the candlelight as a chorus of slightly inebriated voices echoed, 'Queen Charlotte!'

In front of her, all down the long table, mouths opened to hail her, hands raised to toast her, and the ruby red of a dozen rings gleamed like fireworks in the air. Charlotte beamed down on the lot of them, giddy with more than wine.

'Do you have any pronouncements for your loyal subjects?' called out Tommy Fluellen, from the lower end of the table, where he was seated next to the pudding-faced Miss Dempsey.

'That I do!' called back Charlotte, deploying her fan like a sceptre. 'Go forth and enjoy yourself mightily.'

Tommy grinned at her down the table. 'A good and wise queen if ever I saw one, eh, lads?'

The lads all agreed.

'Shall we open the dancing, Your Majesty?' suggested Robert, holding out an arm.

Charlotte considered the guests streaming towards the gallery. There would be the usual jostling for place as they formed up for the dance, the endless polite inanities exchanged with dozens of dull acquaintances. That was all very well for the workaday world, but tonight she was queen, daring and reckless, able to command Armadas with a single word. It was too soon to have to go back to mundanity, to being quiet Charlotte in the corner of the ballroom. 'No,' Charlotte said decidedly. 'I have a better idea.'

'Unicorn hunting?' suggested Robert, seeming perfectly content to follow whichever way she should lead.

'It's the wrong season.' She tugged at his hands, drawing him after her. 'Come with me. I want to show you my very favourite place at Girdings.'

Chapter Nine

When his queen commanded, what was a loyal subject to
do but obey?

Swept up in her enthusiasm, Robert found himself hurrying
along as Charlotte grabbed his hand and pulled him in the wake
of the departing guests. At the door of the dining hall Charlotte
veered sharply to the left, down a narrow and barren corridor
lit with tapers at long intervals. Despite the gloom, Charlotte
moved with the assurance of familiarity, one hand still holding
his as she urged him along, her skirts making a cheerful swishing
noise as she danced ahead of him. Robert had to half run to
keep up with her, his boots skidding on the marble tiles of the
floor. For a small person, Charlotte could move very quickly
when she wanted to. Robert grinned at the thought.

'Where are you taking me?'

Charlotte glanced back over her shoulder, spinning a bit to
make the scalloped edge of her skirts flounce. 'You'll see.'

'Kidnapping, is it? What do you think you can get for me?'

'Seven swans a-swimming?' suggested Charlotte blithely.

'Just so long as we don't have to eat them.'

'No, that wasn't one of Grandmama's better ideas, was it?' said Charlotte, stopping short so unexpectedly that he nearly toppled right over her.

'Does the oubliette open here?' asked Robert, catching at the wall to keep himself from falling over her.

'We're going up rather than down,' said Charlotte, not the least bit discommoded by being hemmed between Robert and the wall.

Given certain of his thoughts at the moment, Robert was afraid that he was going very far down indeed, straight to the realms of pitch and brimstone reserved for those entertaining carnal thoughts about young ladies in dark alcoves. Their present position was as dark and secluded as any rake could desire, far from interfering chaperones and indignant duchesses.

Charlotte tilted her head up at him at an angle that would have been perfect for kissing, had Robert been considering kisses, which he most certainly was not. That was the tale he was telling to his conscience, and he was sticking to it.

'Don't you know where we are?' she asked.

'I haven't the slightest idea,' Robert said, and meant it in more ways than one.

He could see only the outlines of her smile in the general gloom, like a portrait done in charcoals, emphasising the Cupid's bow curve of her lips.

'You should,' she scolded. 'We are directly between your bedroom and dressing room.'

From anyone else that might be construed as an invitation. From Charlotte . . . it was nothing more than a geographical observation. It had to be. Didn't it?

'And these,' continued Charlotte, blissfully unaware of

the implications her last words had engendered, 'are the back stairs.'

Groping along the wall, she located a knob and turned it. A door swung smoothly open on well-oiled hinges – there would be no unsightly creaking noises permitted to disturb the duke's slumbers. Robert had to execute an inelegant hop to get out of the way before the wooden panel made straight for his nose, bowling him safely out of the way of his companion.

There was nothing like a blunt block of wood in the face to dispel lascivious thoughts.

Turning to face him, Charlotte beamed up at him in the way of an illusionist producing silk flowers out of a hat. 'This is how the servants get down to your rooms.'

'Right,' said Robert. Well, that did rather put paid to any thoughts of assignations. Coal scuttles and water buckets weren't exactly among the harbingers of romance.

Gathering her heavy velvet skirt in both hands, Charlotte started up the steps, the gold thread on her emerald slippers winking in the occasional glare of the candles placed at infrequent intervals along the stairway. 'My rooms are just above.'

'Are they?' Robert's eyebrows engaged in the sort of acrobatics that would have done credit to Drury Lane.

'Right through here.' With a sweeping gesture, Charlotte indicated a door that led off the next landing – and kept right on climbing. Robert wasn't sure whether to be relieved or disappointed.

'I used to come up and down these stairs all the time when my father was in the duke's rooms,' Charlotte's voice echoed cheerfully down the stairwell. Ahead of him the velvet train of her gown dragged against the steps, the gold threads in the hem an incongruous splash of luxury against the worn wood.

'It was the easiest way to get in and out without Grandmama seeing me.'

The underside of her train caught on a break in the stair where the warped old wood had cracked. Bending, Robert freed the fabric for her, and was rewarded with a grateful smile from on high. Three steps above him, she still looked like a queen, even with her garland tipping down over one ear.

'I forgot those were your father's rooms.'

'It was my father's idea to have me right upstairs – so I wouldn't feel so alone in a strange house. Our house in Surrey was much smaller, you see.'

She spoke without the slightest hint of bitterness. It would, thought Robert, be like Charlotte to have mastered the trick of remembering without rancour, picking out the good and discarding the bad. Bottle that and she could make a fortune.

'Do you ever miss it?' They were four flights up and still she kept climbing, her train swishing behind her like a mermaid's tail.

Charlotte paused with her hand on the rail, an emerald bracelet glinting on her gloved wrist. 'I miss the idea of it, but I don't think I would want to go back.' She smiled jauntily down at him from the lofty heights of the top step. 'I rather like where I am.'

Robert's heart squeezed in a very inconvenient way. 'I think that it would be very hard not to like wherever you are,' he said, and meant it.

What the implications of that were, he couldn't quite bring himself to work out. Fortunately, he didn't have to. With the air of a conjurer displaying a new trick, Charlotte threw open another door. 'Then wait until you see this!'

The immediate results were not auspicious. Cold air barrelled down the stairway and walloped Robert in the chest, cutting through layers of wool and linen.

'Where are we?' he asked as neutrally as he could. He had expected a conservatory, blooming with carefully preserved plants, or a library, blanketed in books. Instead, Charlotte appeared to have brought him to the North Pole.

'The roof,' said Charlotte, skipping over the threshold and taking a long, deep breath of frigid air. 'Mmmm.'

'Mmmm' wasn't quite the expression that came to Robert's mind. The word that presented itself was just as short but far more profane, so he didn't voice it. Instead, he moved with a great deal of cautiousness over the small bump at the base of the door onto the glacial surface of the roof.

'Welcome to my kingdom,' said Charlotte cheerfully, flinging her arms wide in welcome.

The tip of her nose was already beginning to turn pink, but otherwise she didn't seem to notice the cold at all. Robert made an attempt to remember how many times he had refilled her glass at dinner.

'Come see!' His extremities might be beginning to turn blue, but her enthusiasm was infectious, even among the frost-scarred stone.

Up close, the pale gold stone was pitted by the elements, scarred by past storms and stained by soot from the chimneys. But there was an odd charm to the landscape, nonetheless. A terrace ran waist-high along the edge of the roof, high enough to provide an illusion of security. Along its length perched a fanciful collection of historical and mythological personages, hectoring, lecturing, and gesturing to hypothetical persons in the gardens below.

Charlotte greeted each as an old friend. 'This,' she said,

giving Aristotle a brisk pat on the arm, 'is my first minister of state. And this' – she moved on to another robed gentleman whom Robert didn't recognise, although he had no doubt that Charlotte could – 'is my Chancellor of the Exchequer.'

'Chancellor.' Robert nodded in greeting. Being a very grand personage, the Chancellor forbore to respond.

'A bit high in the instep, isn't he?' Robert said.

'Always,' agreed Charlotte, her eyes glinting a pale, clear green in the icy air. 'He utterly refuses to play tiddlywinks and he despises having poetry read aloud. But he's very good at sums.'

Tucking Charlotte's arm against his side – for warmth, of course – Robert strolled along to the corner of the roof, where two satyrs with furry torsos and cloven hooves leant precariously over the edge, playing their panpipes for the delectation of those in the gardens below.

'And who are these rascals?'

'My court minstrels, of course,' said Charlotte.

'Of course,' agreed Robert.

Charlotte leant familiarly against the satyr's furry arm. 'They're arrant knaves, both of them, but they play beautifully.'

She announced it with such conviction that Robert could almost picture the stone arms flex and the panpipes begin to play.

'You've spent a good deal of time up here, haven't you?' he said. He could picture a miniature Charlotte spinning stories for stone statues and offering them a spot of tea.

Charlotte acknowledged the point with a wry smile. 'It was one of the few places where Grandmama couldn't follow. It was the one place that was wholly my own. And it makes a lovely spot for reading in summer,' she added more prosaically. 'I still come up here when the weather is fine.'

Robert slapped his hands against his arms to warm them, his breath making white puffs in the air. 'I can see where it might be nice – when the weather is fine.'

Charlotte wrinkled her nose at him. 'Such a fuss about a light breeze.' She waved a hand at the sky in a sweeping gesture. 'Just look up there. You don't see stars like that in summer. Can't you just imagine the Wise Men travelling through the night by the light of those stars?'

Robert suspected it would have been a hell of a lot warmer in Bethlehem. The stars, however, were everything Charlotte had said they were. In the clear, cold air, they looked close enough to pluck from the sky, like silver apples in a mythological goddess's garden.

If one were bold enough or rash enough to take them. His classical education was spotty, but he seemed to remember that those mythical apples always came with a high price.

'But this,' said Charlotte, manoeuvring him towards the centre of the terrace, where the ornamental pediment surmounting the garden front came to a sharp point, 'is the very best part.'

Robert looked around and saw nothing to justify that statement. There were no philosophers, no satyrs, no mythological figures to enliven the view, just stone.

Charlotte poked him in the shoulder. 'Not there,' she said. 'There.'

Following where she pointed, he looked out over the edge of the roof and found the whole expanse of the gardens arrayed below. Below them stretched patterned parterres and whimsical follies. The topiary capered and posed for their delight; statues raised their arms in graceful arabesque, fighting to be free of their pedestals. At the verge of the garden, the lake glittered with reflected starlight, like gems on a bed of velvet, and the elegant summer house watched benevolently over the whole, its white columns stately in the moonlight, like a wise old chaperone settling back while her charges played.

But there was still more. Beyond that, he could see out over the fields and the patches of forest, down the muddy road, clear through to Dovedale village in the valley below, where the windows of the cottages glowed orange with firelight as, in house after house, the denizens of the village conducted their own celebrations for the last day of Christmas. The whole scene lay before them like a Christmas crèche, an entire world in small, the edges sharp and clear and glittering with a dusting of ice. It was a fairytale kingdom, offered up for the taking. Charlotte's kingdom, to be precise, and she was offering it to him.

Charlotte tilted her head, eagerly monitoring his reaction. 'Isn't it lovely?'

Her carefully arranged curls had been dragged to one side by her crown and whipped to frizz by the wind. Her cheeks were red and chapped from cold, her lips were bitten, and her nose was starting to drip. Robert had never seen anything lovelier. The starlit lake and perfectly trimmed topiary couldn't even begin to compete. 'It's perfect,' he said.

It was quite clear that he wasn't referring to the scenery.

'I am rather fond of it,' Charlotte managed. Robert could feel more than see the slight movement as her gloved hand tightened around the ledge of the roof, unconsciously seeking support.

It was a very odd sensation to be so attuned to someone else's actions that you could divine the movements of her body without sight. In the past, that sort of awareness had only come to him in the presence of enemies, breathing the same breath as the man on the other end of a sword or a pistol, in a contest for one's life.

Knowing that he was plunging into enemy territory, Robert carefully adjusted her garland, setting it farther back on the crown of her head – *that's right*, a nasty little voice in the back of his head whispered, *get it out of the way*. The voice sounded unpleasantly like Medmenham's. Robert ignored it. 'Your coronet is slipping,' he murmured.

Charlotte looked up at him from under her lashes, eager and uncertain all at once. 'It's made of mistletoe, you know,' she said hopefully, tipping her head back at an angle as old as mistletoe itself.

A tender smile pushed at the corners of Robert's lips. 'Is it? In that case . . .'

His hand traced a path from her garland to her cheek, smoothing her tousled hair out of the way. His conscience gave one last, agitated bleat and went still. It wouldn't do to ignore tradition, after all. Not at Girdings. What harm was a kiss, after all?

Charlotte's lashes fluttered down over her eyes. They were touched with gold at the tips, he noticed, inconsequentially, before his own eyes drifted closed and there was nothing but touch. The slide of her hair beneath his fingers, the soft exhalation of her breath in the cold air, the brush of her lips against his, more warming that any number of well-stoked fires. He had meant it to be only a mistletoe kiss, a ceremonial salutation in honour of the season, but perhaps it was the sheer quantity of the mistletoe in the crown that betrayed them, kiss upon kiss multiplying until there was nothing ceremonial about it at all.

Charlotte's crown jangled forgotten to the stone-flagged

floor as she wrapped her arms securely around his neck, kissing him back with kisses that tasted faintly of wine. Above them, the stars whirled in dizzying circles in the perfect night sky and the faint sound of music rose from below like the chime of celestial harps.

They might have stayed that way for hours, drugged by kisses, spellbound by starlight, if the wind hadn't defeated them. Beneath the velvet of her dress, Robert could feel Charlotte shivering. He wrapped his arms more firmly around her, drawing her into the shelter of his body. While her dress might be made of a warm fabric, it left crucial areas uncovered. Robert warmed the exposed skin at her collarbone with a kiss and felt her shiver with something other than cold.

'You're freezing.' For a wonder, he wasn't. For the first time since returning to England, he felt warm. Too warm. That was the harm in a kiss. 'We should get you back inside.'

Charlotte rested her head against his jacket, finding a comfortable hollow beneath his shoulder. 'Must we?' she said wistfully. 'Magic never fares well in the real world. I'm afraid that once we go downstairs, the enchantment will all fade away.'

'What makes you think it will fade away?' Robert asked, knowing he was flirting with danger. 'What if it's real?'

Charlotte blinked up at him, her voice slightly muffled by his waistcoat. 'Do you mean that? Or are you just trying to get me inside so I don't turn blue?'

Robert tucked a finger under her chin and tilted her face up towards his. 'I like you in blue.'

He kissed her before she could point out that he hadn't answered the question. He kissed her, knowing that it was a knave's trick, designed to buy time. He kissed her to avoid having to acknowledge that the most frightening answer of all was the true one.

When their lips finally parted, neither showed any inclination to move. Instead, they stood in comfortable silence, Charlotte's head tucked beneath his chin, looking out over the sleeping gardens with their rosebushes tied up in burlap, over the dry fountains with their frost-scarred bottoms laid bare to the elements, over the lake from which all the swans had fled – presumably to avoid being turned into a ducal dinner. In summer, the view must be dazzling. For a moment, he allowed himself to entertain an image of what it would be to stand so in summer, with the flowers blooming below and the fountains sending up their fine spray and the sun reflecting golden off the tips of Charlotte's eyelashes.

Summer was a very long time away. In the meantime . . . Robert didn't want to think of the meantime, of Staines and Medmenham, of promises still unfulfilled and dark deeds unpunished.

'We should go in,' he said, brushing a kiss across the top of Charlotte's head to soften the sentiment.

'I know,' agreed Charlotte, and nestled deeper into his waistcoat.

'We could make a house up on the roof,' Robert suggested, only half jokingly. 'And send down baskets for food.'

Reluctantly, Charlotte peeled herself from his side and shook out her skirts. 'It would have to be a very long rope. And you would be very cold.'

'Shall we?' said Robert. There was, he noticed, a crease in her cheek from the seam of his coat. He lifted a hand to smooth it away.

Charlotte caught his hand and pressed the curled fingers to her lips. 'Let's.'

For all that it was warmer in the stairwell, he could feel a chill settle upon him as soon as they closed the door to the roof behind them. Charlotte's hand nestled trustingly in his as they meandered very slowly down the long stair. He could feel the weight of it like a tug at his conscience. Would her hand rest so comfortably in his if she knew him for what he really was? If she discovered that he wasn't at all what she believed him to be, not a Sir Galahad but – well, a man. A man with a cluttered, untidy past and a million minor transgressions to his discredit.

She had hit far too close to the bone at dinner that night, when she asked about his departure from Girdings. He could still hear the clink of coins in his satchel as he had stolen away from Girdings that night, slinking off like a common thief with the four hundred pounds he had needed to purchase his commission as an ensign in the army. His father would have called it 'borrowing against his inheritance,' which was probably why Robert preferred to think of it as it was. Stealing. He had spent years trying to sweat out the taint of it by working twice as hard as any other officer in the regiment, volunteering for the most exhausting treks, the most dangerous missions, the most tedious administrative duties. He had been promoted from subaltern to captain on his own merits – his own merits and the backing of Colonel Arbuthnot. It was a pretty sort of punishment that there was no way to make proper amends; the person to whom he would have to pay that initial money back would be himself.

What would Charlotte say if she knew? Would she care? He remembered her praise of that long-ago Lansdowne who had taken such shameless advantage of Sir Walter Raleigh and allowed himself to hope that she might see it in that light, as an expedient to a greater end, unimportant in itself. But even if she saw it through rose-coloured glasses, he knew otherwise. He knew what he was and what he had done.

But he didn't let go.

It was too tempting to hold on to Charlotte's hand and her vision of what he might be, as though believing hard enough might make it so. He kept the conversation light as they strolled down the narrow stairway, hand in hand, sharing silly stories about nothing in particular and pausing frequently in dark corners. Robert knew he would have to pay the piper sooner or later, but for now, the shadows kept inconvenient realities at bay.

'I should fix my hair,' said Charlotte, dawdling on the first-floor landing, no more eager than he to abandon the shadows. She indicated the way to her rooms with a tilt of her decidedly lopsided coiffure. 'And try to make myself presentable.'

Robert followed her into a wide hallway dotted with majestic-looking doors, not as majestic as the state bedrooms on the ground floor, including the gloomy ducal chambers that he currently inhabited, but still far grander than anything to which he had ever aspired. Accustomed by long usage, Charlotte didn't even seem to notice.

Her sitting room looked just as he would have imagined it, decorated in airy pastels, with papers scattered pell-mell on a writing table and books falling open on every available surface. He thought he recognised the battered binding of the book he had seen her reading in the gallery last week. *Emmelina*? No, *Evelina*. The memory brought a smile to his lips.

'Shall I wait for you?' he asked.

Charlotte clung to his hand as though she were going to

agree, and then reluctantly released it. 'It would probably be best if we went back separately. Just so that people don't talk.'

She looked at him so expectantly that Robert wondered if he was supposed to argue with her and insist on not leaving her side, or whatever else it was that a proper knight errant would be expected to do. But what she said made sound sense. They had undoubtedly been missed by now. Tongues would have begun wagging, dowagers would be whispering behind their fans. Charlotte knew this world far better than he.

'All right,' Robert said, planting both hands on her shoulders and drawing her close for one last kiss. 'I bow to your superior judgment.'

'The ballroom?' she said.

'I get the next dance,' said Robert. 'Whatever it may be.'

This time, he had clearly said the right thing. Charlotte beamed at him. 'It's a promise.'

With a flurry of flounces, she flung her arms around his neck for one more last, absolutely the last, very last kiss. It turned into an almost the very last kiss, instead.

'The ballroom,' Charlotte repeated breathlessly, once the absolutely last kiss had been kissed.

Detaching Robert's hands from around her waist, she swirled through the door of her sitting room, giving the impression of flying rather than walking. Flying did have its hazards. Robert caught a last glimpse of frothing petticoat and heard a muffled 'Ouch!' as she stumbled over a book, and then the door swung shut behind her and he was left staring at a plaster panel.

Not just staring at it, beaming fatuously at it like the most mawkish sort of lovesick schoolboy. Robert hastily rearranged his face into more acceptable ducal lines.

Shaking his head at himself, he forced himself to move

away from the door, step by determined step. Served him right to always be mocking Tommy and then to be hit by the fatal arrow himself. That it was fatal, he had very little doubt. Maybe Charlotte was right, maybe it was all an enchantment. If it was, it felt like a very durable one, solid as the stone of Girdings. Just so long as he could keep the past at bay.

Like the pictures in an all-illustrated paper, he could see their future all laid out, with captions. 'Duke and Duchess of Dovedale Visit the Tenantry,' 'Duke and Duchess of Dovedale Relax in the Library,' 'Duke and Duchess Take Little Dovedales Unicorn Hunting.' Funny, how the prospect of being duke became a great deal less daunting when Charlotte was in the picture as duchess.

He was too busy mentally moving Charlotte into the ducal chambers to hear the sound of footsteps in the hallway behind him. And he was far too engaged in imagining what might come after to notice the long shadow fall across the floor in front of him.

He didn't notice anything at all until a red-ringed hand descended upon his shoulder.

Chapter Ten

Robert grabbed for a pistol that wasn't there. One tended not to wear arms in one's own home, but his home, until now, had been an army tent, and there, one did. How in the blazes could he have allowed himself to go off in the clouds like that? That was the sort of lapse that could get a man killed.

Reality came raging back with the force of a fist to the vitals. With a sickening wrench, Robert realised that he had come within an inch of forgetting everything that had brought him back to Girdings in the first place. Domestic bliss didn't come into it.

'Ah, Dovedale,' drawled Sir Francis Medmenham. 'Just the man I wanted to see.'

Robert couldn't quite bring himself to echo the sentiment. Something about the arch tone of his voice grated on Robert even more than usual.

'Medmenham,' he managed to say, with every imitation of pleasure. 'Enjoying the party?'

'Not so much as you, I expect,' said Sir Francis Medmenham, with an eyebrow arched in the direction of the bedroom doors. 'A bit far afield from the ballroom, aren't we?'

Robert managed to keep smiling, although he was not quite sure how. 'You wanted to see me?'

Having found him, Sir Francis seemed in no hurry to state his business. 'The little Lansdowne has also been conspicuously absent from the ballroom.'

Robert's fists ached with the visceral need to seek out Medmenham's face. He managed a shrug. 'Crowded places, ballrooms. It's hard to see everyone.'

Sir Francis's smile was too knowing by half. 'Indeed.'

Placing one hand on the other man's elbow, Robert steered him firmly away from Charlotte's door. 'Were you looking for me, or for Lady Charlotte?'

Sir Francis made a show of polishing his ring against the side of one perfectly cut sleeve. 'Under the circumstances, I had rather thought I might kill two birds with one stone.'

Men had been called out for less.

There was nothing Robert would have liked more than to suggest rapiers at dawn – or, even better, cannons at twenty paces – but he had no right to dice with Charlotte's reputation. And he couldn't afford to alienate Medmenham. It was, he assured himself, the former that concerned him more than the latter.

'You don't think that I and – good Gad, Medmenham!' Robert affected a hearty laugh. '*Charlotte*? I'm certainly very fond of her, but . . . no.'

'No?'

'No,' repeated Robert quite firmly. 'She's not the sort of girl one dallies with, is she?'

That much, at least, was quite true. Courted, yes; dallied, no.

'And I imagine her grandmother would have something to

say about any man who came calling. She's a dear girl, but not worth slaying dragons for, eh, Medmenham?'

'That,' said Medmenham, 'would depend on the size of her dowry. A dragon's hoard might be worth a certain amount of effort.'

'Not this dragon,' said Robert repressively. 'What exactly was it that you wanted to see me about?'

'A suggestion I think will interest you. I have a little proposition to put to you . . .'

Charlotte danced her way down to the ballroom in the sort of perfect happiness that only occurs once in a lifetime.

This was the very apex of joy, the peak of happiness, the desired ending of every novel. Happily ever after had finally arrived and it was just as glorious as she had dreamt.

They would be married, of course. That went without saying. A spring wedding would be perfect, Charlotte thought, with all its promise of the world coming again into bloom. It had a rather nice symbolic resonance to it. On a more practical level, she was promised to Queen Charlotte – the real Queen Charlotte – to serve as one of her maids of honour from the middle of January to the end of April. Fortunately, her duties would be light and maids of honour were no longer so secluded as they had been in the past. Due to crowded conditions in the royal residences, the queen had decided several years ago that it was no longer necessary for maids of honour to reside with the royal family during their tenure. While the royal household was in London, Charlotte would live at Dovedale House.

The Duke of Dovedale would presumably reside at Dovedale House as well.

In between her duties to the queen, there would be plenty

of time for walks in the park, afternoons in the library, evenings at the theatre, and – Charlotte went a happy pink – many long hours in convenient alcoves. Dovedale House was well furnished with those, although Charlotte had never had any need of them before. Lovely, deep alcoves, shaded with heavy velvet curtains.

Downstairs, champagne burbled from a specially constructed fountain in the hall, monitored by white-wigged footmen in the distinctive green and gold Dovedale livery. The ground floor was mobbed with the most elite of the fashionable world, all of whom had gone trotting out to Girdings at the duchess's command. Charlotte threaded her way through the crowd towards the gallery, smiling and nodding, brimming with affection for the whole of mankind. Even Lord Vaughn and his haughty bride, of whom Charlotte had always been more than a little afraid, earned a beaming smile that left them both completely baffled.

For Charlotte, the enchantment, far from fading, appeared to have followed her down into the gallery. The entire assemblage glowed as though touched with fairy dust. Jewels glittered like pendant stars, silks ran rippling like rainbow streams, the very champagne in the glasses scintillated like condensed sunlight, conveying benefaction to whosesoever lips it touched. She had never seen so many beautiful people, so many brilliant costumes, so many graceful dancers. Even Turnip Fitzhugh had an exuberant charm about him that not even his appallingly high shirt points could mar.

In the midst of it all, Charlotte felt as though she were floating, borne on her own personal, gold-spangled cloud. Her feet barely touched the ground as she sparkled her way through the hall and down the long corridor into the gallery.

As one gnarled dowager shouted to another, 'The little Lansdowne is in looks tonight, ain't she?'

'With that sort of dowry,' bellowed the other, 'who wouldn't be?' And they both cackled happily over their own wit.

Charlotte found Henrietta at the far end of the gallery, on the side farthest from the musicians, chatting with the new Viscountess Pinchingdale, formerly Miss Letty Alsworthy, who had come up from London with her husband for the festivities.

It took only one look at Charlotte's face for Henrietta to hastily detach herself from Letty and scoot Charlotte off into the most remote corner she could find, wedged between a shoulder-high cupid carrying candles and old Lady Featherstonehaugh, who had dozed off in her chair, her mouth open to reveal a truly impressive array of false teeth. Their remove offered only the illusion of privacy, but the din of the music and hundreds of voices chattering provided a far more secure safeguard.

After so many years of friendship, there were times when mere words were redundant. Henrietta grasped both of Charlotte's hands in hers. 'I don't even need to ask. But I will. Well?'

Charlotte beamed. 'Life *can* be better than fiction. Better than *Evelina* even!'

Henrietta's hazel eyes widened. 'This *is* serious.'

'Oh, Hen, it was splendid. We were up on the roof—'

'The *roof?*'

'It was my idea.'

Henrietta shuddered. 'He really must love you. It's frigid out.'

'Neither of us wanted to come back inside. Even though our fingers were turning blue.'

Henrietta collapsed in a fit of choking. 'So you're frostbitten, but very much in love.'

Charlotte felt that that was an accurate summary. 'Essentially.'

'Oh, darling, you are mad,' said Henrietta, and proceeded to give ample evidence of the same herself by laughing, crying, embracing, and generally bouncing around in place.

Fortunately, most of the guests were too involved in their own affairs to wonder why the granddaughter of the Dowager Duchess of Dovedale and the daughter of the Marquess of Uppington were engaging in their own private jig in the corner of the Gallery of Girdings.

'Where is your duke?' asked Henrietta, once the requisite jumping and squealing had been accomplished.

This time, Charlotte didn't contest the appellation. 'He's supposed to meet me in here,' she said, standing on tiptoe to scan the crowd. Given that the gallery was crammed by hundreds of guests, most of them taller than she, it was not the most effective of gestures. Charlotte was nothing daunted. Love's compass would guide Robert to her. Besides, being much taller, he could actually see over the crowd to find her. 'I've promised him whatever dance he likes.'

'Oh, just a *dance*, is it?' teased Henrietta, making Charlotte blush. 'Is it all settled between you, or do I need to make Miles demand his intentions? Miles does loom so well,' she said fondly, sparing a glance in the direction of her own husband, who was less looming than leaning, propped against the wall like a human replica of the Leaning Tower of Pisa as he engaged in a conversation with his old friend, Pinchingdale-Snipe.

'I believe we can spare Miles,' said Charlotte happily. 'I can't believe it was all this easy. I had always thought that the path of true love was supposed to be strewn with challenges and dangers. But Mr Shakespeare seems to have got it entirely backwards. When it's right, it *is* easy.'

'Some of the time,' said Henrietta, whose courtship had been anything but easy. 'Is he going to speak to your grandmother?'

'I suppose so.' Charlotte's face broke into a smile. 'He can't very well speak to himself. Can't you just imagine that conversation?'

Henrietta grinned. 'When he applies to himself for your hand?'

'I hope he grants it to himself!' exclaimed Charlotte. 'Oh, Hen, I'm half afraid that if I pinch myself, this will all go away. I'll wake up in my own bed and Robert will still be in India and all of this will have just been a particularly splendid dream.'

Henrietta made a sympathetic face. 'I dreamt about him before, you know. All those years that he was away. I used to imagine that he would come back from India riding on an elephant and sweep me up behind him and carry me away.'

'Squishing tenants and cottages in your way?' laughed Henrietta.

'Well, I was only twelve,' said Charlotte sheepishly. 'Or thirteen. It made sense at the time.'

'Many things do,' Henrietta agreed sagely.

'And it can't even be my dowry that he wants. He gets nothing from me that wouldn't come to him already.'

'Except your grandmother's personal fortune,' Henrietta felt compelled to point out.

Charlotte wafted that aside without a qualm. 'It's nothing to what he's already inherited. The entailed estate is far greater. And I just couldn't see Robert gambling away his patrimony at cards or spending it all on – well, whatever gentlemen spend it on.'

'In Miles's case, cravats,' said Henrietta cheerfully. 'He must go through at least ten a morning. It drives his valet mad.'

They smiled at each other in perfect understanding, leaving Charlotte feeling as though she had just been admitted to membership in a private club she hadn't even known existed, a secret society for happily settled women. She and Henrietta had always discussed all sorts of things – books and plays and the meaning of life and whether that yellow dress was really a good idea – but Henrietta did not, as a rule, share personal details of her husband's habits.

It was a little disconcerting to realise that she didn't have any personal details to share in return. At least, not yet. She didn't know how many cravats Robert went through a morning, or whether he preferred to sleep with the window open or closed, or how many lumps of sugar he liked in his tea. But she did know that he was kind, and that he cared for her (even if the word 'love' hadn't yet made an appearance), and that she heard trumpets whenever he smiled – and shouldn't that be enough? The rest could be learnt by and by. Couldn't it? That was what marriage was for. Charlotte glowed at the thought.

'Will you still be joining the queen's household?' Henrietta asked.

'It's only for three months,' said Charlotte, 'and Grandmama firmly believes that every Lansdowne woman must spend her time in the royal household to advance the interests of the family.'

The two women exchanged a sceptical glance. The days when personal attendance on the royal family led to power and influence were long since past, but if the duchess had done it, by Gad, her granddaughter was going to do it, too.

'You can stay with us if your grandmother doesn't want

to come to town. I promise to be a very easygoing sort of chaperone.'

'That would be splendid.'

'I assume your duke will be coming to town, too?'

'I don't know,' admitted Charlotte. 'We didn't discuss any of that.'

In fact, they hadn't discussed much of anything at all, other than – what had they discussed? Charlotte found she couldn't remember any of it at all. There had been silly trivia about her childhood games on the roof, a short discussion about the geography of Girdings, speculation about the antics in the ballroom in their absence, but nothing that might have any bearing on their future.

Charlotte craned her neck to peer around the ballroom. It was taking Robert an awfully long time to find her. Of course, he did have to stop and say hello to people and do his duty as nominal host. A newly returned duke was a novelty not to be ignored by the *ton;* there would be many who would want to detain him in conversation after his long time abroad. But she did hope he would appear soon. Their promised next dance had already become the next and the next and there was still no sign of him.

Henrietta was also craning to see through the crowd. 'Look!'

Charlotte looked, fizzing with anticipation.

'There's Penelope!' Henrietta finished, gesturing and waving. 'I haven't seen her since supper.'

A little of Charlotte's fizz went out of her. It wasn't that she wasn't glad to see Penelope, but the longer Robert tarried, the more like a dream their interlude on the roof became.

'M'lady.' It was one of the liveried footmen, bearing a silver tray. Instead of a glass, the tray bore a folded note. There was no seal on the note and no address. 'For you, m'lady.'

Puzzled, Charlotte lifted the small piece of paper and opened it. In a bold, scrawling hand were written all of two words. *Forgive me.*

For what?

'Who gave this to you?' Charlotte asked, trying very hard not to sound as anxious as she felt. There was a very unpleasant buzzing in her ears, like a whole horde of mosquitoes.

The footman stood, straight-backed, staring directly in front of him, as he had been trained. Charlotte had always found it distinctly disconcerting conversing with someone forbidden to look you in the eye; it felt doubly so now. 'The duke, my lady.'

'Did he have any further message for me?'

'He said to tell you that circumstances required him to depart Girdings, my lady, and he did not know when he was to return.'

'I see,' said Charlotte, although she didn't see at all. Paper crackled between her fingers. 'Thank you. That will be all.'

'He's left?' demanded Henrietta. 'Tonight?'

Charlotte couldn't bring herself to look at Henrietta, but stared as straight ahead as the footman. 'So it would appear.'

'But why? What does the note say?'

Charlotte held it up in nerveless fingers. *Forgive me.*

For leaving?

There had to be a logical excuse. An emergency. What else would necessitate so precipitate a departure in the middle of one's own party? A friend might have been taken ill. He might have received an urgent summons from his old regiment. Charlotte's mind churned out a multitude of soothing plausibilities. She would have preferred if Robert had made some indication of when he might return, but at least he had contacted her before he left. That had to count for something. With so haphazard a departure, there wouldn't have been time to write anything more. In fact, she should consider herself honoured that he had taken the time to write anything at all. It showed he had been thinking about her, that he cared about her, that he knew she would worry when he didn't appear, that he wanted her forgiveness.

It all made her feel a great deal better. Charlotte rubbed her cold fingers against the velvet of her skirt, forcing the blood back into them.

Forgive me.

Of course, she would. It was all perfectly understandable – or would be, once he came back and explained the whole story.

'I don't understand,' mourned Henrietta, brooding over the note.

'Understand what?' Penelope's hair was mussed and her eyes were very bright. She looked, in fact, like someone who had just been soundly kissed.

Charlotte found herself seized with an anxious desire to find a mirror and make sure she didn't look like that. Not that it was the same, of course. What she had with Robert was worlds away from Penelope's casual encounters. It was happily ever after, she was sure of it. Even if Robert had mysteriously decamped. Again.

Charlotte fought away a vague sense of unease.

'There's nothing to understand,' she said, making the best of it as best she could. 'Robert was unexpectedly called away.'

Penelope narrowed her tea-coloured eyes. 'Was he?'

'Sometimes these things just can't be helped,' said Charlotte, as much for herself as Penelope.

'Oh, yes, they can.' Penelope folded her arms across her chest with the air of one girding herself for battle. 'Would you like to know where your Sir Galahad has gone? He's off with Sir Francis Medmenham, prospecting for greener pastures.'

'Oh, for heaven's sake, Pen—'

Penelope shook off Henrietta's hand. 'Well, it's true! I heard it myself. I heard your precious duke tell Sir Francis Medmenham that you weren't the sort he'd be interested in dallying with. And then they went off together.'

Charlotte's throat felt very dry. 'When was this?'

'Upstairs, just about an hour ago. Sir Francis saw him near your room and commented on your both leaving the ball at the same time.'

Charlotte's lungs expanded with sheer relief. 'That explains it, then. Robert was protecting my reputation.'

'He was protecting his own—'

'Pen!'

'He wouldn't want Sir Francis to know we were upstairs together,' explained Charlotte hastily, before open warfare could break out between her friends. 'It all makes perfect sense. What else was he to tell him under the circumstances?'

'I can think of a few things,' said Penelope.

'Well, so can we all,' broke in Henrietta, in a conciliatory tone that made Penelope's eyes narrow dangerously, 'but he's only a man, after all. And he was trying to protect Charlotte.'

'By leaving,' said Penelope flatly. 'By going off to carouse with Medmenham.'

Charlotte shook her head so emphatically that a hairpin fell out. 'If he left with Medmenham, it was only to distract him. He doesn't like Medmenham. He's told me so.'

'He's told Medmenham the same about you.' Penelope

rolled her eyes in frustration. 'He *left* you, Lottie. He ran off without saying goodbye.'

Charlotte stiffened at the sound of the old nursery nickname. 'He sent me a note.'

'Not much of one.' Penelope grabbed both of her hands. Charlotte could feel the crush of her fingers through both their pairs of gloves. 'I just don't want to see you make a mistake out of – romantic blindness! You can have him if you like, but don't have him thinking that he's something he isn't.'

'He isn't. I mean, I don't.' Yanking her hands free of Penelope's, Charlotte seized on a simpler point. 'What were you doing upstairs?'

'The same thing you were,' said Penelope with a bluntness that made the colour creep into Charlotte's cheeks. She hadn't thought of it in quite those terms before. It made her feel oddly unclean.

'Upstairs?' said Henrietta despairingly. To go off into alcoves was one thing, bedrooms quite another.

It gave Charlotte a slightly squirmy feeling in the pit of her stomach to realise how carelessly she had been dicing with her own reputation. If she and Robert had been discovered upstairs . . . No wonder Robert had blurted out whatever he had to Medmenham.

Penelope looked off across the room, over the long row of couples circling in unison as they performed the final figure of the dance. In profile, her expression was carefully blank.

'The alcoves were all occupied, so we went upstairs instead.'

The violinist drew his bow across the strings one final time. Throughout the room, gentlemen bowed and ladies curtsied to signify the end of the dance. With her back to the dance floor, Penelope failed to notice.

'I was with Freddy Staines,' finished Penelope, in a tone deliberately designed to provoke. 'In his room.'

The words echoed with unnatural loudness down the suddenly silent room.

Henrietta's face went ashen.

Like an animal scenting fire, Penelope's eyes darted from side to side. Beneath Penelope's still, straight posture, Charlotte could sense the panic coming off her in waves, the frozen panic of a trapped animal that knows it has nowhere left to run.

'You mean Fanny's room?' Charlotte said very loudly. 'Fanny Stillworth?'

There was no such person as Fanny Stillworth, but it was the best she could think of under the circumstances.

As if realising their gaffe, the musicians struck up again, plunging into a rather frenetic quadrille, but almost no one was dancing. They were all too busy watching the dreadful drama unfolding at the far end of the gallery, where one of their own had just willfully flung herself outside the bounds of polite society. Halfway down the room, Penelope's mother looked ready to imitate some of the less attractive sorts of Greek gods and devour her own young.

'You heard what I said.' Penelope's face was a tragic mask, like the bust of Medea in the library, carved into lines of bitter satisfaction. She looked like a queen on the scaffold, staring down the peasantry. 'Everyone heard what I said.'

Without another word, she turned on her heel and strode out of the gallery, her flaming head held high.

'Pen—' Casting an anguished glance over her shoulder at Charlotte, Henrietta hurried out after her.

Charlotte made to follow but she was yanked to a stop by

a hand on her arm. Mrs Ponsonby's pudgy fingers tightened around her sleeve with surprising force.

'No!' declared Mrs Ponsonby, in ringing tones that carried clear over the efforts of the sweating musicians and the dancing couples, her fingers digging painfully into Charlotte's arm. 'Do not go after her! *We* do not know her now.'

Mrs Ponsonby's bosom swelled with self-righteous zeal and not a little bit of selfish satisfaction. She had had her eye on Lord Frederick for her own daughter, Lucy, and everyone knew it.

She was not the only mother who had disliked Penelope on those grounds. They all clustered in now, like savages for the kill, ready to grind their spears into whatever vulnerable flesh they could find.

The murderous haze in the air made Charlotte's stomach turn in a way that had nothing to do with Mrs Ponsonby's poor choice of perfume.

'Perhaps *you* don't,' said Charlotte, shaking off Mrs Ponsonby's clinging grasp, and followed after her friends.

'You can't touch pitch without being tarred!' Mrs Ponsonby called shrilly, if inaccurately, after her.

Hastening after friends, Charlotte refused to give her the satisfaction of looking back.

Mrs Ponsonby was wrong. She might be naive, but she knew enough of the world to know that it took a great deal of pitch to blacken a duke's daughter. Not like poor Penelope, who didn't even have an 'Honourable' in front of her name to scrub her reputation clean.

Charlotte's heart wrenched for her friend. It was so like Penelope to try to protect her and land herself in a stew because of it. So generous and yet so entirely wrongheaded. Because, among other things, she didn't need protection from Robert. Whatever he might have said to Sir Francis, whatever his reasons for leaving, his intentions towards her were honourable.

She was sure of it.

Chapter Eleven

As the boat drew him across the River Styx, Robert knew he was truly in hell.

It had been four days since he had left Girdings, four days since he had stood on the roof with Charlotte, four days since he had struck his own Mephistophelean bargain in the hallway outside Charlotte's chambers. It felt more like four years. The descent from the roof of Girdings to the subterranean caverns of West Wycombe had to be measured in more than miles. The distance between the Dovedale domains and those of Medmenham felt as vast as that between paradise and inferno. Once one began the descent, one didn't go back.

At the time, it had seemed like a logical enough decision. An offer of immediate initiation into Medmenham's Hellfire Club meant that he could find Wrothan that much faster. The faster he found Wrothan, the faster he could return to Girdings. Quick, clean, over.

Fast, however, didn't seem to be in it. Whatever the way to hell was, it wasn't speedy. They had been three days on the road from Girdings to West Wycombe. Once at Wycombe, notices needed to be sent out and preparations made. Robert fervently hoped those preparations included summoning Wrothan from whatever rat-hole he was currently occupying. It wasn't until a day later that the whole party had donned their ceremonial vestments and processed, torchbearers to the fore, from the confines of Wycombe Abbey to the vast Gothic folly Medmenham's cousin had built to mark the entrance to his subterranean caves, home of homegrown Eleusian mysteries and the devil only knew what else.

Upon entering the caves, the others had gone off to prepare, leaving Robert cooling his heels in an upper cavern. He had been instructed to contemplate his sins with the aid of a course of 'religious readings.' These turned out, upon inspection, to be nothing more than a folio of expensive French pornography, done up at the edges with gold leaf and illuminated capitals in a mockery of medieval devotional literature.

As Lord Henry had promised, nothing but the best for their orgies.

Like the mock Book of Hours, the ceremonial garb he had been given to put on was also a survival from the club's earlier incarnation as the Monks of Medmenham. It was a replica of a monk's habit, cut out of rough brown wool, supplied with a belt of thin and flexible leather with curious metal tips. The belt was, in fact, a whip. Robert preferred not to think too closely about that, although he supposed it might come in handy if he had to fight his way out of the caves.

In addition to being draughty, the robe was extremely itchy. Robert knew that his sojourn in the cell was meant to fill him with prickles of anticipation, but instead he just felt prickly. By the time his guide arrived, to conduct him down to the nether regions for his initiation, Robert was strongly wondering whether it was all worth it. There surely had to be other ways to find Wrothan. Ways that did not involve absurd excursions into subterranean amateur theatricals.

The figure gestured to Robert to put up his hood. When Robert would have spoken, he drew a finger sharply across his lips – or the area where Robert presumed his lips must be – indicating silence.

Feeling as though he had stumbled unwittingly into one of Horace Walpole's Gothic novels, Robert followed his guide down into the catacombs. The path sloped steeply downwards, winding this way and that like a drunkard trying to find his way home. Lanterns cased in red glass hung from the ceiling, casting jagged bursts of flame along the chalk walls and turning the ground beneath their feet an unpleasant reddish brown. Crudely carved horned gods leered at them from the walls as they passed.

The path meandered downwards with no apparent direction. Off to the sides, grilles shielded private alcoves, rounded rooms reminiscent of monks' cells, carved out of the earth. In the uncertain light, Robert received only a fleeting impression of lurid wall paintings and jumbled bedclothes. In one, he glimpsed paired skulls, perched like memento mori on the bedposts. The skulls' soundless laughter pursued them as they passed.

Robert made a mental note never to consult Medmenham on matters of interior decoration.

They had, he reckoned, covered roughly a quarter of a mile by the time the path broadened, opening into a vast, vaulted chamber, banded on one side by a shallow stream. In a small boat on the near bank, a boatman waited.

'Ready, Dovedale?' asked Sir Francis Medmenham.

Robert's brown-robed guide faded off into the web of

tunnels. 'With all due reverence and humility,' drawled Robert, matching his tone to his host's. 'Whither do we sail?'

Medmenham raised a brow and the boat pole, all at the same time. 'Across the River Styx and down into Hades.'

'Rather a Greco-Medieval mix for an Order of the Lotus,' Robert commented as Medmenham poled the boat to the other bank.

'Thrift, thrift, my dear Dovedale,' replied Medmenham, managing the skirts of his robe with the ease of long practice as he climbed out of the boat. 'We are an accretion of generations of sin.'

'And all the more sinful for being so?' Clambering about in a habit wasn't nearly so easy as Medmenham made it look. Robert inadvertently showed a good deal of leg as he swung out of the boat onto the bank. It was a decidedly humbling feeling – which was no doubt the intent.

Medmenham smiled a closed-lipped smile. 'It's not quantity of sin but quality to which we aspire. Decadence, after all, is an art. When done properly.'

The brass doors blocking their path did, indeed, bear out that statement. Clearly from an earlier incarnation of the group, they were a work of art in their own right, featuring a bas-relief of Bacchanalian orgies, where tipsy maenads in disordered robes offered their attentions to Bacchus, a herd of satyrs, and one another in a staggering array of wanton combinations. The only concession to the new order was a knocker surmounted on the older panels, its brass jarringly bright in contrast to the mellowed patina of the maenads. It was an elephant's head. The angle of the elephant's trunk left no doubt as to its priapic connotations.

Lifting the ring hanging from the elephant's open mouth,

Medmenham let it fall against the brass doors once, twice, three times. On the third swing the doors swung open, propelled by invisible hands – or, far more likely, by some sort of pulley system. Incense billowed out, sifting like mist across the river, only scented as no mist had ever been, redolent of exotic ports and foreign temples.

Through stinging eyes, Robert could just barely make out the bodies in the haze, rank upon rank of them, it seemed, all in identical brown robes with hoods shrouding their features and whips at their waists. With an ironically courtly gesture, Medmenham gestured him forwards into their midst. The silent brethren shuffled back to form a semicircle around him, blocking off his means of egress. How many were there? Robert tried to count, but the smoke was in his eyes, blurring his vision and his senses. Fourteen or fifteen, maybe, it was hard to tell when one looked much like another and the purple-blue smoke belched from braziers slung from the ceiling on thick brass chains.

Medmenham urged him forwards, into the centre of the room, directly beneath the room's sole lantern, so that the light fell directly on his hooded head, placing him in stark relief while leaving the rest of the room in shadow.

Ahead of him, at the far end of the cave, loomed an immense altar. A great stone slab was surmounted by an arch that might have been stolen from an Indian temple – or simply manufactured with that in mind. All around the arch, in minute carvings, lush concubines attired in little more than strands of beads engaged in a variety of acrobatic erotic activities. Not just any concubines; some of the fertility goddesses portrayed in the carving had the bodies of voluptuous women, but their heads were formed of the overlapping petals of the lotus flower.

'Initiate!' declared Medmenham, in thrilling tones, once the meeting had been convened to order with proper pomp and a roll call of assumed names. 'Do you come here of your own free will?'

'I do,' intoned Robert.

'Do you come of an impure heart?'

'I do.' Just not the sort of impure heart Medmenham had in mind.

'Have you any sins to confess to the company?'

So that was part of Medmenham's game – or Wrothan's. Robert had heard of such a club when he was in India, among the British community at Poona. As an initiation rite, members confessed their sins, usually of a sexual nature. They subsequently found themselves at the mercy of less scrupulous members of the society.

Robert marvelled, as always, at the idiocy of his fellow men, willing to sacrifice their dignity on the promise of little more than a bit of slap and tickle.

'I confess,' declared Robert thrillingly, and paused for good effect, 'that I am sinfully eager to sample the pleasures of the evening.'

That played well with the crowd. Lord Henry Innes roared his appreciation, pounding his large fist against his thigh. Robert would have known that guffaw anywhere, just as he recognised the braying laugh unique to Lord Freddy Staines. The one edging closer to Medmenham, always seeking to be closer to whatever he deemed the centre of power, that had to be Martin Frobisher. That combination of arrogance and obsequiousness was unmistakable, even shrouded in brown wool.

That made four, four out of fourteen whom Robert could identify at a glance. Who were the others? And where in the hell was Wrothan? He might be one of the brown-cloaked figures, but it was impossible to tell. For a moment, Robert thought he caught an elusive whiff of jasmine, as delicate as a ghost in the smoke-haunted chamber, but beneath the heavy reek of incense it was impossible to be sure, and even less possible to trace the source. Robert's shoulders tightened with impatience. Where was the bloody man? Nothing was going as he had planned.

Medmenham yanked on the end of a tasselled cord, sending up a shrill clanging that reverberated through the small chamber. 'We call on the god to bring us the elixir of immortality!'

Claret, no doubt, thought Robert. Or brandy. His head was beginning to ache from the incense, and the ground was gritty and cold against his bare feet. As sin went, this was a fairly ramshackle affair. He wondered if they had mustered a more impressive performance back when they still called themselves the Monks of Medmenham. He doubted it. It would have been inverted crosses then, rather than elephant heads, but it all boiled down to the same thing: a stage set for an otherwise unimaginative bout of drinking and wenching.

It all made him feel very old and very tired.

With a tinkling of beads and a rush of air, a dozen giggling girls scrambled through the arch over the altar, each done up in pseudo-Oriental costumes of strategic straps of chiffon held together with strings of beads that clattered as they moved. Bracelets dangling silver bells circled their ankles and wrists. The exotic costumes sat oddly with flushed pink skin and masses of hair in shades ranging from blond to mid-brown. They were clearly village girls done up to look like temple dancers, preening and giggling as they jangled their bells and pushed out their chests. Their gyrations bore about as much relation to a genuine nautch dance as a jig to the ballet.

One by one, they ranged in an obviously choreographed formation around the base of the altar, posing with their hands clapped above their heads in poor imitation of the figures on the arch above them.

Lord Henry, who had, God help him, appointed himself Robert's personal sponsor, struck Robert's shoulder with a familiar hand.

'The handmaidens of the god,' he rumbled, in the worst stage whisper since Garrick's Hamlet had a spot of bother over whether to be or not to be. 'Just you wait. Here it comes!'

There was more?

Apparently, there was. Innes wasn't the only one bouncing on his heels in anticipation. One of the girls giggled and was hastily hushed. Robert could practically hear the quivering of taut muscles as everyone in the room strained towards the door, waiting for something – or someone. Robert could feel the tension beginning to infect him. His eyes burnt from the smoke and his ears rang in the expectant silence.

Someone began a chant and the others took it up, intoning, in unison, 'So-ma, so-ma.'

It wasn't a name Robert recognised. Clever nonsense, perhaps, cooked up to sound foreign? It was certainly eminently suited to a chant. The low sound echoed through the vaulted room, whirling around and around like a serpent chasing its own tail, over and over again in endless refrain, until the syllables blurred together and one voice was indistinguishable from the next.

Far off – or perhaps it merely sounded like it, through the chanting and the smoke – a pair of cymbals clanged.

Behind him, Robert could hear Lord Henry draw in a rough breath in anticipation. The sound was echoed all around the room. The chanting grew ragged, then faded off entirely, as all eyes focused on the lotus altar. A great blast of smoke blew through the beaded curtain and swirled through the room, a thick, blue-tinged smoke that carried with it a sickly sweet aftertaste that made his tongue feel thick and clung unpleasantly to the back of Robert's throat.

In its midst stalked a creature out of myth.

Through the smoke, he appeared at least seven feet high. His tunic and baggy trousers were of cloth of gold, sewn with bits of metal that caught and reflected the light, so that he seemed to glitter with living flame. A curved sword hung from one hip, the hilt a full six inches high, set with rough chunks of lapis lazuli, carnelian, jasper, and tourmaline in a display of barbaric splendour. A gaudy gold pectoral hung across the creature's chest, from which dangled a single chunk of red glass on which was etched, with a great deal more care than on the members' rings, the insignia of the society.

But that was the least of it. Above the pectoral reared, not a human head, but a grotesque ritual mask, an elephant's head, fully three feet high, with immense ears that spanned a yard on either side and an arrogantly curved trunk that arched up to reveal a great, gaping cavern of a mouth, painted with thick, red lips. But it was the eyes, the eyes that were the most distressing. The area around the eyes had been decorated as though for a festival day, painted a bluish white and outlined with gold beads, like a Venetian carnival mask. But within the ovals carved out for the eyes, all was black. There was nothing inside.

Medmenham's voice rang out high and clear through all the corners of the room. 'We bring, O Great Lord, a humble novice to your service in pursuit of the elixir of immortality.'

Despite himself, Robert couldn't help but feel a frisson of superstitious fear as the sightless elephant head swung in his direction. There was something distinctly eerie about that hollow stare. There had to be eyeholes concealed somewhere else in the mask, somewhere one wouldn't expect, especially when distracted with billowing clouds of blue smoke and a costume that scintillated like a royal fireworks display with every minor movement. Somewhere near the trunk, perhaps, where a viewer would be least likely to look.

From a niche in the wall, the creature produced a two-handled chalice and offered it out to Robert with hooves rather than hands looped through the handles.

Not Indian, that, thought Robert cynically. The bowl was of French enamel, hastily doctored with rough gemstones in an attempt to give it an Oriental air.

'Drink,' intoned the creature.

The word clanged through the corners of the room and seemed to reverberate in the cluttered corners of Robert's brain.

His hands, he was alarmed to see, were trembling as he reached for the bowl. *Good for verisimilitude's sake*, he thought fuzzily. Let them think he went in trembling of their god. It would be nicer, however, if he weren't trembling quite so much. The scented smoke scraped the inside of his nose, making his eyes swim. All around him the sound of chanting rose from the assemblage, louder this time, more forceful, pounding into his skull with every blunt syllable.

'*So-ma!*'

'*So-ma!*'

Wrapping both hands around the baroque curls of the handles, Robert raised the chalice above his head in tribute. The simple action brought beads of sweat to his brow. He found, to his alarm, that his arms were shaking, his muscles fighting him as though the cup were weighted with lead rather than liquid. In front of him, through the corrosive smoke, the elephant mask gave nothing away. Fighting for control, through pure willpower, Robert held the chalice suspended in the air. The room tilted around him, rocking from side to side like a boat in a squall. His stomach twisted, fighting a bitter battle with the remains of his supper.

One thing was for sure. It wasn't claret in the cup. Inch by painful inch, he lowered the cup to his lips. Whatever was inside moved sluggishly as he tilted the chalice, too thick to be wine. It had a golden sheen to it, like mead, and a honeyed smell with a medicinal tang beneath its sweetness. Robert fastened his lips around the rim, made a barrier of his tongue, and tilted the cup.

It was harder than he would ever have thought to try to make it look as though he was swallowing while allowing none of the liquid into his mouth. The effort of swallowing nothing made him want to gag. A few trickles of liquid slipped past his tongue. Even that small amount made his throat tingle and his head swim. Robert tipped the cup farther back. Liquid dribbled down the sides of his lips, trailing in sticky streams down the matted wool of his habit.

At a nod from Medmenham, two of the dancing girls flung themselves on their knees beside him, greedily licking the fallen drops of elixir from his robes, working their way up his body as they went.

In the ever-shifting smoke, they seemed as insubstantial as ghosts but for the very human pressure of their small, plump hands on his thighs. Were they swaying, or was he? Robert found himself rocking like a mast in a high wind, twining his fingers into the disordered hair of his handmaidens, clinging like a sailor to the rigging. They tilted their heads back to stare up at him, eyes glazed, their pupils so dilated that their eyes were nearly as black as the great, empty holes in the elephant mask.

It wasn't the elixir; he hadn't had enough of it for it to work so quickly. Nor had they, unless they had been guzzling behind the altar. But they hadn't looked like that when they first danced in, giggling and posturing. There must be something in the smoke. There was a blankness to their wantonness that chilled Robert to the bone even as his body responded mindlessly to their touch.

Shaking their tangled hair over their shoulders, the dancing girls licked their way up his body, tracing the honeyed path of the elixir up his neck, their bare breasts rubbing against his side as they pressed themselves against him. In automatic reflex, Robert's arms wrapped around their waists, feeling warm flesh beneath his fingers, the generous curves of waist and hips. They ventured further, following the line of liquid up over his jaw, sucking the last of the sweetness from the corners of his lips. He wasn't sure who moved first, or who gave way, but with no more thought than a rutting animal, his fingers were tangled in someone's hair, his lips moving against hers as her tongue sought out the last of the golden potion.

It was like falling into a dark cavern. He scarcely knew who he was or what he did. It was mindless, meaningless, a matter of pure physical reaction. Behind him, somewhere beyond the cavern of his flesh, he gradually became aware of noises. Catcalls and ribald shouts. Comments on his performance – largely favourable ones. The blood slowly began to return to Robert's brain.

The hair under his fingers suddenly felt coarse, the touch

of it lacerating his palms. It wasn't Charlotte's hair; it wasn't Charlotte's lips; it wasn't Charlotte's breasts or hips or thighs or any of those other bits he had been so mindlessly enjoying. He had one woman twined around his neck, another wrapped around his waist, and his body was convinced that this was a perfectly splendid thing.

Behind him, others felt much the same way. He could hear fabric rending, beads shifting, flesh meeting flesh as the smoke continued to snake down from the braziers and the revellers set to coupling in an orgiastic haze.

Robert stumbled back so quickly that both women went sprawling. Their bells jangled discordantly in protest. He scrubbed the back of his hand against his mouth, but it didn't do any good; he could still taste them, along the roof of his mouth, coating his tongue, sickly sweet like rot.

'I have to—' He pressed the back of his hand against his mouth and wobbled a bit. The wobble was exaggerated; the nausea was heartfelt. What in the hell had he just been doing?

The girls backed away with flattering promptness. As they jangled their way over to a group enthusiastically making a beast with three backs, Robert hoisted himself up onto the altar, took the beads in both hands, and hauled himself hastily through the opening.

There was fresh air coming through. For a moment all he could do was stand with his back against the wall, drawing deep, gasping breaths into his labouring lungs, his stomach roiling like a ship on the high seas. Oh Lord. What in the hell had he been about to do? Was he no better than that? No more loyal, no more honourable, no more true? Five more minutes in that smoke . . .

Whatever it was that Medmenham was burning, it was more

than mere incense. Even away from the smoke, he felt oddly light-headed, and his eyes showed an annoying disinclination to focus properly.

Focus. He had to focus. He had to remember why he had come here. It was the least that could be salvaged from the whole cursed affair. It was better than thinking of what had happened in that room, or what had almost happened.

Rubbing his eyes, he levered himself away from the wall and took stock of his surroundings. In niches in the wall, two braziers still smouldered slightly – the source of the smoke that had bellowed out in front of the elephant god. Water sloshed about on the bottom. The so-called god must have poured water over the burning coals to create those bursts of smoke that had preceded his entrance.

The god had also left behind his mask, hanging from a peg on the wall. It was an oddly homely thing, that peg, hardly appropriate to a deity, even a minor one. Discarded, the mask was a trumpery thing, nothing more than painted plaster of Paris, garishly decorated to show to good effect in the uneven light. Robert found the eyeholes just where he had suspected, right below the trunk.

Had Wrothan worn it? Or someone else?

A clever man might hand the starring role to someone else while hiding himself in the anonymity of a brown monk's robe.

At the end of the cell, a path sloped sharply upwards, leading to the source of the fresh air. Robert took it. His legs weren't quite so steady as he might have liked and his tongue still felt fuzzy, but his mind appeared to be clearing. It would be like Wrothan to slip away once the festivities were safely under way. Wrothan had little interest in orgies on their own account; his sole ambition was the power he could glean through them. That debilitating smoke that sapped the energy from muscle and mind alike wouldn't be to his liking at all. But what better time to slip away and conduct a little business? Given the activities in which he had left the others, Robert doubted either he or Wrothan would be missed for some time.

Just thinking about it made Robert's stomach turn again. He could feel the press of the dancing girls like sores in his flesh. He could still taste them on his lips, feel the slide of their tongues painting lines of shame across his skin. Robert scrubbed a hand against his jaw, as if the mere friction could rub off the taint. It felt like a profanation to have gone from Charlotte to . . . this.

And, yet, he almost had. Five more minutes and he would have had them both on the floor, rutting by instinct, as mindless as an animal. Just like his father.

Good God. That was an even more sick-making thought, to ponder the possibility of his father having sown the same field, so to speak, a generation ago, wearing the same brown robes, mindlessly coupling on the same gritty floor in the same vaulted room. The coarse wool of the monk's habit scratched at his bare skin like a hair shirt.

How proud his father would be, after all this time, to know that the apple hadn't fallen that far from the tree after all.

His path came to an abrupt end. Robert found himself facing a sheer chalk wall, but above him, all the way up, he could see the sky, black, practically moonless, and devilish cold, but open sky for all that. He had never been so happy to see it. In front of him, metal bars jutted out from the wall at even intervals, forming a ladder. Hoisting his skirt out of the way, Robert began to climb, resolved of one thing.

He didn't want Medmenham anywhere near Charlotte. Or

Staines or Frobisher or Innes or any of the lot of them. Including himself. He could feel the filthy reek of that subterranean room grinding into his flesh, marking him as surely as a brand.

As he climbed, he could smell jasmine again, the scent of betrayal, as thin as a reed, a phantom, a token, taunting him with all his failures, all the people he had loved and betrayed.

Was it merely his guilty conscience producing the elusive hint of jasmine? Or was it something else? As he left the incense of the lower chambers behind, Robert could still smell jasmine, stronger now in the winter night. No matter what occult powers Medmenham might claim, even he couldn't make jasmine bloom in the English countryside in January. But there were such things as colognes, trapping the essence of the flower in alcohol. Very few men favoured feminine scents like jasmine. But Robert knew of one.

Moving faster, Robert climbed the final few rungs. The ladder let out into a bizarre womb-like marble edifice. It took Robert a moment to identify it as the inside of an urn. It seemed a rather Medmenham sort of joke, to house human asps within immense marble jars, just waiting to crawl into some waiting Cleopatra's breast.

The urn had been cut out on one side, not entirely, just enough of a hole for a man to crawl through. It was as he was contemplating the hole that he heard the voices. Voice, rather. One voice.

It wasn't the sort of voice one would generally remember. It had a common enough timbre, not too high, not too low, with an over-particularity of pronunciation designed to mask an origin more common than the speaker cared to confess. Robert would have known it anywhere.

Robert crawled very carefully through his hole, the scrape

of his robe against the stone sounding, he hoped, like nothing more sinister than the rustle of the wind through the dry winter grass. The massive urn provided the best of all possible screens and there was a wall behind his back, made of rough flint. He was, he realised, in Medmenham's mausoleum, a vast, open-air edifice scattered with memorial monuments, with urns and arches and ornamental columns, in a macabre pleasure garden for the dead.

The dead weren't the only ones enjoying it tonight. The wind carried their words as effectively as the acoustics of the Whispering Gallery in St Paul's.

'There is the small matter of my payment . . .' Wrothan's voice was a touching mix of the obsequious and the importunate.

'Don't fret yourself.' His companion was unimpressed. Unlike Wrothan's, his accent was pure, effortless Oxbridge, save for the faint tang of a foreign accent. 'You will have your gold. When you fulfil your end of the bargain.'

Robert eased around the side of his urn, but to little effect. An ornamental column blocked his view. All he could make out was the skirt of a monk's habit, identical to all the others.

Wrothan's voice took on a wheedling note. 'I imagine that the Home Office would pay a pretty penny to know about your activities. They might even pay better than you.'

Fabric rustled and coins clattered together, ringing too true to be anything but gold. 'A deposit. There will be nothing more until we see results. And if I find that you have played us false . . .'

'Kill the goose that lays the golden eggs?' Now that he had his blunt, Wrothan was all that was jovial. 'Not I.'

His companion was less effusive. 'See that you don't. Or else your goose will be – how do you say? – cooked.' His tone was perfectly matter-of-fact, and all the more chilling for being so.

'General Perron never had any complaints,' countered Wrothan.

In his hollow, Robert's brows drew together. *Perron* was Wrothan's employer? When the colonel had told him Wrothan was selling secrets to the Mahratta, he had never specified to whom. Perron might be nominally employed by one of the Mahratta leaders, but he took his real orders from France.

'Names, Monsieur le Jasmine, names,' said the Frenchman, in suffering tones. *Monsieur le Who*? Robert wondered, and cautiously lifted his head away from the stone in an attempt to hear more clearly. 'If this is how you carried on in India, I am surprised indeed that Monsieur le Marigold kept you on.'

'The Marigold' – Wrothan seemed to have some small difficulty emitting the word – 'had no cause for complaint of me. And nor shall you. If I succeed in this . . .'

'It will be a cause for great rejoicing,' said the Frenchman politely, squelching Wrothan as neatly as a society hostess speeding a parting guest. 'Then. Good night, Jasmine.'

He really had said Jasmine, hadn't he? As in the flower. It took Robert a moment to realise that the Jasmine in question was Wrothan, but he didn't have time to muse on the Frenchman's pet name for his favourite traitor. Grass crackled underfoot as the man strode away from Wrothan – straight towards Robert's urn.

Robert hastily ducked around the other side, grateful for the all-concealing robe that blended so well with both winter-dry grass and granite walls. Hood up, huddled against the base of the urn, he played at being a rock, thankful for the lack of moon that swathed him in darkness. The anonymous monk with the accent disappeared into the urn and down the secret passage.

By the time Robert deemed it safe to look up, both Wrothan and the Frenchman had gone. Only the scent of jasmine lingered in the damp night air.

Robert hunkered back on his haunches, drawing his fingers through his sweat-sodden hair. His head still pounded with the after-effects of the drug, whatever the drug had been, and he lifted his face gratefully to the night air, letting the damp air buffet his aching head.

Jasmine. What in the blazes were they playing at? Robert wished his mental faculties were in better working order, or that Tommy had been there, too, to hear and judge. The Frenchman had said Jasmine.

Robert wondered, for the first time, if that conspicuous sprig of jasmine Wrothan had affected in India had been more than just a dandy's foolish nod to fashion. It was a pity, thought Robert grimly, that he had spent so much time concertedly not noticing Wrothan. It made it that much harder remembering his habits. But he did remember joking with Tommy about the migration of the flower, one day on Wrothan's hat, the next day in his lapel. They had put it down to experiments in fashion. But what if it had been something else? What if it had been a signal, a message? It might have been a call to an assignation, a symbol that he had news to share, any number of things. All of them entirely sinister.

Wrothan wasn't just raising a little extra blunt selling secrets to the Mahratta. He was playing for higher stakes than that. He was playing with the French.

There had been rumblings about revolutionaries while Robert was in India, whispers of French plots and schemes, but for the most part, those, like Robert, who had been many years away from England had shrugged it off. Everyone knew the

Governor-General, Marquess Wellesley, was practically potty on the topic of French threats; he saw Frenchmen under the bed the way small children imagined monsters. There had been a brief stir the year before when Bonaparte had sent a ship of men and arms to India at the request of General Perron, but Wellesley had sent them packing. And Robert had always believed that was that. One failed attempt. They were five months from England by sea. How much interest could they have in the affairs of England and France, or England and France in them? He had assumed that Wrothan's treachery was a local affair, with purely local consequences.

The damp was seeping through the wool of Robert's robe, but it wasn't just his nether regions that were feeling the chill. He might have found Wrothan, but the victory was a Pyrrhic one. There would be no nice, tidy revenge, no easy dispatch of a retired traitor. Instead, he had stumbled upon a hydra, that beast of classical fiction that sported new heads whenever the one was lopped off.

And all the heads were shaped like flowers.

Chapter Twelve

They say that eavesdroppers seldom hear good of themselves.

It's been my experience that eavesdroppers seldom hear anything of themselves at all, since most people aren't as interested in you as, well, you. This time, however, I was absolutely positive that Joan Plowden-Plugge had been talking about me. Me and Colin, that is. Her voice takes on a special sneer when my name comes up. It's rather flattering, considering that I've met her all of three times.

As I dusted my hands off against my pants, and automatically checked to make sure that the zip was where it ought to be, I wondered exactly what it was that I was expected to take badly when I found out. There was, I admitted to myself, as I pushed open the door of the ladies' room, the remote possibility that Joan and Sally might have been talking about another couple entirely. But, come on, who would really believe that?

What I needed to do was get them talking. It shouldn't be too hard to get Joan making barbed little comments. The problem would be making sure they were barbed little comments about whatever it was that Colin did for a living and not about me, my job, my Americanness, or my hair.

I ventured out of the dark cavern of the bathroom hallway (I wonder if there's a regulation that pub bathrooms must always be in a dark cul-de-sac), feeling like the Duke of Dovedale about to infiltrate a meeting of the Hellfire Club. As I quickly scanned the small group of people scattered around the table in front of the bow window, I was forced to reconsider. Can the Hellfire Club really be an appropriate metaphor when there's a vicar involved?

It made me feel all warm and fuzzy that instead of seating himself, Colin was standing next to the table in that way you do when you've only stopped to chat for a moment, declaring to all and sundry his intention to abandon them and cleave unto me – at least for the length of our dinner.

Slipping into the space next to him, I smiled cheerfully all around. 'Hi, all! Mmmm, thanks.' I gratefully accepted the drink Colin handed me. The paper napkin wrapped around the glass was already damp with condensation from the melting ice.

'How long are you here?' asked the vicar, clearly enjoying needling Joan. Joan turned her chair slightly away with the lofty air of one who does not intend to allow herself to be needled.

'Only the week,' I said. 'That is, unless I make some sort of major breakthrough in the archives and have to beg Colin to let me stay on.'

'I'm sure you won't have any trouble convincing him.' The vicar waggled his eyebrows impishly. He reminded me of Puck from *A Midsummer Night's Dream*, all good-natured mischief. I wasn't sure that was generally recommended in a vicar, but I certainly enjoyed it.

'Doesn't Colin have his own work to do?' Joan said acidly, although whether the dig was aimed at me or Colin was hard to tell.

'Nothing that won't keep,' said Colin neutrally. 'Half the time, I don't even know that Eloise is there. She just slopes off into another century and leaves me to my own devices.'

'You make me sound like Dr Who!' I protested.

'But prettier.'

'That's all right then. You know, it's unfair. You all know what I do, but I don't know what any of you do – well, except you,' I added to the vicar.

What was his name? I knew he had been introduced to me by something other than just 'vicar,' but I couldn't for the life of me remember it. Geoffrey? Godfrey? Sigfried? I was probably safer just sticking to vicar.

'Hazard of my profession,' he said sadly. 'It takes all the mystery out of me.'

'Except for the *Eucharisticum Mysterium*,' Colin pointed out, stretching lazily. 'I should think that counts.'

'Yes, but that's not me, is it?' protested the vicar. 'That's all God, and you don't compete for His thunder, not unless you want a plague on your cattle.'

'You don't have cattle,' Sally said, blowing froth off her beer.

'Chattel, then,' said the vicar. 'It's almost spelt the same.'

'Not unless you're using an Elizabethan primer,' interjected Colin.

Sally chuckled. 'Your chattel, then. I can just see your CD collection coming out in boils. Ooooh. Scary.'

We were straying a bit afield from where I had been trying to go. I made a last-ditch attempt to wrench the conversation back on course. 'What about you, Sally?' I asked hastily. 'What do you do?'

'Estate agent,' she said, and it took me a moment to remember that in this century, that meant Realtor rather than a land manager. She nodded to her sister. 'And Joan writes for *Manderley.*'

Joan was a writer? If anything, I would have had them pegged the opposite way around, with Sally as the artsy one and Joan as the pushy real estate broker. But you never can tell, can you? I know grad students who dress like lawyers and lawyers who go all bohemian in their spare time.

Then the name of the magazine registered. 'You write for *Manderley?*'

'Yes.'

Named after the fictional manor house in Daphne du Maurier's *Rebecca*, the magazine was a cross between a glossy like *Country Life* and a serious academic journal, devoted to the conservation of England's major and minor manor houses. Each issue featured articles on subjects ranging from attempts to muster support to save this or that historic site to in-depth looks at restoration projects to more esoteric examinations of material history, such as the spread of chinoiserie textiles in the eighteenth century, with special reference to their sociocultural implications.

As you can tell, I'd done more than my share of guilty newsstand browsing. It wasn't the sort of thing I could quite justify buying, but some of the articles were just enough over the edge into my field to almost qualify as research.

'I love that magazine!'

Joan crossed one long leg over the other. If she had had a cigarette, she would have blown smoke rings. 'Many people do.'

She sounded as though she couldn't quite see the point of it herself. I wondered if it was an act. She was the one who worked for the magazine, after all. Although I hated having to admit there might be something interesting or likable about her.

Well, maybe not likable.

Taking advantage of the lull, Colin seized his moment to whisk us away. 'Brilliant stumbling into you,' he said, steering me back from the table, 'but we're famished. No lunch,' he explained mendaciously.

I suppose from a boy perspective, cheese and crackers in the car doesn't really count as real food.

'Hmph,' said the vicar. 'We know when we're not wanted.'

With a backwards wave, I submitted to being led off to a small round table all the way in the far corner of the room, as tucked away as we could be. The table was blackened with age, nicked by generations of knives, forks, and goodness only knew what else.

The waitress flicked a couple of cardboard beer mats down in front of us, dropped two plastic menus, and departed.

So far, I was getting an F for my attempts at espionage. Mata Hari need have no fear of losing her place in the spy pantheon.

'You know,' I said, setting my vodka tonic down on the beer mat and leaning my elbows on the table, 'we talked about everyone else, but never what you do.'

'You're in a wet patch,' pointed out Colin, his menu covering his face right up to the eyes.

For a moment, I thought that might be an outré way of saying, 'Don't tread here; you're on marshy conversational ground,' or something like that. But it only took the feel of damp seeping through the wool of my sweater to make me realise that, no, he was referring to a literal wet spot.

'Damn!' I snatched my elbows off the table and tried to twist it to peer at the damp patch – which, if you've ever tried it, is an exercise in futility, and doesn't make you any less damp.

Colin ran a finger over the shiny spot on the table. 'Only water,' he decreed, gallantly scrubbing dry the rest of the tabletop with his own napkin. 'Now, what do you want to eat?'

I'm ashamed to admit that what with one thing and another (fisherman's pie and chicken tikka masala), we never made it back to the topic of Colin's occupation. It wasn't just that I'm easily distractible – although I am – or that my previous attempts had been about as successful as trying to batter down a door with a feather duster. There were so many other things to talk about, from silly one-liners to world affairs to books we'd both read or hadn't read but thought the other person should read. We were on to coffee before I could remember lifting a fork to eat my fisherman's pie.

But, in the end, it was the inherent mundanity of the scene that made my earlier wild suppositions seem so impossible. There was something so warm and cosy and incredibly commonplace about everything, from the battered wood tables to the soggy cardboard beer mats to the frayed green wool of Colin's sweater, which looked as though it had been washed, well, by a boy. He didn't look like England's next answer to James Bond. He looked like what he was: a thirty-something English landowner with laugh lines from squinting at the sun, a falling-down old house, and a splash of curry on his sleeve.

It probably had been the word 'sties' that I had heard. It was a bit like playing a game of Mad Libs, trying to reconstruct a sentence with words missing. I tried it out in my head. Joan had said, 'I wouldn't want *my* boyfriend gurgle gurgle gurgle sties.' That could easily translate to, 'I wouldn't want *my* boyfriend playing with pig sties.' Even if Colin didn't have literal pig sties, that could be her way of casting scorn on him for giving up his big city job to take up land management, much the same way my mother liked to refer to several holdover hippie cousins of mine as 'living in trees,' although as far as I could tell (having never visited them), none of them actually lived in a tree house. It all made a lot more sense than 'gurgle gurgle gurgle spies.'

Besides, if he really was a spy, how would Joan and Sally know? It wasn't exactly the sort of thing you rushed to tell the neighbours. Unless the whole village was in on it! And that really would be too, too absurd, like something out of *The Avengers*. I drank my coffee and pushed the whole topic out of my mind.

By the time dinner was over, spies, even of the historical variety, were the farthest thing from my mind. Breathless with cold and laughter, I hopped up and down while Colin opened the doors of the Range Rover. It all felt very normal and very domestic, driving home together along twisty country lanes in the dark, singing along to silly eighties music on the radio as Colin deliberately got the words wrong to some, and I – not so deliberately – got the words wrong to others. Who knew that the words to that Erasure song were really 'I'm your lover, not your rival' rather than 'I'm your lover, not your Bible'? I thought my version made much more sense and told him so.

After he had checked the answering machine and locked the door and kicked the front hall rug back into place (it bunched when you walked on it) and all those other little just-getting-home things that are three-quarters instinctive, we cracked open a bottle of cheap Italian red – real Italian red, brought back from his trip to visit his mother over New Year's – and settled down in a room I hadn't seen until then to cuddle up on the couch and watch silly movies.

For the first time since the bedroom debacle, I really felt as though I were home. Unlike the rest of the house, the room wasn't a decaying example of late Victorian arts and crafts movement; it featured a squashy, comfy couch with a plaid afghan tossed over one side. There were still dog hairs clinging to the side of the couch, relics, Colin admitted, of an elderly family dog who had gone to his reward that past October.

'Right before I met you,' he said, gazing soulfully at me over his wine.

I clinked my glass with his. 'I hope you're not considering me as a replacement.'

He picked a strand of red hair off his shoulder. 'You are shedding,' he said, handing it back to me.

'Um, thanks. But don't expect me to play dead.'

In one corner of the room, an open cabinet – IKEA or the equivalent, at a guess – housed a large collection of videos, in battered cardboard holders. From the looks of it, they were a composite selection. I assumed *Fiorile*, the Italian art film, was Colin's mother. *The Godfather* movies were definitely Colin. And *Four Weddings and a Funeral, Pretty Woman*, and everything ever done by Errol Flynn were undoubtedly the property of his sister, Serena. I wondered if she imagined herself as Maid Marian defending herself against Prince John's tribunal in that amazing courtroom scene. It's so much easier to live the lives we'd like for ourselves when they're printed on celluloid in two-hour-long packages.

I did get Colin to agree to the movie of my choice but, try as I might, I couldn't quite get him to see the finer points of the Errol Flynn *Robin Hood*.

As Robin flung open the doors of the Great Hall of Nottingham Castle, Colin made a snorting noise. 'If I came home with a whole deer slung over my shoulders like that, what would you say?'

I didn't even have to think about it. 'Get that unhygienic thing out of the house!' I snuggled deeper into the couch cushions. 'But when Errol Flynn does it, it's different.'

'He's dead, you know,' said Colin darkly.

'He was also gay. But who cares? He still looks splendid in tights.'

Colin made a grumbling noise that came out sounding somewhat like, 'Yes, if you like effeminate men.'

I supposed I should have been relieved that he didn't. I knew far too many men in college who liked Madonna, Errol Flynn, and Platonic aesthetics (not necessarily in that order). Let's just say that they all came tumbling out of the closet sometime around junior year.

'I took fencing, too,' he said, watching critically as Errol Flynn – looking particularly dishy in his green tights, I might add – cut Prince John's men to ribbons at triple normal speed.

'Have some popcorn,' I said, shoving the bowl at him.

'Can I throw it at the screen?'

'It's your carpet.'

'Hmm,' said Colin, and put it in his mouth instead, by which I gathered that he enjoyed vacuuming about as much as I do.

All in all, it was a perfectly lovely evening. We fell asleep in a happy haze of red wine and extra-connubial canoodling, curled up against the cold beneath Colin's utilitarian blue duvet. It may have been ugly, but it did know its business. For the first time since I'd come to England, I wasn't cold. Having a boy in the bed is better than having one's own space heater.

I was dreaming quite happily of Colin striding into the Great

Hall of Nottingham Castle with a large pig thrown over his shoulders – 'Back to the sties with you!' shouted Prince John, banging his fist on the trestle board with rage – when the Sheriff set off the castle alarm, the portcullis came crashing down, and I was jolted brutally and finally out of sleep.

Half strangling myself in the covers as I flailed into wakefulness, I realised blearily that it wasn't the castle alarm system after all, but the double ring peculiar to English phones. Someone was phoning.

I would have loved to have dropped whoever it was down the nearest oubliette, but since I'd been so nastily jarred out of my castle fantasy, there was no oubliette to be had. Just the phone, which kept ringing and ringing, pausing after each double ring as though gathering its breath. It showed no signs of stopping.

Like most men, Colin could probably have slept through the charge of the Light Brigade as they thundered right over his pillow. Since I was on the side with the phone, I groped sleepily for the receiver, picked it up upside down, and had to reverse it, getting slightly tangled in the cord in the process.

'Hello?' I murmured sleepily, before I had time to wonder whether I should really be picking up Colin's phone in the middle of the night. What if it was a family emergency? I wouldn't want his mother to think I was a loose woman.

Instead of saying 'hello' back – or 'cheers' or whatever – the person on the other end of the phone muttered something in a foreign language and the connection clicked off. I couldn't recognise the language, but it definitely wasn't a Romance language or one of the Nordic ones. Whatever it was, it involved a lot of slurring sounds.

In other words, it was clearly a wrong number.

Oh, well. At least it wasn't Colin's mother. Or his sister.

'All righty, then.' I put the phone back in its cradle, tugged some quilt away from Colin (Ha! He did hog the blankets), pulled my pillow over my head, and prepared to go back to sleep.

The phone instantly started ringing again.

This time it was I who muttered something uncomplimentary.

'Hello?' I snapped, picking up the phone. Didn't he realise it was three in the morning?

It must not have been three in the morning wherever he was. I could hear the sound of traffic, horns blaring, people chattering, taxi drivers cursing. I might not have been able to identify the language, but taxi drivers cursing sounds the same the world over. Trust me, it's true.

But the person on the other end of the phone didn't say a word. 'Hello?' I repeated. *Click* went the phone.

'Well, same to you,' I said, and thrust the receiver down. I missed the cradle, of course. Not that the crazy mis-dialler on the other end could hear it. Now I was awake, awake and annoyed. Colin, of course, was still fast asleep. To add insult to injury, in those crucial two minutes he had managed to wrap himself mummy-like in those few feet of blanket I had so painstakingly extracted from him.

I resisted the ignoble urge to poke him in the ribs. I couldn't find his ribs, anyway. They were too thickly wrapped in *my* side of the blanket.

Grumbling to myself, I half climbed, half rolled out of the bed, sliding until my feet touched the floor. Screw seductive, I was putting on my flannelest flannel. Colin had lost the right to skimpy nightwear when he had stolen my half of the blanket.

I stomped barefoot across the prickly old carpet towards the chest of drawers, my eyes by now having adjusted enough to the darkness to at least make out the shape of large pieces of furniture.

As I was passing Colin's side of the bed, his night table began to shriek at me.

After I jumped half out of my skin, I realised that I hadn't set off some sort of outré girlfriend alarm, it was just his cell phone, which he had forgotten to switch to silent when he went to bed. Admittedly, we both had our minds on other things at the time.

Being a meat-and-potatoes sort of bloke, Colin had never bothered to install one of the music ring-tones; instead, it was just your basic ring, shrill and insistent. If Colin's phone had been one of those flip-top kinds, I would never have looked. It would have been tantamount to opening his mail. But there it was, just lying there, screen side up, all lit up by the call. It was practically thrusting itself in my face. What was I supposed to do, shut my eyes?

On the glowing screen, the country code read '971.' I've always been more than a bit baffled by international dialling, but I knew enough to know that that was not the UK. It wasn't America, either, or anywhere in Europe. Where in the hell was 971? Someplace where people might still be out on the street and taxis might still be driving, perhaps?

The ringing stopped abruptly. A few moments later, the phone gave a double beep, like an electronic belch, to signify that a message had been left.

I didn't check the message, of course. The fact that I didn't have Colin's voice mail access code was entirely immaterial. Good relationships, as we all know, are based on trust.

Blah, blah, blah.

Trust and, in my case, a hearty dose of curiosity.

It couldn't hurt to just find out what the country code was. After all, I was wide awake now (I hurled an accusatory glance at the lump on the bed happily wrapped in all the blankets and sleeping away), and scrolling through directory numbers could have a soporific effect. It would be like counting sheep without the sheep.

Colin had told me there was Internet access in his study. I could look it up there. And while I was at it, I could check my email. Yes, that was what I was doing, checking my email. Nobody was saying anything about snooping. If I had been home and wide-awake in the middle of the night, of course I would go check email. It was immaterial that the email happened to be in Colin's study.

If I had ever learnt how, I probably would have been whistling with my hands stuck into my nonexistent pockets.

Oh, this was just silly! There was nothing wrong with going on a quick email check.

Pulling my thick old flannel nightgown over my head, I tiptoed out of the bedroom, pulling the door softly shut behind me.

Chapter Thirteen

'Charlotte!' In the mad crush of the Queen's Drawing Room, Lady Uppington manoeuvred her hoops expertly around broad skirt and a protruding sword to embrace Charlotte. 'Your grandmother told me you were at Court.'

Charlotte smiled shyly at her best friend's mother. 'I'm in waiting on the queen,' she said unnecessarily.

The egret feathers in Lady Uppington's hair wagged in sympathy. 'I was, too, you know, oh, ages and ages ago. Being a maid of honour was quite different in those days, not like it is now. We all lived in the palace, with that dreadful old dragon of a Mrs Schwellenberg hounding us, just sniffing for the slightest whiff of impropriety. That's why it was such a scandal when – well, never mind that.' Lady Uppington waved away whatever she had been about to say with a dramatic sweep of her lace-edged fan. 'The queen has been kind to you?'

'Tremendously,' Charlotte was able to say with complete sincerity. 'And the king has been all that is kind. He – this will sound very silly, but it was the kindest thing.'

'Yes?' said Lady Uppington encouragingly, as she had when

Charlotte and Henrietta were very little and the girls would run to her to show off their drawings.

'I had my battered old copy of Volume I of *Evelina* with me. His Majesty caught sight of it and asked me if I knew that Miss Burney had been an old friend of theirs. We agreed for a bit on what a wonderful writer she was, and I thought that was all. But then the next day, when I arrived at the palace, there was a package waiting for me, and in it was a splendidly bound set of the books, all done up in morocco leather with my name tooled in gold on the front. It's so fine that I'm half afraid to read it.'

Lady Uppington tilted her head reminiscently. 'That is very like the king. He was always good at the small gestures of munificence.'

Charlotte clasped her hands together over her fan. 'He's given me leave to use his library at the Queen's House whenever I like. It's splendid. Thousands upon thousands upon thousands of *books*.'

Lady Uppington's lips twitched. 'Books always have been the surest way to Their Majesties' hearts. So you're happy, then?'

'Ye-es,' said Charlotte, hesitating only a bit. And she was happy, really she was. The queen asked only that she stand behind her at Assemblies and read to her from time to time; the king had made her up a book in his own private bindery and promised she should have all three volumes of *Cecelia*, too; and the Princess Mary had promised to teach her how to paint on velvet. It would all be quite perfect – if only Robert were there.

She had imagined his return a hundred times since that night at Girdings. He would come galloping down the alley to Girdings. Swinging off his horse, he would dash up the steps to the entrance. 'Where is Lady Charlotte?' he would demand of the first footman to open the door. 'Gone to London, Your

Grace,' the footman would reply, looking neither right nor left. 'To London!' Robert would cry, with visions of rakes, rogues, and seducers wreaking havoc in his breast. Flinging himself right back onto his horse, he would ride *ventre à terre* to the capital, where he would charge into the Queen's House, flinging lackeys right and left, and sweep Charlotte up into his manly arms.

Of course, that was only one version. Sometimes, Charlotte permitted him to change his linen before riding to London. Nor did he always storm the Palace. Sometimes, he would be waiting for her in the sitting room of Loring House, where she was staying with Henrietta. 'Someone to see you,' Henrietta would say, with that impish Henrietta glint in her eye. She would shove Charlotte into the sitting room, slam the door behind her, and there he would be – ready to sweep her into his manly arms. Many of the details of the daydream might change, but the manly arms bit was always the same.

It worried her, from time to time, that there had been no word from him. While the grand imaginings of his racing to her side were all very well, she would have been just as happy with a prosaic note, even if all it said was, 'Held up on business, miss you, back soon. R.' But there had been no note.

Of course, if he had sent her anything, it had probably gone to Girdings, where, for all she knew, it might be gathering dust on her dressing table because Grandmama hadn't seen fit to send it on. One never could tell with Grandmama. For all that Robert came with both Girdings and one of the most coveted titles in the kingdom, it would be very like her to take it into her head that it would be a mesalliance ('mesalliance' being one of Grandmama's very favourite terms, applied frequently to Charlotte's parents). No one had ever gone into details over who Robert's late mother had been, but it had been made quite clear that she was of a sort who Would Not Be Received.

Even so, the lack of a message did make Charlotte just a little bit squirmy. Penelope's voice (it was always Penelope's voice) came at her at odd moments, saying things like, 'If he really loved you, would he have gone off like that?' and, 'He knows how to use a quill, Charlotte. He would if he wanted to.' That last one was bona fide Penelope, voiced over tea just the other morning.

Technically, like Robert's late mother, Penelope ought to be on the list of those who were No Longer Received, but the dowager duchess considered Penelope her own personal project (or, as the dowager put it, 'Reminds me of me at that age! Good stuff in that gel!'). A twist of the arm – or, more accurately, a well-placed thump of the cane – had elicited a marriage proposal from Lord Freddy Staines; the promise of a title, even if only a courtesy one, had placated Penelope's mother; and the dowager's influence had ensured that the newlyweds would have a comfortable posting in India, where they would make their home until the worst of the gossip rumbled down.

Robert's friend, Lieutenant Fluellen, had also offered for Penelope, more than once. Penelope remained firm in her refusal. It would be, she said, a nasty trick to drag an innocent bystander down with her just because he was fool enough to fancy himself in love. Penelope had always had her own sort of honour.

Meanwhile, Charlotte couldn't help but wonder, if Lieutenant Fluellen were back in London, proposing to Penelope every alternate morning and twice on Tuesdays, where was Robert?

Lieutenant Fluellen wasn't the only one to appear in London. Not only was Lord Freddy Staines back in town, preparing for his imminent nuptials to Penelope, but Martin Frobisher had been seen making improper proposals at an Assembly on Tuesday, and Lord Henry Innes was right in the next room, crammed into knee breeches, in attendance on the king. London, it seemed, was a very popular place at the moment. Except for the Duke of Dovedale.

He wouldn't have gone back to India, would he? Not without telling her, at least. A transcontinental voyage would, she would think, require a bit more than a two-word 'forgive me.'

With an effort, Charlotte dragged her attention back to Lady Uppington. Fortunately, Lady Uppington was just as happy speaking to herself as to anyone else, and was politely taking Charlotte's glazed stare as a sign of interest rather than abstraction as she reminisced about her own short spell at Court.

'Of course, the queen was much younger then,' she was saying. 'But then, weren't we all? Ah, but these hoops bring me right back,' she said, patting the protrusions at her sides.

'I rather like them,' Charlotte admitted, swaying a little to make her skirt swish. The sweep of her train against the carpet made a most fascinating sound. Skimpy, faux-Grecian dresses might be all the rage in the streets of London, but to gain entrée into St James, the old-fashioned hooped skirts of the previous century were de rigueur. The full-skirted style suited Charlotte far better than the fashions currently in vogue. Long columns of cloth weren't terribly flattering unless one were a long column oneself, which Charlotte decidedly wasn't.

She just wished Robert were there to witness the effect.

'And the men look awfully dashing with their swords, don't they?' said Lady Uppington wickedly. 'There's nothing like a long blade to lend countenance to a man.'

Henrietta would have been rolling her eyes by now, as she

always did when her mother made outrageous statements. Blushing, Charlotte said, 'They do look quite dashing.'

'Speaking of dashing,' said Lady Uppington, her green eyes twinkling like a girl's. 'I just had the pleasure of making the acquaintance of your mysterious cousin.'

'My . . . cousin?' Charlotte's heart began hammering against her stays.

Lady Uppington looked downright mischievous for a woman of fifty-odd. 'Tall man, blond hair, ducal bearing? I believe you might be acquainted with him,' she said so blandly that Charlotte knew, just knew, that Henrietta had been telling tales.

But all that was immaterial next to the crucial point. 'You mean Robert? Er, the Duke of Dovedale? He's here?'

Lady Uppington was enjoying herself hugely. 'Very much here, all present and accounted for, sword and all. I am pleased to say that he wears his sword with panache. But not too much panache,' she added thoughtfully. 'That would be common.'

'Did you – did he ask about me?' Charlotte was craning her neck wildly, knowing that she was behaving appallingly, but not caring in the least.

'Why don't you ask him yourself? The last time I saw him, he was' – squinting, Lady Uppington peered about the crowd, gave a little nod of satisfaction, and levelled her fan like a cavalry captain signalling a charge – 'right through there.'

It was hard to see in the mad crush, with so many wide skirts and plum-coloured coats shifting like the pattern in a kaleidoscope, but with the fortuitousness of the sun breaking through a cloud, the pattern shifted, the heavens parted, and there was Robert. Or, rather, Robert's back, but Charlotte was quite sure she could recognise him at any angle. He looked ridiculously handsome in the plum-coloured coat and knee breeches that were required of men at court, with dark blond hair neatly brushed and gleaming with hidden glints of gold.

'Charlotte?'

Charlotte jerked abruptly back to life as Lady Uppington nudged her in the ribs with her fan.

'Yes?'

Lady Uppington gave her a maternal shove on the shoulders. '*Go.*'

Charlotte went.

Heedless of her hoops and train, Charlotte hurried across the room, skirts swishing. Pride had no place in true love. And it was true love, true with a capital T, truest of the true, truer than the truest . . . well, that was the general idea. Charlotte all but flew over a protruding train, dodging sword hilts with love-borne ease. He had come for her! He must have gone to Girdings and heard she'd come to Court and . . .

The man he was speaking to tapped him on the arm and indicated Charlotte, whose precipitous progress was eliciting more than one amused smile behind a fan. Charlotte caught the word 'cousin,' and then the man faded discreetly away, leaving Robert to his familial responsibilities.

As Robert turned, his sword turned with him like a compass's needle – pointing away from her. Charlotte decided to ignore that bit. After all, not everything in life could be accounted an omen. Only the happy things.

'Robert!' Without pausing for breath, she held out both hands, skidding to a stop before him, flushed and happy. 'I'm so happy you've come!'

Robert bowed, managing his sword with credible prowess. 'Charlotte.'

Was it her imagination, or did he seem slightly less thrilled to see her than she was to see him? No matter; men were silly about things like public displays of affection. It was his first time at Court, after all, so maybe he was nervous about committing a breach of etiquette. Not that he would ever admit it. As Henrietta was fond of saying, men were about as likely to admit they were nervous as they were to stop and ask for directions, which was why one found so many hopelessly lost courtiers wandering around the tangled by-ways of the Palace after a levee, tripping over their own swords and desperate for a chamber pot.

Realising that she was babbling in her own mind, Charlotte promptly bottled it all up and turned all her enthusiasm on its proper source.

'Did Grandmama tell you I would be here?' she asked breathlessly, beaming all over her face. 'I left a message for you at Girdings, but I wasn't sure if you would see it, especially if your business kept you away longer than you expected.'

'I haven't been back to Girdings,' he said shortly. 'Not since—'

He broke off abruptly, looking as though he had just accidentally sat on the business end of his own sword.

'Since Twelfth Night?' Charlotte filled in for him, smiling at the memories that evoked. 'Are you staying at Dovedale House?'

'No,' he said curtly, looking over his shoulder as he said it. 'I thought it best to take bachelor quarters. So that I can pursue, er, my own pursuits.'

'I . . . see,' Charlotte said, even though she didn't see at all, and Robert knew it. He always knew.

Robert laughed raggedly, as though the sound had been torn

out of his very guts. 'No, you don't see, do you, Charlotte?'

'Then tell me,' she said simply.

For the first time, she noticed that there were deep circles beneath his blue eyes, and that the hair that had been brushed so neatly into place framed a face stripped of all its usual vitality. There was a sallow tinge beneath his tan, and lines along the sides of his lips that hadn't been there two weeks before. Charlotte racked her brain for where she had seen that look before. It had been, she realised, on second sons, just come down from Oxford or Cambridge, who had found themselves playing too deep in the pleasures of the capital.

Charlotte took a deep breath, her eyes never leaving his face. 'Robert, if you're in some sort of trouble, don't keep it to yourself. Let me help you.'

'Help me,' he said flatly.

'Yes.' She could feel her high-piled hair weighing her back as she tipped back her head to see him better. 'That's what people who care about each other do. As I care for you,' she finished, a little awkwardly.

Against the granite of Robert's expression, the sentiment sounded mawkish and flimsy, like rhymes worked by a fifth-rate poet. It had sounded much better in her head.

'I'm sure whatever it is, we can work through it together,' she tried again.

Without saying a word, Robert took her arm and led her through the crush, towards a relatively untenanted window embrasure. It couldn't by any stretch of the imagination be called private, but it was as private as could be found in the crowded room. Charlotte's broad skirts provided a flimsy barrier against the rest of the room.

Robert rested an elbow against the window embrasure,

the lace on his wrists spilling in an expensive stream along the painted sill. In the unforgiving afternoon light, his face looked unutterably tired. 'Charlotte, what happened at Girdings . . .'

Charlotte tilted her head eagerly up at him, already hearing the words she wanted to hear. *Come live with me and be my love.* She had been waiting for this moment for weeks. Her heart hammered unevenly against her corset. 'Yes?'

Robert pressed his eyes shut. 'It was a mistake.'

'A what?' Charlotte's mind refused to process the word. Unless, of course, he meant that it was a mistake to have left so hastily, with which she absolutely agreed. They should, she thought dizzily, have never left the roof. They could have stayed up there and lowered down a rope for food, built a little bird's nest among the statues, watched the garden start to bloom . . .

'A mistake,' he repeated. 'A bit of Yuletide madness.'

'Madness, maybe,' said Charlotte, hating the pleading note she heard in her own voice, 'but a very lovely sort of madness.'

Robert looked at her with regret. The expression she saw there chilled her to the bone.

'Lovely,' he said softly, 'in its place. Remember what you said about enchantments, Charlotte? You were right. They can't survive in the workaday world.'

Even now, the sound of her name on his lips sounded like a caress. Charlotte shook her head very hard, so hard her ears rang with it. 'Not all of them, perhaps, but this one . . .'

'Is over,' he said with gentle finality.

It was the gentleness of it that ripped through Charlotte's composure, piercing her straight to the very core.

She lifted her head, her ostrich plume standing high. 'I don't believe you,' she said, with all the dignity she could muster. 'You wouldn't have' – she twisted over her shoulder and lowered her voice to a whisper. There was no point in being ruined like Penelope – '*kissed* me if you hadn't meant it. I know you, Robert.'

'Do you?' That had clearly been the wrong thing to say. Something dangerous flickered beneath the cerulean surface of his eyes, something dark and unpleasant, like a sea serpent stirring under otherwise placid waters. 'Do you really, Charlotte?'

There was a barbed undertone to his silken voice that suggested that answering would be a very bad idea.

'How long did we have together at Girdings? Ten days? Twelve?'

'Fourteen,' blurted out Charlotte, a little too quickly. She had counted over each one hundreds of times, thumbing through her memories like beads on a rosary.

'Fourteen,' acknowledged Robert. 'A whole fortnight.'

Put that way, it did sound rather paltry.

'A whole fortnight to see directly into someone else's soul.'

'Sometimes it doesn't even take a fortnight,' said Charlotte stubbornly. 'Sometimes you just know. As I know you. Good heavens, Robert, I've known you since we were children!'

'For all of, what, a month? Two months? Twelve years ago?'

'Character doesn't lie,' Charlotte said doggedly. 'You were so kind, so good to me—'

'Who else was I supposed to talk to? Your grandmother? You were my only option.'

'As I was this time?' Charlotte demanded, making a face at him to underline the absurdity of it all. They had been surrounded by a house party full of people, for heaven's sake. Admittedly, some of them, like Turnip Fitzhugh, weren't exactly in the running for an England's Best Conversationalist competition, but it wasn't as though anyone had twisted his arm and forced him to seek her out at the breakfast table or sit with her in the library for hours every afternoon.

Robert, however, seemed to miss the humour in it.

He looked at her long and hard, his face as impassive as the guardsmen stationed by the doors. 'Yes.'

Charlotte could only stare at him, in complete bewilderment. Who was this, and where had he hidden the real Robert?

Robert saved her the trouble of saying anything more. Bowing over her nerveless hand, he said smoothly, 'Thank you, Lady Charlotte, for enlivening an exceedingly dull sojourn in the country. I don't believe our paths need cross in town.'

Over Robert's bowed head, Charlotte could see his friend Medmenham approaching. What was that Penelope had said, five hundred years ago? Something about the company Robert kept. Penelope had been right. Didn't animals tend to run with their own kind? So, apparently, did rakes.

In a voice like dead leaves, Charlotte said tonelessly, 'So I was simply your country entertainment. Like a mummers' play.'

'Only much prettier,' he said matter-of-factly. 'Ah, Medmenham. My cousin was just leaving.'

Medmenham lifted her fingers lingeringly to his lips. 'Pity,' he said.

As if from a very long way away, Charlotte could hear Penelope again, in the ballroom at Girdings. *I heard your precious duke tell Sir Francis Medmenham that you weren't the sort he'd be interested in dallying with . . . He left you, Lottie. By going off to carouse with Medmenham . . . going off to carouse with Medmenham . . . with Medmenham.*

Charlotte could feel colour rising in her cheeks, not out of shame, but rage. Two could play at that game, couldn't they? 'Yes, isn't it?' she said, and her voice had a shrill edge that hadn't been there before. 'Would you walk with me, Sir Francis?'

Medmenham waved a languid hand. 'To the ends of the earth.'

'I had in mind the end of the Presence Chamber.' Charlotte smiled winningly at Medmenham, unshed tears making her eyes brilliant. There was nothing like heartbreak to lend colour to the complexion. 'Will you excuse us, *Cousin* Robert?'

Even now, when she found she knew nothing about him at all, she knew enough to tell that her erstwhile betrayer was decidedly not happy. Displeasure exuded from the sudden stiffness of his shoulders, the belligerent angle of his jaw. Short of making a scene, however, there was nothing at all he could do.

'All right,' he said smoothly, 'but just this once.'

There was something in his tone that said that he meant it.

Charlotte took Medmenham's arm, holding her head so high, it hurt. So he didn't want her monopolising his friends, did he? Well, too bad for him. He wasn't the only one who might find her 'entertaining.' Charlotte's heart clenched painfully at the memory. At least Medmenham was an honest rogue. He had never pretended to be a knight in shining armour. Charlotte blinked back angry tears.

'Do forgive me, Sir Francis,' she said thickly. 'A spot of dust in my eye.'

'Indeed,' agreed Sir Francis. 'The Court is confounded . . . dusty.'

'But peaceful,' said Charlotte. It was peaceful, usually. Too peaceful. She thought of the king's daughters, kept at Court in perpetual monastic confinement, and had to suppress a shiver.

'As the tomb,' agreed Sir Francis. 'And you know what the poets say about that.'

'One poet, at least,' said Charlotte. 'But not one, I think, of whom Their Majesties would approve.'

'Do you base *all* your actions on the approval of Their Majesties?'

'When I am under their roof, it seems the least I can do.'

'Roof' had been the wrong word to choose. In the back of Charlotte's head, drooping nymphs crooned an elegy about the illusions of love. That night on the roof, she had been so very happy, so very sure that Robert had meant everything he said. It wasn't even so much what he said, since, in retrospect, he hadn't said so very much, but the way he had looked as he had said it, tenderness written in every line of his open, honest face.

So much for that.

All this while, she had thought she was living out *Evelina*, where the heroine's virtue and charm won the admiration and love of the honourable Lord Orville. Instead, she seemed to have dropped into *Clarissa*, seduced by the rake Lovelace for his own amusement. She had always thought herself able to tell the one from the other. And Robert had always seemed so honourable, so truthful – so kind.

If she let herself start believing Robert didn't mean what he had said just now, she *would* go mad. Like Ophelia. There was a heroine she most certainly did not want to emulate.

Medmenham ducked closer. 'Is the presence of a roof your sole criteria for the moderation of your activities? What about the royal courtyards? Or the Palace gardens? Would you forebear to gather your rosebuds there for fear of offending your monarch?'

'I believe,' said Charlotte solemnly, 'that, like balconies, gardens and courtyards must be taken as extensions of the overall structure, and dealt with accordingly.'

'Your scruples become you, Lady Charlotte.' The glint in Medmenham's eye said that before the night was out, he would have ten to one in the books at White's that he could overcome them. He, at least, was an unmistakable Lovelace. And, as such, no danger to her.

Charlotte inclined her head in silent acknowledgment, all that was virginal and aloof. After all, if he was playing Lovelace, she might at least do her bit as Clarissa. Especially if Robert was still watching them.

Medmenham rose to the bait. The more she looked away from him, the closer he leant. Charlotte desperately hoped that Robert was watching. But why? What was the point? If he were, he wouldn't care. He had made that quite clear. Charlotte's head swam with the confusion of it all. Just twenty minutes ago, she had been galloping towards happily ever after, in love and loved; now she was . . . what?

Medmenham was still buzzing around her ear, like a fly. 'Do you return to Girdings? Or shall you stay in London to grace the gatherings of the metropolis?'

'As long as Their Majesties are in London, I will be, too. I wait on Her Majesty,' Charlotte explained, pulling herself together. 'It's my three-month turn as maid of honour.'

'I trust, then, that I may wait on you.'

Trust. The word had a bittersweet echo to it. Charlotte could hear herself, like a fool, prattling to Robert in the chapel antechamber, bragging that to trust was to render someone worthy of trust. And Robert, all those long weeks ago, replying, *'That sounds like a very dangerous philosophy.'*

He must have known, even then, what he had intended to do.

Rotten apples, indeed!

Charlotte busied herself with the leaves of her fan, which had been painted with a charming scene of Richmond Palace. 'Never trust, Sir Francis. It's a dubious venture.'

'Will you, then, give me leave to hope?'

'Shall we say, instead, that you may hazard a visit?'

'That,' said Sir Francis, 'would be a wager very much to my taste. For you, dear lady, who could fail to hazard far more?'

One name came to mind.

'I imagine that for a hardened gamester, one wager does as well as another,' Charlotte said honestly. 'And that the determining factor would be which first comes to hand.'

If she hadn't been there, would it have been Penelope or one of the others singled out for the new duke's attentions? It was like looking at the world reflected in the back of a spoon, everything upside down and out of proportion.

'I had never thought you a cynic, Lady Charlotte.' Sir Francis sounded like he very much approved the change.

Charlotte lifted a hand in instinctive revulsion. 'Say practical, rather than cynical.'

'Two words for the same thing.'

'No.' Caught up in the philosophy of it, Charlotte nearly forgot she was talking to Medmenham. 'A cynic looks for the worst. A pragmatist merely weathers it when he stumbles upon it.'

'Or *she*?' asked Lord Francis, a little too knowingly.

Charlotte took refuge behind her fan. 'Does it make any difference? Life makes little distinction for one's sex in these matters, I should think.'

'Radical notions for a member of the queen's household, Lady Charlotte,' drawled Medmenham. 'Have you any others?'

That almost made Charlotte smile. There was nothing

the least bit radical about her. In fact, she was the most conventional creature alive. She believed in true love, and loyalty to one's monarch, and death before dishonour. It was just that, sometimes, things didn't quite turn out as one would have wished. In those cases, there was nothing to do but carry on. And on and on and on.

Charlotte smiled achingly up at him. 'No, Sir Francis. Not radical notions. Merely practical ones.'

Chapter Fourteen

'A pleasant girl, your cousin.'

Medmenham's voice pounded against Robert's aching head like the devil's own hammers. That had not gone well.

In fact, it was hard to imagine a way in which that could have gone any worse, short of flood, fire, or a large batch of locusts. What in all the blazes was Charlotte doing in London? In his imagination, Charlotte was perpetually at Girdings, leaning over the parapet of the roof with the wind playing through her hair. That was the point of towers, after all. They kept their princesses safe. She was safe at Girdings. Safe from him.

Three weeks later, he could smell the reek of the caves rising off his skin like rot. He had spent years trying to remake himself, trying to scour the stench of the tavern from his skin. But when it came down to it, for all his years of self-abnegation, he was no better than his father, whoring his way through life without moderation or honour.

Charlotte deserved better than that.

'You think so?' Robert adopted the bored drawl that was de

rigueur among Medmenham's set. After three weeks, it came as easily as breathing. 'I'm sure she's pleasant enough, but it is the utter end of tedium to be constantly burdened with attendance on a young relation. Especially when there are so many more entertaining companions to be had.'

He deliberately let his gaze linger on a particularly buxom countess, who giggled and turned to whisper behind her fan to a friend.

Medmenham, unfortunately, was not to be distracted. Folding his arms across his chest, he contemplated Charlotte with the lazy scrutiny of a gentleman considering the purchase of a new mare. 'I might be willing to take her off your hands, Dovedale. For a large enough douceur, of course.'

'Angling for a dowry, Medmenham?' Robert didn't bother to keep the sharp edge off his voice.

Medmenham was unperturbed. 'Which of us isn't?'

'There are greater heiresses in London.'

Medmenham's inscrutable gaze followed Charlotte as she, curtsying, handed the queen a dropped handkerchief before falling back into ranks with the other maids of honour. 'Perhaps I find myself in want of connections at Court.'

'Your friend, the Prince of Wales, will be disappointed to find you gone over to his father's camp.'

'My dear Dovedale, I inhabit no camp but my own. I believe I shall ask your cousin for a ride in the park tomorrow. She can ride, can't she?'

'The topic has never come up,' Robert said shortly, wondering how in the devil Medmenham managed to make absolutely everything sound like a double entendre. 'I see Innes waits on the king.'

'Yes,' said Medmenham idly. 'His brother procured him the

post, believing that time spent in the royal monastery would reform Innes's disposition. A foolish notion, that.'

'Especially with you on hand to effect a counter-reformation.'

Robert managed to make it sound more compliment than criticism. 'Does the Order meet again soon?'

'Patience, patience, good Dovedale. In a week, I think. That should be time enough.'

Time enough for what?

It was all Robert could do to paste on the requisite expression of jaded ennui when all he wanted to do was shake Medmenham until he told him what he needed to know. He bitterly loathed clinging to Medmenham's coattails but tentative forays into finding Wrothan on his own had confirmed him in the unhappy conviction that the only way to Wrothan was through Medmenham. No one else seemed to know the least thing about a man answering to his description – and Robert was afraid to ask too much for fear of giving the game away. Espionage, he realised, was not his forte.

The project that had begun as a simple plan to find and exterminate Wrothan had changed into something far more dangerous and complex. To kill the man who had killed his mentor, that was one thing. But now, knowing that Wrothan was actively plotting with the French – or, at least, a Frenchman – Robert knew there was no way he could just run Wrothan through and walk away, leaving Wrothan's contact free to coolly carry on with whatever dastardly doings he had in train. How could he ignore something that might cost more lives? It wasn't just the colonel anymore or the other men who had died due to the sale of intelligence before Assaye. It could be whole battalions of men at stake. Lord Henry had a position at court; Lord Freddy's father was one of the king's ministers; even the loathsome Frobisher had a brother at the War Office. All had access to secrets of state; all might be stripped of those secrets for the price of a gallon of strong cider or a whiff of drugged smoke in a subterranean chamber.

If Wrothan and his French contact were using the Order of the Lotus's orgies as a means of meeting, that would be the best place to catch them, truss them, and haul them off to justice. As soon as he knew where and when the meeting was to be, he could put his plans into operation. And then he could leave. Leave London, leave England, leave Europe. The ultimate location didn't matter, just so long as it was a very long way away, away from Charlotte and Girdings and this bizarre homesickness for something that had never been his to long for in the first place.

Despite himself, Robert's eyes wandered to the cluster of ladies around the queen, drawn, as always, to Charlotte. She was smiling at something one of the others had said, smiling too broadly for it to be anything but false. And he knew, without knowing how he knew, that she was as aware of him as he was of her, and would be, no matter where in the room he roamed.

It was only a matter of weeks, Robert reminded himself. Then Wrothan would be found, his work here would be done, and Charlotte could marry the sort of man she was meant to marry.

Just so long as that man wasn't Medmenham.

As soon as the queen released her, Charlotte did what she always did in moments of great emotional distress. She made straight for the library.

The pages and footmen and guards who peopled the Queen's

House already knew Charlotte by sight. They let her pass without comment, which was a very good thing, since Charlotte wasn't sure quite what would come out if she opened her mouth. She had kept it pressed very tightly shut all through the long afternoon at the queen's side, smiling, smiling, smiling. She had smiled through the end of the reception, smiled through the trip from St James back to the Queen's House, smiled as Princess Augusta read aloud from *The Lay of the Last Minstrel*, smiled until she wanted to scream from the strain of smiling, all the while reliving, in excruciating detail, every second of the past few weeks, from Robert's arrival at Girdings through his stunning defection just now.

At the end of it, all Charlotte was left with was the sense of having been terribly, horribly wrong. For someone who prided herself on her ability to read, she had painfully misread everything that had happened, every word, every gesture, every embrace. That almost kiss hadn't been almost because he didn't want to sully her; it had been almost because he just wasn't that interested. As for the roof . . . good heavens, she had all but kidnapped him. He had even called it a kidnapping. Then, once she had him alone and poised on the edge of a sheer five-storey drop, she had practically attacked him.

Charlotte managed a sickly smile. There was something funny about the image of a strapping army man cowering in terror from the amorous advances of a diminutive debutante. 'Demmed fierce things, those debutantes,' she could hear them telling one another in their clubs. 'Gotta watch out for the little ones. Get you around the knees and don't let go.'

Charlotte swallowed a laugh that sounded a bit too much like incipient hysteria for comfort.

That would cause a scandal, wouldn't it? 'Queen's New

Maid of Honour Goes Batty at Buckingham House.' Charlotte glanced carefully left and right as she slipped out of the queen's apartments, but no one seemed to have noticed anything out of the ordinary.

Charlotte's train whispered along the marble stairs behind her as she descended to the ground floor. She no longer found its swishing quite so satisfying as she had before. All around her, painted into the walls along the Great Stairs, murals depicting the sad career of Dido and Aeneas leered down at her.

Had Aeneas simply been amusing himself, too? Beguiling the long hours in Carthage with the first willing woman who came to hand? Given the smug expression on Aeneas's face, just where the double flight met and turned into a single one, Charlotte rather suspected as much. Like Robert, Aeneas had simply turned and run in the middle of the night. And yet men called him a hero. Surely there was something wrong with that?

According to legend, England had been founded by another Trojan, a comrade of Aeneas's named Brutus. If Robert was any indication, the old strain bred true.

Charlotte winced at the recollection of how slavishly adoring she had been, doting on his every word and painting pretty daydreams about knights in armour. She had, she realised, had an entire romance with an object out of her own imagination. Take one reasonably handsome man, paste on armour, and, voilà! instant hero.

He had even tried to warn her, with all that business about rotten apples. But she had been too intent on being adoring to pay the least bit of attention to what he was actually saying. No wonder he had decided to take what was so willingly offered! Until the novelty of playing hero palled. Was that why he had left so abruptly? Did he find her adoration too stomach-turning cloying to bear for another hour?

Well, she was no Dido to fling herself onto a pyre, even if she felt dazed and battered, as though she had just tumbled off the edge of a fairy tale into a strange new world where none of the old happy certitudes held sway.

Crossing into the complex of rooms that housed the king's apartments, Charlotte manoeuvred her hoops through the doors of the Great Library, just one of three vast rooms constructed by the king to house his remarkable collection of books. Court dress might be charming in a drawing room, but it vastly complicated one's interactions with doorways and furniture. Narrow dresses might not be nearly so glamorous, thought Charlotte, squishing her hoops as she squeezed through the door, but they were a good deal easier to move about in.

Charlotte breathed in the library smell like a tonic, the comforting scent of fresh leather bindings and decaying old paper. At this time of day, there were no visitors to goggle at her in her Court dress, no scholars to glower at her for invading their intellectual precinct. Even the king's librarian had left his post at the vast desk on one side of the room. Even the desk had been designed to do its part for storing books. The sides housed immense folios, each as high as Charlotte's hips.

It wasn't the folios Charlotte was after. Taking her candle, she held it up to the long rows of books that lined the walls. She was in search of a heroine.

All her life, Charlotte had picked books on which to pattern herself, trying on heroines the way other girls sampled new dresses. All through the four long years of successive Seasons, she had worked so very hard to turn herself into Evelina – eager, wide-eyed, innocent Evelina – in the assurance that, in the end, virtue would reap its own reward and patience would be rewarded with true love, just as Evelina was rewarded with Lord Orville.

Charlotte felt bitterly betrayed, and not just by Robert.

Evelina had lied to her. Evelina and Pamela and all the other companions of her solitary hours at Girdings, all the dusty books of her mother's youth with their dewy-eyed heroines whose unassailable virtue won the affections of the hero and drove the villains to long deathbed speeches of abject repentance.

Where was the heroine for her now? She didn't want to be Dido or Cleopatra, dead by their own hands. She rather liked living, even if her knight in shining armour had turned out to be an asp. Somewhere in the king's wealth of books there had to be another model to be found, a heroine scorned who didn't bury her knife in her breast or fling herself off a parapet or go mad when told to get herself to a nunnery.

Dismissing the books in front of her, Charlotte turned restlessly, holding her candle high, only to fall back with a cry as a hideous apparition shambled into the light. With a harsh, indrawn breath, Charlotte managed to get control of herself and the candle, which danced a little jig in her hand before she managed to grasp the base. In those moments, shape separated from shadow, making it clear that it wasn't a beast after all, but a man, and not just any man.

It was the king, but the king as she had never seen him. His jacket was undone and his shirt had come untucked from his breeches, the ends trailing untidily down. His silk stockings were rumpled, and his hair stood up sparse and grey on his poor, wigless head. He looked like a broken old man, turned out on the parish, but for the great Star of the Garter that shone on his breast.

'Emily?' he called out in a wavering voice, his pet name for his youngest daughter.

The Princess Amelia was exactly of an age with Charlotte, slight and fair. It was an easy enough mistake to have made, but it still made Charlotte feel like an imposter intruding on a private moment, especially with the king in such disarray.

'No, sir.' Charlotte stepped out into the light of the fire and dropped a hasty curtsy. 'It's Lady Charlotte. Lady Charlotte Lansdowne. You said I might use the library.'

'Lansdowne . . . Lansdowne.' The king mulled over the name. 'I knew a Lansdowne once. A good fellow, Lansdowne.'

'I believe you refer to my father, sir,' ventured Charlotte.

For a moment the king looked confused. 'Yes, yes,' he said at last, shuffling closer and squinting at her as though he were having trouble seeing. Appropriating Charlotte's candle, he held it so close to her face that it was all Charlotte could do not to flinch back. Against the dancing flame, his pupils were oddly distended, turning the king's protuberant blue eyes nearly black. 'You are the little Lansdowne, eh what?'

'Yes, sire.' Charlotte kept her spine straight and her voice soft.

The candle wavered in the king's hand as he mercifully fell back a step. Dark spots danced in front of Charlotte's eyes where the flame had burnt on the retina. 'The little Lansdowne,' he repeated. 'The little Lansdowne who likes Burney. You do like Miss Burney, eh what?'

'Very much, sir.' Now did not seem to be the time to voice her latent reservations about Fanny Burney's portrayal of human nature. 'You were kind enough to make me a very pretty present of her books.'

'Miss Burney was a friend to me, a true friend.' To Charlotte's shock, tears began to wander along the weathered cheeks. 'Where is one to find such friends again? Lost, lost, lost, all lost.'

The sheen of tears in the folds of his face glittered in ironic counterpoint to the gleaming Star of the Garter on his breast. An icy weight settled in Charlotte's stomach. She felt frozen in horror, watching the broken shambles of the monarch who had only hours before affably received various notables and asked after her grandmother's dog.

Had it begun this way before? No one at the palace liked to talk of it, but the memory of it was like a palpable presence in the palace at all times, there in the quick, sideways glances when the king began speaking too quickly, or the strain that sometimes entered the queen's face when she looked at him when she thought no one else was watching. Although the royal household had tried to keep it quiet, Charlotte knew that the dreadful mania had emerged again only three years ago. Leaving state acts unsigned, the king had been taken off to Kew, 'for a rest,' it was said, but the mad-doctors had gone with him.

'Sire . . .' said Charlotte helplessly. 'Are you . . . are you quite well?'

The king pressed a trembling hand to his stomach. 'The foul fiend does bite me in the belly,' he whispered hoarsely. 'The little dogs and all, Tray, Blanch, and Sweetheart, see, they bark at me.'

The dogs were clearly straight out of *King Lear*, but the grimace that transfigured the king's face left no doubt that the stomach pain was more than a literary allusion. 'Sire,' said Charlotte again, 'if you are ill—'

'No!' he said, so violently that she fell back a step. 'I will not be ill. Don't let them make me ill, Lady Charlotte.'

'No, sire,' Charlotte whispered, feeling tears well in her own eyes. 'I shan't let them, I promise.'

Surely it had to be a good sign that he had remembered her name? From all accounts of his previous illnesses, they had all begun with a rapid spate of speech. The king wasn't speaking quickly now. If anything, his words had a sluggish quality to them, like a man who didn't know whether he woke or dreamt.

The veined old hands closed around her own, weak as parchment. 'You are a good friend, Lady Charlotte,' the king said brokenly. 'A good friend.'

He spoke with such touching affection that it was all Charlotte could do not to give way to tears herself. 'It would be hard not to be a good friend to Your Majesty when you have always been so good to me.'

Please let him not be mad, she prayed. Please let him just be tired and sick. Anyone might be tired and sick and confused . . . just not mad. If the king were to be mad again, the possibilities were horrifying. All state business to grind to a halt, the hideous struggles over who should take the reins of government, the Prince of Wales's ghoulish glee at his father's incapacity, and, worst of all, the sorrow of the queen. It was said that last time her desolation had been terrible to behold.

'This is why it is best to have daughters.' For a moment, Charlotte thought that he had confused her again with the Princess Amelia, but he added, in a stronger tone, 'Never have sons, Lady

Charlotte, or they shall publish your letters in the papers.'

'Yes, sire.' The reference was clear. Not a month before, the Prince of Wales, in a fit of pique, had made public all his correspondence with the king, whining about the king's treatment of him.

'Monstrous unnatural creatures, eh what? Eh what? Has the world ever seen such pelican sons?'

'No, sire.' It was all Charlotte could do not to rise up on her toes and wave in relief as the door to the king's bedchamber burst open and a decidedly harried figure in knee breeches and plum coat came hurrying out.

She was less relieved when she saw who it was.

'Sire!' panted Lord Henry Innes, resting his large palms on his knees. 'You haven't finished your tonic.'

'A stomach tonic?' Charlotte asked hopefully.

Lord Henry dismissed her with a glance.

'This way, Your Majesty,' he said with forced joviality, as though she weren't even there. 'The doctor is waiting for you.'

Blinking in the light, the king followed him obediently enough, but the lost expression in his eyes was enough to make a stone weep.

As Lord Henry handed him over to a white-wigged attendant, the king glanced piteously over his shoulder at Charlotte. 'You won't let them make me ill again, will you, Emily?'

'No,' Charlotte whispered as the king was whisked away out of sight. 'No, Your Majesty.'

With the king safely away, Lord Henry braced himself between Charlotte and the door, standing like Henry VIII with his legs spread wide and his hands on his hips. It was a pose that worked better in a doublet and tights, with a ham haunch in one hand.

'Apologies for that, Lady . . . er . . .'

Charlotte's wide-skirted Court dress and single egret feather provided the indication of her rank, but otherwise he was at a loss. Charlotte imagined he didn't spend much time looking at ladies' faces, at least not if the way his gaze was angled towards her neckline was any indication.

'Charlotte,' said Charlotte. 'Lady Charlotte Lansdowne. I'm in waiting to the queen.'

Charlotte forbore to add that he had just spent the Christmas season living in her house. That would only cause unnecessary confusion, and Charlotte was far more concerned about the king than a man who had obviously been dropped on his head as a youth. Repeatedly.

And this was the sort of man with whom Robert chose to spend his time? That ought to have warned her, if nothing else had.

Lord Henry might only be capable of one idea at a time, but whichever he held, he held doggedly. 'If you're with the queen,' he said, with the air of a man pronouncing a mathematical theorem, 'shouldn't you be upstairs?'

'I came down for a book.'

'Book?' Lord Henry looked blankly around the library as though it had only just dawned on him that that was what the room was for, and that the little rectangular thingies embedded in the walls weren't just another decorating motif. 'Ah, right. Don't have much use for the things myself. Bit late for a book, isn't it?'

Now wasn't the appropriate moment to give him her speech on how good fiction transcended time. Other matters demanded more immediate attention. Charlotte felt slightly sick at the thought of it, but it had to be faced.

'Is his Majesty' – Charlotte couldn't bring herself to voice the dreaded word – 'in need of assistance? Should I fetch the queen?'

'No, no,' Lord Henry said heartily, waving his huge hands in negation. 'No need to disturb the queen. Don't want to raise a ruckus, eh what?' Apparently, the king's speech habits were catching.

Charlotte carried on doggedly. 'But if—'

'Nothing of the sort!' exclaimed Lord Henry, a little too hastily. 'His Majesty only had a bit of a stomach upset. Took a little too much rich food today. Doctor's on hand. Nothing to be worried about.'

'But he seemed to be wandering in his speech . . .'

Lord Henry shrugged in a way that implied a little woman had no business bothering an important attendant of the king with trivialities. 'Nothing like pain to make us all a little loopy, eh? Don't want to keep you. Best be going back to the queen, what?'

Stepping back across the threshold into the king's rooms, he started to push the panel closed.

'One thing, Lord Henry.' Lord Henry's hand stayed on the door panel and his eyes rolled back in his head in an oh-no-here-it-comes gesture. 'Should his Majesty's . . . stomach upset worsen, you will send word to the queen, won't you?'

What Lord Henry really wanted to send for was a muzzle for use on interfering maids of honour. He did not exactly have the most guarded of countenances. He must, Charlotte thought irrelevantly, lose a fortune every time he sat down to cards.

'It's just a stomach upset,' he repeated. 'No need to concern yourself.' He didn't exactly add 'bloody interfering female,' but the words were implied. And, then, in a last burst of lucid speech, 'Tell that cousin of yours I'll be seeing him next Thursday!'

With a concatenation of wood against wood, Charlotte found herself staring at a closed door.

She felt a powerful urge to kick it.

Chapter Fifteen

The next day dawned clear and bright. In the light of morning, with the sunlight streaming through the east-facing windows of her borrowed bedroom at Loring House, the events of the night before seemed nothing more than a hideous phantasm, too outrageous to be real.

Curled up in her comfortable nest of linen and down, with the branches of the trees in the square waving a cheerful good morning, Charlotte couldn't help but feel that she had been extremely silly. She indulged in a moment of gratitude that she hadn't acted on her first impulse and run tattling to the queen. With her spirits already in turmoil from her interview with Robert, carried away by the Gothic atmosphere of books and candlelight, she had given way to exaggerated imaginings fuelled by – what? Nothing more than the king confusing her, in a dark room, with his daughter Amelia, and complaining of stomach ache, albeit in somewhat florid terms. Candlelight played all sorts of tricks.

Goodness only knew her powers of perception hadn't been anything to boast about of late.

Rolling over, Charlotte buried her face in her pillow. The down billowed comfortably around her face. Perhaps she could just stay here. For a year or so. She felt sore all over, in that hollow way one did after an emotional crisis once the storm had already flooded through. It was easier to be angry than to be hollow, but the anger just wouldn't seem to come. Oh, but she had been an idiot!

With a resolute shove, Charlotte emerged from the bedclothes flushed but determined. No more calling herself names – even if she had been utterly, entirely idiotic to have believed . . . well, that was all beside the point now, wasn't it? She had had a long, teary session with Henrietta the night before, but that was all over now. There was nothing to be done but to take the whole, sorry incident as a salutary lesson and never, ever behave so foolishly ever again. No more tears, no more regrets, and absolutely no more Robert.

She supposed she would have to see him again from time to time in the normal course of things, but there was no reason to dwell on it. Girdings had twenty-two bedrooms and twelve major reception rooms; they could live in the same house for years without so much as passing each other in the hallway.

Rolling out of the bed trailing the bedclothes along with her, Charlotte squinted shortsightedly at the china clock on the mantelpiece. Eleven o'clock! Henrietta must have left orders she wasn't to be disturbed. Either that, or the entire staff was still engaged in laundering the flotilla of handkerchiefs she had gone through last night, while Henrietta patted her arm and repeated 'but I don't understand' until Charlotte didn't know whether to hug her or kick her in the ankle; Miles hovered just outside the drawing room door with the air of a man who would like to be helpful but doesn't know how, popping in from time to time with bloodthirsty and unhelpful solutions like keelhauling, horse-whipping, and light braising in boiling oil, which at least had the benefit of making Charlotte hiccup through her handkerchief with snotty gasps of laughter in between bouts of concerted sobbing.

At least the keelhauling had been preferable to Henrietta's determined incomprehension. 'But he seemed so devoted!' didn't do anyone the least bit of good, no matter how well Henrietta meant by it.

Hopping in her haste, Charlotte kicked off a bit of sheet that was unaccountably clinging to her ankle and shimmied into her chemise, managing to get it wrong way round on the first go. The maid must have come while she was sleeping and cleared up the discarded debris of her court dress. Not so much as a crushed egret feather remained on the floor as a reminder of the night before. Someone had even removed the broken quill she had left lying next to her diary and replaced the stained blotter. Her poor diary had taken quite a beating the night before.

But that was all done with. Charlotte defiantly donned a bright red spencer over her white muslin dress. The queen liked red, after all. And she wasn't going to skulk around in mourning just because her fairy tale had turned out to be nothing but an extended fit of self-delusion.

But she wasn't supposed to be thinking about that, was she?

Grabbing up her reticule, Charlotte hurried down the front stairs, dodging a length of drapery that someone had unaccountably left hanging from the banister. Henrietta was in the process of redecorating Loring House from the ground up, so one had to be alert for ladders, lengths of fabric, and bits of miscellaneous masonry. Not only Henrietta and Miles but the entire staff of Loring House had been lovely about adopting her as a surrogate daughter of the house. Fortunately, the servants seemed to find her habit of leaving books open on odd surfaces more endearing than annoying.

As Charlotte made her way to the door, buttoning her gloves and expertly navigating around three chairs that usually lived in the south drawing room, a carefully calculated cough brought her up short. Miles's butler Stwyth had mastered the art of exhalations that, at the same time, managed to be both unassuming and yet resonate through an entire room. It was a most impressive talent.

'There is a gentleman to see you, Lady Charlotte,' he intoned. Stwyth's displeasure at this social irregularity was displayed only in the quivering tufts of hair above either ear, which served as a fairly reliable barometer of the old retainer's moods. 'I have taken the liberty of showing him into the morning room.'

A gentleman, was it? Sir Francis Medmenham must have made good his promise to call. It was rather flattering that he had been quite so prompt. Charlotte doubted Lovelace would ever have hauled himself from his bed before noon, just to pursue Clarissa.

'Thank you, Stwyth,' she said with a smile that made Stwyth thaw ever so slightly. 'Good morning – *Robert*?'

If she had tufts of hair like Stwyth's, they would have been quivering for England.

'Charlotte,' he acknowledged, turning away from his perusal of the French porcelain on the mantel to greet her. The morning light wasn't kind to him. Fatigue – or more likely dissipation, Charlotte reminded herself – had riven deep purple patches beneath his eyes. 'I take it you were expecting someone else?'

'I certainly wasn't expecting you,' blurted out Charlotte, jolted into honesty. 'I thought our paths weren't to cross.'

'Consider this more of a brief and necessary uncrossing.'

It was like looking at a stranger, but a stranger wearing a loved one's face. It wasn't fair, Charlotte thought furiously, for him to look so familiar and yet be so strange. It was one thing to know that the man she thought she saw wasn't the man she was seeing; it was another thing to teach her heart to believe it. Even now, part of her still wanted to coo and flutter at him.

Charlotte crossed her arms tight across her chest, a makeshift sort of armour against an insidious enemy. 'To what do I owe this uncrossing, then?'

Robert pushed abruptly away from the mantelpiece, very rudely presenting her with his back as he stalked with jerky movements towards the window. All the practiced gallantry he had displayed at Girdings seemed to have disappeared along with his pretended affections. But it wasn't his gallantries that Charlotte missed the most; it was those moments when he was at his most matter-of-fact, too plainspoken to be anything but sincere. It had been an excellent act.

Robert braced his hands on the windowsill, staring fixedly into the square. It would be a pretty view in summer, with the park in the middle of the square, but now the trees were black and barren, as knobby as witches' knees, and the only pedestrians promenading were white-capped nannies and their heavily bundled charges.

'Sir Francis Medmenham intends to ask you riding,' he said to the windowsill.

Charlotte stared at his back in wide-eyed disgust. 'And he sends you as emissary?'

It was one thing not to want her himself, but to so coolly pass her along to a friend, to turn from lover to pander within the space of a month . . . Bile rose in Charlotte's throat. Even Lovelace wouldn't have behaved so.

'No!' Robert jerked around to glower at her. 'He isn't aware I've come to see you.'

'How shocking.' Relief made Charlotte acid. 'I hadn't thought you went anywhere without him.'

Her bolt hit home. Robert's knuckles whitened around the windowsill. 'I have come to request that you decline Medmenham's invitation.'

'Oh, have you?'

'Yes,' Robert said stiffly.

Charlotte might not have wanted to go riding with Medmenham before, but she did now. Despite having grown up in the country, she had never been much of a rider. Horses tended to realise when you were thinking about something else entirely and had a tendency to use those moments to dump you in the nearest hedge. But she wouldn't miss this ride for the world.

'Do you think I can't keep my seat?'

Robert's blue eyes darkened. 'Not on a ride such as this.'

'Don't worry,' said Charlotte flippantly. 'If I take a tumble, I won't come crying to you.'

Robert's lips moved, but no sound came out. She appeared to have rendered him incapable of speech.

Charlotte had never seen outrage quite so profound, and all because she had made a comment about falling off her horse, which didn't seem like it ought to be the sort of thing to make a man start breathing gusts of flame.

As she watched Robert's face move from tan to crimson, it belatedly occurred to Charlotte that tumble might, just might, have more than one meaning.

Charlotte went pink straight to the tips of her ears. 'Oh, no. He couldn't think . . .'

He clearly did.

'I meant off my *horse*!' she all but shouted.

'I know that,' Robert snapped.

'That's not what you were thinking,' she muttered.

Could a duke blush? This one seemed to be colouring up nicely. 'You don't know what I was thinking,' he gritted out.

'No, we've established that, haven't we?' said Charlotte brittlely. 'Several times.'

'Then I'll make myself very plain this time.' Robert spoke very slowly and clearly, as though to the village half-wit. He was still breathing heavily through his nose. He might not want her for himself, but the notion of her dallying elsewhere clearly discommoded him.

Charlotte lifted her chin and regarded him haughtily, in her best imitation of her grandmother squishing the peasantry. 'And what are your pronouncements, O Master?'

Enunciating every syllable, Robert pronounced, 'If Sir Francis Medmenham asks you to marry him, don't.'

Charlotte blinked. She had missed a vital link there. So, as far as she could tell, had Robert. Since when had a ride in the park become a euphemism for matrimony?

Charlotte abandoned her duchess impression to wrinkle her nose at her erstwhile lover, who had clearly gone utterly mad. Or maybe he had always been utterly mad and she just hadn't realised. Much more of this and she would go utterly mad.

Madness must be in the air.

'He hasn't even asked me to go riding yet. I only have your word on it. And we both know what *that* is worth.'

'Well, if he does, don't.'

'Go riding with him or marry him?' Taunting Robert was actually rather fun, once one got into the swing of it. Poking him with little sticks would probably be fun, too, but there weren't any to hand. Too bad.

'Either.' If Robert gritted his teeth any more, they were going to fall out. Charlotte watched the process with fascination and no little satisfaction. Serve him right to be a toothless wonder. That would put a spoke in his future seduction plans.

'I don't see by what right you tell me to do – or not to do – anything.'

'By my *right* as the head of the family.'

'Oh, naturally!' Charlotte wafted her arms in the air. 'The same right you exercised oh so diligently all those years while you were away in India. The same right you employed with such stunning' – Charlotte ground to a stop, momentarily at a loss for a suitably scathing noun – '*conscientiousness* by running away.'

A wry expression settled across Robert's face, painfully reminiscent of the man she had known at Girdings. 'Which time?'

'Either,' Charlotte shot his own word back at him. 'You needn't pretend you have the slightest concern, however minuscule, for my well-being or happiness. You just don't want your little friend being diverted by matrimony.'

If she hadn't known better, she might have thought that he looked . . . sad. That was nonsense, of course. 'Right. Naturally. You've hit it entirely,' he said tonelessly. 'Will you grant me my request?'

'No.' Some inner devil prompted Charlotte to add, 'I haven't so many suitors that I can afford to lose one. Even if he is yet another piece of rotten fruit.' She let that sink in before continuing, 'But at least he makes no pretence about it. He's never pretended to be anything else. Now may we consider this interview at a close?'

It would have been a very impressive speech if her voice hadn't cracked at the end. With a flourish, she gestured towards the open door into the hall, where, she had no doubt, Stwyth and at least two under housemaids would be busy dusting the wainscoting along the side of the door.

Robert briefly closed his eyes, in a gesture indicative of unspeakable weariness. Without moving, he said, 'I'm sorry I hurt you. If you believe nothing else I say, believe that.'

'You're right,' Charlotte said, and waited deliberately, cruelly, before adding, 'I don't believe anything you say.'

Plunking her nose firmly in the air, she turned on her heel and swept out, nearly tripping over a crouching maid in the process.

Robert didn't make any attempt to pursue. She could see him reflected in a vast Baroque mirror propped against the wall awaiting rehanging. He didn't move. His expression didn't change. He just stood there in Henrietta's blue and white morning room, watching her walk away.

She should have felt triumphant. She had said all the sorts of things she had always intended to say, but never actually did. And it had been easy. They had just come pouring out. But instead of feeling victorious, she just felt drained. And very, very confused. How could he say he hadn't meant to hurt her when he had? Why come and bedevil her when he had made it very clear he hadn't wanted anything to do with her? Charlotte's gloved hands curled into fists at her sides. It just plain wasn't *right*.

Tripping down the front steps, Charlotte took a deep breath

before letting a groom hand her up into Henrietta's carriage. She just needed to put it all behind her. It was all over. Nothing Robert said had any power to move her. If she repeated it to herself often enough, she might even begin to believe it. Grimacing, Charlotte sank back against the blue satin cushions.

At least it would be peaceful at the Queen's House.

At the Queen's House, all was havoc.

The queen's pages greeted her with wide, frightened eyes as she passed down the halls. One of Princess Mary's ladies stumbled past, crying, her handkerchief over her eyes. Apprehension quickened Charlotte's steps until she was all but running, her slippers padding against the varnished wooden floors.

In the Warm Room, so called because it boasted one of the only carpets in the palace, Princess Sophia was pacing maniacally back and forth, her butter-blond curls sticking out at odd angles from their bandeau. On seeing Charlotte, she turned a tear-ridden face her direction. 'Oh, Lansy,' she moaned. 'It's happened *again*.'

'What has?' Charlotte asked breathlessly, fearing that she knew very well what.

'Papa! He's gone . . . well, you know.'

Charlotte sagged heavily against the back of a gilded chair. 'Oh, dear.'

Princess Sophia cast a nasty look in the direction of her mother's dressing room, '*She* drove the darling to it, I have no doubt. You'd best go in to her. *She* is having her own hysterics. As if she really cared!'

Princess Sophia's tone implied that the queen had no right to any hysterics, much less hysterics of her own. The animosity Princess Sophia bore for her mother only seemed to intensify with every day Charlotte had spent at the palace.

That, however, was no business of Charlotte's. Releasing her death grip on the chair, she resolutely shook out her skirts. 'I'll see what I can do,' she promised.

'You're an angel, really,' said Princess Sophia. 'Not that *she* deserves it.'

Charlotte smiled fleetingly and was gone, through the door into the queen's dressing room. If the queen had had hysterics, she wasn't anymore. She drooped in her chair, still wearing her dressing gown. Her face was so grey that it seemed as though the crimson walls had drained all the life out of her. Next to her hovered Princesses Mary and Elizabeth. Above her head, six portrait miniatures of Charles I gazed mournfully down from their case on the wall in sad commentary on the perils of bearing the crown.

Princess Mary, always so calm, was as disarrayed as her mother, her fair face flushed and her usually immaculately arranged hair straggling in wisps around her face. Dropping her mother's hand, she made her way to Charlotte.

'You've heard, I take it?' she asked, in a low voice, as the Princess Elizabeth continued to hover over her mother's shoulder, patting her arm and making soothing noises.

'Princess Sophia just told me.'

'It's dreadful,' said Princess Mary heavily. 'Just dreadful. Worse than last time, even. It was so sudden.'

Charlotte thought of what she had seen the night before, but held her tongue. There could be no use in mentioning it now.

'They won't let Mama in to see him,' Princess Mary continued despairingly. 'Papa has dismissed all his pages and his Lords of the Bedchamber. At least, they say it's by his own wishes.'

Charlotte's eyes widened. 'Surely, the doctor—' she began.

'They have appointed a new doctor,' said Princess Mary. 'They say Papa doesn't want the Willises anymore, not after the way they treated him last time. They wouldn't allow Mama's physician in to see him.'

'They?'

'He, rather,' Princess Mary corrected herself, with a shrug to show the futility of syntax at such a time. 'My brother's man, Colonel McMahon.'

'Oh,' said Charlotte. And then again, 'Oh.'

The Prince of Wales had apparently lost no time in securing his hold over the household.

'Mama is frantic for lack of news. And,' the princess admitted, 'so are we. Poor Papa!'

'Have you sent to the Prince of Wales?' asked Charlotte tentatively.

'He is probably too busy celebrating to take any notice,' said Princess Mary, who was usually quite fond of her brother, bitterly. 'Why must this happen again and again? Papa is so *good*. Why must he be afflicted so? Why must *we* be afflicted so?'

'Is there anything at all I can do?' asked Charlotte. 'Any assistance I might render?'

Princess Mary sighed. 'Unless you can persuade my brother to lift his ban . . .' With a shrug at the futility of it, she suggested, without much enthusiasm, 'Perhaps you might read to Mama. Mama?'

'I should not do the listening justice.' The queen's voice was hoarse and cracked, as frail as her skin. 'Not now.'

It was enough to make anyone think decidedly nasty thoughts about the Prince of Wales. How could he be so abandoned to filial feeling, much less common human decency?

He had done the same before, grabbing charge of the king's household and forbidding his mother and sisters access to the king. It was said that on those previous occasions, the prince had done everything possible to arrest the king's recovery in the hopes that if his father's mind remained deranged, he would be granted all the powers of a regency.

The notion that someone would be willing to sabotage his own parent's sanity for personal gain made Charlotte's skin crawl.

As she looked at the pathetic figure of the queen, a germ of an idea fluttered through Charlotte's brain. 'The king's bedchamber is next to the Great Library!' she blurted out.

The two princesses looked at her as though she were the one to have run mad.

'Yes,' said the Princess Elizabeth. 'Where it has been these thirty years.'

'If Your Majesty were to desire me to read to you,' Charlotte suggested haltingly, 'a new book might need to be procured for your amusement. It is the merest coincidence that the library opens directly into the king's chamber . . .'

The queen's dull eyes lifted to Charlotte's, comprehension lighting in their depths. The royal spine straightened.

'Fetch me a new book, Lady Charlotte,' the queen commanded in her charmingly accented English. 'I find I desire to be read to.'

Chapter Sixteen

To promise daring deeds was one thing; to actually accomplish them quite another.

Even though it was the same route she had walked a hundred times before, Charlotte felt dreadfully conspicuous as she made her way from the queen's apartments to the Great Library. How did proper spies manage? Charlotte couldn't help feeling like her purpose must be blazoned in fireworks above her head for all to see. But no one else appeared to notice anything out of the ordinary. They were all too busy whispering about the king's health to bother with her – 'I heard he jumped right out of bed and built an ark in the middle of the night!' she heard one footman whisper excitedly to another. 'Calls himself Noah and runs around looking for animals to put on the ark!'

With news of the king's madness already spread, the library was completely deserted. It would, Charlotte supposed, take rather a lot of cheek to go on reading Plautus or Livy with the king suffering in the next room.

Feeling like a poor excuse for an emissary, Charlotte placed a palm carefully to the surface of the door to the king's room and pushed. The door gave without the slightest murmur, moving soundlessly. With the door merely an inch open, Charlotte paused, listening for all she was worth. There was nothing to be heard, no footsteps, no voices, nothing – except for a low mumbling monologue like water running over the rocks of a stream, an indistinguishable burbling punctuated by low sobs and a sort of rustling sound.

Throwing caution to the winds, Charlotte pushed the door the rest of the way open and beheld a sight to stir the hardest heart. In a sodden nest of disordered linens, the king lay curled into a protective ball, knees tucked up to his chest. The poor royal legs were bare beneath his nightshirt, pitted with goose pimples in the merciless cold of the room. Charlotte's nose wrinkled at the reek of an unemptied chamber pot.

Had the servants never come? The fire was still banked from the night before and the room was dreadfully cold, with the bone-aching January chill that fires could keep at bay but never quite eliminate. With his covers off, the king was all but exposed to the elements, shivering and crying and sweating despite the cold, crooning to himself in a low, continuous monotone. Charlotte stood frozen with pity and horror.

How, oh, how was she ever going to tell the queen? Surely, such things couldn't be allowed to happen. Not to a monarch. The servants must be called and scolded, the fire stoked, the linens changed, a soothing draught of some sort prepared . . .

But all that faded into insignificance next to the most horrifying sight of all. As the king floundered among his sheets, Charlotte at last saw just what it was that made him move so awkwardly and lie so strangely. His arms were twisted and tied around his chest in a hideous contraption of a waistcoat, holding his upper body all but immobile.

Charlotte must have made some noise, of horror or pity, because the king paused in his whimpering and, with an effort that made the veins of his neck stand out, twisted his head in a pitiful effort to try to see.

'Emily?' he called, in piteous echo of the night before. 'Oh, Emily, why won't you save your father? Take off this cursed waistcoat, my Emily! Emily . . .'

Charlotte didn't know what she might have done. Her automatic instinct was to take the king away, free him from his bonds and spirit him up to the queen, where his poor shrinking flesh would be covered with warm robes and his anxious daughters would lavish him with every attention that might soothe and heal. But in that instant the sound of another voice was heard through the door that led to the king's dressing room.

'I say,' someone called. 'What was that?'

It was too late to escape back to the library; the door lay clear across the room. Without stopping to think, Charlotte dove for a squat mahogany cabinet in the corner of the room, decorated with an elaborate design of garlands and flowers, all made out of tiny pieces of inlaid wood. The side curved inwards in the rococo style, leaving a space just large enough for Charlotte to crouch. On its squat ormolu legs, the cabinet was nearly flush with the ground, leaving no telltale gap underneath.

The king thrashed uncomfortably in his bonds, jerking his neck from side to side in an attempt to see her. 'Emily?' he called. 'Emily?'

'This way, Doctor,' said a voice she didn't recognise, a smooth, almost too-polished sort of voice. 'And you'll see what we've been telling you about.'

Charlotte scooped in the last, betraying fold of her skirt and pressed herself as small as she could make herself between the curve of the cabinet and the wall. She was ridiculously grateful that today wasn't a Drawing Room day; the spreading hoops of her court dress would have been impossible to hide. There was nothing to be done about the white muslin of her dress, but at least her red spencer blended nicely with the crimson hangings of the wall behind her.

The floor, uncarpeted like most of the palace, vibrated beneath the sudden onslaught of footsteps. Charlotte could feel the floorboards quivering beneath her fingertips.

'Emily?' moaned the king, jerking like a fish on the line. 'Emily?'

'As you can see, Dr Simmons,' said the first voice again. A pair of booted legs strode past Charlotte's hiding place, polished to a mirror sheen and smelling of leather, champagne, and horse. 'The situation is dire.'

'How long has he been like this?' It must be the doctor this time, with snagged and dirty stockings and buckled shoes with the crossbar of one buckle missing. Mad-doctoring was seldom a lucrative calling.

More shoes, this time shiny buckled ones, attached to heavily muscled legs, every step thundering down like a giant trampling on a village. 'Since last night.'

Charlotte froze stiff as a board against the side of her cabinet. She knew that voice.

'He grew agitated last night, so we had to restrain him. Upon his Royal Highness's orders,' Lord Henry added, with the instincts of a born coward. 'I found him with one of the queen's maids of honour. He appeared to be making, er, indecent conversation.'

The very idea! Charlotte rolled her eyes in the general

257

direction of Lord Henry. It wasn't a very satisfying response, but it was all she could do without giving herself away. As if the king would do such a thing!

'As he has before,' said the smooth-voiced man with crocodile regret. 'I am sure we all recall his fascination with Lady Pembroke the last time this . . . unfortunate situation occurred. Both Her Majesty and Lady Pembroke were most embarrassed by it. And then, of course, there was the incident with Mrs Drax on His Majesty's yacht at Weymouth.'

'You mean when he told Mrs Drax she had a pretty ass and demanded that she bring it over so he could pat it?' Lord Henry sounded as though he wished he had thought of that. 'It's good to be the king, hey?'

'There is no need,' said smooth-voice chillingly, 'to go into details. But you can see, Doctor, why the prince thought it necessary that his father be restrained.'

Smooth-voice, Charlotte realised, must be the prince's man.

'Well done.' The doctor's voice vibrated slightly, as though he were nodding. 'I approve your reasoning entirely, Colonel McMahon – and that of the prince, your master, of course.'

Toady, thought Charlotte, glowering at the cabinet wall.

'The only way to tame a madman is by constant use of restraints,' the doctor continued, in a lecturing tone. 'I hear you have a chair of correction?'

The mention of the chair had a terrible effect on the king, who began thrashing about with his legs, trying to get off the bed.

'At Kew, I believe,' Colonel McMahon replied smoothly. 'That was the last place it was used. It can be sent for, if you so desire.'

'Indeed,' agreed the doctor. 'Have it sent for at once.'

'Emily?' the king called, rolling wildly from side to side on the bed. Desperation threaded his hoarse voice. Despite the chill of the room, the sheets were soaked with his perspiration, emitting a thin, sour smell. 'Emily? Don't let them take me to the chair, Emily . . . Emily?'

'Hallucinating again, I see,' said the doctor. 'Well, that was to be expected, given his earlier episodes. I gather last time he thought his Chancellor of the Exchequer was . . . a pigeon?'

'A peacock,' Colonel McMahon corrected briskly. 'But I fail to see why the species of bird—'

'Interesting,' said the doctor, advancing on the king. 'Very interesting. You must recognise, Colonel, it helps to understand his mania in order to control it.'

'Control or cure?'

There was a moment of fraught silence reeking with the stench of the king's fear. Beneath it, Charlotte fancied she could detect the sickly sweet scent of treason. Treason smelt remarkably like the champagne on Colonel McMahon's boots.

'We'll just have to see as we go on, shan't we?' said the doctor coyly.

Charlotte didn't like the sound of that.

'Get him cleaned up,' ordered the doctor. Two more pairs of legs, previously stationary by the far wall, began moving. These were pedestrian sorts of legs, wearing heavy shoes and wool stockings. 'And build up the fire. No need to freeze him to death.'

'But the Willises—' began Lord Henry, referring to the doctors who had served the king in his two prior illnesses.

'The Willises aren't in charge any longer. I am.'

'I saved this for you.' Charlotte heard the slosh of liquid as

Lord Henry presented the doctor with a brimming chamber pot.

The doctor recoiled, his nostrils flaring. 'And to what do I owe this honour?'

'I had thought . . .' Lord Henry made the mistake of gesticulating with the chamber pot and both gentlemen shied back. 'Er, I had thought you might need it for your medical analysis.'

The doctor sniffed, remembered the stench, and thought better of it. 'That is antiquated stuff,' he said loftily, 'poking about at stools and dabbling in urine. I am a man of modern science.'

'So we've been told,' drawled McMahon. 'You came recommended most highly by Sir Francis Medmenham.'

'Ah, yes,' said the doctor. 'Sir Francis. I had the care of his great-aunt. A fascinating case. She stripped naked, painted herself blue, called herself Boadicea, and attempted to invade Hadley-on-Thames.'

McMahon cut him neatly off before he could reminisce further about his brief brush with the Queen of the Britons. 'That, I am relieved to say, does not appear to be His Majesty's problem. How will you proceed with him?'

The soiled stockings prowled along the side of the bed. By dint of leaning sideways and cricking her neck, Charlotte was able to get her first look at more than the doctor's legs. He looked like a Drury Lane caricature of a mad-doctor, in his old-fashioned black frock coat, shiny from wear, and his equally old-fashioned horsehair wig, which came down too low over his forehead, as though he had bought it too big for his head. A rumpled white stock, none too clean, appeared to have eaten his chin. To be fair, most of his patients probably couldn't care the slightest about his appearance, unless they wanted him to paint himself blue and join in the fight against the invading Roman legions.

The edge of the frock coat moved and Charlotte hastily ducked her head again, attempting to impersonate a very large mouse.

The king whimpered weakly from the bed. Charlotte heard a rustling noise, as though the king were trying to bury himself in the bedclothes, away from the impudence of prying eyes. 'We will start with a course of hot vinegar applied to the feet, to draw the humours down through his body,' announced the doctor. 'If the king continues restless, we will follow it with an emetic of tartar to purge the humours via the rectal corridor.'

'And then?' asked McMahon.

'Blistering,' said the doctor firmly. 'Blistering of the arms, legs, and head, combined with a preparation of musk and quinine to be taken internally.'

McMahon gave it his nod of approval. 'All sounds quite sound to me. I will relay your recommendations to His Royal Highness. In the meantime, I see no reason you should not begin treatment.'

'Excellent.' The doctor rubbed his hands together, undoubtedly in glee at having obtained a royal patron. 'I must return briefly to St Luke's, to leave instructions for my patients there, but my men know what to do. With your leave, gentlemen, I would have them begin with the vinegar at once.'

'I trust you will return as quickly as possible.' From McMahon's lips, the words had all the force of a direct order from the Prince of Wales. 'I must return to His Highness. In the meantime, we leave His Majesty under Lord Henry's capable supervision.'

Lord Henry didn't look best pleased at being delegated to stay. Charlotte could see him shift his weight from one shoe to the other as though he were squirming. 'I say, doesn't vinegar have a powerful tang?'

'All part of its healing powers,' said the doctor soothingly. 'The forceful aroma rises through the nostrils into the brain, driving down the evil humours, while the application of heat to the soles of the feet allows the humours to puddle in blisters, which then may be safely drained.'

'Modern science is, indeed, a wonderful thing,' said Colonel McMahon sagely.

It was easy for him to be sanguine; he wasn't going to have to smell it in progress. Charlotte, however, was beginning to fear that she would. The bed was between her and the door. And all attention was very much centred on the bed. Next time, she would have to pick a hiding place nearer the door. Not that she intended there to be a next time for this sort of escapade, but just in case.

With much noisy clumping against the floorboards, Lord Henry ushered McMahon and the doctor out of the room. That would have been all very well and good but for the two attendants who had been left behind to begin the dreaded vinegar treatment. The king sounded even more unhappy about it than Charlotte. From beyond her hiding place, she could hear the sounds of the fire being vigorously stoked. Her corner by the wall began to feel uncomfortably warm.

'There, now, Your Majesty,' one was saying, in a thick St Giles accent. 'We'll soon have this over with. You got the vinegar, Billy?'

Billy, it appeared, had not got the vinegar or, as he preferred to put it, the bleeding vinegar. A long discussion ensued.

Charlotte crouched in her hiding place, hands braced against the floor, wondering just how long it would be until Lord Henry came back and if he were really quite stupid enough to believe that she had accidentally wandered in while looking for a book and fallen asleep beneath the cabinetry.

'Doctor said to apply the bleeding vinegar before he got back,' said the one who wasn't Billy. 'We'd better get it.'

'Should we leave 'im, do you think?' Billy asked in hesitating tones.

The other emitted a coarse chuckle. 'He ain't going anywhere, is he? Come on.'

The floor vibrated again, and was still. Poking her head up like a turtle out of its shell, Charlotte peered over the edge of the cabinet.

All the doors were ajar, and the fire was hissing and crackling, but the room was empty of human habitation save for the helpless form of the king. Charlotte couldn't believe her luck. However, there was no guarantee that her luck would hold. The doctor's assistants might be back at any moment.

Stumbling on limbs gone numb, Charlotte squeezed herself willy-nilly out of her corner, catching at the edge of the cabinet to keep from tripping over the hem of her own dress. With her right leg all pins and needles, she lurched towards the door in a lopsided lope until the thready sound of the king's voice brought her up short.

'Emily?' They had rolled the king onto his back, and his rheumy eyes gazed pleadingly up at Charlotte. Tears leaked helplessly down the withered cheeks. 'Do . . . not . . . leave . . . me . . .'

'I must,' Charlotte whispered. 'I will fetch help. I promise.'

As he continued to call piteously for his Emily, Charlotte

fled through the connecting door into the library, not slowing her pace until she had achieved the hall beyond. She would go to the queen; that much of her promise, at least, she could keep. But what help could there be for the king if the prince himself ordered it otherwise?

Stumbling on her skirts in her haste, Charlotte scrambled back up the great marble stairs to the queen's chambers, where she breathlessly poured out her report to the queen and princesses.

Princess Sophia inveighed heavily against her older brother. 'Does he really fancy, because he is the rising sun, anything he says is to be swallowed whole? How dare he treat the dear angel so! And not even to do it in person – but by proxy! It is too beastly.'

'It is beastly, but it may be necessary, Sophie,' said Princess Mary tiredly. 'They did the same last time, you remember, with the restraints and the blistering. And it brought him back, didn't it?'

'Yes, last time,' said Princess Sophia mutinously. 'But what do we know of this new doctor? For all we know, he could be an utter charlatan. Much anyone here would care.'

That last was clearly intended for her mama.

'Lady Charlotte,' said the queen, ignoring her turbulent daughter. 'I believe I may have another commission for you.'

'Why exactly do you want me to go to a madhouse with you?' asked Henrietta forty-five minutes later, adjusting the ribbons on her bonnet as the carriage racketed down Clerkenwell Road towards Dr Simmons and his hospital. 'Not that I mind, but it does seem an odd way to spend an afternoon.'

'It's not a madhouse, exactly,' hedged Charlotte. 'More of a mad hospital.' Without thinking, she scrubbed her gloved hands together like Lady Macbeth. Beneath the kid, she fancied she could still smell the reek of the king's sickroom on her skin, that acrid stench of sweat and despair.

'Isn't that the same thing by a different name?'

'I just like the sound of it better,' Charlotte confessed. 'It sounds less . . .'

'Mad?' Henrietta supplied. From beneath the brim of her bonnet, she peered keenly at Charlotte. 'This doesn't have anything to do with—'

'No!' With more dignity, she added, 'I'm not asking you to check me in, if that's what you mean. Going mad for love went out of fashion several centuries ago.'

'I'm not implying that you're going mad,' Henrietta began carefully. 'But you have had something of a, well . . .'

'Shock?' With as much conviction as she could muster, Charlotte said, 'That's all done with. It's over. Finished.'

Fiddling with the buttons on her glove, Henrietta said with false nonchalance, 'Stwyth informed me that you had a caller this morning.'

'Stwyth *told* you?' Charlotte wasn't sure who she was more irritated with, Robert for calling or Stwyth for tattling. On closer consideration, Robert. Definitely Robert.

'Well, I am technically your chaperone,' pointed out Henrietta. 'I need to know these things.'

The notion of Henrietta, dear though she might be, monitoring her meetings made Charlotte's shoulders tense in automatic negation. After all the years of whispering and giggling in the corners of ballrooms, conducting emergency hair repairs and pinning up hems that had come down, to have one act as an authority over the other just felt wrong. Charlotte was perfectly content to let Henrietta enjoy her new position as a young matron, but not if it meant an alteration in the way that Henrietta treated her. Was this what had sent Penelope storming out onto the balcony with Freddy Staines?

'What about being my friend?' asked Charlotte quietly.

'Even more reason to know!' exclaimed Henrietta expansively. Her voice dropped a little, betraying a deep vein of genuine hurt. 'I just can't believe you didn't tell me yourself.'

Charlotte took refuge in the scenery, although she couldn't have said with any honesty what they were passing. 'There was nothing to tell. Nothing worth telling, that is. Honestly. If there had been, I would have told you.'

'He didn't—' Henrietta began hopefully.

'Apologise?' filled in Charlotte. 'No.'

'Oh,' said her best friend, her voice full of disappointment.

Henrietta's disappointment was nothing compared with her own. It would be too tempting to let herself believe that Robert had come because he couldn't stay away, that the strange note in his voice had been a sign of repressed emotion, that his concern about Medmenham was a sign that he still wanted her for himself.

This, thought Charlotte despairingly, was the problem with the world outside the cover of a book. She couldn't craft Robert's dialogue for him, putting the words she wanted to say into his lips. She couldn't control the direction of his emotions. All she could do was attempt to discipline her own.

Reaching out, Charlotte squeezed Henrietta's hand. 'I'm fine. Really. It's the king who is in difficulties.'

'The king?' Henrietta's voice dropped to a whisper and she darted a glance at the panel that separated them from the coachman. 'He's not . . .'

It was every subject's worst nightmare, that the king should go mad again. Memories of the regency crisis of sixteen years before still ran strong. If the king should go mad, the government would be in disarray, with the prince fighting the king's ministers for power, Parliament drawn into warring factions over a Regency bill, and no one to conduct the basic matters of state. It had already happened twice before.

Charlotte nodded. 'The king has been secluded by the Prince of Wales's orders. The queen is frantic.'

'I should think so! Her poor Majesty.'

'The Prince of Wales even appointed a new physician. Her Majesty wants me to speak with him and see if he can be persuaded to report to her on the king's condition.'

'Of course he must!'

'Not necessarily,' said Charlotte. 'During the king's first illness, one of his doctors refused to speak either to Her Majesty or her ladies. It might be like that again.'

'It's monstrous!'

'Welcome to life at Court,' said Charlotte wryly. 'Grandmama claims it was the same in her day, with the king and Prince of Wales always feuding – only then, it was a different king and a different Prince of Wales. And no one was going mad. At least, not in the literal sense.'

'It will be madness if the prince is allowed to filch the throne,' said Henrietta darkly. Henrietta's family were all stalwart Tories, staunchly opposed to the Prince of Wales and his party. Lord Uppington had been instrumental in blocking the prince's last Regency bill, in 1788. As for Lady Uppington, her views about the prince didn't bear repeating in polite company, the mildest of them involving the phrase 'bloated bunch-backed toad.'

Henrietta's own feelings towards the prince were scarcely milder. 'Can't you just see it already? The first thing he'll do is clamour for an increased income, the selfish toad. And what will become of the war with France?'

'He did ask the king to let him go fight,' Charlotte pointed out in the interest of fairness.

'Merely because he fancies himself in uniform,' Henrietta sniffed. 'He's entirely at the mercy of that dreadful Charles James Fox, and we all know where *his* sympathies lie. Jacobin to the core!'

'Let's not borrow trouble yet,' said Charlotte soothingly. 'The king has recovered each time before. It was jarring to see it for myself, but by all accounts it was equally awful each other time, and yet His Majesty has always pulled through.'

'Hmm,' said Henrietta. 'I hope you're right.'

'I hope so, too.' Charlotte righted her bonnet as the carriage rolled to the halt in a paved courtyard, set slightly back from the road. 'That's what we're here to find out. I do hope Dr Simmons will consent to speak to us.'

'Oh, he'll speak to us,' said Henrietta, sailing out of the carriage like an entire cavalry charge rolled into one blue muslin dress. 'Hello! You! Over there!'

Two men, wearing identical uniforms of dark brown wool, halted at Henrietta's halloo. One carried a bucket and mop, the other seemed to just be along for a chat. They must, Charlotte assumed, be orderlies of some sort, employed by the hospital.

'Where can we find Dr Simmons?' Henrietta demanded.

Between her imperious tone and her pearl earbobs, Henrietta was clearly a lady of quality. The orderlies immediately snapped to.

'I'll just fetch him for you, shall I, miss?' said one, and disappeared around the side of the building, leaving his companion to mind the two ladies.

Charlotte noticed that he made no move to invite them into the building. Because the sights in there wouldn't be fit for their eyes? She wasn't sure she wanted to think too deeply about that.

From the outside, all seemed neat and tidy enough – as long as one ignored the bars on all the windows. But there was an unfortunate smell hanging about the place. It wasn't any one odour one could identify, but a combination of unpleasant scents, not unlike the king's bedchamber that morning, compounded of sweat and fear and unwashed bodies and strange medicinal compounds. From one of the windows came a series of sharp, shrill cries.

'Won't be a moment, miss,' the orderly said to Henrietta just a little too loudly, in a clear attempt to draw her attention away from the rhythmic shrieking. 'The doctor's like as not out in the garden. Won't be a tick.'

'There are gardens in the back?' Henrietta asked in surprise. The shrieker put her all into one final cry and then went still, whether at her own volition or at someone else's being entirely unclear.

'Yes, miss.' The orderly smiled, displaying several missing teeth. Charlotte wondered if they had been missing before, or gone missing due to his work at the mad hospital. 'So the inmates can exercise, like. The ones as ain't too wild, that is.'

'What happens to those?' Henrietta asked, looking repelled and fascinated at the same time.

The orderly's eyes went up to the barred windows above. 'We keeps them safe, miss – don't you worry.'

'I'm sure you do,' said Henrietta reassuringly, and widened her eyes in horror at Charlotte behind the orderly's back.

'Righty-ho! There's the doctor now!' With evident relief,

the orderly pointed at two men coming around the side of the building. 'There's your Dr Simmons, miss, and I 'ope 'e can be of 'elp to you and yer poor sister.'

'Oh, it's not for her, precisely.' Henrietta was hedging, while Charlotte gave an excellent impression of being quite as mad as the orderly clearly thought her by staring for all she was worth at the pair of men approaching them along the length of the building.

One was the other orderly. He was of no interest to Charlotte. The other was clearly the doctor. His coat was black, but plainly cut and neatly buttoned across the chest with a double row of buttons over a plain white stock, simply tied. Rather than a wig, he wore his own greying hair pulled back and tied into a queue, making no effort to conceal the receding of the hairline over either temple. His stockings were immaculate.

In short, he was a distinguished-looking man, not at all what one would expect from a mad-doctor. And he bore absolutely no resemblance to the man Charlotte had seen in the king's bedchamber that morning.

'That,' whispered Charlotte to Henrietta, 'is not Dr Simmons.'

Chapter Seventeen

Henrietta looked at Charlotte as though she suspected her of being a little mad after all. 'That *is* what the orderly just called him.'

Charlotte did her best to speak without moving her lips. The result was not an entire success. 'That isn't what I meant. That is not the man I saw in the king's bedchamber.'

'You mean . . .'

Charlotte wished she knew what she meant. 'I don't know. There must be some mistake.' Abandoning Henrietta, she ventured towards the approaching men. Raising a hand, she called out, 'Dr Simmons?'

He certainly appeared to be under the delusion that he was Dr Simmons.

'Yes?' he asked slightly impatiently. 'I am informed that you wish to speak with me.'

It would be tempting to believe that it was a delusion, that he was a patient whose madness had taken on the form of impersonating his own doctor. But too many details militated against that theory. Even if the orderlies hadn't deferred to him, his clothes were too expensive and too neatly kept to belong to one of the patients. His expression, while irritable, was eminently rational.

Who wouldn't be a bit annoyed at being dragged from his work to attend a pair of flighty young ladies? He was probably afraid they were there for an afternoon's diversion, touring the cells of the insane for sport, as they did in Bedlam, where, for a penny, anyone could enter to gawk and jeer. Charlotte had heard visitors were even permitted to bring long sticks with which to poke at the inmates. From the way the orderlies had ranged themselves on either side of the door, it was clear that such behaviour was not allowed at St Luke's.

But if he was Dr Simmons, who was the man back at the Palace?

On an impulse, Charlotte batted her eyelashes at him and said in a fluttery sort of voice, 'I had hoped I might trouble you for a consultation. It is my grandmother, you see. I fear she may be . . .'

'No longer possessed of all her proper faculties?' the doctor finished helpfully.

'I fear so,' said Charlotte sadly. 'She has taken to having herself carried around her own home on a gilded palanquin, striking out at any who dare approach her with a sort of sceptre.'

Next to her, Henrietta's bonnet brim quivered.

'I see,' said the doctor briskly. 'In essence, your grandmother suffers from violent delusions.'

Henrietta stuffed her hands against her mouth to contain a fit of coughing that escaped around her gloved fingers in a series of explosive snorts. The doctor took a discreet step back.

Charlotte followed him, winding her bonnet string coyly around one finger and doing her best to look adoringly daft.

But not too daft. She didn't want to find herself in hot vinegar up to her ankles. 'I have heard that in such cases,' she said breathlessly, 'where the subject is prone to violence, that a form of restraining waistcoat might be applied.'

'Ah,' said the doctor. 'You mean the straight waistcoat. I highly recommend it as a means of convincing the patient that violent behaviour will not be tolerated.'

'What do you think of vinegar treatments? I've heard wonderful things of vinegar treatments as a means of moving the humours. And blistering. In multiple places.'

'Each of those may be efficacious in its proper application. The blistering, in particular, often does wonders to drive away delirium. Of course, I should need to see the patient before recommending a course of treatment.'

'That would be delightful, Dr Simmons!' Charlotte clapped her hands together in a very ecstasy of delight. 'I shouldn't like to take you away from your other patrons, though, if you were engaged elsewhere.'

'That shouldn't be a problem, Miss—'

Charlotte began backing away towards the carriage. She hoped he didn't know enough about the peerage to recognise the crest on the side. 'Oh, thank you! I really must be getting back. We don't like to leave Grandmama for too long. She starts throwing things,' Charlotte confided in a stage whisper. 'Coming, Dulcinea?'

'Dulcinea?' demanded Henrietta as they collapsed breathless back in the carriage.

'I had madness on the mind,' said Charlotte apologetically. 'So Dulcinea seemed to fit.'

'I suppose I should be grateful that you didn't make me Ophelia!' Henrietta impatiently yanked at the ribbons of her bonnet and tossed it carelessly onto the seat beside her. 'Now will you tell me what that was all about?'

'I think,' said Charlotte thoughtfully, 'we can safely say that Dr Simmons has not been retained by the Prince of Wales. If he had been, he wouldn't have been nearly so eager to treat my poor, dear Grandmama.'

'And the straight waistcoat and all that?'

'Currently in use on the king.'

'Oh,' said Henrietta, sobering.

'If this Dr Simmons is to be believed, everything being done to the king is medically sound.'

'It still sounds like torture to me,' said Henrietta, with a shudder.

'And to me,' admitted Charlotte. 'Especially having seen it.'

A sombre silence fell over the inside of the carriage as the two friends contemplated the plight of their king.

When Henrietta finally spoke, she voiced what they were both thinking. 'If this Dr Simmons isn't treating the king, who is? There couldn't be two Dr Simmonses, could there?'

That would be by far the simplest explanation, but it also seemed the least probable. 'Not at St Luke's Hospital for Lunatics, I shouldn't think. The doctor treating the king specifically mentioned returning to his patients at St Luke's.'

'Perhaps your Dr Simmons got the name of the hospital wrong?'

'What doctor mistakes his own hospital?'

'Hmm. Good point.' Henrietta lapsed again into silence.

Staring out the window, Charlotte struggled to recall that uncomfortable interlude scrunched up against the side of the cabinet, scrounging for any clue that might unravel the bizarre tangle. What *was* she going to tell the queen? Her simple assignment had suddenly become very, very complicated.

Outside, the early winter dusk was already falling. Charlotte could see her own face reflected in ghostly double in the windowpane. She frowned, and her shadow self frowned back at her.

A seemingly insignificant detail niggled at the back of Charlotte's mind. 'Colonel McMahon said that it was Sir Francis Medmenham who had recommended Simmons.'

'The real Simmons, or the false one?'

'I don't know,' said Charlotte. 'He might have recommended the real one, never knowing an imposter would interpose himself. Or he might have put forward the false candidate for purposes of his own.'

'What cause would Medmenham have for inserting an imposter into the king's household?'

'He is a member of the prince's party,' said Charlotte slowly, 'and should the king go mad, he might benefit immensely from it.'

'You're not implying—'

A bizarre sort of picture was beginning to form. Charlotte wasn't sure if it was the true one, but it did make its own sort of sense. 'If the king goes mad for long enough, the prince will advance another Regency bill. And if he becomes Regent—'

'Medmenham will have his pick of plum positions,' Henrietta finished for her. 'If it's power that he's after.'

'I can't really see Sir Francis necessarily serving in an official capacity, can you? He's no Charles James Fox. But it might be enough for him to be the silent power behind the throne. He would like lording it over a prince regent, wouldn't he?'

Just as he obviously enjoyed lording it over a certain duke

of her acquaintance. If a mere duke was a coup, how much more so the ruling power in the realm?

'We need to know more about Medmenham,' pronounced Henrietta, in the air of one delivering a royal command. 'Besides, I find him oddly intriguing.'

'Henrietta!'

'Not that kind of intriguing! I meant as a potential villain. I have excellent instincts when it comes to spotting wrongdoers.'

'We don't know that Medmenham is a wrongdoer. The real Dr Simmons may very well have cured his aunt.'

'Does he have an aunt?' asked Henrietta.

Charlotte raised both hands in a gesture of helplessness. 'For all we know, he might have a dozen.'

'That's easy enough to find out,' Henrietta said decidedly as the carriage drew up before Loring House. The waiting footmen advanced to open the door and unroll the folding stairs.

'It may be even easier than you think,' said Charlotte, gathering her skirts to descend. 'I hear that he intends—'

A dark figure loomed up out of the night. Charlotte caught at the steadying arm of the footman as she nearly tumbled off the second step.

Blending with the bushes beside the house, he seemed huge, a monster out of myth, the dark cousin to the unicorn. As he stepped into the square of light cast by the drawing room windows, it became clear that it wasn't a monster but a man. When she saw which man it was, Charlotte wasn't sure she wouldn't prefer the monster. At least a monster had a certain élan to it. Perfidious men were as common as the muck on the street.

'Charlotte?' Henrietta came careening down the steps after her. 'What – oh.'

The Duke of Dovedale bobbed stiffly at the neck. He looked as though the high points of his shirt collar pained him. 'Lady Henrietta. Cousin Charlotte.'

'To what do we owe this . . . er . . . ?' Henrietta looked from Robert, stiff as the iron railings, to Charlotte, prickly as winter rosebushes, and lapsed into silence. Not even the most optimistic hostess could possibly call his appearance a pleasure.

'I fear that when I visited this morning, I inadvertently left a bagatelle behind me.'

'Your dignity?' suggested Charlotte, her breath misting like smoke in the cold air.

Behind her, she could hear Henrietta's swift intake of breath, half horrified, half amused. Charlotte didn't care.

Something like appreciation flashed through Robert's blue eyes. Or perhaps it was just the light from the torchères burning on either side of the door. 'My snuffbox.'

Charlotte folded her arms across her chest. 'I don't think it's in those bushes.'

'My dignity, you mean?' said Robert blandly.

Charlotte narrowed her eyes at him, hating him with every bone in her body. It was unforgivable of him to sound like that, amused and urbane, so very like the man with whom she had fancied herself in love.

'Your *snuffbox*,' she said, a little too forcefully.

'Well, that's easily solved, isn't it?' Quickly interposing herself between them, Henrietta threaded her arm through Charlotte's in a mingled gesture of support and restraint. With a swooping gesture, she indicated that the duke should precede them through the open door, where the footmen waited on either side, silently storing up every detail to repeat in the servants' hall later that evening. 'I'm sure Stwyth will be happy to help you recover it – your snuffbox, I mean.'

Turning back to Robert, Henrietta asked, 'Where did you leave it? The snuffbox, that is.'

With Robert in it, the entry hall, which could easily fit at least two of Charlotte's grandmother's tenants' cottages, felt ridiculously small.

'I left it in the morning room,' he said, speaking to Henrietta, but looking at Charlotte. 'This morning.'

'Morning *is* an excellent time to use the morning room,' commented Henrietta to no one in particular. 'And the snuffbox is—?'

Robert frowned in that way men do when asked to describe trumperies. 'A snuffbox?'

'Stwyth?' commanded Henrietta.

Taking his cue, Stwyth shuffled off to hunt for what Charlotte was sure would be the latest in invisible snuffboxes. If you couldn't see it, could it still be in the height of fashion? Goodness, she was so angry she was positively giddy with it.

Her only saving grace was that Robert, for all his vaunted urbanity, looked as uncomfortable as she did. Good. Charlotte took a small, malicious satisfaction in his catching his foot on a roll of drapery fabric that was unaccountably lying half unrolled just inside the front door.

'Oh, dear,' Henrietta clucked, making distressed hostess noises. 'That really shouldn't be out here. Will you excuse me for a moment?'

'Of course.'

'I'm sure Charlotte will entertain you in my absence.'

Charlotte wasn't feeling the least bit entertaining, unless one was talking about the sort of entertainment that involved goring gladiators.

'I don't think that would be a good idea,' she said, not looking at Robert. It wasn't quite so easy as it sounded. Not looking at Robert made the corners of her eyes hurt.

'Nonsense,' said Henrietta blithely. 'I'll be right back.'

With a swish of petticoats, she was gone, off to run an errand as imaginary as Robert's snuffbox. Charlotte looked grimly after Henrietta's retreating back. She knew exactly what her best friend was doing. Finding Robert on her doorstep twice in one day, Henrietta had obviously concluded that the pull of true love had overcome whatever temporary madness had driven Robert from Charlotte's side. Or, as Henrietta would put it, that Robert had finally come to his senses. And she had left them alone to get on with the grand reconciliation she was sure would ensue. Knowing Henrietta, she was probably currently planning what to wear to the wedding. Charlotte was not amused.

She had had enough. Completely, utterly, up to here, enough with everyone thinking they could run her life for her, from Henrietta, who tried to marry her off by leaving her alone in an entry hall, to ridiculous Robert, who couldn't decide whether they were speaking or not speaking but definitely knew that he didn't want her to go riding with Medmenham.

As far as Charlotte was concerned, they could all take a long, cold bath in the Thames.

Buoyed with righteous anger, Charlotte turned on her sometime knight in shining armour, who was as much the possessor of a snuffbox as she was the queen of England. Did he really think she was ninny enough to buy that ridiculous story?

A nasty little voice in the back of her head reminded her that she had, in fact, been more than willing to swallow any story he cared to tell her not so very long ago. The thought of it only made her angrier.

'Why are you really here?' she demanded, glowering at him like a grand inquisitor with a heretic in his sights.

If Robert was taken aback by her tone, he didn't show it.

'I'm rather fond of that snuffbox,' he said mildly. 'It has a very attractive painting of Carlton House on the lid.'

Charlotte doubted he even owned a snuffbox. Robert made a most unconvincing dandy. The finicky clothes he had adopted since coming to London sat oddly on his athletic frame, like someone trying to swaddle a sword in lace draperies. Unless, of course, this lace-clad Robert was the real Robert, and the rough-and-ready soldier the act he had put on for her at Girdings. Which was real? Trying to sort it out made her head spin. That just made her even crankier.

'Did you take snuff much in India?' she jeered. She had never known that she had it in her to jeer. It was amazing the new talents one discovered under duress.

Robert wandered idly towards a marble-topped table, where the day's correspondence sat piled on a silver tray. 'Perhaps my new station demands new habits.'

'Do you change your habits so easily as that?' Charlotte didn't bother to hide the scorn in her voice.

She was punishing him, she knew, for not being what she had wanted him to be. It might not be fair of her, but it wasn't any more fair of him to keep coming back when he had promised to stay away. Funny, to think she would once have given almost anything for his promise to come back. Now, all she wanted was for him to leave her in peace.

Perhaps, if she repeated that to herself often enough, she might even start to believe it. She had, unfortunately, got into the habit of daydreaming about him. While his habits might change easily, hers never had.

His eyes met hers, reflected in the hall mirror. It was rather uncanny, looking at his reflection instead of the man. But wasn't that what she had been seeing all along? Only a reflection and a distorted one, at that, as pocked by untruths as this one was by the bevelling in the Venetian glass.

'No,' he said at last, his eyes constant on hers in the mirror. 'In fact, I find my habits very hard to change.'

Charlotte kept her voice hard. 'I hope you are not going to make a habit of this. Of visiting here, I mean.'

Robert thumbed idly through the letters and invitations piled in the silver tray, lowering his head so that she couldn't see his face, even in reflection. 'Is that what you really want?'

It was very disconcerting speaking to the mirrored top of someone's head. She could see the pale gilt where the Indian sun had streaked his hair and the darker hair beginning to grow out beneath it under the influence of a colder climate.

Charlotte spoke more loudly than she had intended. 'I hadn't realised that what I want is of any consequence.'

She didn't need to see his face to see his shoulders stiffen as her words hit home.

'Charlotte, I didn't mean—'

He turned so abruptly that she automatically took a step backwards, even though there were several feet between them. He turned so abruptly that he forgot about the letter in his hand that hadn't quite made it all the way into his sleeve.

She could see her name – or at least the half of it that wasn't hidden beneath the lace-edged cuff of his shirt – on the top fold. It was a heavy cream paper, subscribed in a bold, masculine hand, sealed with a blob of midnight blue wax. Charlotte didn't need to break the seal to know who had written it.

Amazed at her own boldness, she tapped Robert smartly on the arm before the note could disappear entirely into his sleeve. 'I'll take that.'

Robert made no move to hand it to her. 'I wish you wouldn't.'

Was there nothing about him that was true? So that was why he had come back – not because he couldn't stay away from her, or for an illusory snuffbox, but to intercept any correspondence from Medmenham. His mission this morning having failed, he had decided to try a surer way.

Tipping her head back, Charlotte regarded him accusingly. 'There never was any snuffbox, was there?'

Before Robert could even open his mouth to respond, a surprisingly heavy tread announced the reappearance of Henrietta's butler. Having heard Stwyth move as softly as a cat when he felt like it, Charlotte was sure the interruption was quite deliberate.

Stone-faced, Stwyth extended a small, octagonal object covered with panels of painted porcelain. 'Your snuffbox, sir.'

'Thank you – Stwyth, is it?' Robert raised an altogether too smug eyebrow in Charlotte's general direction. 'You were saying?'

'Enjoy your snuff,' said Charlotte tartly. She hoped he choked on it.

Tucking the snuffbox neatly away in his waistcoat pocket, he retrieved his hat and gloves from Stwyth. Hat in hand, he smiled ruefully down at Charlotte. 'I don't believe I will. It isn't really to my taste.'

'Then why take it?'

'Call it penance. Good evening, Charlotte.'

Clapping his hat on his head, Robert turned on his heel. But he paused before he reached the door. Stwyth, who had scurried to open it, hastily pushed it closed again against the arctic air.

Tripping over his own words, he said, 'I can't promise our paths won't cross. But I won't come here again if you don't want me to. You see, what you want is of some consequence after all. At least to me. Good night.'

It took Stwyth a moment to open the door. He studied Robert quite suspiciously before he would consent to do so, as though suspecting him of intending another abortive exit that would require more false openings and closings. But this time, Robert had clearly said all he intended to say. He all but collided with the door panel in his haste to leave. And Charlotte, perversely, having wished him gone, found herself wanting him to stay.

It wasn't until Stwyth had triumphantly and with great finality shut the great door behind him that Charlotte realised that Robert had successfully made off with Medmenham's note.

Chapter Eighteen

Medmenham's letter crinkled reassuringly in Robert's waistcoat pocket as he trudged down the stairs of Loring House.

'Did the old snuffbox dodge work?' A dark shape detached itself from the corner of the house, falling in step beside him. They were already late for an appointment at an exclusive gentlemen's club on St James Street.

'Beautifully. I owe you one.' Robert made the mistake of looking back. Through one of the long windows, he could still see Charlotte, in silhouette, standing where he had left her.

Grabbing his arm, his companion tugged him to one side, narrowly saving him from collision with a decidedly unfriendly lamppost.

'By my count, you owe me about two hundred. Including that one. But what are a few favours between friends?' said Tommy airily. 'Did you get Medmenham's note?'

Robert patted his waistcoat pocket. 'Safely tucked away.'

'And the lady?'

Robert kicked at a bit of loose paving, sending pebbles

scattering down the street. 'Still thinks I'm lower than dirt.'

Tommy was unsympathetic. 'You did rather do that to yourself, you know.'

'For good reasons!'

Tommy stuck his hands in his pockets and tilted his head back to stare at the sky. 'You just keep telling that to yourself.'

'They seemed like good reasons at the time,' Robert mumbled. Even to his own ears, he didn't sound anywhere near convincing.

How had he managed to make such a monumental muddle of things? Fresh from the Hellfire Caves, the stench of brimstone still scouring his nostrils, it had all seemed so simple. In a fine glow of self-abnegation, he resolved to take the noble and lonely path, sacrificing his own happiness to keep his princess safe in her tower. For 'noble,' substitute . . . 'misguided,' Robert decided, ignoring the various riper adjectives Tommy had suggested, among the milder of which were 'pig-headed,' 'addlepated,' and 'just plain stupid.'

'Seems my friend,' said Tommy wisely, 'is a very dangerous creature. Like a tiger, only with even more spots. Great big spotty spots.'

Robert reminded himself that there was nothing to be gained by throttling his closest friend, even if he was asking for it. 'There's no need to belabour the point.'

'Or the spots? All right, all right. I'll leave you to make yourself miserable in your own way.'

'What happened to pots and kettles?' demanded Robert, stung beyond endurance. 'How many times have you proposed to Penelope Deveraux in the past week?'

Some of the mirth faded from his friend's face. Tommy managed to shrug without taking his hands out of his pockets.

'Ten at last count. I try to get in at least one proposal before lunch and another after supper. But she won't have me. She says she won't drag me down with her.'

'Then why do you keep trying?'

'Why in the hell did you leave that damned snuffbox?'

Robert wasn't sure he would call it quite the same thing, but Tommy had made his point.

'Fair enough,' he said brusquely. 'We're both besotted fools.'

'The difference,' said Tommy, delicately scratching the side of his nose, 'is that you still have a chance.'

He might have had a chance once, but he had trodden it beneath his horse's hooves on that hasty midnight ride from Girdings, trampling it away in the slush and the mud. However good his intentions might have been, there was no going back, no wiping the slate clean, any more than one could turn slush back into snow.

Irritation made him sharp. 'Because "I never want to speak to you again" so often means "I love you." No, Tommy. It's just not on.'

'There is a very simple solution,' Tommy pointed out. 'Tell her the truth.'

'Before or after our next drunken orgy?' asked Robert sarcastically.

'Just because you go doesn't mean you participate.'

'Brilliant,' said Robert, ducking out of the way of a very rapidly moving sedan chair. 'I'll just tell her I was surrounded by drugged smoke but I didn't inhale.'

'Well, when you put it that way . . .'

Robert rubbed the back of his hand across his eyes, knowing that he was being deliberately difficult and wondering if maybe, just maybe, Tommy might have a fragment of a point. His grand and noble gesture had been a colossal failure. What would Charlotte say if he plunked himself down in her parlour and said – what in the hell would he say? 'Everything I told you the other day was a lie'? 'Sorry to break your heart, but I was only trying to protect you'?

He *had* meant to protect her. Protect her and keep her safe for the sort of man she ought to marry. Someone whose education had come out of more than the odd book scrounged from other people's libraries. Someone who didn't wake in the night with sheets soaked with the sweat of memories of horses writhing and men screaming and flies lighting on the open eyes of the dead and dying and black powder smoke drifting over it all as though driven by the devil's own bellows. Someone who would protect her and cherish her and never be anything other than she expected him to be.

After a month moving through Charlotte's world, he began to wonder if he hadn't been the naive one. In the hardscrabble of his youth, he had always imagined his peers – the ones whose fathers hadn't burnt through their inheritances, who hadn't been disowned by their families, who didn't eke out a life lurching from town to town a week ahead of their creditors – leading lives of awe-inspiring gentility, with tutors to tend their minds and servants their bodies. Their food would be taken off china plates, from platters proffered by silent servants, not slopped into tin. Conversation would be conducted at a level scarcely louder than the genteel click of silver against porcelain. No shouting, no banging, no waving drumsticks to emphasize a point, no loud demonstrations of bodily functions. That was the sort of man Charlotte ought to marry, polished to a fine sheen of civilisation.

Such creatures didn't seem to exist. Over the past month

he had met bruising sportsmen who smelt of the stable even in evening clothes, professional toadies who simpered even in their sleep, and dedicated roués whose encyclopedic knowledge of sin would put a St Giles slumlord to shame. These men, these polished, powdered, pampered men, with their Etonian inflections and towering confections of neckwear, might have cleaner linen than the louts he had known growing up, but underneath they were as coarse, as self-serving, and a good deal less honest.

Who was he protecting by staying away? Charlotte? Or himself?

At the far end of the street, Robert could see the twin Tudor towers of the palace of St James, location of that uncomfortable scene in the Queen's Drawing Room. Even if Charlotte forgave him for that, what if he hurt her again? He had seen his father do it again and again, trampling over the feelings of those nearest to him, not out of malice, but just by being what he was. There was no assurance that he would be able to make her happy, in this world that was so much more hers than his.

Seeing her in the Palace wearing her diamonds and feathers with the unselfconsciousness of long custom, he had felt for the first time the true depth of the chasm that separated them. He hadn't risen to a ducal coronet; it had tumbled down to him. He had seen feathers before, on chickens. Diamonds didn't come into it. When his childhood companions spoke of court, they meant the sort ruled by magistrates, not monarchs. Right now, he was nearly as much a novelty as a unicorn, the rightful heir returned home, cloaked in exotic grandeur from his time in India. But it was all an illusion. In time, she would come to be ashamed of him, and regret the impulse that had made her paint him in brighter colours than he deserved.

Which would be worse? he wondered. Never having her at all, or having to witness the slow death of love by disillusionment?

There was a cheerful prospect.

Robert scowled at the shadows on the pavement. Tommy, wisely, stayed quiet. There were some moods on which a man's closest friends knew better than to intrude.

Talk to her, Tommy had said. What if he did? What if he told her the whole of it, warts and all? Robert felt the familiar twist in his stomach at the memory of that interlude in the underground chamber. Well, maybe not quite the whole of it. But close. Enough to allow her to decide for herself. Back at Girdings, he might have worried that childhood infatuation would unfairly prejudice her opinion of him – but he had certainly put paid to that, hadn't he? He grimaced at the recollection of Charlotte challenging the existence of his snuffbox. She wasn't anyone's fool. Not even his.

As they strode down St James Street, he heard his own voice asking, roughly, 'What if she doesn't believe me?'

'Then you've lost nothing.' Tommy paused to consider. 'Except possibly a snuffbox or two. But you're a duke now. You can afford those.'

Robert shook his head. 'And what if she does? What then?'

'Then,' said Tommy, speaking very slowly, as though to a not-very-bright child, 'you live happily ever after.'

'What if there isn't such a thing as happily ever after?'

'Then I can't really help you, can I?' said Tommy.

Robert paused in front of a wide-fronted stone house, one of the famous gentlemen's clubs scattered along the street. Had he been the sort of duke he was meant to be, he might have been a member. Instead, he came as guest. He wasn't even sure it was the right bloody building. They didn't exactly signpost these things for nonmembers.

Hoping to hell he was in the right place, Robert began climbing the shallow stone steps.

'Nothing can be done until the day after tomorrow, anyway,' said Robert, as much to himself as Tommy. 'We have to catch Wrothan first.'

'Even better,' said Tommy cheerfully. 'Think of it this way. You'll be coming to her a hero, having bagged a vicious traitor and a French spy.'

'Mmmph,' said Robert as noncommittally as he could, struggling to mask the unwarranted surge of hope that Tommy's casual suggestion brought with it.

It was a possibility, at least, the prospect of scouring away all the embarrassments of his past with one pure blaze of heroism. Once redeemed . . . well, he would deal with that when he got there. First, there was a spy to catch. And he hadn't the least idea of how to go about it.

'Our contact said he would meet us here at seven.' Robert raised a hand to rap at the door and hastily withdrew it as the door opened of its own accord. Knocking, apparently, was yet another faux pas.

'Who is this contact of yours?' whispered Tommy as they handed their hats and gloves to a waiting manservant.

'War Office,' Robert whispered back, before raising his voice to give their names to the waiting manservant. It was hard to tell whether or not they were expected; the man's expression remained as impassive as wax. If he poked the man's cheek, the impression of his finger would probably remain.

'Hmm,' said Tommy, looking around as though expecting the head of the War Office to burst through the door.

It had been a struggle to admit that he required reinforcements. But if the colonel had drummed anything into him over the years, it was that fighting a battle one couldn't win wasn't gallant; it was irresponsible.

So he had swallowed his pride and found his way to a ramshackle building on Crown Street, where his years of loyal service to the crown had meant nothing, but his ducal title got him through the door. He was passed along to someone not so junior as to offend Robert's rank, but not so senior as to interfere with real work. In the end, he had been given a name, a contact, someone who (the slightly bored bureaucrat said, glancing at his watch) might help him. To Robert's surprise, it was a name he knew.

The man with their hats melted away, replaced by another black-coated functionary, who guided Robert and Tommy through a series of rooms papered in deep greens and rich reds, redolent of tobacco and freshly ironed newspapers. Up two flights of stairs, at the very back of the house, they were admitted to a square room with only one window. The walls were papered in the same hunter green as the rooms downstairs, hung with paintings of slightly lumpy horses. The heavy drapes had been drawn across the one window, muffling the room from the outside world. After bowing them in, their guide closed the thick oak door securely behind them, leaving them to the man who waited for them, sprawled in a squat leather chair before the fire.

'Dovedale!' Robert's contact bounded out of his chair in a very un-agent-like way. 'Bloody good of you to come. Sit down, sit down.'

Waving them into chairs, he promptly set about splashing brandy into three glasses. A table had been discreetly furnished with an array of decanters and a platter of refreshments.

'Ginger biscuit?' offered their host, brandishing a biscuit. 'As you can see, we have everything we need. You don't need to worry about being disturbed. No one will come unless we call.'

Robert gingerly accepted a biscuit. 'Thank you for agreeing to help us.'

'I couldn't be more delighted. London has been damnably dull since the Black Tulip was put out of commission.'

'The Black Who?' asked Tommy, punching the leather of his chair into a more comfortable shape.

'By Gad, how long did you say you'd been away?' Their host paused with the biscuit in midair to gape at them.

'Twelve years for me,' said Robert drily.

'Well, that explains it, then.' Their host flung himself back in his chair, stretching his long legs out in front of him. Taking a big bite of his ginger biscuit, he followed it with a long swig of brandy, swilling the two together with obvious satisfaction. Thus refreshed, he said, rather indistinctly, 'There's been a vogue this past decade for flower names for spies, English and French. You must have just missed it when you left, Dovedale. We've had the Pimpernel, the Purple Gentian, the Pink Carnation. They've countered with the Black Tulip – nasty one, that – and a rather halfhearted series of Daisies, none of that stuck.'

'You can add a Jasmine to that list,' put in Robert, as the missing puzzle piece clicked into place. 'A Jasmine that might prove rather sticky.'

'So that's it!' exclaimed Tommy. 'Wrothan and his infernal sprig of jasmine. It wasn't just for show.'

Seeing their host's confused expression, Robert explained, 'It all began in India, with a man named Arthur Wrothan.'

'Your Jasmine,' Tommy chimed in, 'who was selling secrets to the Mahratta and, it seems, to the French.'

'Wrothan,' continued Robert, 'attached himself to Freddy Staines in India. It was what he did. He collected young officers with more money than sense and promised them access to all manners of Eastern pleasures.'

'Eastern pleasures?' Their host perked up.

'Usually women with a fringe of opiates,' Robert said bluntly. 'Wrothan appears to have found a similar outlet for his talents here, in Sir Francis Medmenham's Hellfire Club. He appears to be using Medmenham's meetings as a cover for rendezvous with his liaison from France.'

'I see.' Their host frowned into his brandy. 'Medmenham and Staines have been friends since the nursery. Staines would have provided your Mr Wrothan with the introduction to Medmenham. Mr Wrothan sounds like he would fit right into Medmenham's infernal activities. But how does the Frenchman come in?'

'That's what we wanted to find out,' admitted Tommy. 'Wrothan must have met him in India. Or Wrothan's French contacts in India arranged for an introduction once he returned to England.'

'Medmenham's club must have seemed like manna from heaven to him,' put in Robert. 'Think about it. You have the brothers and sons of members of the cabinet, a groom of the bedchamber to the king, and assorted peers, all out of their minds on opiates.'

'Good God,' breathed their host. 'It's the answer to an agent's prayer. Do you think Medmenham's in on it?'

'It's hard to tell,' admitted Robert. 'In those robes, it's deuced hard to tell who's who. The Frenchman might have snuck in without being passed through Medmenham. He might also be known to Medmenham without Medmenham being aware of his other activities.'

'There are certainly more than enough Royalist émigrés moving about society, any of whom might secretly be working for the other side,' said their host frankly, helping himself to another biscuit. 'But if Medmenham doesn't know about your Mr Wrothan's extra activities, what does he get out of all those? Aside from the women and opiates, of course.'

Robert thought about it. 'Power. Influence.' He remembered the rapt look on Medmenham's face as he called forth his papier-mâché deity. It might have been merely the opiates at work, but he rather thought it went deeper than that. He could hear Medmenham's voice at Girdings, speaking of more things than heaven and earth. 'Much as he mocks it all, I wouldn't wonder if Medmenham half believes his own mumbo jumbo. Ridiculous as it sounds.'

'Huh.' Their host kicked back in his chair, balancing his brandy balloon on his stomach. 'We have enough demons in London without his raising more. Your esteemed relation, for example.' He cast a nervous glance over his shoulder as he said it, as though expecting her to pop out at him. 'The dowager duchess.'

'Who is, mercifully, at Girdings,' said Robert. 'And will hopefully stay there until this business is done.'

'Amen,' agreed their host, and got down to business. 'When is Medmenham's next meeting?'

'Tomorrow.' Robert felt duty bound to add, 'The Frenchman might not appear again. It is something of a long shot.'

'My favourite kind!' Their host raised his hand to toast and realised he was holding a biscuit instead of his glass.

Philosophically, he finished it off in two large bites, adding somewhat indistinctly, 'Where's the place?'

'Upon the heath,' said Robert.

'Really?' said their host eagerly.

'No. Not really,' Robert admitted. 'We're meeting tomorrow night at Drury Lane at six o'clock and then departing the theatre at a prearranged time to be led to the ceremonial meeting place, wherever that may be.'

'Midnight?' said their host, reaching for another biscuit.

'Nine o'clock.'

Their host coughed up brandy. 'What self-respecting satanical society meets at nine o'clock?'

'One with an early bedtime?' suggested Tommy.

Robert considered the liquid in his glass. The wallpaper gave it an oddly greenish tinge, like something seen through water. 'Or one with other activities planned afterwards.'

Their host raised his glass to Robert. 'I like the way you think. Tomorrow night it is. To the Hellfire Club!'

Chapter Nineteen

Hallways always seem longer in the dark, especially when you don't know where you're going.

If there was a moon out, it wasn't doing me the least bit of good. The hallway ran along the interior of the house; the only window was the one at the far end. It was so dark that I couldn't even make out where the end of the hall was.

I hoped Robert Lansdowne and Tommy Fluellen conducted their reconnaissance mission more suavely than I was conducting mine.

I had a vague notion that Colin's study – and in it, the computer, the ostensible goal of my quest – was somewhere on the second floor with me. The downstairs was devoted to reception rooms on one side, the kitchen and den on the other, and the long drawing room in the back. With the carpet runner prickling against the soles of my bare feet, I started cautiously down the stretch of hallway Colin had redirected me from earlier.

That sounds nice and Gothic, doesn't it? If I were a Gothic heroine that would be the signal to all attentive readers that something dreadful (and key to the plot) was hidden at the end of the West Wing. Of course, if I were a Gothic heroine, I would also have had a candle dripping wax on one hand and a demented old maidservant popping out of the shadows to moan, 'Beware! Beware! Beware the curse of the Selwicks!' before laughing maniacally and bolting down to the cellars to croon to the corpses of Colin's six murdered wives.

Perhaps it was a good thing I wasn't a Gothic heroine.

At any rate, Colin's injunction about the hallway hadn't been anything sinister or even suggestive; he had merely meant to indicate that the library was in the opposite direction. But I did vaguely recall that he had gone off that way himself once I'd finally been set on the right path library-wards, hence leading to my logical deduction that therein lay the study.

It would have been easier to wait till morning and just ask him, but easy never seems like the appropriate choice at three in the morning when the pipes are moaning and the floorboards are creaking and the very shadows seem to have eyes. Nothing was going to put me to sleep but finding out where on earth 971 was, and then sending a long email to my friend Alex telling her how silly I was being, at which point it would all be out of my system and then I could go back to being a normal (all right, passably normal) human being.

Tomorrow, I knew, I would feel extremely sheepish about the whole thing and wonder why it had seemed so imperative. But that was tomorrow.

With one hand on the hip-high moulding that ran down the length of the wall, I felt my way down the hallway, groping my way by touch through the darkness. I encountered a door frame and kept going. Ahead of me, I could see a faint distinction in the quality of the darkness. Ah, glass. That was a window, one of the windows that looked out over the front of the house (the bedroom had windows on the garden front).

Doubling around, I blundered back to the last door frame. It was only a frame; the door itself had been left open.

Surely, that made any ideas about Colin being double-0-something-or-other even sillier. Any self-respecting agent in any novel would have left his study door both closed and locked. A good thing, too. Unlike the heroines of those sorts of novels, I (a) don't wear hairpins, and (b) wouldn't know how to pick a lock with them even if I did.

Oh, well. I had never really thought Colin might be a spy. It was just one of those titillating what-ifs, a harmless little daydream, like fantasizing about suddenly inheriting a castle from a long-lost relative, or being asked out by Sean Bean after accidentally stepping on his foot in the Marks & Spencer food hall (many was the happy hour I had spent with that one). You know they're make-believe. Even if my heart did always beat a little faster when I entered that Marks & Sparks sandwich aisle. But it was all harmless fun, like imagining that my not-always-mild-mannered boyfriend might secretly be an international man of mystery.

And, hey, as daydreams go, it was at least slightly more likely than winning Sean Bean's undying devotion over an egg and cress sandwich. Hadn't at least three of Colin's great-great-great-great-great-grandparents been in the business? (I was still excited over the whole his-being-descended-from-Miles thing.)

There I went again.

Shaking my head at myself, I shimmied my way through the door of the study, patting down the wall in search of a light switch.

Blinking in the avalanche of light, I twisted this way and

that, like a comical cat burglar in one of the *Pink Panther* movies. What if Colin saw? What if it woke him up? Never mind that the bedroom was down the hall with the door closed; I dashed over to the desk, pulled the chain on the small brass desk lamp, and hastily switched off the overhead.

A gentle light diffused over the scarred wood of the desk and the reddish brown carpet. Ah, that was better. As my heart rate slowed to a reasonable pace, I looked around, taking stock of my surroundings.

It was larger than I had imagined it would be, more of a combination study – sitting room – library than my apartment-bred definition of a study. Bookcases had been set against the walls on three sides of the room, breaking only for the two long west-facing windows and another that looked south, towards the front of the house. On the right was Colin's desk, facing out towards the door, with the promised computer crouching on it like a big beige gremlin. If the desk faced out, that meant the computer faced in, where someone walking into the study couldn't see what was on it.

The other side of the room featured a well-worn sofa, a squashy chintz chair, and a table with drink rings all over the top. Perched on top of a file cabinet sat an electric kettle, one of those white plastic ones without which no British kitchen seems complete, a battered French press with squished coffee grounds on the bottom, and a stained mug, off of which the lettering had been mostly washed by repeated use over time. There was also a biscuit tin with the lid half off.

I automatically shifted feet, scraping the sole of one against the ankle of another. No wonder the carpet beneath my feet felt mildly crunchy. I wondered if that brown in the rug was there by design or was really just splotches of spilt coffee.

Not exactly anyone's image of a den of international espionage.

Crunching my way across the rug, I plopped myself comfortably into Colin's desk chair. It wasn't one of the wheelie kinds, but a plain old four-legged chair with reddish leather padding set into the seat and back. Fortunately, the computer was already on. It was a slightly different model from my own, so I could just see myself taking an hour to find the on switch. All it took was a slight jiggle of the mouse and the screen blinked crankily into life. Apparently, it didn't much feel like being woken up, either.

Like a middle-aged lady donning its housecoat, the computer presented me with a plain blue screen and the option of logging on as Colin, Serena, or Guest. Serena had chosen a lilac as her icon. It suited her, I thought: thin and willowy and graceful. Surprisingly, Colin had also gone with the flower option. His was little and pink. It looked, in fact, remarkably like a pink carnation. Hmm.

Oh, no, I wasn't starting that again. Not even if it did remind me of that bit in *The Scarlet Pimpernel* where Marguerite spies the small red flowers on her husband's crest and it all clicks into place for her. Fiction, I reminded myself. They call it fiction for a reason. And could you really imagine James Bond with biscuit crumbs?

All the same, I couldn't quite resist casting a casual eye over the contents of the desk as I waited for the Guest setting to boot up. The computer was making the huffing and grunting noises that indicate that it might do what you want but it will have to think about it for a while first. Idly, I flipped through the papers that had been piled to the far side of the mouse, held together at the top with a large binder clip. They were all newspaper clippings. I squinted at the tiny print in the top right-hand corner. And recent ones, at that. The top one was dated last week; the others were all dated within the past month. They came from a wide variety of papers. I saw *The Daily Telegraph*, *The Guardian*, *The Times of London*, the *Daily Mail*, articles in French from *Le Monde*, in Italian from *Corriere della Sera*, and in German from something with a very long compound title that I won't even bother to reproduce.

It was nice to be dating a man who not only spoke his own language properly, but others as well.

The article on top reported that Dubai banks had been used to wire money to Al-Qaeda. So did the article underneath it. Others concerned undersea communications cables located in the Persian Gulf outside Dubai; the Dubai engineering boom; the influx of German engineers to Dubai (this in the German paper with the unpronounceable name); the percentage of the world's cranes currently in Dubai; and so on. Every single article touched in some way on Dubai. Maybe his former company had investments in Dubai. I hoped he wasn't thinking of looking for a job out there. I doubted it, though. He seemed too attached to Selwick Hall to ever really leave.

Logging into Hotmail, I quickly checked my email – a 'Hi! Where are you?' from a grad school friend; a longer email from Alex that I saved to read later; a three-liner from my mother; and five emails, all in the exact same block letters, offering to help me enlarge my penis – and then went to *Google.com* to try to find the source of the elusive country code. To be honest, it had become more a matter of boredom than burning interest at that point. It took me a while to find a site that would just give me the country codes without trying to sell me phone cards, but, eventually, there it was. The country code for the

United Arab Emirates is 971. In other words, for Dubai.

I looked sideways at the pile of articles. OK, so that was just a little bit weird.

There weren't any other articles on the desk, but there were Post-it notes scattered here and there, and others that looked like they had been torn carelessly out of a notepad, scribbled with notes in Colin's henscratch handwriting. Some looked like phone numbers, only they were longer than any phone numbers with which I was acquainted, with the dashes in odd places. More international numbers?

The country code finder was still up on the screen, so I typed one of the numbers in, just because. 'Russia,' announced the computer.

Curiouser and curiouser, as Alice would say.

But where in Russia? It had been hard enough finding the country code site; I didn't have the patience to hunt around for city codes – and, to be honest, I wasn't quite sure which bit of the number was the city code. As an American studying English history, I had the New York-to-London calling routine down by rote, but I'd never had to tackle calling internationally anyplace else. Not so with Colin, apparently.

Twisting in his desk chair, my nightgown bunching around me, I squinted at the bookshelves behind the desk. 'DUBAI' was splashed in lurid green letters down one binding, next to a Fodor's guide with 'United Arab Emirates' in more discreet lettering down the spine. There were half a dozen guides on Dubai alone, others to the UAE, Oman, Qatar, Bahrain, and Saudi Arabia. Farther down the shelf, Moscow elbowed Saint Petersburg for shelf space, cramming Kazakhstan, Uzbekistan, and Kyrgyzstan all the way into a corner. Kyrgyzstan? Who had ever heard of Kyrgyzstan?

Colin, apparently. Not only did he own the one and only official guide, but it had evidently been well read. The binding was cracked in three places. As I tugged it out of the shelf, the book fell instantly open to the description of a city named Osh. Colin had underlined a section about Osh's proximity to the Uzbek border and resultant raids by an Uzbek militant Muslim group. Wow, everyone seemed to have their own homegrown terrorists these days.

Frowning, I shoved the book back into its corner on the shelf. By this point, I was up on my knees on Colin's desk chair, my back to the computer, leaning over the back of the chair to try to see the books in the farther shelves. There was a whole shelf dedicated to nothing but dictionaries, dictionaries in languages I had never seen before. Oh, some were perfectly mundane and extremely well used – French, German, Latin, Greek, all presumably relics from Colin's school days – but others were shiny and new, with lettering that looked even more like hieroglyphs than Colin's handwriting.

I had leant out too far. The chair tipped precipitously forwards, sending me whapping stomach-first into the crossbar as I caught at the edge of the shelf to keep from going over. After a few wobbly moments, the chair steadied and I settled safely back down on my haunches, staring with narrowed eyes at the bookshelves. The row I was facing was all biography and cultural history. A biography called *Sultan in Oman* about Sultan Qaboos, another on the conflict between tradition and modernisation in the Middle East, and so on.

All right, I told myself, feeling for the ground with one foot as I wiggled backwards off the desk chair. Calm down. So Colin was interested in other countries and cultures. So were many other people. He might have been an international relations major in college or, rather, read international relations at university as they put it here. Perfectly normal, perfectly innocent.

Only he hadn't, had he? Hadn't he told me that he had read economics at Oxford? Or was I making that up? Between the lateness of the hour and everything else, I was so muddled that I was finding it hard to distinguish between what Colin had actually told me and what I had merely assumed. I had had so many imaginary conversations with him in my head over the past few weeks that it was very hard to sort them out from the real ones. Let's be honest; we all do that. Aren't there times when you're sure you've told someone something and then remember you'd only intended to tell them? Or that you assume one thing until they tell you another?

Right, let's say Colin had been an econ major. Everyone needed a hobby. Maybe he just liked the study of languages and their corresponding cultures. Maybe he just had time on his hands after leaving his City job and needed something to do. Maybe.

Feeling a bit like Catherine Morland in *Northanger Abbey* pouncing on the Tilneys' old laundry lists in the hopes that they were mouldering manuscripts, I attacked the drawers of Colin's desk, yanking them open one by one. If he came in – well, I was just looking for paper and pen to scribble down some dissertation ideas. Ignore the fact that I had paper and pen of my own in my bag in the bedroom.

The top drawer had nothing but the usual office effluvia of stretched-out paper clips, capless pens, boxes of spare staples, eraser-less pencils and pencil-less erasers. The second drawer was more promising. Hands unsteady, I reached for the first of the hanging files. 'Business Expenses,' it read. Business expenses for what? What business? The first batch were all estate related, reports of land taxes paid, necessary repairs made, machinery bought. No pigs, I noticed.

Feeling considerably less excited, I eased the file back into the folder and drew out the next one. This really was turning into Catherine Morland with her laundry list, wasn't it? I was all ready to dismissively tuck away this file as I had the last one, closing the drawer on the files and the whole embarrassing episode, when something made me stay my hand.

Unlike the last file, there were no neatly printed-out spreadsheets of estate accounts. Instead, it was just a bunch of receipts shoved haphazardly into a folder. The one on top had been folded three times and tucked into a blue holder that read 'Hilton Dubai Jumeirah.' Jumeirah? On an impulse, I tugged down one of the UAE books from the shelf. And there it was. Jumeirah, one of the outlying areas of rapidly developing Dubai. The guidebook listed the hotel as 'moderate' and enthused that it was 'a bargain for the beachfront.' Hmm. What was Colin doing going to beachfronts in Dubai? Pre-me, I hoped.

Easing it out of its holder, I unfolded the hotel receipt. It hadn't been pre-me. In fact, it had been this month. Colin had stayed there for a week, one of the two weeks he had been out of London 'on business.' Other receipts in the pile were for various restaurants in Dubai, drinks at Vu's, lunch at Bastakiah Nights, taxi rides, coffees, bus tickets, the usual petty expenses of travel.

Well, that explained how brown he had got over Christmas. He had spent enough of his youth in the sun that he had one of those perma-tans, a permanent overlay of brown over a naturally fair skin that probably signalled melanomas later in life, so it hadn't been striking enough to warrant questions; if anything, I had ascribed his heightened colour to the effects of his ski trip with his mother and her husband when he had visited them in Italy over the New Year.

I wondered where he had spent the other week.

If I delved deeper into the folder, I would no doubt find receipts for that week, too, in some other exotic location. Moscow, perhaps, since that seemed to have occasioned the second largest pile of guidebooks, or Bonn, or maybe even Kyrgyzstan. It was all straight out of an old-fashioned thriller. Our Man in . . . Sussex.

Huh.

Didn't quite have the right ring to it, did it? Besides, if he really was involved in something top secret, why would he leave all his background materials out where anyone could see them? The dictionaries and guides were right there on the back wall, in plain view from the door – except where they would be obscured by the computer monitor and the back of the chair, but that didn't really count, since all you had to do was walk around them. Shelves are meant to display, not hide. And then there were the receipts in the drawer. The unlocked drawer. Everything was right out there in the open.

But open to whom? That was the question. We were in West Sussex, isolated at the end of a not-very-well-kept road (my posterior, still bruised from the ride down it earlier, suggested stronger adjectives). The books might be right there on the shelves and the receipts right there in the drawer, but they were all the way up on the second floor in a wing off the main block of the house. All the reception rooms were downstairs. Even if he had people over, they probably wouldn't go up above the ground floor. And if they did go upstairs, this room was all the way at the end of a wing that contained nothing else but the master bedroom and bath.

When I had stayed last time, as guest, my bedroom had been in the main block, the library all the way over in the other wing. I had had no idea that this wing – or this room – was even here. Why would I have? And if I had ventured this way, I would probably have spotted Colin's bedroom, realised I was trespassing, and gone no farther.

It was all more than a little perplexing.

Tucking the folder back into the drawer, I nudged it shut with one knee and reached for the bottom drawer. It didn't budge. I tried again, getting a better grip on the brass handle. It rattled a bit, but wouldn't move. So this one *was* locked. I knelt down beside the desk to get a better look, my nightgown spreading out along the carpet around me, the bright green flannel with its splashy pink flowers incongruous against the faded and stained Persian carpet. Closing one eye and putting the other against the keyhole, I thought I could make out *something* in there – but I couldn't tell what. Probably just the rest of the keyhole.

Settling back on my heels, disgruntled, I spotted something I had missed. There was a fragment of paper on the carpet beneath the desk, right near the edge of my nightgown. It really was just a fragment, with ragged corners, roughly the quarter of the size of a standard piece of paper, as though a document had been torn in two and then torn again. It read:

'—*llowed them as far as the gold souk where*—'
'—*back alley behind a vendor selling fake hand*—' (I really hoped the next missing word there was 'bags.')
'—*crawled beneath a display of gold chains into*—'

'—*nversation between them in the back room*—'
'—*elves safe, made little effort to keep their voices*—'
'—*Dublin, in four days, and then from there to*—'
'—*this gun, a Jericho 941 F double action semiauto*—'
'—*idn't stand a chance at point-blank range. After*—'

And there it ended, infuriating, inconclusive, all but unintelligible.

What in the hell?

I held the piece of paper under the bulb of the desk lamp, as though more light would somehow illuminate the contents or make the missing words reappear. Even if they did, how was this to be explained? It was Colin's handwriting; I knew it by now, every awkward, angular scratch of the pen. But the contents . . .

No, I thought. No. This was supposed to be *Northanger Abbey*, not *The Spy Who Loved Me*. I might imagine these things, but I was never supposed to actually find corroboration. I rubbed one cold palm against my nightgown: flannel, warm, safe, and mundane. Spies didn't exist in worlds with flowered flannel nightgowns and coffee-stained carpets. Those things were normal; they were real. Spies were for television, for movie screens, for the old Ian Fleming paperbacks in the library. All fiction, all imaginary. Except some of them weren't imaginary.

I looked at the piece of paper trembling in my other hand, in the glare of the bulb of the desk light. It looked pretty real, too. So had all those receipts in the drawer. And then there was that two-week period when Colin was out of London, leaving 'Miss you!' messages on my voice mail at odd hours, but never there when I called back. I thought back to Sally's and Joan's odd comments in the ladies' room; Colin's caginess when asked about his occupation; that pink flower icon guarding the files on his computer.

I let the scrap of paper drop to the floor where I had found it, among the biscuit crumbs and spiky bits on the carpet where coffee had spilt and dried. It lay there looking perfectly innocent, like any other fragment of paper accidentally torn and dropped.

Only I knew better.

Why hadn't anyone told me that I was dating 007?

Chapter Twenty

'We can try again tomorrow,' Henrietta said soothingly. Muslin brushed against velvet as Charlotte sank down into a chair beside her best friend in the Dorringtons' box at Drury Lane. The opulence of the gold embroidery on the hem of her white muslin dress and the rich sheen of the velvet upholstery stood in stark contrast to her distinctly muddy mood.

'But what if tomorrow is too late?' she protested, dropping her fan so that it dangled limply from her wrist.

'How could it be too late?' Henrietta asked sensibly.

As Henrietta had pointed out earlier that day, it wasn't as if the king was going anywhere. Nor, unfortunately, was the false Dr Simmons. With the queen's connivance, Charlotte had spent the whole of the afternoon lying in wait for him, but no matter how Charlotte haunted the library, Dr Simmons hadn't put a single broken-buckled shoe out of the king's chambers.

Charlotte shrugged helplessly. 'I don't even know.'

'Don't know what?' asked Miles, tromping happily up behind them.

It had been Miles's suggestion that they go to the theatre, and Charlotte couldn't think of a reasonable reason to refuse. If she were Penelope, or even Henrietta, she might, she thought, have claimed a headache and doubled back to Buckingham House to lurk in the shadows until the false doctor emerged from his lair. But, being herself, she couldn't imagine creeping out after dark without a chaperone. It just seemed like poor sense. And more than a little bit daunting. Lurking in the library was just about the extent of her daring.

Her grandmother was right. She didn't have any gumption.

'Anything,' said Charlotte glumly.

'Cheer up, old thing.' A large hand descended on her head in a casual gesture of friendship that broke her egret feather and drove two pins into her scalp. Happily oblivious, Miles continued, 'Dovedale told me he'll be here tonight.'

That was supposed to improve her mood?

Egret feather wagging drunkenly, Charlotte narrowed her eyes at her best friend's husband. 'You spoke to Robert?'

'Why wouldn't I?'

The more appropriate question was why would he. They did not exactly move within the same circles.

Charlotte looked to Henrietta, but Henrietta only widened her eyes in a silent protestation of innocence.

Charlotte was not convinced. 'You didn't invite him, did you?' Charlotte asked suspiciously.

'No.' Miles seemed genuinely surprised by the question. But, then, Miles always seemed vaguely surprised. By everything. 'He's making one of Medmenham's party.'

Medmenham. Always Medmenham. Charlotte was sick unto death of Sir Francis Medmenham, whose fingers were far too busy in any number of pies, attaching himself to Robert, recommending new doctors for the king. In fact, when she searched for the base of all the sources of confusion in her life, it always seemed to come back to Medmenham.

Despite herself, Charlotte found herself turning towards Medmenham's box, peering myopically at the confusion of gentlemen who were sorting themselves out among the small gilt chairs. One box over, she could see the blur of Penelope's red head, in company with her soon-to-be husband, her mother, who was positively moulting feathers, and her father, who was only visible as a long pair of legs and a tilted program covering his face. Staines leant over the partition to speak to someone in Medmenham's box and the configuration shifted, revealing Robert at the very back. Even blurry, he looked somewhat grim. Or maybe that was just the effect of his stark black-and-white evening clothes.

'I wonder why Dovedale didn't use the Dovedale box,' Henrietta was saying to Miles over Charlotte's head.

'I expect he didn't know he had it,' said Miles matter-of-factly.

Charlotte cocked her head at him. 'What do you mean?'

Miles shrugged awkwardly. 'Well, it's not exactly as though the dowager is relinquishing anything, is it? I put him up for my club, but he refused,' he added as an afterthought. 'Said he didn't have the blunt to pay the fees.'

'But—' Charlotte began, and broke off.

Miles looked at her quizzically, but Charlotte just shook her head, the words she had been about to say all jumbled in a lump at the back of her throat.

But of course he has the funds, she had been about to say. It was all his. The opera box, the houses, the horses, Girdings, everything, down to the very honey in the beehives. Only it wasn't, was it? Not while her grandmother held the keys. By law, it had been all Robert's for over a decade, but he hadn't had any use of it, of any of it.

'He isn't even living at Dovedale House, is he?' Henrietta asked curiously, as if it were a matter of purely academic interest.

Charlotte knew the answer to that one. 'Bachelor lodgings,' she croaked. She wasn't quite sure why her throat had suddenly gone so dry. 'He told me he took bachelor lodgings in the Albany.'

As if he didn't intend to stay. Or, she realised, with a sinking feeling, as if he never felt like he could stay in the first place.

Charlotte looked across the way, at the bustling box where Medmenham's cronies were amusing themselves with ribald jokes and scurrilous stories. Medmenham presided with quizzing glass in hand, entirely at home among the velvet and gilt. Robert, in contrast, kept to the back of the box, to the shadows, as though primed for a quick retreat. As he had retreated from Girdings all those years ago?

Her grandmother certainly hadn't done anything to make him welcome.

And she was just as bad. Charlotte could feel her cheeks burn with two bright flags of colour. What had she done to make him feel at home in his own home? She had never stopped to think of how strange it might be for him, any of it, of how big and daunting Girdings might seem, or how utterly alien the code of behaviour that governed the small world of the *ton*. She hadn't thought about him at all; she had simply used him for her own purposes, first as playmate and then as a repository for her romantic fancies.

Old anger wrestled with new guilt in a writhing mass of

313

undigestible emotion. To have kissed her and then fled wasn't the act of a gentleman – but what had her part been in that?

He had tried to tell her. Charlotte's restless hands crushed the lace edge of her fan as she remembered their conversation in the dining room on Twelfth Night, and how she had brushed away his tentative admissions about his own inadequacies as duke, too preoccupied with wondering what he thought of her, only concerned with how whatever he said related to her. In retrospect, her own behaviour struck her as embarrassingly childish and more than a little selfish.

'I wonder if it is all very strange for him,' she said tentatively, half hoping that Miles would say no. 'Coming back to all this, I mean.'

'I can't think how it wouldn't be,' said Miles, casually heaping coals of fire on her head. 'And your grandmother has been known to make grown men jump out of drawing room windows.'

'It was a ballroom window,' said Charlotte defensively. 'And I don't think Percy Ponsonby really counts as a grown man.'

'Fair enough,' said Miles equably. 'But you can't deny that the dowager tends to inspire the urge to emigrate. I used to think I wanted to run away and join the army,' he added reminiscently.

'You also thought you wanted to be a woodcutter,' reminded Henrietta caustically.

'I like chopping things down,' said Miles cheerfully.

'He chopped down Mother's favourite rosebush,' said Henrietta to Charlotte.

'It wasn't her favourite,' Miles protested. 'And it grew back.'

Their familiar bickering faded into a blur in the background. Charlotte feigned interest in the stage, but she did not see the brightly costumed actors any more than she heard Miles and Henrietta's banter. Instead, she was busily realigning the past few weeks within her head, worrying at them, turning bits and pieces upside down to create an entirely new picture of events. Maybe Robert wasn't a Lovelace, or an Orville, either, but something entirely different. For once, Charlotte could think of no literary counterpart into which she could slot Robert's behaviour.

Girdings and the town house were both his. He would have been well within his rights to dispossess both her and her grandmother. Her grandmother had her dower property and a comfortable allowance of her own. Nobody would have condemned him for it, or even thought anything of it. It was the way the world worked.

Instead, he had behaved as though he were the interloper, rather than they, attending the house party at Girdings more as guest than host, never indicating by word or deed that he minded the usurpation of his rightful place. The only liberty he had taken was in kissing her. And as for that . . . Charlotte's hands tightened on her fan as it all began to make a very unpleasant sort of sense. After he had been made to feel like the rankest of interlopers, it must have been terribly tempting to find himself the object of adoration of the not-entirely-ill-favoured daughter of the house. Add a windswept parapet, a sky full of stars, and a good deal of wine at dinner, and she didn't wonder that he had kissed her.

Or that he had thought better of it afterwards. She knew her own limitations.

Charlotte was jarred out of that unpleasant line of thought as Henrietta's chair bumped against hers as its occupant scrambled to stand.

'Penelope!' Henrietta exclaimed, leaping from her seat and hurrying to the back of the box.

Dropping her mangled fan, Charlotte saw that they had visitors. Penelope pushed into the box, tugging her fiancé along behind her like a dog on a leash. Inevitably as the night follows the day, Medmenham, Innes, and Frobisher followed along behind him, although Charlotte noticed that Frobisher had the good sense to stay to the back of the group, well away from Henrietta and Miles. Was Robert there, too? In the confusion of coats and cravats, gleaming quizzing glasses and frothing linen, it was difficult to tell.

For the first time, Charlotte thought she could see why Robert might have attached himself so strongly to Medmenham. For a man who had been abroad so long, shunned by his own family, Medmenham's company provided an instant fraternity of his fellows. A rather frightful fraternity, but a fraternity nonetheless. When was the last time she had gone anywhere without either Henrietta or Penelope in tow?

Lord Freddy stumbled as Penelope let go of him, catching at a chair back for balance.

Penelope regarded her fiancé with a jaundiced eye. 'Really, Freddy. How much have you had?'

Even bloated with claret, there was something undeniably winning about Staines's smile. His were classic British good looks, ruddy cheeked, with that unique dark blond shade of hair peculiar to the British Isles. 'Can't a gentleman have a drink?'

'Not if he can't hold it without being foxed,' said Penelope rudely.

Staines caught her around the waist. His colour was high as he yanked her close in a grasp too intimate for a public place. 'A fine thing for my affianced bride to say.'

Penelope gave him a light shove. 'We're not married yet.'

'Are you promising to descend into docility once that blessed day arrives, Miss Deveraux?' drawled Medmenham, baring his teeth at Penelope as though she were the star attraction in a bear baiting. His tone was as gently needling as a pointy stick.

'I shall mend my ways,' said Penelope sweetly, 'when Freddy mends his.'

Medmenham affected a bow. 'A very pattern for matrimony.'

Not liking the way the conversation was going, or the dangerous glint in Penelope's eye, Charlotte asked hastily, 'When do you leave for India?'

'A week Thursday.' If Penelope had any trepidation about travelling halfway around the world, she certainly didn't show it. She might have been referring to a trip to Almack's. 'Two days after the wedding.'

'I wish I could come,' Charlotte said wistfully. 'You'll have to be sure to write regularly.'

For a moment, Penelope's face softened. 'By every packet,' she promised. 'You can bring them to Henrietta and laugh over my misadventures.'

'Or exult over your triumphs,' Charlotte amended gently. 'I'm sure you'll have maharajas bringing you rubies as big as your palm and besotted British officers leaving leopard skins at your feet.'

'I should hope not,' scoffed Penelope. 'The skins would probably smell.'

Charlotte squeezed her hands. 'It will be an adventure,' she said softly. 'You'll see.'

Penelope shrugged. 'Perhaps.'

Her own troubles momentarily paled into insignificance beside Penelope's, off to a strange continent with no one for comfort but her husband. No matter how well Penelope hid it, she had to be nervous. Charlotte knew she would be.

It might, thought Charlotte hopefully, be the making of Penelope's marriage. Charlotte glanced back over her shoulder to where Freddy Staines was passing a silver flask back and forth with Henry Innes. Penelope had noticed, too. Her eyes were narrowed in an expression of mingled condescension and irritation.

Maybe not.

'I could come with you,' Charlotte suggested, only half joking. 'You could be my chaperone.'

Penelope laughed raggedly. 'And ruin you, too? I don't think so. But – thank you.'

Before Charlotte could say anything else, Penelope swept up the train of her skirt, a catlike smile curving the corners of her lips. 'I'd best be removing myself,' she said meaningfully. 'You'll have company enough without me.'

'Pen?' Charlotte rose to follow her and bumped smack into a dark suit of evening clothes.

There was a man within the evening clothes, a man tall enough that her eyes were on a level with the stickpin in his cravat. There were no pearls or diamonds or rubies for him, none of the ostentatious decoration affected by the other gentlemen in the box. The stickpin was a plain gold oval, a familiar family crest incised into the metal. The lines of the crest were worn with age, but Charlotte would have known it anywhere: a dove in flight with a sprig of rosemary in its mouth. Rosemary for remembrance. Charlotte had never been entirely sure whether the dove was flying towards home or away.

Charlotte backed up a few paces, catching at the railing of the balcony before she found herself flying into the pit. In the light of the thousand chandeliers, his face seemed as bright as the golden oval, but it was considerably harder to read.

What had become of his promise not to come until she called? Perversely, she was more pleased than not that he had disobeyed.

Charlotte abruptly squashed down that thought. There was no future there. That dove had flown.

'Robert,' said Charlotte, struggling to keep her tone light. 'I hadn't thought to see you here.'

'I could disappear again,' he offered.

'Yes, you do that very well,' said Charlotte without thinking. Flushing, she amended, 'I didn't mean—'

'Of course, you did,' said Robert lightly, as though they were talking about nothing more meaningful than the movements on the stage. He bared his teeth in a polished social smile. 'And I deserved it.'

Charlotte pleated the folds of her fan. 'Most of it,' she mumbled. 'You were not entirely without assistance.'

Looking up from her fan, she found him watching her, his expression intent and curiously vulnerable.

Shifting from one foot to the other, he said in a rapid undertone, 'If I were to call on you tomorrow afternoon, would you receive me?'

Charlotte didn't know what to say. There was a tightening in the back of her throat, not of anticipation, but of dread.

'It *is* your choice,' he added levelly. 'If you tell me to stay away, I will. Although I very much hope you won't. I should like – well, to talk to you.'

That could only mean one thing.

Charlotte let her gaze drop to her mangled fan. What a fool she was. She should be glad that he wanted to make amends, to be – oh, what a lacklustre word! – friends. They could put all of her silliness and all of his missteps behind them and start over again, as they should have in the first place.

It was all for the best, she assured herself. But right now she wasn't sure she wanted to sit through an explanation of what a lovely person she was and how very sorry he was to have kissed her. The very thought of it made her chest tighten in silent protest.

'If I'm not at the Palace,' she prevaricated.

He didn't seem all that thrilled with her response, but he accepted it as a deserved rebuke. 'I will await *your* pleasure,' he said quietly.

It was an exceedingly unfortunate choice of phrase. Charlotte experienced an intense urge to stamp her foot and shout, *It's not my pleasure*! But ladies didn't do that sort of thing, especially not Lansdowne ones, so instead, she inclined her head in a genteel nod, while her insides churned in silent rebellion.

Was he really that thick? Didn't he realise there were few conversations she would less rather have? That no matter how much she tried to convince herself otherwise, she was still ridiculously, childishly infatuated with the very idea of him?

And not just the idea – it would be easier if it were just the idea of him. She was ridiculously, childishly infatuated with the actuality of him, too. It was there in the way he leant just that little bit forwards when he spoke to her; the way his lips turned up on one side and not the other when he smiled; the way he was looking at her right now, as though he actually cared what she thought or felt. It was absurd that in a theatre loud with the din of singing, dancing, and talking, she could hear the rustle of his sleeve as he stirred; that in the midst of burning beeswax, orange peel, gingerbread, and a dozen different perfumes, she could still distinguish the particular smell of him, all clean linen and sandalwood and just a hint of saddle leather. There was no play, no party, no pit below. The entire world was narrowed to the span between her body and his, bounded by the curve of his arm on the balcony.

'Dovedale!' The word careened into their kingdom like a cannonball, shattering the strange silence that bound her to Robert.

Sir Francis Medmenham strolled over like Charles II favouring a pair of fortunate courtiers with his presence. Charlotte practically expected to see spaniels nipping at his heels, instead of just Frobisher and Innes.

'Do stop monopolising your little cousin, Dovedale,' he casually commanded. 'It's unfair on the rest of company.'

And then Robert did something very curious.

Instead of standing aside to allow Medmenham to pass, he turned so that his body was ranged between Charlotte and Medmenham, and said, very deliberately, 'We are scarcely cousins. The connection is a very distant one. Isn't it, Charlotte?'

'Through half siblings more than a hundred years ago,' Charlotte confirmed. 'You see, our great-great-grandfather married six times,' she began, but Medmenham did not seem to be paying attention to the intricacies of the Lansdowne family tree. Which was a pity, because Charlotte had always found the story of their great-great-grandfather and his multiple marital misfortunes a singularly diverting one.

Smiling charmingly, Medmenham said, 'In that case, Dovedale, all the more reason for you to step aside.'

Robert drew himself up in a way that made Charlotte think of knights and gauntlets and the clash of swords on shields. She could practically hear the trumpets sounding in the background. The two men were roughly of a height, but Robert was broader, his muscles honed with years of marches and physical work, while Medmenham was as lean and rangy as a kitchen cat.

'I still have a responsibility as the head of my house,' Robert said pleasantly, but there was a bite beneath it.

Beneath his genial mask, Charlotte was suddenly quite, quite sure that Robert's feelings for Medmenham were anything but cordial. Then why was he playing at being his friend?

Medmenham had games of his own to play. 'Are you sure that's all it is, Dovedale?' he asked, smiling faintly as though there was something he knew that Robert didn't. Whatever it was, it pleased him mightily. He looked like Penelope right after a jaunt to a balcony.

'And what would that be to you, Medmenham?'

'That,' said Medmenham lightly, 'remains to be seen.'

'I don't believe that there is anything more for you to see here.'

'Certainly not the play,' Charlotte burst out. 'I don't believe anyone is even making a pretence of watching it.'

Deliberately cutting Robert out of the conversation, Sir Francis smiled intimately at her. 'Why would they? I've seen better acting from the inhabitants of Bedlam.'

It was a rather odd metaphor to pick. It was, Charlotte remembered, Sir Francis who had recommended Dr Simmons to the Prince of Wales. The real Dr Simmons, or the false one?

Charlotte was very aware of Robert's eyes on her as she said, with forced gaiety, 'Do you habitually frequent mad hospitals, Sir Francis?'

'Why would I need to when I can find the same entertainment closer to home?' Sir Francis's gesture encompassed the entirety of their party, saving only Robert, who stood tight-lipped beside them as though unsure whether to intervene.

It might not be so very bad for Robert to have to play chaperone to her and Sir Francis, thought Charlotte, with a pleasure not without malice. Now that they were to be *friends*. It was all for the good of the king, after all, she reminded herself piously.

'As you know,' said Charlotte, batting her eyes at Sir Francis over her fan, 'the taint of madness runs in some of our best families.'

'Some more than others,' contributed Robert flatly, looking straight at Medmenham.

Medmenham acknowledged the point with admirable sangfroid, leaning one elbow on the wrought iron balcony that edged the box. 'Do you refer to my cousin or my aunt?'

It had been Medmenham's aunt, according to Innes, who had employed the services of Dr Simmons. If Medmenham did have an aunt who had run mad, wouldn't that imply that Medmenham had meant to recommend the genuine Dr Simmons? On the other hand, if it was Medmenham who supplied Innes with the story, nothing Medmenham said proved anything at all.

'I believe I may have heard of your aunt . . .' hedged Charlotte.

Medmenham smiled lazily. 'You would be unusual if you hadn't.'

'I haven't,' said Robert tightly.

The others both ignored him. 'And your cousin?' Charlotte asked prettily, more to annoy Robert than anything else.

Medmenham's lips curled with unholy amusement. 'There your esteemed kinsman may have a little more knowledge.

My cousin was a noted eccentric of his day – and he was good enough to leave me his house.'

Robert made an abrupt movement, but Charlotte rushed in first. 'Of course! You mentioned before that you have a very well-known house. Is it anything like Sir Horace Walpole's Strawberry Hill?' she asked, referring to the famous monument to the Gothic style the author of *The Castle of Otranto* had erected.

'It has something of the Gothic to it,' drawled Sir Francis. 'Wouldn't you agree, Dovedale?'

'I would not presume to judge,' Robert said stiffly. 'My knowledge of . . . architecture is limited.'

'But growing,' said Sir Francis genially. 'Under my careful tutelage. I am sure there are many among your friends who would be glad to give a good report to Lady Charlotte of your *architectural* education.'

Robert went as stiff as though Medmenham had threatened rather than complimented him. What *were* they talking about?

Well pleased with the effect of his words, Medmenham turned back to Charlotte. 'Have you ever considered taking up the study of architecture?' he asked caressingly. 'I should think that you would have a taste for the . . . picturesque.'

Something in the way he pronounced the last word made Charlotte squirm in her seat. The trail of innuendo beneath his words made her feel vaguely unclean and more than a little bit indignant.

'I have every admiration for a pretty prospect,' said Charlotte, choosing her words carefully. 'But not all follies appeal to me. Some are too decadent in their design.'

'You shouldn't dismiss them until you have sampled them,'

Sir Francis said condescendingly. 'Although some say one must go to the Continent for a true education, you would be surprised at the number of places of interest buried away in our own English countryside.'

'With Girdings to hand,' said Robert firmly, 'I don't believe Lady Charlotte need look any farther.'

Charlotte had reached the limits of her patience with both of them. While she had no desire to accede to whatever it was that Sir Francis appeared to be offering, she certainly didn't intend to be cloistered at Girdings merely because the man who repented kissing her decreed it so.

'But Girdings is yours, *Cousin* Robert,' she said sweetly. 'I shall have to look elsewhere eventually.'

Let Robert grapple with that one, she thought defiantly. He and Medmenham weren't the only ones who could speak in double entendres.

Sir Francis bowed low over Charlotte's hand. 'A loss to Girdings but a gain to the rest of us. I think you should find Medmenham Abbey greatly enlightening, Lady Charlotte, should you care to honour it with your presence.'

'I am quite sure I should,' she murmured demurely.

'If,' said Robert pointedly, 'your attendance on the queen permits it. Since it has such a dampening effect on your social engagements.'

Charlotte lifted her chin, looking him straight in the eye. 'That depends on the engagement.'

With the conversation no longer centred on him, Sir Francis Medmenham had had quite enough. 'I am afraid,' interjected Medmenham smoothly, 'that we have another engagement this evening. Haven't we, Dovedale?'

Robert twisted abruptly away from Charlotte. 'For my sins,'

he said, and the words seemed to mean something more to Medmenham than to Charlotte, because he laughed as if at a private joke.

'Not just yours,' he said. 'Lady Charlotte.' With a final bow, Medmenham took his leave as carelessly as if nothing out of the ordinary had happened at all. And perhaps it hadn't.

Charlotte looked to Robert. He was frowning, two lines incised into the space between his eyebrows.

'Tomorrow,' he said heavily, and turned on his heel as though he didn't trust himself to say anything more. The click of his heels echoed through Charlotte's ears.

The rest of the party were also taking their leave. Penelope had already been returned to her parents. In the corridor, Charlotte could see Penelope's mother's mouth open in one of her endless reproaches, while Penelope yawned behind a hand that emphasised more than concealed the gesture of disrespect.

'Well!' said Henrietta, coming up beside Charlotte on the balcony. 'I thought I was going to have to intervene before they went for their pistols.'

'I don't think they had pistols,' said Charlotte.

'Chairs, then,' said Henrietta, dismissing the choice of weapon as irrelevant. 'You always did say you wanted men to duel over you.'

'Not with furniture.' Charlotte regarded her best friend with troubled eyes. 'And it would be somewhat more flattering if I were quite sure they were squabbling over me.'

'What else?' asked Henrietta.

Charlotte stared out over the balcony, down over the restless sprinkling of humanity below. The Drury Lane had been waning in popularity ever since the new building had been constructed

326

ten years before; last year, even Mrs Siddons and the Kembles had deserted the theatre for the more hospitable Covent Garden theatre and no number of ingenious spectacles had contrived to recapture the crowds the theatre had once known. The pit was all but deserted.

'I wish I knew,' Charlotte said, watching an orange seller attempt to wheedle a sale from an unresponsive patron. 'It was all very oblique.'

Henrietta's eyes lit up. 'Could it have something to do with the king? If Medmenham was involved in hiring the false doctor . . .'

Charlotte looked up at her in surprise. 'How could it? Robert has nothing to do with any of that.'

'Unless,' said Henrietta dramatically, 'he does. That would explain why he has spent so much time with that lot,' she said excitedly, warming to her own theory. 'What if Dovedale was sent to investigate Medmenham?'

'By whom?' demanded Charlotte. 'And all the way from India? No.'

Fortunately, she was spared further protests by Miles, who loomed up over Henrietta's shoulder like a very large jack-in-the-box. He tapped Henrietta's shoulder.

'Do you mind if I leave you here?' he asked, all in one breath. He belatedly added, by way of explanation, 'Card game.'

Henrietta flapped a hand at him. 'Enjoy,' she said.

Miles hovered for a moment. 'Are you sure?'

Charlotte angled away, trying to afford them a spot of privacy. Leaning over the balcony, she watched the pattern created by the shifting patrons in the pit, marvelling at Henrietta's ridiculous notion about Robert. She might be prepared to believe many fantastical things, but not that

Robert was some sort of – well, some sort of spy. It was too fantastical, even for her. It was true that he was behaving oddly, but there were more than enough explanations for that without bringing in espionage. Henrietta, thought Charlotte complacently, just had espionage on the brain.

It wasn't surprising. Henrietta's brother had for years and years confounded the French under the flowery sobriquet of the Purple Gentian. Charlotte had never had terribly much to do with that part of Henrietta's life. Given the current situation with the king, she rather wished she had. If she had paid more attention to Henrietta's brother's tricks and stratagems, perhaps she would have a better idea of how to go about tracking down the identity and origin of the false Dr Simmons.

Below, in the pit, the unresponsive patron had detached himself from the clinging hands of the orange seller and was beginning to push his way out. Charlotte blinked against the glare of the candles. In profile, he really did look very much like Dr Simmons. Charlotte made a face at herself. She clearly had Dr Simmons on her mind; she was starting to see him everywhere, the way Henrietta saw espionage. Without taking her eyes off the pit, Charlotte appropriated Henrietta's opera glasses. It couldn't hurt just to check.

'Just leave me the carriage,' Henrietta was saying.

Miles beamed at her. 'Done.'

'Hen.' Charlotte tugged on Henrietta's arm, keeping the opera glasses trained on the dark coat of the moving man.

'Hmm?' said Henrietta, blowing a kiss to Miles as he dashed out the back of the box.

'Hen, look,' Charlotte said urgently, pointing her fan down into the pit. 'Down there.'

'Down where?' Henrietta fumbled her opera glasses back from Charlotte.

'The man who just passed the orange seller. Not there. A little more to the right. Do you see? With the bad wig and the lumpy nose?'

'Ye-es.'

'That,' announced Charlotte, 'is the false Dr Simmons.'

Chapter Twenty-One

'It's a very good thing we kept the carriage then, isn't it?' said Henrietta, sweeping up out of her chair and pulling Charlotte along behind her.

'Oh, no,' began Charlotte. 'We can't—'

'It's the perfect opportunity,' said Henrietta firmly, swinging her cloak over her shoulders and hurrying them both along towards the stairs. Charlotte had just time to grab up her own cloak before following. 'We can follow him straight to the people who hired him. My money is still on the Prince of Wales.'

'He might just be going home,' protested Charlotte, catching at her long skirt as they skidded down the stairs.

'That's nearly as good,' said Henrietta. 'If we can find his lodgings, we might be able to find out who he is. And then you can report all to the queen. Do you see him?' she demanded as they paused breathless outside the theatre.

Snow fell in large, light flakes, creating a pattern like lace on the dark blue velvet of Charlotte's opera cloak. It had begun to accumulate on the ground, creating a fine layer of grey mush over the cobblestones, while the horses of waiting carriages lifted their hooves in protest and the waiting chairmen shivered at their posts.

'There,' said Charlotte, pointing towards Russell Street, where a line of sedan chairs waited for customers. 'There he is.'

Beneath an old-fashioned black hat, the man's crimped wool wig rested against his shoulders like two drifts of snow. His chin was tucked away as far as it would go into the folds of a long muffler, and a caped greatcoat obscured his clothes. She might not be able to make out his features, but there was something decidedly smug about his movements as he sauntered through the night. He avoided the line of chairs for hire, stopping at a point slightly beyond them.

'Is that a sedan chair he's getting into?'

Henrietta's head bumped Charlotte's as she leant in for a closer look. 'It doesn't look like a hired one, does it? But the chairmen aren't wearing livery, either. How odd.' By odd, she clearly meant suspicious. 'It's like hiring an unmarked carriage.'

'How will we find yours?' asked Charlotte.

Cravenly, she almost hoped it would take them too long. Then they could just go back to Loring House and a hot fire. Adventure was all very well and good, but it was frigid cold and the slush was seeping through the fragile fabric of her slippers.

There was no such luck. The carriage was waiting for them right near the entrance to the theatre, one of a line of carriages awaiting the end of the play. Henrietta instructed her coachman to follow the sedan chair at the very end of the row.

'I don't expect the doctor will go far,' she said to Charlotte, sinking back against the cushioned seat while Charlotte burrowed under a pile of lap rugs. 'If he meant to go any distance, wouldn't he have called for a carriage rather than a sedan chair?'

'Not necessarily,' said Charlotte. There were still streets in London too narrow for a carriage to pass, places where only a sedan chair would do. They were not neighbourhoods she usually had occasion to visit.

It was too late to back out now, though. Ahead of them, the chairmen had hoisted their burden, choosing their footing carefully on the snow-slick cobbles. The initial flurry had melted into the ground, but a fine dusting of snow was beginning to stick, not enough to create drifts, but just enough to make walking treacherous. It was, as the saying had it, a night fit for neither man nor beast.

Charlotte felt the familiar quiver as the coachman coaxed the horses into movement, sending the carriage swaying on its narrow wheels. The false doctor had hired a linkboy to light his way. As they edged along a discreet distance behind, the small burst of light winked in and out of the snow like a shooting star reflected through an astronomer's lens.

Through the shifting snow, Charlotte spotted the old Savoy Palace on the Strand and briefly recognised her surroundings, but then the sedan chair shifted sharply sideways, down a side street, and Charlotte was lost again. All she knew was that they weren't in Mayfair anymore.

The carriage lumbered deeper and deeper into a tangled warren of streets that seemed to twist and turn in on themselves like the strands of a spider's web. Charlotte had never actually been to a stew or a rookery, but this was how she imagined one must look, with the upper stories of buildings tilting haphazardly over their bottoms. Any closer, and the carriage wouldn't be able to pass. As it was, it was a tight fit.

Charlotte was only glad that the weather had prompted the residents to take refuge indoors, behind bolted shutters. She doubted this was a neighbourhood in which carriages passed often.

'I suppose conspiracies can't very well meet in Mayfair,' she said, catching at the side of the seat as the carriage lurched across a rut.

'I don't see why not. It would be so much more convenient.'

'For us.' Charlotte doubted that this was the conspirators' primary concern. 'What if he means to go somewhere the carriage can't follow?'

Henrietta glanced ruefully at her evening slippers. They were stylish, but not terribly sturdy. 'Then we follow on foot.'

Charlotte looked dubiously out the window. 'What if it's not safe?'

With an air of unnerving competence, Henrietta whipped something out from beneath the seat. 'That's why I keep this in the carriage.'

It was long and metallic and had pretty mother-of-pearl inlay that sparkled in the light of the carriage lamp. Not all the mother-of-pearl in the world, though, could disguise the deadly purpose of the rounded barrel and elegantly curled trigger.

Charlotte instinctively ducked. 'Do you know how to use it?'

'Oh, Richard and Miles taught me ages ago.' Henrietta hefted the firearm with a nonchalance that made Charlotte scoot back against the seat. If she could, she would have crawled into the seat, just for the extra padding. 'Of course, it has been a while, but it should act just as well as a deterrent without our actually having to fire them.'

'Them?' Charlotte didn't like the sound of that.

'For you,' said Henrietta benevolently, pressing the twin of her pistol into Charlotte's hand. 'You point. They run. Don't worry! Yours isn't loaded.'

The butt of the gun felt very cold, even through Charlotte's glove, and surprisingly heavy. The weight of it bent her wrist back at an uncomfortable angle.

'Should that make me worry more, or worry less?' she asked, frowning at her firearm. If one was going to deal in the hideous things, one might at least have the use of it.

'I really did just bring them along as a precaution,' Henrietta hastened to reassure her. 'I don't think we'll have to use them.'

Charlotte regarded the slim piece of steel dubiously. 'I hope you're right.'

Between the decaying buildings, the strong smell of sewage, and the firearm in her hand, this was all beginning to take on just a little too much of the taint of reality. It was all very well to theorise about a bit of ladylike eavesdropping from the comfort of Henrietta's morning room, but it was another thing entirely to find oneself, at dead of night, in a decidedly dodgy bit of London with a pistol dangling from one hand and a smell one didn't like to think too much about battering insistently on the windowpanes. In that, at least, the cold was probably a blessing. Charlotte didn't want to imagine what it would have been like in summer, with people reeling out of tavern doors and the stench of unwashed flesh magnified by the humid air.

This, she realised, was probably what Penelope had meant when she argued that Charlotte was mad to want to go back to the Middle Ages, pointing out that the stench of a midden would undoubtedly outweigh the thrill of a joust. For the first time, Charlotte had an inkling of what Pen had meant. Some things worked far better in imagination than reality. In imagination, she was intrepid and resourceful; in reality, she wished she were home, wrapped in a quilt.

Down a dark and crooked street, the unmarked sedan chair drew to a halt in front of a building where broken shutters had been augmented by the addition of boards of wood hammered over the windows. A wooden sign creaked from a pole above the door, indicating its occupation as an alehouse. On the crudely carved sign, a potbellied ape sank his teeth with obvious enjoyment into an apple whose red paint had long since flaked off, except for a few sanguinary flecks of red adhering to the monkey's teeth. The red flecks gave the ape a decidedly carnivorous air.

Next door, an old church sank into its foundations, as if wearied by the evidence of original sin. Even the stones in the graveyard could not be bothered to stand up straight; they tilted dispiritedly to one side, worn by time and pocked with snow.

The man who emerged from the sedan chair had undergone a transformation of his own. Gone were the cracked buckles on his shoes, the tricorne, the wig. Instead, the king's physician was enveloped in a covering of dark fabric from his ankles all the way up to his hooded head. In one hand, he held an old-fashioned lantern, shuttered on three sides.

In the dark interior of the carriage, Henrietta and Charlotte exchanged a long look. 'This just gets odder and odder,' whispered Henrietta.

'Is that a *cassock*?' whispered back Charlotte. 'Why would he be wearing a cassock?'

'I don't know! Do you think we followed the wrong sedan chair?'

Instead of entering the Ape and the Apple, the hooded figure crunched his way through the dead weeds and bits of cracked crockery that littered the old graveyard. The light of his lantern disappeared with him into the side of the church. There had to be a door there, Charlotte rationalised. The crackle of crockery underfoot had been too crisp for their hooded friend to be anything but corporeal.

'What could he possibly want in there?' demanded Henrietta. 'It is a little late for Evensong.'

Henrietta's lip curled. 'I don't think that church has seen Evensong for quite some time. Just look at it.'

Whatever stained-glass windows the church had possessed had been long since broken, the empty embrasures covered with the same boards used to bolster the drunken shutters of the alehouse on the other side of the graveyard. No light showed through the gaps in the boards. The church lay dark, still, and abandoned, isolated from the surrounding buildings by the scraggly churchyard.

'Do we go in?' whispered Charlotte, contemplating the long and twisty street with disfavour. There didn't seem to be much distinction between street and gutter in this part of the town. Even blurred by snow, the alley was pitted with ruts and strewn with debris. Dark gaps showed between the houses and shops, like slashes in the fabric of the street. They made ideal crevices for footpads to lurk, ready to pounce on unwary ladies from Mayfair.

Looking no more thrilled by the prospect than Charlotte, Henrietta set her jaw bravely. 'If we want to know what he's doing there.'

Charlotte took that as a yes. 'If I go through the front, will you go around the back?'

'That seems to make the most sense,' Henrietta agreed. 'You have your pistol?'

Charlotte lifted it in silent assent, pleased to notice that it didn't wobble any more than one might have expected from its weight. Now that the moment had come, she wasn't displeased to have it. Leaving the carriage around the corner, the two women slid out of the carriage, moving awkwardly on limbs stiff from sitting in the cold. Henrietta slipped on a slushy patch of snow, and Charlotte caught her arm before she could go skidding down into the gutter.

'Just practising,' whispered Henrietta.

Charlotte nodded beneath her hood. 'We'll do better from now on.'

The sign of the Ape and the Apple swayed above her head, the chains creaking like a raven cawing in the night. She could hear movement within the tavern as they passed, laughter muted by the wooden boards and a sour reek she assumed must be ale, but no one flung open the sagging door and demanded to know their business. Perhaps hooded women skulking down the street wasn't quite so unusual as one would expect. Charlotte concentrated on keeping her footing and avoiding the most suspicious-looking protrusions beneath the snow.

The churchyard looked even more derelict up close, the scraggly remains of the summer's weeds crawling over the broken stones. The air whistled sharply through the cracks between the buildings, stirring the sodden weeds and sending broken shutters thumping back and forth. It played auditory tricks, carrying the sounds of voices and laughter from the tavern and swirling them through the churchyard like the faint cackling of malicious spirits.

Imagination, Charlotte assured herself. It was all imagination and the wind. Who would possibly be in a ruin of a church by night? Except for the king's false physician, that was. Charlotte turned her mind from ghostly revels and tried to focus on him instead.

Freeing one arm from her cloak, Charlotte reached out to squeeze Henrietta's hand. 'Are we ready?'

'I'll see you inside.' With an answering squeeze, Henrietta disappeared around the side of the church while Charlotte stepped gingerly onto the broken flagstones leading up to the stone stairs.

The faithful must have walked that same path to Sunday prayer once upon a time, but now the paving stones were little more than pebbles, cracked and broken, and the stone stairs sagged in the middle from the press of generations of feet. Charlotte put her hand carefully to the warped wood of the door and was surprised when it gave with no sound at all. Charlotte had heard tales of miracles of oil, but none involved hinges.

It was darker inside than out. In comparison to the snow-grey sky, the interior of the church pressed down on her like a heavy fall of black cloth, textured with the lingering scents of old incense and damp stone, as though the very air had grown mould. Charlotte groped her way past the door, feeling only rough wall, bare of paintings or statues. In the blackness, space had no meaning; it was a struggle simply to determine the shape of the space around her. The church had been stripped long ago, the only sign of any habitation the looming bulk of the heavy pillars that marched double file down the centre of the nave. Any pews had long since been stolen and broken up for firewood. If there had ever been a confessional, it had gone the same way. Charlotte didn't like to think where the baptismal font must have got to.

It was dark, but not silent. All around her, Charlotte

could hear the distant rumble of voices, low voices, masculine voices, talking all at once, the peculiar acoustics of the vaulted ceiling projecting and echoing the sounds like a song sung in round.

Charlotte started nervously as the first clamorous stroke of a bell reverberated stridently through the nave. The sound was almost palpable in the darkness; it seemed to be swinging straight towards her. Again it tolled and again, the noise filling the blackness, making Charlotte's head ring even as her nose twitched with the scent of incense, which appeared, inexplicably, to have grown stronger. At nine strokes, Charlotte expected the bell to stop ringing, but it kept on, battering against the walls of the church, marking something more than the hour. It rang out a thirteenth peal before finally echoing into unnerving silence. A superstitious shiver ran down Charlotte's spine.

There was no time to dwell on ghost stories. Before the final peal had ceased to ring, a door burst open in a flare of light. Through the incandescent gap processed a shadowy line of dark-robed men.

For an insane moment, Charlotte wondered if she had stumbled through a gap in time, falling backwards into a London of long ago, well before King Henry's Reformation, when skirted friars held their ceremonies in chapels lit by sputtering candlelight. But there were no vespers being sung by this congregation, no holy chants. Instead, Charlotte could hear the low mutter of decidedly modern conversation, scented by a strong tang of spirituous liquor below the pervasive reek of scented smoke. There was nothing insubstantial about these phantoms. Their feet shuffled and their robes scratched and their breath misted in the air.

Charlotte pressed as close as she could to the nearest pillar, moulding herself to it as though she could become a part of it. Thank goodness her evening cloak was a dark colour! Hopefully, if anyone looked her way, they would just think it was a particularly lumpy pillar. Charlotte drew as much comfort as she could from that thought.

Along the length of the nave, the friars had drawn themselves into double ranks. Even in the poor light, Charlotte could see that their costume was careless at best. Polished black boots protruded beneath some robes and bare feet from others. Only one or two had elected the roped sandals of their pretended order. Now, as one, they turned their hooded heads towards the glowing door.

The light lurched forward like a living pillar of flame. Charlotte ducked behind her pillar. Not a living flame, Charlotte realised, carefully peering from behind her pillar, but a living man carrying a torch nearly as tall as he was, with a centre twice as wide as the head of a man. It made him look as though he were wearing a fiery headdress rather than the same monastic attire as all the others.

Striding to the centre of the long line of friars, he thumped the base of his torch twice against the flagged floor, sending the flames waving through the air like pagan dancers.

Holding the torch in two hands, he raised it high above his head, his long sleeves falling back from a pair of elegant wrists, circled in barbaric gold bracelets that appeared to twist up and up and up, ending near the elbow in stylised elephant heads.

'Welcome, my brimstone brethren!' he roared, and the congregation roared back, an earthy sound that resounded through the arched ceiling and made Charlotte's cold limbs tremble. 'Well met by moonlight!'

Charlotte's fingers tightened on the fluted stone of the pillar. She knew that voice. Charlotte had an excellent memory for voices. She had always thought it must be nature's way of compensating for making her so very bad at recognising faces. It was a voice more suited to Almack's than to pagan ceremony. And it had been whispering innuendos into her ear only hours before.

'I don't see a moon, do you?' someone called out. Lord Henry Innes! That was quite definitely Lord Henry.

'You want a moon, I'll show you a moon!' someone else rejoined, in slurred tones that suggested he had supped on more than moonlight. Bending over, he mimed what was obviously meant to be a vulgar gesture.

'Gentlemen! Gentlemen!' the master of ceremonies admonished, and this time there was absolutely no doubt as to who it was. 'Would you defile the court of the elephant god?'

Elephant god? Charlotte felt as though she'd taken that tumble Robert had prophesied, right off her horse onto the hard winter ground in Hyde Park. Her chest felt very tight, as though all the breath had been knocked out of her, and her lungs refused to function properly. Nothing made the least bit of sense.

That was Sir Francis Medmenham. Sir Francis Medmenham and Lord Henry and the false doctor and goodness only knew who else. Charlotte froze behind her pillar, as still as a stone saint. They mustn't find her here. The scandal surrounding Penelope's betrothal would be as nothing to this. Whatever her defiant words to Robert, Charlotte had no desire to find herself the brimstone bride of Sir Francis Medmenham. With the torch in front of him, his face seemed made of flame, more demon than man.

Feeling her way back towards the wall, moving as softly as she could, Charlotte began inching towards the door. If she could just keep her back to the wall and silently slip out while they were all occupied with Sir Francis . . .

Charlotte bumped backwards into the wall, giving silent thanks for the shadows cast by the pillars and the general dark decrepitude of her surroundings. Just a few yards to the left and she would be safe. All she had to do was find the doorknob, turn it, and dart into the night. And then she was never going to do anything like this ever, ever, ever again. No matter what Henrietta or anyone else said. Adventure was for heroines, and Robert had proved quite conclusively that she wasn't one.

In the centre of the room, Sir Francis raised his torch high again, sending the light scorching across the upturned faces of his comrades, across the blunt features of Lord Henry and the cleancut good looks of Lord Freddy Staines. Heavens, thought Charlotte, what would Penelope have to say about that? Did she know? Would she even care?

With profound relief, Charlotte felt the change that signalled the shift from plaster to wood, from wall to door. Her hand jammed into something hard and rounded. The knob! It was all she could do not to sob in gratitude. She didn't even begrudge the broken fingernail.

Her arm fully extended at an awkward angle, Charlotte folded her fingers carefully around the heavy bulk of the knob. One twist, that was all that was needed, one twist and then a mad dash to freedom.

Halfway down the nave, Sir Francis was entertaining his congregation, keeping their attention focused mercifully on him rather than her. 'Gentlemen! I give you . . . the sacred flame!'

It was the perfect time to flee. With her breath burning in her lungs, she sprang for the door, giving the knob a brutal twist just as light exploded through the room.

Fireworks cartwheeled through the air, streaking it with ribbons of flame, catching Charlotte in their glare as sure as a fox in a snare.

Chapter Twenty-Two

Bacchanalian orgies had never been intended for a cold climate.

Outside, the snow still fell. Instead of casting a purifying veil over the scene, it turned to slush as it touched the tainted ground. Robert considered it an appropriate indictment on their activities, yet more proof that one couldn't touch pitch without being defiled.

Inside, the illustrious members of the Order of the Lotus were stripping off in preparation for their latest orgy. It was not an inspiring sight. From the variety of physiques revealed, not everyone spent his days boxing with Gentleman Jackson. While more than adequate for one vicar, the former vestry of the Church of St Ethelred the Unsteady was decidedly inadequate for twenty grown men, most of whom were incapable of finding the fastenings of their own trousers without the aid of a valet. There was much hopping on one foot, flailing of arms, and airing of language that turned the consecrated air blue.

Unfortunately, the close quarters worked against him rather than for him. It was nearly impossible to pick out one voice in the cacophony of the whole and even harder to identify a set of familiar features beneath the close-draped hoods. A dozen colognes clashed for precedence, along with the ghost of ancient incense, masking any one scent. If Wrothan was there, he hadn't yet done anything to betray his presence. He might, Robert concluded, be the elephant god, which would explain why he hadn't yet put in an appearance. Or he might simply have had the good sense to keep his mouth closed and his head down. It was impossible to tell.

A particularly hearty elbow whapped into Robert's ribs. This elbow, however, had been an intentional elbow.

'Looking forward to the evening, eh?' beamed Lord Henry Innes.

Robert managed to duck out of the way just in time to avoid a brotherly whack on the back. For whatever reason, Lord Henry still appeared to consider himself a sort of de facto godfather to the group's newest member. A devil father? Robert was unclear on the appropriate nomenclature. The society seemed to veer between Satanism and paganism with no clear creed from either.

Despite the pretence of anonymity, Lord Henry's hood was thrown carelessly back. Like Lord Henry, many of the members appeared to have no qualms about their identity being known; they called one another frankly by name and chatted openly about this ball or that rout and whether the next satanic celebration could be scheduled so as not to conflict with someone's sister's come out. 'I expect you all to dance with her!' bleated the fond brother. 'Or m'mother will have my head!'

There were, however, a handful of members who hung back from the general conviviality, staying close to the corners of the room, their dark robes like blots against the rough whitewash of the walls.

Robert poked Lord Henry in the arm and nodded towards the wall. 'I don't believe I've been introduced to that lot.'

Lord Henry shrugged with every appearance of unconcern. 'Introductions ain't quite the thing here, you know. Air of mystery and whatnot.'

'But what if' – Robert lowered his voice conspiratorially – 'an intruder were to slip into our midst and spy on our revels? It would be deuced hard to tell in these robes, now, wouldn't it?'

Lord Henry's brow wrinkled. 'Intruder? Can't say the problem's ever occurred, has it, Medmenham?'

Damn. Damn, damn, damn. The last thing Robert wanted was Medmenham involved in the discussion. It was too late now, though.

Medmenham smiled lazily. His teeth looked unnaturally white against the dark frame of his hood. Although he had kept his hood up, there was no mistaking who he was. The barbaric bracelets affixed to his arms proclaimed his identity as surely as any sigil. 'Afraid of exposure, Dovedale?'

'If I were, would I be wearing this?' Robert gestured irritably to his robe. No need for them to know that he was still wearing his evening kit beneath it. Given the temperature of the stone floor, he wasn't the only one to have kept his shoes on. Those brave few who had gone barefoot looked decidedly uncomfortable. 'I am, however, still a stranger to society. I wasn't sure . . .'

'How our activities would be received?' The concept appeared to amuse Medmenham mightily. 'My dear fellow, the days when one might be banished from court for one's naughty behaviour is long since past. These days, there's scarce a court to be banished from.'

'Deuced dull at court,' Lord Henry agreed. 'No scandal, no intrigue, and not a woman worth seducing.'

'Not one?' Medmenham raised a brow at Robert.

Robert clamped down on his temper. 'Don't tell me you mean to promote the charms of Lady Pembroke,' he drawled. 'You may have to fight the king for her, though.'

The mention of the queen's ageing lady-in-waiting had the desired effect. The king's recurrent sexual fantasies about the determinedly virtuous sixty-seven-year-old had everyone deeply baffled.

Medmenham laughed with genuine humour. 'She certainly appears to have an aphrodisiac effect on His Majesty. I, however, fail to see the appeal. We shall find far better entertainment here tonight, I promise you.'

Robert craned his neck in a pretence of eagerness. 'Where is this, er, entertainment?'

Medmenham's lips curved in a slow, satisfied smile. This was his drug, the ability to manipulate his peers with the promise of pleasure, rewarding with access, punishing by withholding. 'Not so hasty, Dovedale. As anyone will tell you, *entertainment* is best savoured slowly.'

'It's hard to savour what isn't here,' riposted Robert. If Medmenham had his dancing girls stashed away elsewhere, what else did he have hidden?

'All in good time.'

'Is it time to start yet?' Innes bounced on his heels like a dog waiting for his master to throw a stick.

Medmenham cast a practised eye around the room. The majority of the members had managed to make their way into their robes and were beginning to make inroads on the flasks concealed on their persons.

Cassocks, Robert had learnt, afforded excellent hiding places for a multiplicity of items, including pistols and knives or, in Medmenham's case, a small silver bell of the sort one might use to summon a servant. Raising it, Medmenham jingled it in a prearranged signal.

Far above them, in the bell tower, a deep tolling answered the soprano call of Medmenham's bell.

In the Robing Room, the members, like greyhounds at the slip, began jostling into place, attempting to form the two straight lines in which they would process into the chapel. Even the antisocial souls propped against the wall abandoned their secluded havens to join in the general throng.

Robert focused his gaze on the men who had kept to themselves during the robing. If he hadn't, he would never have seen the signal, the barely perceptible tilt of the head that summoned one of the hooded figures to meet another at the very end of the line. In that brief moment, as the man's hood slipped ever so slightly, Robert saw all he needed to see. That was Wrothan on the left side of the room, perched by a pile of mouldering Books of Common Prayer. Robert recognised the bump on the nose, a bump that Wrothan had always claimed was the result of ambush by the Mahratta but that Robert was more inclined to ascribe to a barroom brawl in the days before Wrothan had developed his pretensions to gentility and his following among the younger and more corruptible members of the aristocracy.

Wrothan's contact was more adept. He moved smoothly into line with no betraying movement of any kind, his face perfectly hidden by the fall of his hood.

Robert wriggled himself into the line directly in front of them. Sound, after all, travelled forwards, and there was nothing to be gained by a view of the backs of their hoods. He exchanged terse nods with his partner in the line, whom he recognised as Miss Penelope Deveraux's affianced. Lord Frederick Staines's upcoming nuptials appeared to have had no visible effect on his extracurricular activities. Robert just hoped Tommy hadn't spotted him.

With an unhurried movement, Lord Freddy adjusted his hood over his gleaming hair, easing his features into shadow. Robert twitched his own hood back the other way. Not enough to attract notice, but just enough to free his ears from the heavy fabric.

Between one stroke of the bell and the next, he heard one of the men behind him murmur, 'I have your price.'

Between the reverberation of the bell and clomp and shuffle of two dozen variously shod male feet, the words were all but indistinguishable. The conspirators had chosen their moment well.

'Oh, no,' countered Wrothan, a little too loudly. Robert recognised the tone of his voice. He had heard it before, in the officers' mess, when Wrothan knew himself to hold a winning hand. Wrothan's whisper was shrill with repressed excitement. 'I don't believe you do.'

The Frenchman spoke sternly. He was, it was clear, not accustomed to being disobeyed. Unlike Wrothan, his pitch was perfect; although Robert stood directly ahead of him, he had to strain to hear. 'The price will be what we agreed.'

Ahead of them, the door to the nave had been thrown open. The first row of false monks processed in two by two. 'I don't think so. Not if the prize is no longer in the palace. The game has changed, monsieur. I hold all the cards. Or, should I say, *the* card?'

'Very amusing, sir.' The Frenchman sounded anything but amused.

Wrothan, on the other hand, was enjoying himself immensely. 'I couldn't be more serious.'

The Frenchman's voice was sharp as a well-honed blade. 'You mean to say that you have—'

'*Yes.*'

Have *what*? Robert wanted to shout. What had Wrothan filched from the palace? State papers seemed the most obvious answer. Secrets of the sort that could be sold for a high price. Unless, of course, the Frenchman was not working for his government at all. In that case, the prize could be nearly anything. The queen's diamonds alone could keep a man in frog legs for quite some time.

'How do I know that this card is not a mere jack?'

'Would I bluff?'

'If you thought you could – yes.'

'Well, I'm not.' Robert, for one, was inclined to believe him. Wrothan positively buzzed with self-satisfaction. 'This time, I have the king in my hand.'

Behind them, the bell tolled for a tenth time. On cue, Robert and his partner stepped through the arched door into the church, nearly missing the Frenchman's terse whisper. 'Where?'

The bell tolled again. Eleven.

'That,' said Wrothan smugly, 'would be telling. You pay, I tell.'

The twelfth peal rang. 'I see.'

There was something in the Frenchman's voice that suggested he saw altogether more than Wrothan might like, but Wrothan, flying high on his moment of triumph, was immune to nuance. 'I thought you would see it my way.'

'How much?'

'What is a king's ransom these days?'

The thirteenth peal shuddered through the chamber. They had nearly reached the point where the pairs divided, filing down opposite sides of the nave to form an honour guard for the high priest of the elephant god. 'Shall we discuss this – outside?'

Wrothan must have made some gesture of assent. 'During the fireworks. There's a side door in the nave, on the left.'

The Frenchman's voice was heavy with irony. 'I see you have left no detail to chance.'

'I pride myself on my planning.'

'You must indeed be . . . very proud.'

The Frenchman wheeled to one side, Wrothan to the other. Robert followed along behind the Frenchman, to the right side of the chapel. If he were Wrothan, he would be more worried than proud. The Frenchman's initial alarm had quickly faded to something else.

He had been, at the end, nearly as smug as Wrothan. The Frenchman clearly had another card up his sleeve. Robert was exceedingly glad that Tommy and their War Office agent were standing guard outside.

Impatiently, he waited behind the Frenchman as Medmenham strode to the centre of the room, torch held high. He was eager to have it all done with already. In a matter of minutes, Wrothan and his accomplice would be caught red-handed, dealing in whatever they were dealing in in plain sight of an agent of the War Office. With three against two, there shouldn't be any difficulty subduing them and hauling them back to Crown Street for questioning.

Three friars down, Henry Innes made some sort of bawdy

comment. Robert's lips tightened with impatience. Why didn't they just get on with it?

Once Wrothan was in custody, his debt to the colonel would be done. Only a month ago, the possibility of his quest coming to an end had left him with a hollow sensation, like falling off the end of the earth. Now he craved that resolution. Once this night was done, he need never wear a cassock again. He could break with Medmenham and his whole gruesome crew. He could try to make things right with Charlotte.

That, he knew, was the root and stem of all his impatience, not the burning desire to avenge the colonel, but the need to see this all done so he could make his amends to Charlotte. The future wasn't a desert anymore, or an endless sea fraught with serpents; it was a garden to be tended, a pleasant place away from the rest of the world, with unicorns to be courted and flowers to be plucked. It was Girdings and Charlotte and everything from which he had been running all these years.

If she would have him, that was. After the events of the past few weeks, that was by no means a foregone conclusion.

In the centre of the nave, Medmenham raised his torch high, angling it towards a deep bowl that had been hung where a chandelier must have been, long, long ago. His sleeves fell back from his arms, revealing two red-eyed elephants, whose trunks twined down his forearms.

'Gentlemen!' he called out. It was, Robert thought, a singularly inappropriate term under the circumstances. 'I give you . . . the sacred flame!'

Across the aisle, Wrothan inclined his head in a barely perceptible nod. Next to him, the Frenchman nodded back.

As fireworks shot into the air, cartwheeling through the high, arched ceiling, the swish of a monk on the move was barely perceptible through the crackle of the fireworks and the catcalls of the members. Robert automatically cast a quick glance around as he prepared to follow, and nearly tripped over his own habit as he saw what the explosion of light had illuminated. One by one, the babbling voices fell into silence as the hooded body of men stared, as one, at one small girl huddled at the far end of the nave, clutching at the door handle with one gloved hand.

Robert's triumph turned to ashes in his mouth. It wasn't just any girl. It was Charlotte. Even in a shapeless dark cloak, with a hood shading her face, he knew her. He would have known her anywhere.

Had she followed them? Guilt rose, acrid and viscous, in Robert's throat. If he had brought her to this, however unintentionally . . .

'My, my,' drawled the amused voice of Sir Francis as the last of the rockets exploded, unleashing a shower of sparks that made Charlotte shrink back against the door. 'The great elephant god is nothing if not quick with his rewards!'

Beneath the raucous laughter Robert could hear a pitiful squeaking sound. It was the leather of Charlotte's glove, scraping against the doorknob as she struggled to get it to turn. Abandoning all subtlety, she turned her back on the company and used both hands to tug at the knob. It was no use. The door was stuck. And so was she.

From the left side of the church came a decided click as the door to the churchyard swung shut behind Wrothan and his companion, prepared to implicate themselves in all manner of dastardly plans. It was the moment Robert had been waiting for since the colonel's death, the culmination of months of painstaking plotting and tracking. He had dreamt of this moment during the long voyage from India to England; the prospect of it had kept him warm against the biting winds of the endless ride to Girdings. His revenge was finally at hand.

Robert didn't have to think twice.

He sprinted forwards, grabbing Charlotte around the waist and hoisting her up over his shoulder so that all his fellow friars could see were a pair of rapidly kicking legs in silk stockings. Let Tommy and the War Office man deal with Wrothan.

'Mmmrph!' bleated Charlotte into his back.

He decided to take that as 'Thanks, awfully, for saving me' rather than 'Put me down right now!'

'Sorry, my fault!' Robert announced, making sure to keep any bit of Charlotte that might be the least bit recognisable between his back and the wall. Since there was only one bit of Charlotte that anyone in the room ought to recognise, that was simple enough. 'This one's mine. I forgot to tell her to go round the back.'

He could tell the exact moment she recognised his voice. Her hands stopped clawing at his back and her legs ceased their kicking. In that one moment, she went entirely rigid, with a stiffness born of shock.

A sucking sense of despair settled somewhere in Robert's middle, like low-lying fog. The game was up. There would be no making it up to her now, no explanations that would suffice. How could she not despise him after seeing this? It would have been one thing to tell her about his recent activities – with suitable ameliorations – quite another for her to have seen it with her own eyes. He had always known the gods were cruel. He had just never realised quite how cruel.

The only slight saving grace was that Medmenham looked even worse than he. It was scant comfort.

'No fair hogging her!' one of his brethren called out in

354

raucous tones. 'Share and share alike, that's our motto!'

Robert could have sworn that their motto was 'only the best for our orgies,' but a low rumble of assent greeted the man's statement.

'I say, pass 'er over!' shouted out Lord Henry, losing his aspirates in his enthusiasm for female flesh. 'Looks like a ripe 'un.'

'Ripe but not ready,' parried Robert, miming a hearty pat to Charlotte's backside. In for a penny, in for a pound, after all. Her gasp of indignation was lost somewhere in the folds of his cassock. 'Can't you see she isn't properly costumed? Besides, we can't have the girls before the ceremony. The god wouldn't like it. And if the god doesn't like it . . .'

Charlotte hung heavy over his shoulder, so still, she seemed to be scarcely breathing. He could feel her listening with every fibre in her body, listening as though her life depended on it. Didn't she even trust him to get her safely out?

But, then, why should she? Robert asked himself with brutal honesty. His record so far hadn't exactly been one of spotless knight errantry. The truth of it stung like sharpened steel thrust straight through the vitals.

'I'll just go deposit her in the back, shall I?' Robert suggested. He didn't wait for anyone to propose an alternate plan. Instead, he lurched towards the door to the vestry as fast as he could go, with Charlotte jouncing against his back with every step, twisting her out of the reach of an inebriated monk who made a grab for her temptingly displayed posterior.

'No sampling the goods early!' he snapped.

'Someone needs to teach you to share,' pronounced Medmenham provocatively, hefting his torch.

'Would you share?' demanded Robert with deliberate

insolence. With the resultant burst of laughter as a shield, he slipped through the door to the vestry, clipping one of Charlotte's shoes against the door frame in the process. Charlotte made an irritated choking sound.

Fighting for balance, Robert kicked the door shut behind them. It wouldn't stymie pursuit, but it might slow it.

Charlotte immediately began to indicate that she wished to be set down.

'Not. Now,' Robert gritted out, tightening his hold on the backs of her legs. 'Do you want them to have you?'

With any luck, the members of the society would be too eager for the promised pleasure of their magical elixir and multitalented dancing girls to care to pursue, but he wouldn't feel properly safe until there was a good mile between Charlotte and the brethren. Make that two miles, he amended.

Through the thick wooden door the chanting was beginning, calling for the elephant god. Medmenham must have used the torch to light the braziers. Scented smoke began to seep beneath the door frame, making Robert's stomach heave in memory.

Maybe it wasn't just the smoke making his stomach heave. Robert kicked open the door on the side of the vestry, taking out some of his anger on the unsuspecting planks. This was *not* how this was supposed to have gone. What in all the blazes was Charlotte doing barging into the Hellfire Club? Serpentlike, he could hear Medmenham's voice urging Charlotte to improve her acquaintance with 'architecture.'

Bending forwards from the waist, Robert eased Charlotte to the ground, trying to keep her from tumbling over into the mud of the churchyard.

Charlotte stumbled as she landed, swaying in place as she

tried to get her bearings. One hand lifted to her head while the other came to rest against the church wall. Lowering her head, she took a deep breath, then another, sucking in the cool, damp air.

'Are you all right?' he demanded in a rough whisper, grasping her by the arms. He resisted the urge to examine her for broken bones, an absurd notion. Any bruises were undoubtedly internal rather than otherwise.

Charlotte ducked her head, still fighting for breath. 'Fine,' she wheezed, and then came the question he had been dreading. 'What was—'

'You shouldn't be here,' he said quickly, knowing he could only delay, not avoid. 'We need to get you away. Before they come after us.'

How was he even to get her away? He had come with Medmenham, in Medmenham's carriage, which was now the devil only knew where.

'What in the blazes are you doing here?' he demanded belatedly. His hands tightened on her arms. 'Did Medmenham invite you?'

'No! I hadn't known he would be here. Or you. Or even where here is.' Charlotte blinked a few times, as though she were still having trouble focusing. 'What are *you* doing here?'

He hardly remembered. 'I'll tell you the whole story,' he promised. 'Later. After we get you home. This is no place for a lady.'

'But—' began Charlotte.

'Did you come in a carriage? A sedan chair? This is no neighbourhood to walk about in.'

It was already too late. A crunching in the underbrush alerted him to the fact that they were no longer alone.

Whirling around to face off French spies, treacherous Englishmen, and drunken monks of any nationality, Robert found himself facing a medium-size female in an expensive silk cloak lined with swansdown.

'Um, Charlotte? Oh, hello, Dovedale.' Lady Henrietta Dorrington flashed him a winning smile while Robert attempted to realign his jaw with the rest of his face. 'I do hate to interrupt, but there is something you ought to see.'

Charlotte had brought a *friend*? Robert bypassed guilt and went straight to anger.

'Does either of you realise that this is not Almack's Assembly Rooms?' Robert gritted out.

'Of course,' said Charlotte, as if Robert were the one being silly. 'There's no ratafia.'

Robert found himself entirely incapable of speech.

Now he understood why their early ancestors had expressed themselves entirely in grunts. No other noise could quite encapsulate his current level of shock, anger, and general disbelief. Anger surged to the fore, trumping shock, when Charlotte, seemingly oblivious to the fact that he had just rescued her from the proverbial fate worse than death, blithely turned to her friend, dismissing him entirely.

'Did you find the doctor?' Charlotte asked eagerly. The who?

'I'm afraid so.' Lady Henrietta's face was as grim as it could get. Swinging her lantern, she gestured, not towards the street but towards the back of the church, where pitted gravestones clustered close together in the lee of the drooping eaves. 'Follow me.'

With mud slurping around his boots, Robert followed. His only other choice was to fling Charlotte back over his shoulder and bear her bodily forth into the street. It was an attractive option, but not one that Charlotte was likely to approve.

Did it matter what she approved anymore?

'Who,' Robert demanded tersely, 'is the doctor?'

'This is,' said Lady Henrietta soberly, pointing to the gap between two tombstones. She lifted the shutter of her lantern, and what Robert had perceived as merely a fallen log took on a hideous resolution.

'Or, rather, this was,' she amended.

A man sprawled between the tombstones. Like Robert, he wore the simple brown wool cassock of the Order of St Francis, tied at the waist with the regulation leather belt, tipped with twin prongs of metal. A pair of old-fashioned buckled shoes protruded from beneath his robe, any gems that had been set into the buckle long since prized out of their frames. His hood had fallen back from his head, revealing close-cropped dark hair and a face too thin for fashion.

The light of Lady Henrietta's lantern reflected off the glistening surface of his eyes. For a moment, Robert expected him to speak, to lever himself up, to make a dash across the tombstones, through the churchyard. But the eyes were fixed, open, unmoving. It was only the treacherous lamplight that gave the illusion of life to eyes that would never blink again.

Someone had beaten Robert to his revenge.

Chapter Twenty-Three

'**G**ood heavens,' Charlotte whispered. 'It's Dr Simmons.'

Henrietta took a step back, leaving room for the other two to get a better view. 'I'm afraid I . . . well, I stepped on him. Not that it can hurt him now.'

Nothing was ever going to hurt him again. Blood mingled with the slush and mud, creating an unpleasant musky smell that made Charlotte's stomach churn, overlaid with the faint, delicate scent of a foreign flower. The incongruity made Charlotte's stomach churn. Catching on to a tombstone for balance, she backed away, shutting her own eyes to block out that fixed and glittering stare. The dead features were frozen in an eternal gloat.

'At least he died happy,' said Charlotte faintly, doing her best to cultivate an expression of sangfroid and failing miserably. Dead bodies weren't something she generally encountered.

Robert swung towards Henrietta. 'Did you see who did this?' he asked sharply.

Henrietta shook her head. 'I heard a thud—' she began,

when two men pounded around the side of the tavern.

'Hullo!' The larger of the two waved a hand in the air as he vaulted – quite unnecessarily – over a tombstone to land within a yard of the doctor's body.

'I see you've found him,' Miles gasped, resting his hands on his thighs and bending over to catch his breath. 'We chased the chap who did it, but – Hen?'

'*Miles?*' Recovering first, Henrietta clamped her hands on her hips. 'I thought you had a card game!'

Miles was the picture of outraged dignity, marred only slightly by a patch of mud on his cheek. 'I thought you were still at the theatre!'

Charlotte hastily interjected herself between the two. 'This is a sort of performance,' she said soothingly. 'Like a masque.'

'Looks more like a farce to me,' commented Lieutenant Fluellen sagely, earning a glower from his best friend.

'What in the – er, what are you doing here?' Robert demanded, turning his glower on Charlotte instead.

'What he said,' Miles seconded, looping an arm firmly around his wife's waist before she could get away again. 'Including what he didn't say.'

Charlotte cocked her head at Miles. 'What he didn't say?'

She tried not to notice the way that Henrietta leant against Miles, her head fitting comfortably into the crook of his shoulder. Even while ostensibly arguing, they still gravitated together. It would be so lovely to be able to lean against someone like that, with all the unspoken support it implied. Not to mention the warmth. Out of the corner of her eye she could see Robert standing next to her, near enough that the hem of his cassock brushed against the side of her pelisse. He radiated heat, too, but it was all of the wrong kind. Tension and irritation rolled off him in palpable waves. Charlotte felt her own shoulders stiffen in reaction.

'Never mind that,' said Robert brusquely. 'Why are you here?'

'We were following the king's doctor,' Charlotte explained defiantly.

'The king's who?' Miles demanded of his wife.

'You first,' Henrietta said. 'You still haven't told us why you're here.'

'Are we really going to have this conversation here?' Grimacing, Lieutenant Fluellen waved a gloved hand at the doctor's crumpled form.

'Well, we don't need to worry about him eavesdropping,' said Miles cheerfully, earning a poke in the ribs from his wife. 'Ouch!'

Lifting an eyebrow at Miles, Robert took charge before further horseplay could ensue. 'Perhaps we should search him,' he suggested. Coming from Robert, the suggestion had the force of a command.

'Jolly good idea!' Miles hunkered down next to the body like a dog with a particularly juicy bone. 'I say, do cassocks have pockets?'

'Sometimes,' said Robert, patting down the area around the wound. 'If the owner bothered to have them put in.'

'Unless the other chappie relieved him of any burdens before sticking him.' Lieutenant Fluellen crouched down beside them, inspecting the dead man's shoes for concealed hidey-holes.

Charlotte hastily stepped back to give them more room. Next to her, Henrietta stood on her tiptoes, craning her neck to try to see over the men's bent backs.

'He had no time,' said Robert tersely. 'Unless he lifted

something off Wrothan in the Robing Room beforehand.'

'Wrothan?' asked Charlotte, head swimming in a flurry of masculine pronouns. The gentlemen all seemed to understand one another perfectly, but she had no idea who was meant to have stabbed whom.

'The dead one,' supplied Miles helpfully.

'You mean Dr Simmons,' corrected Henrietta.

'Unless,' said Charlotte, 'Mr Wrothan is Dr Simmons.'

Robert pushed himself to his feet, scrubbing his hands against his robe with a compulsive gesture that reminded Charlotte of Lady Macbeth. The movement only smeared the blood rather than removing it, giving him, in his medieval cassock, the appearance of something out of a novel by Mrs Radcliffe.

'Dr who?' he demanded.

Lieutenant Fluellen lifted a restraining hand. His were streaked, too, but with mud rather than blood. 'May I suggest we exchange stories somewhere more hospitable? By a fire, perhaps?'

'Oh, yes, please!' said Henrietta. 'We have a carriage waiting at the end of the road.'

Miles staggered to his feet. '*Our* carriage?'

Charlotte glanced over her shoulder at the figure lying between the tombstones, nothing more than a shadow among shadows, shrouded in dirty snow. 'But, surely,' she said uncertainly, 'we can't just leave him like this.'

Taking possession of Charlotte's arm, Robert marched her briskly forwards. 'Why not?' he said, and his voice was as cold as the slush seeping through Charlotte's slippers. 'It's no more than he has done to others.'

Numb with cold and confusion, Charlotte darted a glance up

at him. 'What—' she began, but Lieutenant Fluellen intervened as smoothly as though it had been planned, saying soothingly, 'He's on consecrated ground, at least.'

As though to underline his point, incense seeped through the gaps in the boards on the church windows, redolent of ancient mysteries.

There was something oddly familiar about the smell of the smoke coming from the church. Frankincense? It did smell a bit like incense, but there was a sickly sweetness beneath the exotic herbs that was nothing like the smell of Sunday mornings.

'Wait.' Charlotte tugged against Robert's arm. 'I've smelt that smoke before.'

Robert stretched an arm across her back, marching her forwards. There was nothing the least bit personal about the touch. His arm felt like an iron bar across her back. 'I sincerely doubt it.'

'On the king,' Charlotte clarified, scurrying to keep up with him and trying to sniff the air at the same time.

'You can hardly mean to suggest that the king is an opium eater,' Robert said shortly, picking up his pace.

'Is that what that was?'

'Part of it.' Robert hoisted her into the carriage so energetically that Charlotte went careening straight to the far side of the seat. 'I suspect there's some belladonna in there, too.'

Charlotte sank back into her nest of lap rugs, which were, alas, now as cold as she was. 'That would explain so much.'

'What would?' asked Lieutenant Fluellen, settling down across from her. Henrietta climbed in after him, with Miles attached to her other side like a very large cushion.

'Opium,' provided Charlotte as Robert took the only

remaining seat, the one next to her. She wondered if Henrietta had done that by design, but there was no way of asking. 'It seems that's what I smelt on the king the other day.'

'You think the king is smoking opium?' said Lieutenant Fluellen curiously. 'I find that hard to imagine.'

'Not of his own accord,' explained Charlotte. 'I believe Dr Simmons gave it to him.'

Robert looked to Henrietta rather than Charlotte. 'Let's start at the beginning, shall we? Who is Dr Simmons?'

Charlotte and Henrietta exchanged a long look.

'That's what we've been trying to find out,' explained Henrietta. 'A man calling himself Dr Simmons has been treating the king for, er—'

'A return of his old complaint,' Charlotte put in.

'You mean he's gone around the bend,' translated Miles. 'Again.'

'Something like that,' agreed his wife, snuggling into the crook of his arm. 'The queen asked Charlotte to have a word with Dr Simmons about the king's condition, so we both went to seek him out. That's how we discovered that Dr Simmons wasn't Dr Simmons.'

'You're saying there's a real Dr Simmons?' Miles tried to look down at Henrietta and went cross-eyed.

'Yes. And he wasn't the man lying in that churchyard.' Henrietta shuddered, partly for dramatic effect, partly from cold. Miles gave her a comforting squeeze.

Charlotte wouldn't have minded a comforting squeeze, but there didn't seem much chance of one, not even of the cousinly sort. Robert maintained a grasp on the side of her pelisse much as a parent might hold on to a small child. It was about as comforting as cod-liver oil.

Lieutenant Fluellen, who was, Charlotte had always maintained, a Very Nice Man, leant forwards to pat her hand. 'Not a pleasant sight, was he?' he said sympathetically.

'The man you knew as Dr Simmons was in reality Mr Arthur Wrothan,' Robert blurted out so loudly that Charlotte's ears rang with it.

'He's the chap we were pursuing,' put in Lieutenant Fluellen helpfully, smiling beatifically at Robert over her head. He clearly had found something terribly amusing. Whatever it was, Robert didn't share the joke. He had gone as stiff and cold as an iceberg. A very icy iceberg.

'But who was he? Aside from impersonating Dr Simmons, that is.' Lady Henrietta tilted her head up at her husband. 'And how did you get involved?'

'War Office,' Miles declared proudly.

Henrietta wrinkled her nose. 'They've let you loose again?'

Miles's last foray into espionage had not exactly been an unqualified success. While Miles had many virtues, subtlety wasn't one of them. It wasn't exactly Henrietta's strong suit, either, but Charlotte would never offend her friend by telling her that.

'Ouch!' Miles clapped a hand somewhere in the vicinity of his heart. 'That hurts.'

'Not as much as a knife in the ribs,' said Robert acerbically. 'We can weep over your wounds later. Once we've sorted out this tangle.'

Henrietta beamed at him. 'I knew I liked you.'

'Who was Mr Wrothan?' Charlotte demanded hastily before Henrietta could say something embarrassing. Like proposing on Charlotte's behalf.

'Other than a scoundrel?' Robert settled back against the

seat, releasing his grip on Charlotte's pelisse. 'Wrothan was a first lieutenant in the Seventy-fourth Foot. I have reason to believe that he augmented his income by selling secrets to the Mahratta in India.'

'And the French,' put in Miles, not to be left out.

'And the French,' agreed Robert. 'Although what he was selling to them remains unclear.'

'Is that why you came back to England?' asked Charlotte, twisting in her seat to see him more clearly. 'To pursue Mr Wrothan?'

'Yes,' Robert said shortly, and left it at that. The stony set of his profile did not invite further questions.

Charlotte frowned down at her gloved hands as the past rearranged itself yet again like a mosaic that had been misassembled.

He hadn't come home, then, to take up the ducal mantle and settle comfortably into the peaceful flow of life at Girdings. He hadn't come home to come home at all.

And she – she didn't really have much of a role at all, did she, in this new, larger tale of betrayal and retribution? It was very lowering to be not just a side character, but a minor side character, little more than a footnote in someone else's story.

Fortunately, no one else seemed to notice her abstraction. Henrietta, comfortably ensconced at the centre of her own narrative, was busily trying to align this new information. 'So,' she said, 'your Mr Wrothan pretended to be the king's doctor and insinuated himself into the king's household in order to glean secrets to sell to the French.'

'Lucky for him that the king should go batty again,' commented Miles comfortably.

Charlotte lifted her head. 'Unless it wasn't luck,' she said. She might be a side character, but there was no need to be an entirely insignificant one.

For the first time that horrible night, Robert looked directly at her. 'The opium,' he said.

Their eyes locked in a moment of complete mutual comprehension.

'Would you mind explaining for the rest of us?' demanded Miles.

'If someone were to drug the king with opium,' Charlotte said, not altogether coherently, 'they might be able to simulate something akin to madness. Everyone at Court is so afraid of another bout that the least little aberration in behaviour would be taken as a recurrence of his old illness.'

'And he would be treated accordingly.' Robert's words fell into the fraught silence like footsteps in a graveyard.

'A doctor would be called in,' confirmed Charlotte. 'And not Dr Willis. The king has expressly stated that he will not allow himself to be treated by Dr Willis ever again, and the Dukes of Kent and Cumberland have expressed their resolves to bar any attempt by Dr Willis to enter against their father's wishes.'

'Meaning,' translated Robert delicately, 'that a new doctor would have to be appointed. Someone unknown.'

Henrietta's almond eyes had gone nearly as round as Charlotte's. 'That would explain Dr Simmons. Once in the king's apartments, he could steal all the secrets he liked.'

For a moment, there was complete silence in the carriage as they all sat staring at one another, speechless at the sheer audacity of the scheme.

'Good God,' breathed Miles.

'Not God,' said Charlotte. 'The Prince of Wales. He has the power to appoint the king's physicians in these . . . well, these interludes. And the Prince of Wales is friends with Sir Francis Medmenham.'

'Who knew Wrothan,' Robert finished grimly. 'As you've now witnessed for yourself, Medmenham maintains a . . . secret society of sorts.' He looked at her as though daring her to elaborate on his description. 'Wrothan was a member.'

'A secret society?' echoed Henrietta.

'Hellfire Club,' elaborated Miles.

That explained the monks' habits and the bizarre ritual. 'Then the only question,' said Charlotte, 'is whether Medmenham deliberately sent Wrothan to impersonate Simmons or whether Wrothan heard through Medmenham that a new physician was being appointed and interjected himself.'

'Not exactly the only question,' put in Lieutenant Fluellen equably. 'For the sake of argument, let's say the king was being drugged with opium before they called for a doctor. How did they get it to him in the first place?'

Charlotte remembered that first night, Lord Henry Innes standing irritable and anxious at the door of the king's bedchamber. 'Henry Innes is a member of Medmenham's secret society, isn't he?' she asked, looking to Robert.

He confirmed her hunch with a distant nod.

Charlotte soldiered on. 'Lord Henry was in attendance on the king. If someone – like your Wrothan – were to give Lord Henry something and tell him it was a nerve tonic or a cure for stomach upsets—' From the expressions of the others, Charlotte could see they understood. She hurried on. 'I saw the king the night he was first taken ill, before the doctor was called. He didn't act quite as he was reported to in his other illnesses.

Rather than being hurried and agitated, there was something almost . . . dreamy. His eyes didn't seem to want to focus quite properly.'

Lieutenant Fluellen looked at Robert. 'Sounds like opium to me.'

'But why' – Miles leant forwards, bracing his hands on his knees – 'would your Frenchie kill Wrothan? Wrothan was his entrée into the palace.'

'Unless,' suggested Charlotte wildly, 'he had another false Dr Simmons lined up. There might be a whole regiment of them. A monstrous regiment of Dr Simmonses.'

'Or,' countered Robert in a voice that effectively quelled Charlotte's desire to giggle, 'he had already extracted what he wanted. I overheard the two of them talking tonight. Wrothan was bragging that he had removed something from the palace.'

'Did he say what?' asked Henrietta.

Robert held up both hands in a gesture of defeat. 'He compared it all to a game of cards. He kept talking about having the king in his hand.'

Charlotte remembered the king as she had seen him: entirely helpless, strapped into a straight waistcoat, denied the use of his limbs, weak and wasted.

'What else did he say?' Charlotte asked urgently, shoving her lap rugs out of the way.

Robert smiled grimly. 'Wrothan was waxing poetic today. When the Frenchman asked his price, he demanded a king's ransom. I imagine Wrothan thought he would get more if he left it to the imagination.'

'Turn the carriage around,' Charlotte said breathlessly.

'What?' said Miles.

'Please.' Reaching out, Charlotte caught at his arm. 'Tell

your coachman to go to the Queen's House. As fast as he can.'

'Isn't it a bit late to go calling at the Palace?' said Miles cautiously, in the sort of tone one uses with small children and excitable maiden aunts.

Looking around the circle of faces in the carriage, Charlotte encountered identical stares of incomprehension. Didn't even one of them see what she saw? Perhaps it was because they hadn't been there. Or perhaps it was because they didn't read as many novels. On the face of it, she realised, it did sound absurd, but she couldn't think of a better explanation for the events of the evening. And if she was right . . .

Charlotte squashed her hair back behind her ears with both hands and stared imploringly at her companions. 'Don't you see? They can only have been talking about the king. Not *a* king, *the* king.'

As they all stared at her uncomprehendingly, the level of her voice rose. 'If the false doctor was planted by the French spy to secure something that the doctor then ran off with to hold it for ransom – not just any ransom,' Charlotte continued relentlessly. 'A *king's* ransom.'

'No,' said Robert flatly. 'No. It can't be.'

'What else can it be?' Charlotte twisted the lap rug so hard that it nearly ripped in two. 'Your Mr Wrothan has kidnapped the king!'

Chapter Twenty-Four

'We don't know that,' said Robert forcefully, when the furor had died down enough for him to make himself heard. 'We don't know anything of the kind.'

Charlotte's small hands were clasped as if in prayer. 'What else is there in the Palace worth stealing?'

'Aside from state papers, priceless art, a king's ransom in silver and jewels . . .'

Charlotte waved all that aside. 'Why else drug the king into a state of insensibility?'

'I can think of a number of reasons,' said Robert grimly. 'You can have your pick. There's simple theft, the Prince of Wales's reversionary interest, or an attempt to sow discord by our friends across the Channel.'

'Any of those might have been the original plan. But' – Charlotte took a very deep breath – ' what if your friend decided to take it a step further?'

'He wasn't my friend.' Robert wasn't sure why he felt the need to specify that, but he did. 'He was never my friend.'

'Your enemy, then. Suppose your enemy double-crossed his

conspirator and, finding himself in a position to do so, made off with the king. It needn't have been a well-thought-out plan,' she added, as an afterthought. 'He might simply have seen the opportunity and seized it.'

'Like a boy with a plate of unguarded jam tarts?' Robert saw the quick flash of recognition before Charlotte's eyes dropped again.

'Rather larger, but otherwise the same idea,' acknowledged Charlotte, not quite meeting his eyes. 'He saw his opportunity and seized it.'

It would be like Wrothan to snatch up whatever fell conveniently into his path, whether it belonged to him or not, but Robert had difficulties with the logistics of it. One didn't just walk off with a monarch.

'It's one thing to seize a jam tart and quite another thing to seize a king,' Robert pressed. 'As you said, the king is larger. And, one would presume, would be more likely to protest at being carried off.'

'You have to admit that he has a point,' said Miles, who had been watching the exchange like a spectator at a sporting match. 'My pudding seldom protests. People do.'

'Not if they're bound and drugged. The people, I mean, not the puddings.' Charlotte cast an imploring glance around the carriage. 'None of you saw the king. I did. Anyone could have walked in, tossed him over his shoulder, and walked out with him.'

'With the king,' Robert said incredulously. 'Aren't there guards? Attendants? Something?'

Charlotte shook her head. 'The king prides himself on not surrounding himself with guards. He says he doesn't like to be separated from his subjects. As for attendants, as soon as he fell ill, all his pages were dismissed. His most loyal gentlemen of the bedchamber were barred from him. The queen, too,' she added. 'We were told it was all by his own orders.'

Miles pounded with one large fist on the hatch leading to the box.

'The Queen's House,' he instructed the coachman. Looking sheepish, he said, 'I suppose it doesn't hurt to check. Just to set Charlotte's mind at ease.'

'Charlotte is all appreciation,' murmured Charlotte, although she looked anything but at ease. Her hands were clasped so tightly in her lap that it was a wonder they didn't crack. She looked, Robert thought, like the more fragile sort of porcelain shepherdess, in danger of shattering at a careless touch.

'How do you intend to get in?' asked Robert brusquely as the carriage drew up by St James's Park. He knew he was being surly, but he couldn't seem to help it. Too much had happened, and none of it the way he had planned it. Wrothan was meant to be dead by *his* sword, not by an assassin's knife. And Charlotte . . . Charlotte was meant to be safe at home, not tracking murderers by moonlight. 'I imagine one can't just stroll in to the king's apartments.'

'One can, actually,' Charlotte said demurely. 'If one knows how to go about it.'

'Lead the way, O Captain, my captain,' signalled Miles, with an extravagant salute.

And she did. It was Charlotte who took the lead, Charlotte who guided them through the snow and the slush, down a long avenue shaded by lime trees to a square courtyard. They passed a dry fountain, the stone statues around its edge huddling in on themselves against the cold. Locating an entrance half obscured in the shrubbery, Charlotte guided them downstairs, through a warren of subterranean rooms that smelt pungently of glue and leather.

'This is the king's personal bindery,' Charlotte explained in a whisper. 'It connects to the library.'

'Rather careless of him, isn't it?' asked Robert, thinking of sentries and pickets and the hosts of armed guards attendant on Eastern potentates.

Charlotte shook her head, looking very serious. 'It was quite intentional. He wanted his library to be available to scholars at all times, without their having to go through the Palace. Dr Johnson used to study here,' she said proudly.

She led the way up a narrow flight of stairs to the centre of a vast wing that seemed entirely made up, as far as Robert could tell, of rooms filled with books, levels upon levels upon levels of books of all shapes, colours, and sizes. It made the library at Dovedale House look positively puny by comparison. Charlotte, however, appeared to know exactly where she was going. Ignoring an octagonal room with a soaring ceiling that looked more like an observatory than a library, she shepherded her flock into a rectangular room with a square desk that itself appeared to be constructed largely from books.

There was a light in the library, not from the coals in the fireplace, but from the brackets on either side of the door on the far side of the room. They illuminated, with pitiless clarity, the man lounged at the door connecting to the king's personal chambers.

'No visitors!' barked the man, before Charlotte could say anything at all.

From behind her, Robert could see Charlotte's back go very stiff.

'May I ask by whose authority?' she asked, in a dangerously polite tone.

The guard made no such attempt at civility. 'No,' he said insolently.

Charlotte regarded the guard thoughtfully. Robert recognised that expression quite well. Without another word, Charlotte simply walked straight past him and reached for the door handle.

'Don't,' said Robert, grabbing the guard by the scruff of the neck before he could make a move to stop Charlotte. 'I wouldn't do that if I were you.'

'I wouldn't do that if I were 'er!' whined the guard, but it was too late. Charlotte swept regally through the door, walking with all the assurance of four centuries of semi-feudal power. The dowager duchess herself couldn't have done better.

'Too late,' said Robert genially, letting him down as their small party bustled into the king's chamber behind Charlotte. The guard, assessing the odds, wisely decided not to argue, shuffling in meekly behind. Robert doubted he was being paid anything sufficient to warrant his cutting up a fuss. Judging by the man's slovenly attire, he was not on the ordinary palace payroll.

From inside the room came a low, keening moan, followed by a rustling that reminded Robert of snakes in the sand. Robert pushed his way through to Charlotte, who had come to an abrupt halt in the centre of the room. There, in the royal bed, lay the figure of a man. He looked scarcely a man, twisted into a fetal position, slithering against the bed linens in a manner more animal than human. But, even bloated and ill, his features were still, Robert fancied, recognisably those that had been reproduced on thousands of coins across the realm.

'Oh,' said Charlotte.

The king was a pitiful sight, unshaven, sweat-stained, his limbs wrapped around him like a baby in swaddling. 'Help poor Tom,' he crooned, glaring at them through bloodshot eyes. 'Poor Tom's a-cold.'

'Ah,' said Miles, stopping short so suddenly that Henrietta and Tommy racketed into him.

There, thought Robert, went the kidnapping theory tossed into a cocked hat.

The attendant crossed his arms smugly across his chest. 'His Majesty ain't in no fit condition for visitors.'

Charlotte's wide grey-green eyes roamed from the bed to the attendant and back again. 'I know what visitor His Majesty would most like,' she said quietly, in a voice that didn't sound quite like hers.

'Visits from Her Majesty are strictly forbidden!' barked out the attendant. 'Order of the prince.'

'Not Her Majesty,' said Charlotte, in the same singsong voice. 'The Princess Amelia. The king is always calling for her, the poor thing.'

Miles shot her a puzzled glance. Robert hoped he had the sense not to let his own confusion show on his face. What in the devil was she about? That she was up to something, he had no doubt. Robert regarded her closely, but her placid countenance provided no clue. She exuded serenity. It made Robert distinctly nervous.

'That's what His Majesty did last time,' Charlotte said conversationally, never removing her eyes from the king. 'He called and called for Princess Amelia. It broke the heart to hear it.'

As if on cue, the figure on the bed began to thrash back and forth, bleating, 'Amelia! Amelia!'

The attendant stumped forwards, thrusting out his jaw belligerently. 'Now look what you've done!'

Robert hastily moved between them, prepared to intervene for his lady's honour, but Charlotte appeared entirely unperturbed. There was something almost fey about her, as she tilted her head at the guard, staring him down with her wide, nearsighted eyes.

'Not me,' she said enigmatically. 'At least, not that way.'

She gestured towards the pathetic figure on the bed, and Robert noticed that, for all her appearance of calm, her hand was trembling.

But there wasn't the slightest quaver in her voice as she announced, with complete conviction, 'That man is not the king.'

Even the king forgot to croon as everyone stared, open-mouthed, at Charlotte.

'Is she—?' The attendant jabbed one finger at his temple in the universal gesture for 'absolutely barmy.'

Miles rested a brotherly hand on Charlotte's shoulder, although whether for support or restraint was unclear.

'He does look like the king,' Miles said awkwardly. 'Sounds like him, too.'

'But he isn't.' Charlotte quite literally dug her heels into the floor, setting her chin at an angle that brought back memories from that summer all those years ago. Charlotte, Robert remembered, was the most accommodating creature in the world – until she wasn't. She never fought; she never screamed; she just refused to budge. When something touched her stubborn streak, nothing in heaven or earth could move her. Not even the dowager duchess. A mere hospital orderly didn't stand a chance.

'This isn't the king,' Charlotte repeated. 'If he were, he would have called the princess by his pet name for her. He would never have called her Amelia like that.'

Was it Robert's imagination, or had the creature on the bed modulated his thrashing in order to listen?

'But you don't know that, do you?' Charlotte continued gently, addressing the pathetic figure on the bed. 'They never told you.'

'Poor Tom's a-cold,' whimpered the creature that might be king, reverting to King Lear.

Miles, who had been squinting down at the king, suddenly jabbed a finger at him. 'Prendergast!' he exclaimed.

'Prendergast?' Robert echoed. Was that like 'eureka!'? He really had been away from England far too long.

Miles rubbed his hands together happily, his hair flopping all over the place. 'Horatio Prendergast! I thought you looked familiar. I saw your Edgar at Drury Lane,' he informed the thing on the bed. 'Brilliant! For what it's worth, I think you ought to have wound up with Cordelia in the end rather than that king of France chappie.'

'Help poor Tom?' ventured the creature on the bed, but it lacked conviction.

'So what you're saying,' Tommy said slowly as the attendant backed away towards the wall, 'is that this man is an actor.'

'A very good one,' declared Miles, scrupulously awarding credit where credit was due.

'Which is why,' said Charlotte, never taking her eyes from the squirming creature on the bed, 'he was chosen to play the king. Tell me, Mr Prendergast, how did they persuade you to take the part?'

'The foul fiend doth bite me in the back!' whimpered Mr

Prendergast, who did, indeed, look greatly afflicted, mostly by Charlotte.

Not, however, nearly so greatly afflicted as he pretended to be. 'Has anyone else noticed that those blisters on his forehead are lip rouge?' chirped Henrietta, leaning forwards to swipe out one of the offending splotches.

The 'madman' jerked indignantly away from her hand, but not before she had managed to create a long, red smear across his forehead, effectively proving her point.

A good actor knew when it was time to bring the curtain down. Dropping the mad act, the false king struggled to swing into a sitting position, but his straight waistcoat made him flop about like a fish on a hook. Ever the gentleman, Miles put out a hand to help him up.

'Many thanks, sir.' Prendergast inclined his head, the one part of his body he could move freely, in gratitude. 'Both for your aid and for your good notices for my performance. My other performance,' he added, with a wry glance around his audience.

'Well, you were rather hampered in this one,' Miles said generously.

Henrietta waved her husband to silence. 'Then you *are* an actor?' At his nod, she asked intently, 'Why?'

He didn't pretend to misunderstand. 'I was in prison for debt. Rather large debts,' he admitted. 'It is not always easy to live in the style to which one would prefer to be accustomed. A man came to me. He told me the king was ill.'

'Yes?' urged Charlotte, like a child being told a bedtime story.

The actor smiled wryly at Miles. 'Like you, sir, he had seen my Edgar. He told me he wanted . . . a proxy of sorts to stave off speculation that might undermine the government and compromise the war with France. I was told,' he added, 'that it would only be for a few weeks, while the real king recovered elsewhere, free from the baneful influence of prying eyes.'

'So you agreed to play the king,' Charlotte summarised.

'For the good of the country,' the actor said piously, before adding, 'and my debts paid in full.'

'Who hired you?' demanded Robert.

The actor shrugged, nearly overbalancing himself in the process. 'A doctor. Dr Simmons.'

'Who was as much a doctor as you are a king,' murmured Robert. 'Was there no one else?'

Having learnt the dangers of shrugging, the actor shook his head. 'Not that I saw. The doctor came alone.'

'When did all this happen?' Charlotte broke in, moving around Robert to address the actor directly. 'When did you come here?'

The actor smiled at her as winningly as a man could when strapped into a straitjacket. 'Yesterday evening. I had just been given my supper when Dr Simmons came for me.'

'Yesterday?' The cause of Charlotte's distress was equally apparent to all of them. Wrothan had had more than enough time to conceal the real king.

Charlotte turned to Henrietta. 'The false Simmons must have made the substitution while we were talking to the real Simmons.'

'Or later that night,' countered Henrietta, looking equally shaken. 'If we'd only known—'

'How could you have?' interrupted Robert, not liking the stricken expression on Charlotte's face. He turned back to the man on the bed. 'Did you hear where he was being taken?'

The actor affected a rueful expression. 'Simmons said something about his recuperating at Kew.'

Charlotte touched a hand tentatively to Robert's arm. 'Kew is where the king recovered from his last illness. Simmons – the false Simmons, I mean – wouldn't have taken him there.'

'No,' agreed Robert abstractedly, 'he wouldn't.'

Where would Wrothan, newly returned to England, stash a kidnapped king? Wrothan had to find some place where he could hide the king from the French and English alike. It was no small matter outwitting the secret service of not one but two nations. The king's face was well-known, not only from his own peregrinations across the country but from thousands of loyal prints and far less loyal caricatures. It was no easy matter to hide a king. Wrothan would need somewhere secluded, somewhere entirely cut off.

Somewhere like the Hellfire caves.

'I think I know where he is.' Robert scarcely recognised his own voice. 'And I'll be willing to wager our Frenchie does, too. He would never have killed Wrothan otherwise.'

Wrothan always had been more cunning than wise. If the answer was obvious to Robert, it would have been obvious to the Frenchman as well. Robert made a note; the next time he kidnapped someone and held them for ransom, he would not hide them in the same place where he had held his secret meetings. It was a distinct gaffe.

'Killed?' The man on the bed looked distinctly unhappy.

No one paid the least bit of attention to him. Miles stampeded towards the door like a one-man cavalry charge, one arm upraised. 'There's no time to lose! To – er.' He skidded to an abrupt halt just shy of the door. 'Where are we going?'

'Wycombe,' announced Robert with grim finality. 'West Wycombe.'

'Why Wycombe?' Miles demanded.

'Hellfire Club,' said Robert succinctly. Now that the club was out of the bag, so to speak, there was no point in hiding it. 'We can leave the ladies at Loring House—'

'Oh, no,' said Henrietta. 'You're not leaving us anywhere.'

Charlotte sidled up beside her. 'I'm the only one who knows the king. If we find him, I should be there. So he won't be alarmed.'

Robert hated to tell her that the king was probably already alarmed – or so deeply drugged that he couldn't be alarmed if they tried. From the set of Charlotte's chin, he knew that if he didn't agree, nothing short of a straight waistcoat would keep her from following. And, so far, her instincts had been better than his.

'Fine,' he said shortly. 'We may find nothing at all, you know.'

Charlotte looked up at him as though trying to decide whether to hire him to bear her standard off into battle. 'But we still have to try.'

Feeling subtly rebuked, Robert got down to business. 'Can we hire a boat?' Medmenham Abbey was on the Thames, a much faster trip by water than by land.

'Shouldn't be a problem,' Miles said, barging towards the door. 'Bloody good thing the Thames hasn't frozen.'

Robert didn't miss the longing look Charlotte cast at the dwindling embers of the coal fire as she disappeared through the door. It was going to be a long, cold trip. But, hopefully, not a fruitless one. Robert didn't let himself dwell on what would happen if the king wasn't at Wycombe.

In that case, he could only hope that the Frenchman would be as stymied as they were.

'What about me?' Horatio Prendergast called after them.

Robert spared a glance over his shoulder. 'You stay right where you are and play your role as though your life depended on it.' He paused for the maximum effect. 'It does.'

Chapter Twenty-Five

In the light of morning, my midnight adventures appeared more than a little bit absurd.

To call it morning might have been pushing it a bit. It was more like noon. What with all my midnight meanderings, by the time I woke up, Colin was long since gone, leaving only a rumpled patch on his side of the sheets and the traditional dent in the pillow. I was wrapped like a mummy in the entirety of the comforter, having apparently taken his departure from the bed as a moment of personal triumph in the quilt war.

There was a note waiting for me on the bedside table, propped against the phone. Groping for my glasses, I squinted at it through a fringe of hair that had decided to take on a new life as a porcupine.

'Didn't want to wake you,' it read. That probably translated as 'Tried to wake you; didn't get far.' I'm a night person, not a morning person. The rest of the note read a bit like a very modern poem. 'Food in fridge. Water in kettle. Happy hunting. C.'

Happy hunting? Oh, right. My death grip on the sheet

relaxed. He meant the archive. As far as he knew, I was only hunting historical spies.

And for all I knew, I reminded myself, they were the only spies on the premises. So to speak, that was.

I brushed my teeth and washed my hair and put on clothing and managed to find my way to the kitchen with only one or two wrong turns along the way.

The door to the study was closed.

I wondered what Colin was doing in there. Had he discovered that fragment of paper beneath the desk? Had he wadded it up and tossed it away? Or shredded it with his special Captain Kangaroo Secret Spy Docu-Shred Ray?

Rolling my eyes at myself, I set about making coffee in the decidedly prosaic mustard yellow kitchen, breathing in the fumes from the French press as though the magical whiff of caffeine might clear my foggy brain.

After all, what had I really seen in there last night? Leaving aside all the atmospherics of the dim light of the single lamp, the long nightgown swishing around my bare feet, the decidedly House of Usher shadows cast by unfamiliar objects. Just some dictionaries, some travel guides, some newspaper clippings, and a scrap of a larger piece of paper that would probably read entirely differently when plugged into the missing three quarters of the page.

I filled my mug with coffee, looked at it critically, and snagged the French press in my other hand before making my way carefully up the stairs to the library. Refills would undoubtedly be necessary.

Henrietta's journals and correspondence were just where I had left them, open to a very cold boat ride on the Thames in the middle of the night. I, apparently, wasn't the only one seized with odd impulses during the wee hours of the morning. In their case, though, Charlotte had a bit more to go on than I did. I still couldn't quite believe someone had had the nerve to substitute an actor for the king.

Wiggling my way into a comfortable position in the squashy old armchair, I flipped open my laptop and prepared to transcribe the salient bits of Lady Charlotte's pursuit of the captured king. As far as I could tell, the Pink Carnation wasn't involved – at least, not yet – but it was still unclear whether or not the Black Tulip, the Pink Carnation's French nemesis, was really out of the picture. Drugging the king to effect a simulation of madness didn't really seem his sort of thing, but who really knew? If the Black Tulip had survived the conflagration that had foiled his previous plot, an attempt to blow up the royal family with a three-foot-high plaster bust of George III crammed with explosives, his agenda might have altered.

But no matter how I tried to concentrate on England in winter, on a cold palace, on a mad king, on the icy Thames, my mind kept straying to blazing desert sands, to gold souks and to semiautomatic something-or-others and to unexplained trips to Dubai. Even the fascinating possibility that George III had been replaced by a decoy king failed to hold my attention. For once in my life, the present seemed a good deal more arresting than the past. I wasn't sure that was a good thing. At least, not for the sake of my dissertation.

After reading the same page over five times without absorbing a word of it, I admitted defeat. Pushing away from the table, I fumbled in my bag for that lifeline of our modern existence, my mobile phone. I'd been too much in the archives, too much among the improbable events of long ago. What I needed was a nice, sane, safe modern voice to bring me back to my senses.

Well, maybe not entirely sane.

Scrolling down through my contacts, I hit the first name to come up in the Ps. If anyone could whip away the cobwebs, it would be Pammy. I had no intention of confiding my embarrassing 007 suspicions to her, but if nothing else, at least she would be a distraction. And she had the added benefit of having gone to school with Colin's sister, Serena, in London for two years. They didn't move in entirely the same circles these days, but if anyone knew what Colin did for a living, it would be Pammy. The woman has the instincts of a bloodhound and the scruples of a Chihuahua.

Pammy doesn't believe in outmoded social mundanities like 'Hello.' Instead, she started right in with, 'You're at Selwick Hall, aren't you!'

'Pammy! Hi! How are you?' I have the social mundanities on autopilot. They just come out, whether I mean them to or not. 'It's me, Eloise.'

Pammy made a noise that would have sounded suspiciously like 'duh!' if 'duh' hadn't gone out several years ago. Pammy is nothing if not *au courant*. 'Who else would be calling from your mobile?'

'Good point,' I admitted.

'So?' piped Pammy. 'How *is* it? Which flavour is he?'

As I so often do with Pammy, I removed the phone from my ear, looked at it, and put it back. It never helps. 'Huh?' I said.

'Which flavour ice cream is he? It's the latest thing. You compare every man you know to his corresponding icecream flavour. Vanilla is your standard City bloke, presentable, but bland. Vanilla bean has a bit more potential, but it's still no chocolate chip . . . You get the idea.'

Hmm. I decided to try this out. 'What's moose tracks?'

Pammy answered without missing a beat. 'Vaguely outdoorsy, from the Midwest in the States or the Midlands here, on the shaggy side.'

'Strawberry?' I asked.

'Super WASP-y, always wears pink Brooks Brothers shirts, on the borderline of gay.'

'Sorbet?'

'Definitely gay. So what's Colin?'

'Mint chip,' I said, without even having to think about it. Cool on the outside, but with all sorts of dark depths. 'Listen, Pams, do you ever remember Serena saying anything about what Colin does for a living?'

'Something in the City,' Pammy said promptly. In the background I could hear the whir of an espresso machine. It takes a lot of coffee to maintain that level of constant exuberance.

'That's what he used to do. Any idea what he does now?'

There was a long, happy exhalation of steam in the background as the espresso maker did its thing. 'Shouldn't you be asking him?'

'It seems kind of tacky,' I hedged. 'And I feel like I should know already.' At least that much was true.

'Hmm.'

I could hear Pammy thinking – and texting on one of her three other phones, but I chose to ignore that bit. Pammy texts even in her sleep; her phones are so much a part of her fingers that they have no impact on her other activities or on her brain.

'I have this friend' – Uh-oh. Pammy always had these friends. Which was this one going to be? The astrologist? The feng shui expert? The Colour-Me-Beautiful woman? – 'who has an agency called ManTrackers.'

'ManTrackers,' I repeated flatly. I had an image of Xena: Warrior Princess stalking her man through the streets of London's financial district. It was straight out of Monty Python. Did they bring back scalps, or just suit jackets?

'They run checkups on new boyfriends, you know, like due diligence, making sure they are what they said and all that.'

'Due *diligence*?'

'Well, just think about it, Ellie,' Pammy said, as though it were all perfectly reasonable and I just a little bit slow, 'you wouldn't buy a flat or a business without first having it professionally checked out, so why expend less care on picking out a man? It never hurts to do your homework.'

'That's not homework – that's stalking.'

'Don't be silly, sweetie. Stalking is when you do it yourself.'

I love Pammy, I do. Most of the time. 'I think I'll hold off on the, er, ManTrackers for a bit.'

'It's your choice.' A bad choice, her tone said. I could practically hear her shrug. 'But I'll just shoot you their number, anyway, yah?'

'Yah,' I echoed absently. 'I mean, yes.'

Easier to give in to Pammy than to argue with her. Disagreement is a form of discourse she does not understand. Not that I ever, ever intended to use this 'ManTracking' madness. What in the hell had happened to romance? To trust?

'You don't use them, do you?' I demanded incredulously.

It was hard to believe it, even of Pammy. Especially of Pammy, who went through enough men per year to form her own private army. I didn't like to think what the bill for that would be if she was having each one checked out individually. Sufficient to put a down payment on a London flat, no doubt.

Fortunately, Pammy had a very large trust fund from a very guilty father.

'Of course! If they were publicly traded, I would buy stock.'

That answered that, then.

'They're really great,' said Pammy seriously. 'They check out his financial records, whether he pays his bills promptly, his taxes, his properties, his exes. Total full service.'

'Great,' I said, because I couldn't think of anything else to say. At least, nothing positive. What next, going through their garbage to see if there were unexplained used condoms? That wasn't the way it was supposed to work. You were supposed to grow to know someone through mutual interactions, communicating with them, not with some bizarre surveillance agency about them. What had happened to trust, for crying out loud?

I was a fine one to talk about trust. There I was scrounging around in Colin's desk drawers in the middle of the night. How was that any different?

Because it wasn't systematic, I told myself. Because I'd felt guilty doing it. Because I wasn't paying someone else to do it.

'It's a jungle out there,' Pammy said seriously. 'You have to protect yourself, Eloise.'

She didn't know the half of it. What would she say if I told her that I suspected Colin was a gun-toting, licence-to-kill-carrying secret agent? Not much, actually. That wasn't the sort of thing Pammy worried about.

Pammy's voice was still streaming through the little holes in my mobile. 'I mean, you'd be surprised by how many men say they're single but really aren't – and you can't just tell by looking for a tan line on their ring fingers! And then there are a lot of them who lie about their financials, or who've cheated on their ex-wives, or—'

I have to admit, I tuned out somewhere after ex-wives. I just didn't want to know. Dating was hard enough. Why create more things to stress about? I was about to say, *You don't seriously worry about all these things, do you?* when I remembered: Of course she did.

Pammy doesn't just come from a broken home; she comes from broken homes, plural. In fact, her mother had practically made a career out of it, trading up husbands. Some of the trading had been done of her own accord. Husband One, a reasonably successful attorney, had been ditched for Pammy's father, a wildly successful King of the Universe, *Bonfire of the Vanities* investment-banker type. Some of the trading had been thrust upon her. After Husband Two did his own trading up, Pammy's mother had moved on to his English equivalent, Husband Three. I was still unclear as to what had happened with Husband Three, but Pammy's mother had come out of it with a choice town house in London, and a 'cottage' in Dorset with fifteen bedrooms and its own tennis courts. The Palm Beach house was courtesy of Pammy's father, as were the various Monets and Renoirs that now decorated the London and Dorset properties.

It's not like Pammy went around talking about it – other than in the most matter-of-fact of ways – and she had never, to my knowledge, sought psychological counselling, or ever, in any way, given anyone to believe that she was anything but perfectly well-adjusted. Mildly crazy, but perfectly well-adjusted. But sometimes even perfectly well-adjusted can cover a multitude of scars.

Maybe it wasn't fair to call them scars. Call it a different world-view, then. Talking with Pammy could be like one of those *Twilight Zone* episodes where you get a peep into a universe that operates on laws entirely differently from your own. Visiting Pammy-land was like travelling through a totally foreign country, one where they didn't take Visa and none of my own expectations applied. Which was funny, since we'd grown up together. We'd gone to the same private school together from kindergarten till her mother whisked her off to England in tenth grade, the same ballet classes, the same skating lessons, the same hideous middle school dances; but our home situations were different enough that we might as well have hailed from different planets.

It was true: I did take for granted having two parents who had met, fallen in love, married – and stayed married. Sure, they'd had their moments, but for the most part they were a united front, aligned against the world, two heads with the same brain, and on and on. My sister, Jillian, and I always joked that telling one something was tantamount to telling the other because after thirty years of marriage, information went back and forth between the two of them like some Discovery Channel program on osmosis.

Unlike Pammy's mother, who had only learnt that her second husband – Pammy's father – was cheating on her when she came home from a trip to a spa in Arizona and found that all her clothes had been cleaned out of the closet and a younger model installed in her bed. When I say younger model, I mean that literally. Her replacement had been a runway model, all silky hair and exposed hip-bones. The resulting divorce had been brutal and very, very bitter.

Pammy had her own reasons for her preoccupations.

It did say something about Pammy that she had always

managed to stay on decent terms with her father. She handled him with the same casual insouciance with which she dealt with everything else in her life, never indicating by word or deed that she resented what he had done to her mother – but she had never had a boyfriend who had lasted more than three months. Most got the boot in fewer than two. Two weeks, that was.

Just enough time for ManTrackers to issue a report.

We all joked about Pammy's infamous two-week rule, but . . . I suddenly felt like the wormiest of worms. 'Thanks, Pams,' I said soberly. 'I'll bear them in mind.'

We hung up with mutual expressions of goodwill. It took me a moment before I realised that I was no better off than before I had called. What with icecream flavours and ManTrackers, I wasn't the least bit closer to discovering what Colin actually did.

Dropping my mobile back into my bag, I wandered over to the long windows that looked out over the gardens. I did have a few options other than ManTrackers. I could (a) continue snooping; (b) talk to Colin's sister or his great-aunt; or (c) just ask Colin.

For a moment, I was tempted by option B. Colin's great-aunt, Mrs Selwick-Alderly, had been the moving force in getting us together in the first place. She had also made some very interesting comments – oh, goodness, what was it that she had said? Colin had been raising a ruckus about my being allowed access to the family papers. Mrs Selwick-Alderly, as poised as an Edwardian duchess, had simply smiled at him and said, 'The one doesn't lead to the other, you know.' Or something like that. What did it mean? What did she mean?

Could she have meant that revealing the identities of

nineteenth-century spies wouldn't clue me in that he was following in the family tradition?

I *did* have her number stored in my mobile somewhere.

No. I folded my arms across my chest so they wouldn't be tempted to reach for my mobile. I wasn't going to do that. I had a choice to make. I could talk to Colin like a reasonable human being and set a pattern for a proper relationship – a real relationship, based on communication and trust – or I could continue skulking around behind his back like a dime store Mata Hari, abusing his trust in me in the process. It might be exciting, it might be titillating (playing with the unknown is always so much more thrilling than dealing with anything head-on), but in the end it meant the difference between something real and something make-believe. At that rate, I might as well call Pammy's ManTrackers and have done with it.

Did I want something real? Up until now, there had always been intrigue of some kind. There had been the whole does-he-like-me/ does-he-want-to-throttle-me dilemma so beloved of Gothic novelists to keep me entertained, and after that, once I knew he liked me, there had been all the euphoria of a new relationship coupled with a transatlantic separation. There hadn't, until now, been any of the real bread and butter of a relationship, the day-to-day getting to know each other. Speculating like mad about the other person behind his back didn't count.

Was it just the dating of a descendant of the Purple Gentian that I wanted? The thrill of being able to go home and tell everyone I'd caught a real, live Englishman – and then thrown him back? Or did I really want Colin, who wrote terse notes and woke up too early and forgot to pick up his socks?

I stared out over the gravelled paths of his garden, past the eighteenth-century follies and the dead rosebushes, all the way to the old Norman tower that stood on its own crest to the east of the gardens. My eyes narrowed on the bulk of the tower. The last time I had been at Selwick Hall, Colin had warned me away from it, explaining that it was an insurance liability to let guests wander around inside. Or something like that.

What if the liability involved didn't have anything to do with insurance?

There had been a big, shiny padlock on the door last time. The big, shiny padlock was probably still in place. But it was becoming quite clear that what I really needed was a walk. There would be nothing like a walk through the damp, cold air to whip my head back into order. Walks are supposed to be good for you, aren't they?

After last time, I already knew the drill. I knew where to find the spare Wellies (and I knew that it would be a very bad idea not to put on the spare Wellies, even if the smallest ones were still a size too big) and I knew the shortest way from the kitchen door to the tower. I virtuously emptied out my coffee grounds and deposited the French press in the sink along the way. And I tried not to think about what I was really doing.

Outside, the countryside was doing its best to demonstrate why so many Britons like to go abroad to other climates during the winter months. Instead of properly raining, the sky was snivelling, leaching down an irresolute moisture that was too thick to be called mist and too insidious to be called rain. The ground was sodden, turning that squelchy black unique to winter, where the entire landscape appears to be etched in shades of black and grey. The tower was the greyest of the lot, a lowering pile of roughly cut stone, dark with damp. Moisture dripped off the padlock, falling with a dull plop to gather in a small puddle below.

The whole thing looked highly unhygienic.

Huddling in my quilted jacket, I contemplated the stone mass. Bizarre to think that people had once lived in here. At some point back in time, there would have been men jostling one another and exchanging bawdy jokes in Norman French. There would have been a solar somewhere up top, with women in pointy hats weaving on their looms. There would have been a hall with a great fire and meat roasting on it. Now, all that was left was a miserable, hollow cylinder of stone.

I might have turned back then. I like to think that I would have. It was those ridiculous water drops that did it, drawing my attention back to the lock, which was, indeed, still very big, still very shiny, and still very much a lock. It was also very unfastened.

To be strictly accurate, it was only slightly unfastened. It was one of those padlocks that involves driving a bit of metal into another bit of metal. There must be some technical term for it, but as you can see, I know roughly as much about locks as I do about medieval solars. What I did know was that the locking bit hadn't been entirely pushed home, so that while the lock still looked closed, there was a crucial gap between the end of the curved piece and the hole it was supposed to go into. Whoever had been inside last had been careless.

Surely it couldn't hurt just to take a quick look inside.

Feeling like Nancy Drew (who, I would like to point out, was also Titian-haired), I eased the padlock open. Despite the shiny newness of the lock, the door didn't open easily. It creaked and protested on hinges made cranky by damp. Either the original roof had survived or a new one had been put on, because there was no light at all in the interior. I hadn't noticed from the outside, but the original arrow slits had all been boarded up, blocked with thick planks of wood.

This was all beginning to look exceedingly suspicious. Or it would have, had I been able to see anything.

Propping open the door with my back, I stood at the threshold, wishing I had possessed the good sense to bring a flashlight. The reluctant winter light, lying low to the ground like mist, scarcely penetrated the door frame. But there was something inside; I could make out that much. If there were any partitions, they had long since crumbled with time. From where I stood, the inside looked like one cavernous circle. But it wasn't empty. Something large and metallic occupied the centre of the room.

Unwilling to relinquish my hold on the door, I sidled closer by baby steps, one hand still braced against the heavy door, propping it open as far as my arm would allow. Whatever was inside there looked like something straight out of *The Avengers*, a diabolical machine bristling with levers and gears.

I was so occupied in squinting at the amorphous shape in the darkness that I didn't hear the steps behind me. All I noticed was that the light, that feeble trail of light coming through the doorway, had suddenly been eclipsed, blotting out what little light there was with a large, man-shaped shadow.

And then it was too late to do anything at all.

Chapter Twenty-Six

It took nearly an hour to find a crew crazy enough to convey them thirty miles along the Thames by night.

On hearing that their party wanted to go farther than just across the river, the first three boats turned them down flat. The river was treacherous by day, they protested; to go by night was a fool's game. Only the promise of ten times their normal fee, in gold, had prevailed with the fourth boat, and even then the boatmen had grumbled on their benches, pulling their oars with visible reluctance.

Burdened with six oarsmen and five passengers, the boat moved slowly through the dark waters of the Thames. A foul reek rose from the river, a compound of all manner of waste that human habitation could devise, all dumped into the murky waters of the Thames. The stench of a cantonment in India in summer was nothing to it.

The ladies had retreated beneath the tilt, or canopy, that formed a rudimentary cabin in the middle of the boat, although the open-walled cabin provided little barrier between them and the unwashed bodies of the boatmen that warred with the Thames for the prize of most noxious stench. Curled up one against the other for warmth, Charlotte and Henrietta had been lulled by the rocking of the boat into sleep. Miles had been the next to go, slumped at his lady's feet like a dog on a medieval tombstone. Even Tommy had succumbed, his long legs stretched out in front of him across the width of the cabin. At least, thought Robert, his presence formed a sort of windbreak for the ladies.

Only Robert remained awake, alone at the prow of the boat, staring sightlessly at the waters ahead while the oars splashed rhythmically in and out of the water behind him. The lanterns hanging from the sides of the tilt did little to illuminate what lay ahead.

He sincerely hoped the boatmen knew where they were going. After all those years away, the Thames was as foreign to him as the Ganges. If the sun had been shining, he still wouldn't know Henley from King's Lynn. One town looked much the same as another to him and the blurry memories of his youth provided no sure guide.

The not knowing where he was scraped at his nerves. It wasn't just the physical landscape that confounded him; it was everything. Nothing had gone the way it was supposed to. An actor played the king, the king played the fool, and Charlotte – his own sweet, unworldly Charlotte – abandoned her tower to rout her dragons herself. The world had turned upside down and his head was spinning with it.

Or perhaps that was just the rocking of the boat. He had never been particularly good with boats. He liked his feet on firm ground.

There didn't seem to be any firm ground to be had. His mind couldn't quite close around the fact that Wrothan was dead. When he thought of the end of his quest, he had always assumed that there would be a duel, pistols at twenty paces or swords on some damp heath, with plenty of time to toy with his enemy, to make him sweat, to regret what he had done, before shouting something suitable to the occasion – like, 'For the colonel!' – before plunging his rapier home. He had never expected to be beaten to the post by a French agent who had driven his knife home without so much as a by-your-leave, with no preamble, no ceremony.

Nor had he ever expected to find himself trailing in Charlotte's wake, following her lead through a maze of palace paths and assumed identities where his sword arm meant less than her calm knowledge of the court. He had been wrong. She wasn't made of porcelain but of wrought iron, deceptively delicate, stronger than stone. It was tempting to believe that this was something new, forged from the strange enchantments that seemed to have turned the whole world on its head. Remembering Charlotte's quiet fortitude in the face of her grandmother's tantrums, Robert thought not. It had always been there. He had simply been too busy basking in the glow of her adoration to pay any notice.

The realisation made him feel oddly bare, stripped of the only role that lent him any hope of dignity. What good was he, if not to slay her dragons for her? What good was he to anyone? He hadn't even accomplished his own revenge. Someone else had seized that for him.

The futility of his vigil – of all his vigils – pressed in around him like the dark waters of the river.

Behind him, a rustling noise caught his attention. He turned to see Charlotte emerge from the tilt.

Hunched over beneath a motley collection of rugs taken

from the carriage, she moved like an old woman, her limbs stiff with cold and sleep. Aside from being slightly blue around the lips, she looked just the same as she always had: slight, soft-featured, defenceless, her hair rough with sleep and her eyes slightly unfocused. She did not look like anyone's idea of a warrior maiden.

'Hello,' she whispered hoarsely. Rubbing the sleep out of her eyes with two hands, she blinked blearily at him as she asked, 'Are we there yet?'

'Close,' Robert lied, although he wasn't sure whether it was precisely a lie or not. They had certainly been on the river long enough – three hours, by his last count. They should be close to Medmenham by now. Shouldn't they? He bloody hated not knowing where they were.

He bared his teeth in a reassuring smile. 'We'll be there soon.'

'G-good.' Charlotte nodded her approval. She was sleepy enough that even that small movement made her sway in place.

Reaching out, Robert hastily caught her by the shoulders. There wasn't much chance of her going over the side, but why risk it? Through the layers of cloak and dress, the bones of her shoulders felt tiny and fragile beneath his hands, like a bird's. She had lost weight since Girdings. Weren't they feeding her at the Palace?

'You're cold,' he said, just to say something, before his undisciplined, sleep-deprived mind could wander off in any more inappropriate directions. Judging her steady enough not to pitch over into the river, he released her.

Charlotte's blue lips cracked into a wry smile. 'I don't think I'll ever be warm again.' She hitched up the blanket that had fallen to the crooks of her elbows, shivering where the cold wool touched her shoulders. Her dress was muslin, thin and entirely impractical for winter, short-sleeved and scoop-necked.

Robert held out an arm, lifting his thick cloak to provide a place for her. It was only for warmth, after all. Soldiers might bunk together for warmth on a cold night, if it meant the difference between death and survival. The cold wind off the river shot through the opening in his cloak, attacking the thin linen of his shirt like a plague of stinging needles. 'Come here.'

Charlotte went very still. Robert was reminded of a rabbit in a field, scenting a predator. The comparison was not a pleasing one. 'No, thank you,' she said, even though her lips were blue and her teeth clattered together as she said it.

Her wariness cut him to the core.

'Are you sure?' Robert held the cloak open, enduring the bite of the wind, willing her to change her mind. It could be so simple, just one step, then another, such a small space to cross to reach where they had been before. He tried to inject some levity into his voice, to camouflage the enormity of what was at stake. 'Don't freeze just to spite me.'

It didn't have the desired effect. Charlotte shook her head, taking a step back, away from him. What had happened to the Charlotte on the roof, the Charlotte who would have followed him anywhere? He hadn't realised how much he prized that trust until he had betrayed it. He wanted it back.

Charlotte tugged at the corners of her rug, hunching her shoulders beneath its meagre shelter. She looked very small and very alone as she said, 'Don't worry. I'm quite all right on my own.'

'I can see that,' he said, trying to substitute humour for hurt. 'I felt decidedly superfluous tonight.'

Sluggish with sleep, Charlotte frowned at him from beneath her rumpled hair. 'What do you mean?'

Robert grimaced, feeling like a churl. 'Consider it a badly botched compliment,' he said. And then, because it was true, he added, sincerely, 'You were magnificent in the Queen's House.'

'All I did was show you the way,' said Charlotte. 'Anyone familiar with the Queen's House could have done the same.'

He was losing her. He could see her starting to retreat into the tilt, angling back towards the shadows beneath the canopy, slipping away from him as quietly and politely as a dream on waking.

'That was hardly all,' said Robert hastily. 'How did you know that the man in the bed wasn't the real king?'

It wasn't entirely a subterfuge; he did want to know. But, mostly, he wanted to keep her talking. It was a poor counterfeit of the intimacy they had had back at Girdings. Robert felt as though he were slowly and painfully scaling the walls of a fortress he had once occupied by right and foolishly abandoned.

It worked. Charlotte paused, leaning one hand against the frame as she looked back towards Robert, weighing the events of the evening.

'It was mostly a guess,' she admitted. 'The man in the bed sounded wrong. He *smelt* wrong. They weren't drugging the false king, Mr – oh, whatever his name was.'

'Pendergast,' Robert supplied. 'Or Prendergast. Even so. I would never have noticed. And neither would any of the others. But for you, the ploy would have worked.'

Had he been too effusive? Charlotte regarded him warily, more nonplussed than pleased. Had he been so chary with his compliments before?

'I – thank you,' she said.

Oh, hell. 'Don't,' he said bluntly. 'It's nothing more than your due.' Feeling suddenly clumsy, he added awkwardly, 'I'm sure the king will say the same. When we find him.'

Charlotte seized on the change of topic. 'If we find him. Do you think he's really at Wycombe?'

It gave him an absurd rush of satisfaction to have her looking to him again for answers, for advice, for reassurance, for anything.

'I don't know,' he admitted, hating being caught out in an admission of fallibility, but knowing that nothing less than the truth would do. He had already dug enough of a hole for himself with lies and half-truths. A bit of cautious optimism couldn't hurt, however. 'It seems like the most logical place, though.'

Charlotte turned to look out over the dark expanse of the river. He wondered what she saw reflected on those dark waters. The king? Medmenham? The torches of the Hellfire Club? 'It's not exactly a logical scenario, though, is it? Any of it. Hellfire Clubs and counterfeit kings . . .'

'Club,' Robert corrected. 'Only one. To my knowledge.' Brilliant. Now he had just established himself as a Hellfire expert.

'And not much of one, at that. I would have thought that the Hellfire Club would have been more . . . well, decadent.' Charlotte glanced back over her shoulder at him. 'Not just cassocks and fireworks.'

Robert sidled a few steps closer. To better hear her. After all, they wouldn't want to wake the others by speaking too loudly. 'I believe the cassocks were originally intended to make an anticlerical statement,' Robert hedged. No need to add that the robes also provided easy access once the prostitutes were brought in, at least for those members bold enough to go bare beneath. 'I gather it was very daring in its time.'

'I suppose it must have been,' said Charlotte, although she sounded less than convinced. 'What was all that about the elephant god?'

'I think,' said Robert, 'that it was Wrothan's attempt to pique the jaded appetites of the Hellfire crowd by offering them something foreign and exotic. He took the basic Hellfire Club framework—'

'Cassocks and fireworks,' supplied Charlotte knowledgeably.

'—and layered it with a lot of faux-Indian mumbo jumbo, including a man in a very large elephant mask pretending to be an elephant god.'

Unlike the gentlemen in the caves, Charlotte was not impressed. 'But what did he do?'

Between the drugged smoke and the pure superstitious terror evoked at having a beast half-man, half-animal suddenly coming at one, a performance would have seemed superfluous. 'Not terribly much. At least, not that I saw. I left soon after he made his appearance.' That much, at least, was true. 'I only joined the Hellfire Club to follow Wrothan. And I didn't enjoy it,' he added idiotically.

Charlotte twisted her head to look up at him. He didn't blame her for looking puzzled. He didn't quite understand what he was doing himself.

'I just didn't want you to think I was the same as those others, Medmenham and Staines and the rest,' Robert tried to explain. 'That's all.'

It wasn't nearly all, but he didn't seem to be doing too well with the English language at the moment.

'I did wonder,' said Charlotte, not quite looking at him, 'why you were spending so much time with Medmenham. I had thought it might be—'

'Might be what?' Appropriating the space beside her, Robert angled his head, trying to see her more clearly. It didn't do any good. With her head bowed, all he could see was a scrap of profile through a mass of tangled hair.

Charlotte scraped her hair back, keeping her hand there to hold it out of the way. 'That you might be lonely,' she said. 'I thought you might be looking for an entrée into the *ton*.'

'With *Medmenham*?' Robert sounded as horrified as he felt. 'Is that what you really thought of me?'

Charlotte looked at him steadily. 'What else was I supposed to think? I had very little evidence to rely on.'

You had *me*, he wanted to say. You should have relied on me.

But why should she have?

Because she was Charlotte, that was why. Because she gave new meaning to the term 'blind devotion.' Because she was the woman who had announced that it was better to trust and be disappointed than never to have trusted at all. It didn't matter that he had warned her against all that, that he had taken her to task about her trusting nature and those who might take advantage of it. It was completely different when he was the one who needed to take advantage of it. God, he was a rotten apple.

Robert braced his hands against the rail. 'I owe you an explanation, don't I?'

It was meant to be rhetorical, but Charlotte didn't take it that way. Cocking her head to one side, she considered.

'You did once,' she said, as though she were considering an

academic proposition involving something very long ago and far away. It chilled Robert to the bone.

'I still do,' he said fiercely. 'Even if it is long overdue. I was . . . you see, I had a personal score to settle with Wrothan. Not just a personal score,' he hastened to correct himself. 'It was more of a pledge.' There, that sounded better. 'To a dying man.'

Was it wrong to bring the colonel into it? It seemed a bit cheap, to be wooing a woman by trotting out the corpse of a friend. Robert frowned out over the river. He could recall something along those lines in a Shakespeare play he had seen years ago, on leave, a suitor applying to a lady over a hero's corpse. 'Was ever woman in this humour wooed?' had been the line. The man, he remembered, had been Richard III. Robert didn't much like the comparison.

In profile, it was hard to tell what Charlotte was thinking, and her voice gave nothing away other than a detached interest in the topic. 'So it wasn't just about the sale of secrets, then?'

'No.' Would the colonel have minded? Robert remembered how, after all those years, the gruff Scotsman had still kept a lock of his wife's hair in his breast pocket, twenty years after her death. When Robert, as a know-it-all sixteen-year-old, had carelessly asked why he didn't marry again – with the consequent improvements in housekeeping and meals – the colonel had simply patted his pocket and said that he was married and would be until he died. At the time, Robert had simply rolled his eyes and gone off drinking with a set of long-forgotten mates. But, now . . . Yes, the colonel would understand. 'I had . . . a sort of mentor in India. More than a mentor, really. He all but adopted me.'

'I'm glad somebody did.'

'I badly needed adopting,' Robert admitted. At sixteen, he had been reckless, belligerent, constantly spoiling for a fight.

It was a fight that had brought him to the attention of the colonel, brawling with a fellow lieutenant. The colonel had decided, like Calvin come to Geneva, that Robert was his cross to bear and, by God, he was going to make an officer and a gentleman out of him if one of them died in the process.

And so he had died. Robert wondered, as he had wondered before, what would have happened if he had had the foresight to prevent it, if he had gone to the appropriate authorities the night before instead of putting it all off till after the battle.

'What happened?' asked Charlotte, breaking him out of his reflections.

'Wrothan shot him in the back. He shot him in the middle of a battle, when he thought no one would know the difference.' And he had almost been right. If Robert hadn't known of Wrothan's treachery, he might have supposed the same himself, and the colonel would have gone down as yet another casualty of war. And Wrothan . . .

Wrothan would still be dead at the Frenchman's hand.

Perhaps it was justice, of a sort. Robert would still have preferred to have administered it himself.

'I knew Staines from India,' Robert hurried on. 'That is, I knew of him. He was part of Wrothan's set.'

'So you followed Staines to Girdings,' Charlotte summed up. 'That was why you came back.'

'Yes.' She was too self-contained, too quiet. It made him nervous. 'I should have told you before. I just didn't want you all tangled up in it.' Given that she was now irrevocably tangled, it seemed a singularly inane thing to have said.

Keeping her eyes on the water, Charlotte asked, as if they were strangers at an Assembly, 'Now that your revenge is all done, will you go back to India?'

Black dread welled up around him, like the river. 'Do you want me to? Is that what you're trying to tell me?'

Charlotte blinked up at him. 'I don't see why what I want would have anything to do with it.'

'Don't you?' Robert braced a hand beside hers on the rail, trapping her between him and the river. It was a hell of a time for a declaration, but he was sick of waiting, of prevaricating. 'It has everything to do with it. If you want me to go, I'll go. If you want me to stay, I'll stay. Just give me my orders, and I'll obey.'

Just so long as she commanded him to stay.

Charlotte eyed him curiously and came to her own conclusions. 'Is this what you wanted to talk about tomorrow?' Robert nodded brusquely.

Charlotte's lips quirked upwards in a lopsided smile, like a tragic-comic mask. 'There's no need for grand gestures, you know,' she said, 'or rash promises to leave the country. I wasn't planning to make any more scenes or to take you to task for things that shouldn't have happened and can't be undone. We can put everything behind us and be friendly again.' She regarded her clasped hands as if they were a book she was weary of reading. 'It will make life – easier.'

'Easier,' Robert repeated flatly. What in the deuce was she talking about?

'Easier,' she agreed. 'Since our paths will, invariably, cross. And I do think we could be friends. As we were. Before. We were friends, weren't we?'

Robert's voice came out harsher than intended. 'I wasn't talking about being friends, Charlotte!'

'Then what—?' Her eyes were wide and confused and defensive. 'I don't understand.' Or she didn't want to understand.

'I've missed you,' he said rapidly, trying to put it as plainly as he could before they went off on cross-purposes yet again. 'I want you back.'

Charlotte held up a hand as though to ward him off, scrunching herself as far back against the rail as it would let her.

'Back?' she said incredulously, with a breathless laugh that broke in the middle. 'You said it yourself. We scarcely know each other. You can't have back what you've never had.'

'Never had?' Robert demanded, his eyes locking with hers. 'Would you swear to that? Can you really, in all honesty, claim that there was never anything between us?'

Charlotte flushed. With temper, rather than shame, from the looks of it. '*You* told me it was all an illusion, an enchantment. Those were your words, not mine.'

'I lied.' That didn't sound terribly good, did it? Damn. Damn, damn, damn. Every time he opened his mouth, he just stuck his foot farther down it. 'I knew I had to stay close to Medmenham and the Hellfire crowd in order to make good my promise. I meant to protect you from them,' he finished lamely. 'I didn't want you hurt.'

Charlotte made a little snorting noise. Robert had to admit that it probably more accurately summarised the situation than anything else she could have said.

'I blundered. Badly. Forgive me?' His voice went up hopefully on the last words. Even to his own ears, it sounded a little weak. But it was worth a try. And it had worked before.

Charlotte stubbornly shook her head. 'You told me it was all an illusion, an enchantment. Enchantments don't last.'

'Perhaps this one can,' he said tenderly, reaching out to brush a finger against her cheek.

Charlotte wrenched away from his touch. '*Don't*,' she said, and meant it. 'Which am I meant to believe? What you said then or what you say now? Or what you might say tomorrow?'

He knew the answer to that one. 'Now,' Robert said firmly. 'Definitely now.'

Apparently, that hadn't been the right answer.

'No.' Drawing in a ragged breath, Charlotte braced her elbows against the rail. 'How can you define when now is? Now keeps changing. *You* keep changing. Then was now then, and now will be then soon. You may think you mean it now, but what happens when you change your mind again next week? Another disappearance? Another "forgive me"?'

'I thought you were a forgiving person,' he said. It was a cheap shot, but he was desperate.

'Not that forgiving.' Unhappiness drew new lines in Charlotte's face. 'I don't have that many forgive me's in me. I wish I had. But I don't.'

'You won't need any more,' he promised. 'This is the last time.'

Charlotte made an instinctive move of negation.

Pretending not to see it, Robert blundered on. 'I want things to go back the way they were. Back at Girdings. We can go back, just the two of us. No Medmenham, no Hellfire Club. We'll send your grandmother off to Bath,' he continued persuasively. He concentrated on weaving a spell with his voice and his words. 'We can row on the pond and hunt for unicorns in the garden. I'll feed you the very choicest bits of my jam tarts. We'll spend every evening on the roof, counting stars.'

His own spell had him fast; he could picture it, down to the smell of Charlotte's hair, the feel of her head pressed against his shoulder, the rough stone of the roof ledge at his back. He could smell the flowers in the garden, the flowers he had only seen as dry twigs wrapped in burlap; he could see them in full bloom, perfuming the whole house with their scent. He could imagine the long dinners in the long dining room, candlelight puddling like molten gold on the polished wood of the table. And then, at the very end of every evening, the walk arm in arm down the marble corridors of the first floor to the curtained opulence of the ducal chamber, where Charlotte's inevitable pile of books would totter on the night table, her dropped pens would leave blots on the carpet, and that ridiculously large bed could at last be put to some proper use.

'We'll spend every night in the ducal chambers, together,' he promised, willing her to see what he saw, the velvet drapes, the crested linen, the glow of the candles. 'You can read me poetry. And I can teach you . . . other things.'

Charlotte's eyes were as wide as saucers and slightly unfocused, as though she, too, were seeing the ducal chamber at Girdings and other things besides. Whatever it was stained her telltale skin a deep peony red.

Robert lowered his voice to the merest murmur. 'All you have to do is say yes.'

'It doesn't work that way,' Charlotte protested, and he had the feeling she was arguing with herself as much as with him. Good. She looked at him imploringly. 'You can't just turn back the clock like that.'

'Why not?' He felt like a demon tempting an angel, stringing her along with dark sophistries and forbidden pleasures. Robert drew his voice from deep within his chest, as dark and compelling as the inside of midnight. 'Why not if we both agree to it?'

Charlotte might be half-entranced, but she was entirely stubborn. 'We haven't both agreed. *I* haven't agreed.'

'But you want to.'

Charlotte's lips pressed together as she glowered at him in

mute frustration. She looked as though she wanted to kick him. 'Of course, I do,' she burst out.

But before Robert could bask in his victory, she hurried on, spitting out the words as though they might contaminate her otherwise. 'But don't you see? That's not the point. The wanting isn't enough. Just because I want you—' Colouring, she bit down hard on her lower lip.

'Yes?' said Robert encouragingly, smoothing an errant curl back behind her ear. 'Just because you want me . . . ?'

Charlotte stared at him pleadingly, the prey appealing to the predator. ' – doesn't mean it won't end badly,' she finished stumblingly.

He had won. He could tell. Or, at least, near enough for a kiss to cement the victory.

'On the other hand,' he murmured, his fingers tangling in her hair, 'it doesn't mean it won't end well.'

They were close enough that he could feel the hurried beat of her heart. He could feel Charlotte's indecision in every word she didn't say and every move she didn't make. She was tense with uncertainty, quivering with irresolution. She might not be leaning into him, but she wasn't pulling away, either.

Running a gentling hand down her back, he tilted that crucial bit forwards, just as a jarring sweep sent them both tottering sideways.

Robert swore, catching at the side of the boat with one hand and Charlotte with the other, grabbing at the side of her dress to keep her from going over. Wiping the spray out of his eyes, he could see the vast bulk of Medmenham Abbey looming above them on the bank, like an evil sorcerer's fortress. Swinging on a wide arc, sending water spraying in its wake, the boat made for the water stairs. They had arrived.

Damn, damn, damn. Even in absentia, Medmenham contrived to thwart his courtship.

Charlotte pulled away, shaking off droplets of water and frantically smoothing her hair. From the look on her face, the argument was far from over.

Robert's throat constricted with the reminder of how badly he had managed to mangle something that could have been so simple. If he had only explained himself at Girdings, if he had only sent more than a two-word message – but he couldn't have, back then, he thought wearily. Part of Charlotte's accusation was fair; he hadn't known her well enough to be sure how she would have received it. He knew now, but now it was too late. There was a certain Shakespearean irony to it.

There was no going back, he reminded himself, only forward. The endless night wasn't over yet. There was the king to be found, and perhaps that might yet be the saving of him, if he could offer up the king to Charlotte as a token of his seriousness of purpose.

At least it would make a more original gift than flowers or chocolates.

Fabric rustled and loud yawns could be heard as the inhabitants of the cabin began to stir.

'Are we there yet?' came Miles's plaintive voice from inside the tilt.

'Not quite,' Robert said drily.

Chapter Twenty-Seven

Charlotte was shaking with more than cold as she climbed out of the barge.

She had lost her lap rug somewhere on the deck of the shallop. Her lap rug and her senses, too. She could still feel the warmth of Robert's fingers in her hair, like a phantom of her own folly. If the boat hadn't turned when it had, quite literally dousing her with cold water . . . she didn't want to think about that bit. Not with the others all waking and milling and stretching. Only so much of the colour in her cheeks could be convincingly attributed to windburn.

Robert offered her a hand to help her out of the barge and she took it, feeling the clasp of his fingers sure and firm around her own. Charlotte glanced fleetingly up at him. He returned her glance with a slight, reassuring smile.

That smile made Charlotte bristle.

Was it her imagination, or was there something ever so slightly smug about that smile? As though he knew he had her in the palm of his hand and could decide to pick her up or drop her as the whim moved him.

Charlotte seized on that tiny, warming spark of anger. What did he think he was playing at? One moment Robert was all compliments and deep, burning looks; the next it would be calm reserve and protestations of indifference. Did he just have a horror of cold places? Charlotte would have laughed if she weren't afraid her frozen facial muscles would crack with the strain. It had been frigid in the chapel at Girdings, too, and on the roof. That would be the most lowering explanation of all, to be wanted not for one's wit or charm but for one's ability to serve as a chest and lip warmer in cold places.

He couldn't keep changing the terms. Charlotte was cold and numb and miserable, but she managed to grasp that one simple concept with her frozen senses. She – she told herself indignantly – had been more than accommodating in her willingness to forgive his last lapse and be friends despite it all. It wasn't fair of him, just as she had worked her way around to understanding and forgiveness, to go and start the cycle all over again. This sort of romantic tangle wasn't meant to *be* a cycle. She didn't think she could bear to keep playing the same scenes over and over again, earnest affection followed by terse words of denial, followed by cautious forgiveness, followed by earnest affection again. It sounded like one of the more inventive torments derived by the Greek gods for their favoured guests in Hades. Sisyphus didn't even begin to compare.

Charlotte would have told him so, but now didn't quite seem to be the time, not surrounded by their raggle-taggle band of adventurers with a king to be saved. Charlotte had always had the lowest possible opinion of those heroines who caused unnecessary delays in the middle of a quest by dragging in their own petty romantic problems.

What she had failed to allow for was that it wouldn't feel

nearly so petty when it was her own. But having a proper Lansdowne temper tantrum at Robert could wait until they had the king safely tucked into his own bed, attended by his own attendants. Minus Lord Henry Innes, that was. Even if Lord Henry had been merely the unwitting dupe of Robert's mysterious Mr Wrothan, he was still not fit to be entrusted with the care of a lapdog, much less the king.

Despite the fact that she was safely on dry land and in no imminent danger of falling over, Robert had taken casual possession of her arm, grasping it through her cloak, just beneath the elbow, as though he had every right to offer that support.

It would not have infuriated Charlotte quite so much if she hadn't caught herself leaning into that gentle pressure, like a dog preening to be petted.

Charlotte pulled herself stiffly upright.

Robert, still casually bracing her arm as though – as though she were a dog he had on the lead (having chosen a metaphor, it seemed simpler to stay with it, as unflattering as it was to her), didn't seem to notice. He frowned up at the stucco façade of Medmenham Abbey.

'Look at the lights,' he said, keeping his voice deliberately low. 'Someone is in the Abbey.'

'Not unusual, surely?' said Miles, vaulting easily over the edge of the boat and landing on the dock with a satisfied thump. Miles had always been particularly fond of jumping over things. 'Medmenham would have left a staff behind. Servants and . . . well, servants.'

Household management had never been Miles's forte.

The lantern light trailed from one window to the next, casting strange plays of light and shadow onto the winter grey grass of the bank. To Charlotte's dazed and dazzled eyes, the light seemed to ripple like the tail of a salamander.

There was something entirely uncanny about the whole scene, something that whispered of old and cruel enchantments. Behind her, she could hear the harsh laughter of the wind whistling through the reeds. It made Charlotte think of Shakespeare's Puck. But this was a very old Puck, an old and a malicious Puck, wheezing with spiteful pleasure at tricks still to be played on a band of self-satisfied and unsuspecting mortals.

Pure fancy, she told herself. But she still drew her cloak more tightly around her, wishing she had some iron in her pocket to touch to keep away the fairies. It might be silly, but it couldn't hurt.

The others were more concerned with human malefactors than malicious spirits.

'Who prowls about at midnight?' said Robert. 'Those aren't servants. Someone is looking for something.'

'Or for someone?' suggested Charlotte, thinking of the king.

His eyes caught hers. 'Or for someone,' he agreed, and for a brief moment Charlotte wasn't sure whether they were discussing the king or something else entirely.

'The Frenchman's men, I'd wager,' said Lieutenant Fluellen lazily, coming up between them. Time returned to its normal pacing. 'Wrothan would know where he had stashed his prize.'

'And the Frenchman had an hour's start on us.' Turning back to the boat, Robert had a brief conversation with the boatmen, involving the exchange of gold from Robert's hands to theirs and assurances given on either side. The breeze carried their words away to the far bank, robbing Charlotte of the ability to eavesdrop.

Within a moment, Robert was done, driving the rest of the group before him like a professional sheepdog.

'Shall we?' he said briskly. 'I suggest we don't let them find us here.'

'I second that,' said Lieutenant Fluellen, falling easily into the secondary place by Robert's side, as he must, Charlotte imagined, have done many times before, away across the seas. It made Charlotte feel staggeringly superfluous. 'Where to?'

'The caves.' Robert led the group away from the Abbey, into the protective lee of the shrubbery. The gravel crunched beneath Charlotte's feet as she hurried along behind, her skirts held up in both hands. Behind her, gargoyle faces glowered from the portico. She very much hoped they were made of stone. Twin harpies, their faces proud and cruel, looked as though they might take flight at any moment, cackling as they tore apart their prey. 'If the Frenchman's lot are still searching the house, there's a good chance they haven't yet looked in the caves.'

'Where are the caves?' asked Charlotte, her breath coming in uneven pants as she struggled to match the others' longer strides. Before her, the gardens seemed to stretch on endlessly, dotted with statues whose white stone gleamed dully in the moonlight and odd follies whose peaked and rounded roofs reared out of the topiary like fantastical beasts in the night. The path twisted and turned back upon itself in unnumbered tangles like a sinner's conscience.

There was no turning back, though. The boat had already pulled away from the dock. With its long oars extended, it looked like a water insect skimming on top of the moonlit river. The lanterns – at Robert's instruction? – had been shuttered.

'The caves are several miles inland, near the family mausoleum and the Church of St Lawrence. We have a long walk ahead of us.' He frowned down at Charlotte. 'Are you – ?'

'I'm fine,' she asserted haughtily. No need to tell him about the blister on her heel or the fact that she could really rather use a few moments alone with a chamber pot. The last thing she wanted was his solicitude. One kind look, one sympathetic gesture, and she would dissolve into his arms in a pitiful little ball of jelly, cravenly crying for warmth and reassurance. She hardened her features to try to prevent any sign of weakness from slipping through. 'Lead the way.'

Robert regarded her closely and Charlotte felt herself unconsciously trying to make her spine straighter, as though posture might be an indicator of stamina.

'Right,' he said. 'Onwards!'

He would have taken Charlotte's arm, but Charlotte evaded him by leaning over to brush an imaginary leaf off her cloak.

Within a very short period of time she began to wish she had been more practical and less proud. No wonder most heroes in stories staged their adventures for summer, thought Charlotte despairingly. There was no romance to their expedition, only grim endurance and gruelling cold that bit through her bones and sapped all energy and strength. Not that she had had much of the latter to begin with.

They stayed close, for safety and the meagre warmth that came of keeping together. Robert took the lead, as by right, and Lieutenant Fluellen the rear, by an unspoken prearrangement as smoothly orchestrated as the movement of the mechanical devices Medmenham kept in his garden to shock his visitors. In the beginning, Henrietta and Miles kept up a quiet stream of desultory conversation, but by the time they reached the wilderness garden, with the willows weeping above their heads, the fronds catching at their cloaks like the fingers of mourning nymphs, and the mulch sopping sloppily beneath their feet, even they lapsed into grim silence, keeping their eyes on the path and reserving their strength for the task of carrying on.

There was no time to brood about Robert; every ounce of energy was expended on simply staying upright as they staggered down the tangled paths of Medmenham's personal maze. Charlotte had thought that nothing could have been more like torture than the gravel paths that pounded her frozen feet through her thin evening slippers, but as they left the formal gardens for a carefully planned wilderness, she discovered that wood chips were worse, sinking unevenly beneath her weight and leaching forth an icy brown liquid that seeped through the sides of her slippers and made her frozen toes tingle painfully.

Charlotte lost all sense of time. They might have been wandering Medmenham's grounds for hours or years, trapped in a sorcerer's silver glass, miming the motions for his amusement.

The moonlight cast an unearthly glaze over the landscape, lending an eerie illusion of life to marble statues and the tortured shapes of trees. The topiary, clipped to resemble all manner of mythical and exotic beasts, seemed to scowl and roar as they ventured past. Griffins arched their unnatural claws and tigers yawned with green-fanged mouths. Charlotte felt as though she had stumbled into a mad poet's disordered dreams. At every turn, a new grotesquerie confronted them. Marble nymphs fled across their path, pursued by a team of grinning, gloating satyrs displaying anatomical properties Charlotte had heard whispers of, but had never viewed in either stone or flesh. Leda disappeared between the wings of an amorous swan, while a sultry Venus beckoned them off the path to a pavilion whose scrolled marble benches glimmered dimly in the moonlight, double the width of any bench that graced the gardens of Girdings and hollowed in suspicious places.

'Medmenham's predecessor was a great patron of the arts,' explained Robert stiffly, hauling Charlotte out of the way of an Apollo who, flinging himself to his knees, had buried his head between Daphne's legs – no doubt in an excess of grief at seeing her turn into a tree. 'He spent a good deal of time in Italy.'

This time, when he took her arm, Charlotte didn't protest. She wasn't quite sure how many more yards she still had in her. Her legs felt disconnected from the rest of her, like a doll she had possessed as a child, made of cylindrical pieces of polished wood with the limbs loosely connected by metal pegs, so that when you picked it up, the doll would dance, legs and arms jiggling disjointedly. That had been before Girdings, before her grandmother declared such simple playthings fit for the tenantry, not for the daughter of a duke. Charlotte had said she would give it away, but she hadn't. She could still remember, then, her mother holding it and making it dance.

Fragmented memories circled through her mind, more real than anything around her. Whispering in the corner of Almack's with Henrietta and Penelope during their very first season; summer days in the gardens of Girdings with *Evelina* for company; Robert, as he had been once upon a time, boosting her onto the edge of the fountain to watch the goldfish swim in the sunlight. And, behind it all, she could see her mother's arms, in blue wool sleeves, holding on to her old wooden doll, making it dance.

With a flutter of anxiety, Charlotte realised she was drifting away into a sort of waking sleep.

With a strength born of fear, she struggled back to reality. Cold, miserable, clammy reality. Charlotte stepped down hard on a stone, feeling the bite of it straight through her sodden slippers. That was real, just as the damp cling of her muslin skirt against her legs was real.

'You don't want one of these statues for the gardens of Girdings, then?' Charlotte's lips were cracked and clumsy, her voice rusty. Talking to Robert would keep her awake, at least. She had a feeling that she looked even worse than she sounded. The hem of her once fashionable dress was caked with mud and it clung to her legs as she moved, making the going even more difficult than it would otherwise be.

Robert's hand tightened on her arm, with a pressure that was unmistakably an embrace. 'And scandalise all your ministers of state on the roof?'

There was a tenderness in his voice that made Charlotte's heart clench in a very inconvenient way.

Irritation, she told herself. It was the intimation of intimacy that irked her. He had no right to be bringing up that night on the roof. He had forfeited the right to that when he changed his mind the first time.

On the positive side, there was nothing like a bit of romantic turmoil to bring one fully awake.

'I don't know,' Charlotte said contrarily, keeping her head down and her eyes on her hem. 'It's been awfully quiet for them up there. A little scandal might do them good.'

'They would probably tumble off their perches with the shock,' Robert replied idly, helping her over a rough patch of ground.

'They might be stronger than that.' Charlotte could feel her heels beginning to dig in. 'Perhaps they want a little variety.'

'Or,' said Robert, missing the point entirely, 'perhaps they're made of plaster and don't really care.'

'Stone,' Charlotte corrected, kicking her skirt out of the way. 'Not plaster. It's stronger.'

She could feel his steps slow as he paused to look down at her. Charlotte resolutely kept her own eyes on the ground, struggling forward one laboured step at a time. If he didn't realise why she was upset, she didn't want to tell him. Especially since she wasn't quite sure why herself.

'We can rest for a moment, if you like,' he suggested, with infuriating solicitude. 'At least get you out of the wind.'

If she stopped, she might never move again. And it would be just as cold wherever they were.

'And let the Frenchman catch us up?' she countered. 'How far are we from the caves?'

Robert pointed directly ahead. Above the trees, an immense golden orb dominated the horizon, shimmering with reflected moonlight. It looked, thought Charlotte, like a sceptre sculpted for the king of a race of giants. 'Do you see that gold ball?'

'It would be hard not to,' she said, and was a little ashamed of quite how snappish she sounded. 'What is it?'

'Medmenham's church,' said Robert. 'I was told that it is positioned directly over the deepest part of the caves, the bit they call Hades.'

Dizzy and miserable as she was, Charlotte appreciated the conceit. 'It's like Dante's *Divine Comedy*, with Inferno below and Paradise above.'

'And Purgatory in the middle.' Robert pronounced the word with a grim relish that made Charlotte wonder, for the first time, if he might not be in a sort of purgatory, too. She risked a sidelong glance in his direction. He had assumed leadership of their expedition so easily, taken charge of her so casually, that she had assumed this must all be little more than a lark for him, all in a night's work. Including the improper proposals.

Before she could find a cautious way of broaching the topic, Robert said briskly, 'Medmenham's mausoleum covers the back entrance to the caves.' Turning his head, he raised his voice ever so slightly to carry to the people behind them. 'As we approach, it's probably best if we try to be as quiet as possible.'

'What's that?' Miles called out.

Robert mimed lowering of voice by raising one hand and bringing it slowly down. Miles looked abashed. Charlotte swallowed her grin before Robert could see it; it looked too much like his own.

At the gates of the mausoleum, the men arranged themselves in a triangular formation. Behind them, Charlotte saw Henrietta ease her pistol out of the folds of her pelisse. Charlotte couldn't quite recall what she had done with her own pistol. She thought she might have left it in the carriage. Since the carriage was back in London, three hours by river, she doubted it would do her much good.

The mausoleum sounded quiet enough to her. All she could hear was the sodden slap of the tree leaves and the laboured rise and fall of her own breathing. But the men were clearly primed for battle, cloaks off, pistols at the ready. Charlotte, who had always dreamt of brave battles with banners flaring, felt at a loss. This was no formal joust at which she could wave her veil and cheer her champion; if anything, it would be an ambush.

But who was ambushing whom? Charlotte's fingernails bit into her palms as the men burst through the entrance of the mausoleum.

They were greeted with resounding silence. There was no scramble of booted feet on wet grass, no jostling for weaponry, no grunts or battle cries, just the sound of their own laboured breathing.

Aside from its scattering of masonry, the grounds of the mausoleum were entirely empty.

Miles straightened from his fighting crouch. 'Where is everyone?' he demanded indignantly.

Charlotte and Henrietta ducked under the archway into the mausoleum. It was as eccentric in its design as the rest of the grounds, open to the elements, dotted with arches and monuments and other classical effluvia, in no particular pattern that Charlotte could discern. Between the granite walls and the barren ground, it did, however, succeed in conveying a decidedly grim impression. That, at least, seemed in keeping with Charlotte's notion of a mausoleum.

'There should be someone here.' Robert prowled around the side of an urn, looking more than a little bit irritated at being balked of his battle. 'Wrothan wouldn't have left his prize unguarded.'

Charlotte saw no need to voice what they were all thinking, that there would only be a need for guards if the king was, in fact, on the premises. After their long, miserable journey, failure didn't bear thinking of.

'He would need someone on hand,' she said instead. 'Someone to bring the king food at intervals.'

'Poor *ton* to starve the king,' seconded Miles.

'Poor business sense, too,' said Lieutenant Fluellen cheerfully. 'You can't ransom a royal skeleton.'

'So where are they?' asked Henrietta, as indignant as a hostess whose guests had failed to appear for dinner.

'Down in the caves with the king?' suggested Miles. 'If I wanted to guard someone, I'd jolly well stay close.'

'There was someone here,' muttered Robert, squinting at the ground around the perimeter. 'Do you see this?' When he straightened, he was holding a long-stemmed clay pipe. 'The bowl is still warm.'

'Cheerful place for a smoke,' commented Miles, grimacing at the funereal monuments.

'But a logical place if one was about to go underground,' said Lieutenant Fluellen thoughtfully. 'The guard must have popped up for a smoke before going back down into the caves.'

'Guard or guards?' asked Charlotte, looking anxiously around her. She kept thinking she saw movement out of the corner of her eye, only to turn and find yet another urn or arch.

Above it all, the gold-tipped spire of the church looked smugly on. The entrance seemed to lie at the other side of the mausoleum. Could the entrance to the caves lie through there? Despite Robert's assertion that the back entrance to the caves lay through the mausoleum, she had yet to see it.

'Three guards at most,' said Lieutenant Fluellen authoritatively. As all the others looked at him, he shrugged. 'Well, it just sounded like a logical number.'

'All down in the caves,' said Miles, rubbing his hands together.

'If they're here,' said Robert repressively. 'We might be barking up the wrong tree entirely.'

'Or down the wrong cave,' said Charlotte.

'What about the church?' asked Henrietta, squinting at the nondescript granite façade of Medmenham's church. With its rough stone, square bell tower, and squat design, it looked more like a fortress than a place of worship. 'If I were your Mr Whatever-His-Name-Was, I would prefer to hide my monarch above ground.'

'Excellent thought!' said Lieutenant Fluellen, a little too heartily. 'You and Lady Charlotte can investigate the church while we inspect the caves.'

'I second that.' Miles's relief was palpable. 'Divide and conquer and all that.'

No one pointed out that it was enemies who were supposed to be divided, not allies.

Henrietta kept quiet because she had already decided that she was right and the others were wrong; Charlotte could tell from the set of her friend's shoulders that she was already planning her 'I told you so' in elaborate and loving detail. Charlotte held her tongue for the opposite reason. If they did encounter a cadre of hardened villains (or even not so hardened villains) down in the caves, she and Henrietta would be more trouble than help. She had no illusions about her own utility in a battle. It might be nice to seize a moment of glory, to strike a blow for king and country as she did in her daydreams, but she knew, realistically, that she was far more likely to trip over her own skirt, walk in front of someone at a crucial moment, or be captured, dragged to one side, and used to make Robert, Miles, and Lieutenant Fluellen throw down their weapons. All things considered, she and Henrietta were more use to the king out of the caves than in them.

Charlotte shivered as the grim reality of their situation set in. Maybe they would be lucky, maybe there wouldn't be any sort of battle. It was difficult to remember that she once thought of battles with a romantic frisson of excitement; now, with the reality looming, the prospect brought only dread.

Their tiny army was already making its preparations, jostling together alongside the massive urn that Robert swore contained the secret entrance to the tunnels. As Miles peered through the hole in the side of the urn, in whispered conversation with Lieutenant Fluellen, Charlotte caught Robert's eye. He immediately detached himself from his fellows and strode towards her.

And Charlotte realised that something rather alarming had happened. She no longer heard trumpets when she looked at him. There were no more fanfares or imaginary banners. He was just Robert, not a mythical knight in shining armour, not a hero in a storybook. The old infatuation had died, but what had replaced it was even more debilitating; like the bitter winter wind, it stripped through all her outer layers, biting clear to the bone.

It was fortunate that he had no idea, Charlotte thought, as he strolled over to her, tall and golden and radiating martial energy. It would hurt badly enough in the morning when he remembered that he was he and she was she and that he really wasn't that enamoured of her after all. It would be even harder if he knew just how much she cared. Harder for both of them. She knew him well enough now for that.

'We're off to slay your dragons,' he said wryly. 'Or dragon, as the case may be.'

Once Charlotte would have thought it a charming turn of phrase; now she felt a whisper of superstitious dread. This wasn't a tale out of one of her books. There was no armour to guard him, no enchantments to protect him, no happily ever after to ensure his safe return.

'Is it very dangerous?' she asked, knowing it was a ridiculous question even as she asked it. Of course, it was dangerous.

'No,' he said, and she knew he was lying through his teeth, lying right through the broad, reassuring smile he donned like armour. 'There are three of us, after all.'

But there might be three of them as well. Their putative opponents had the advantage of knowing their terrain. Down in the darkness of the caves, who knew what might happen?

Nothing had really changed; tomorrow morning would still be tomorrow morning, but all that paled into insignificance against the gaping hole in the side of the urn that led into caves of unknown peril and treachery.

Charlotte clutched Robert's arm, her fingernails biting through the thin fabric of his sleeve. 'Be careful.'

'Rob!' Lieutenant Fluellen called softly, only his head sticking out of the back of the urn. 'Any day now!'

'Coming,' Robert called back, and rolled his eyes for Charlotte's benefit.

Charlotte was in no mood to be so cheaply diverted. 'You should go,' she said, very seriously. 'I won't keep you.'

With one finger, Robert gently lifted her chin. 'Don't worry,' he said softly. 'We'll be back.'

And then, before Charlotte could say anything else at all, he grabbed her to him in a quick, fierce embrace. Although he had removed his cloak and coat, she could feel the heat radiating through his shirt as he clasped her to him, his arms like bars of iron around her back. Throwing caution to the winds, Charlotte wrapped her arms around his neck and kissed him back, kissed him good luck, kissed him goodbye, kissed him forgiveness, kissed him everything she had meant to say and hadn't.

Through it all, the trumpets sounded. They hadn't gone away after all; they had only changed their tune.

As suddenly as he had embraced her, Robert released her, putting her from him with sure, resolute hands, making sure she was steady on her feet before letting her go again. The air felt even more frigid cold without him.

'Good luck,' she croaked.

With one last wave and a jaunty grin, Robert disappeared into the urn and down into the tunnels of the Hellfire caves.

Chapter Twenty-Eight

Charlotte stood like a pillar of salt, staring at the empty urn, until a loud and pointed clearing of the throat shook her out of her reverie.

'Do I take it that you two have reconciled?' said Henrietta.

Reconciled didn't seem quite the right word for it. Despite the lingering tingle on her lips, she couldn't help but remember that night on the roof of Girdings, when Robert had seemed just as attentive – until he disappeared. Just as he had before. It was beginning to look like a habit.

'Not really,' said Charlotte.

Henrietta's eyes glinted like a cat's in the dark as she groped for the handle of the church door. 'Then what do you call that?'

'A lady's favour to a knight going into battle,' Charlotte said honestly. 'I didn't have a scarf to give him, so a kiss had to do.'

'Hmph,' said Henrietta. 'I doubt you'll see him complaining about the substitution.'

The door swung open behind her, moving soundlessly on well-oiled hinges, revealing the oddest sort of church Charlotte had ever seen. In place of pews, there were armchairs, curved and curled at the arms in the Egyptian fashion. Alchemical symbols decorated the font, including a serpent chasing its own tail in an intimation of eternity, and Judas Iscariot leered down from the ceiling as he savoured the Last Supper. But it wasn't the bizarre or even the blasphemous that made Charlotte bump into Henrietta's back as they both froze in the doorway. It was a small and homely detail, one that under any other circumstance wouldn't have warranted the slightest bit of notice.

A lamp was burning at the far end of the nave.

Charlotte felt Henrietta's fingers clamp like a vice around her upper arm. Soundlessly, she pointed upwards. Following her gaze, Charlotte stared in wide-eyed incomprehension. There was a man slowly but steadily climbing down a long ladder propped against the wall. Mercifully, his back was to them. He also had a bulky object hanging from one arm. A bag of some sort?

With a jerky movement, Henrietta yanked on Charlotte's arm, whisking them both around the door in a flurry of damp fabric. Charlotte stumbled and caught her balance on the side of the church, feeling the stucco siding scrape against her palm.

Pointing back at the door, she mimed confusion.

Every muscle on alert, Henrietta reminded Charlotte of nothing so much as a horse about to bolt. 'Guard,' she mouthed soundlessly.

Even without making noise, Henrietta managed to convey a decided air of triumph. Charlotte had no doubt she was inwardly dancing a jig, complete with pipers piping and lots of lords a-leaping.

Charlotte pointed back towards the mausoleum, framing the words, 'Should we . . . ?'

Henrietta gave an abrupt shake of the head. Narrowing her eyes meaningfully, Henrietta lifted her hand and brought it down in a chopping motion.

Charlotte held up both hands palm up. It was all very well and good to talk about knocking out the guard, but with what? He wasn't particularly big or burly – in fact, he looked fairly small and malnourished – but for all that he was small, he might be fierce. And armed. They couldn't very well just bash at him with their reticules until he pleaded nicely for pardon and genteelly submitted to being tied up.

Reaching into the folds of her pelisse, Henrietta whipped out a long, metallic object. At least, she tried to whip it out. The little curly bit – the trigger? – caught on the folds and Henrietta had to pause midflourish to disentangle herself. It was not a sight to fill Charlotte with confidence. But what were their other alternatives? By the time they made their way through the tunnels, the man might be gone, along with whatever information he might have. If they were going to strike, it needed to be now.

Meeting her friend's eyes, Charlotte lowered her head in a brief nod. 'If I distract him,' she whispered, leaning forwards so they were practically nose to nose, 'can you hit him?'

'With the gun or with a bullet?' whispered Henrietta.

'Either,' Charlotte hissed back.

Henrietta paused just a moment too long for confidence before bringing her chin down in a nod. But it was the best they were going to do. The cavalry was all underground.

'Ready?' whispered Henrietta, tilting her pistol at a jaunty, if not exactly useful, angle. 'Go!'

What she lacked in force, she might make up in sheer insanity. They did say beginners were lucky, didn't they? Feeling like an idiot, Charlotte did the most distracting thing she could think of. She swooped down the nave of the church waving her arms above her head and shrieking like her grandmother's maid on a particularly bad day.

The first screech got the man's attention. The second made him lose his grip. Twisting around to see a madwoman flinging her arms in the air, the man on the ladder lost hold of the bundle tucked underneath his left arm. Fumbling for it, his other hand wrenched free, the sweat of his palm leaving a wet trail on the worn wood. An expression of open-mouthed shock transfixed his face as he hung suspended in space, rocking back and forth with his feet on the ladder as he flailed his arms for balance. Charlotte skidded to a stop, her last shriek ending in an apologetic cough. With the inevitability of a tree toppling in the forest, the man went over, striking his head on the stone floor with an unpleasant crunch.

Wincing, Charlotte flung herself onto the ground beside him. There was a bloody spot on the side of his head – a head which, it appeared, had not been washed all too recently – but he was still breathing. He also smelt quite heavily of tobacco. Charlotte wondered if he had realised that he lost his pipe. Of course, at the moment, that was probably the least of his concerns.

'Good heavens. Well done.' Henrietta rubbed her ears with a grimace of remembered pain. 'I had no idea you could hit those notes. I wonder if they heard it down in the tunnels.'

'I doubt it.' Charlotte rocked back on her heels. 'I really didn't expect him to fall like that.'

'Neither did I,' agreed Henrietta, 'but I'm awfully glad he did. It saved me having to use this.' She dropped the pistol on the floor beside the ladder as she knelt next to Charlotte. 'I suppose we should tie him up, anyway, just in case. There goes my petticoat.'

'It's a good thing he wasn't too high off the ground when he fell.' Delicate exploration revealed that the man's skull appeared to be intact, although he would have a dreadful lump. His hair – his very greasy hair – appeared to have provided at least a partial buffer. The blood came from one small graze. Charlotte wadded her handkerchief against it all the same.

'Charlotte,' said Henrietta, wriggling out of her stocking in lieu of trying to tear up her petticoat, 'the man was instrumental in kidnapping the king. You can't feel too sorry for him.'

'I know,' said Charlotte, taking one limp, slightly damp stocking from Henrietta. 'But I still wouldn't want his death on my conscience.'

'Mmph,' said Henrietta noncommittally, tying the man's legs together with her other stocking. The flowers embroidered along the sides looked decidedly incongruous against the rough brown wool of the man's breeches. 'If we capture anyone else, it will have to be your stockings,' she said, standing and wiping her hands off against her skirt. 'I don't think my garters are wide enough.'

'Did you see what he was carrying?' Charlotte asked as she tied a double knot around the man's hands. She doubted it would hold long against concerted pressure.

Henrietta scrunched up her nose, scanning the floor for it. 'It looked like a sack, didn't it? There it is.'

The dun-coloured burlap was discoloured by a damp patch of liquid that had seeped through the fabric. Charlotte yanked her hand out of the bag as her finger grazed something sharp. Thinking better of it, she upended the sack and scattered the contents out along the stone floor. Broken glass shone dully in the light of the man's lantern, discoloured by a coating of a viscous liquid.

'Hen!' Charlotte whispered hoarsely, pointing to the fallen objects on the floor with mounting excitement. 'Look what was in the bag.'

In front of her lay a heel of bread, the rind of a cheese, and a stained cloth. Whether it had been stained before or after the bottle broke was unclear.

Henrietta's hazel eyes lit up. 'Not exactly your usual place for a picnic.'

Reaching out very carefully, Charlotte ran a finger along the moisture filming one of the larger pieces of the broken glass bottle. The liquid made the skin of her finger tingle. Lifting it to her nose, she sniffed cautiously.

'The king,' she said breathlessly. 'Hen, he must have been coming from the king. Here.' She thrust her hand at her friend. 'Smell. It's laudanum.'

Henrietta dutifully sniffed, screwing up her nose at the scent. 'But why the ladder?'

They both looked up. The ladder stretched up and up like something out of a biblical prophet's dream. It ended just below the folds of a disciple's robe in the vast picture of the Last Supper that decorated the ceiling.

'They wouldn't have put him on the roof,' said Henrietta doubtfully.

'No,' said Charlotte decidedly, 'not the roof. But they might have put him in the orb.'

'The what?'

The more she thought about it, the more Charlotte was convinced she was right. 'The ornamental orb on top of the church. It's certainly large enough to house a man. And it would be the last place anyone would look.'

Henrietta craned her head back, looking dubiously at the ceiling. 'I suppose it couldn't hurt to look,' she said, but neither of them made any move to approach the ladder. It was probably no more or less sturdy than any other ladder, but it seemed an uncommonly rickety affair, propped against the wall of the church.

'I can go,' said Henrietta unenthusiastically, moving to kilt up her skirts. 'If you keep watch below.'

'Will you be all right?' said Charlotte doubtfully. 'The last time you tried to climb a tree, Miles had to fetch you down.'

'True,' admitted Henrietta, unsuccessfully trying to tie a knot into the fabric of her skirt. 'I was fine with the climbing part, though. It was only the getting-down part that was hard.'

'The getting-down bit is rather crucial,' said Charlotte apologetically. 'I'll go.'

She hoped she sounded more confident than she felt. Her own experience with tree climbing had been even more limited than Henrietta's. She felt much about trees as she did about horses; pretty to look at, but she felt no desire to climb on them. But surely a ladder would be different? It was meant to be climbed, after all. She was smaller and lighter than Henrietta, which would put less weight on the rails – and the look of relief on Henrietta's face was too obvious to be ignored.

'Are you sure?' said Henrietta, dropping her skirt with obvious relief.

'I don't mind at all,' Charlotte lied. 'And the king knows me. If he is there, it would be better that he see me. Would you hold this for me?'

Wriggling out of her cloak, she passed it over to Henrietta, shivering as the thick fabric lifted off her shoulders. The dress that had been possible in the theatre, with thousands of candles burning, was eminently unsuited to an unheated building of coarse stone that appeared to hoard the cold and damp, magnifying rather than mitigating it. But the extra fabric would pose a hazard while climbing. Charlotte was scared enough as it was, without an extra length of heavy velvet pulling her back.

Tentatively, Charlotte lifted one foot onto the first rung. The wooden bar pressed into the sole of her foot through her slipper. Belatedly, Charlotte wondered if she ought to have removed her shoes and stockings, but she suspected that if she descended the ladder now, she wouldn't have the courage to go back on it again. A few more rungs and her slippers were level with Henrietta's shoulders. Resolutely, Charlotte looked straight ahead, concentrating on the pull of the muscles in her legs, the solid feel of the scratchy wood of the rails beneath her hands. It would not do to think of how long the ladder seemed or how steep or how very far she still was from the top of it.

Her nails had gone purple with cold and she was having trouble feeling her fingers.

'Are you all right?' Henrietta called up, from what felt like an endless way below. Her voice sounded oddly hollow.

Charlotte gave a nervous laugh, clutching compulsively at the rails as the ladder wobbled with her. 'I'll let you know when I get down.'

'How on earth would they get the king up there?' Henrietta's voice was sharp with nerves. 'Perhaps you'd best just come down. We can send one of the men up later. They like climbing things.'

'A very sensible suggestion. Allow me to second that, Lady Charlotte.'

Dizzily, Charlotte clung to the ladder, understanding for the first time how the other man had come to fall as a new voice intruded into their conversation, nearly startling her from her precarious perch.

It was a cultivated voice, polished and amused, with just the slightest hint of a foreign accent. A French accent, to be precise.

Henrietta made a noise of protest that was muffled midsqueak. There was a scuffling noise, which Charlotte deduced had something to do with Henrietta's slippered feet attempting to do the most harm they possibly could and generally missing their mark.

Bland and unruffled, the Frenchman continued with scarcely a pause. 'May I prevail upon you to descend, Lady Charlotte? I shouldn't like to have to shoot you down.'

The elephant god had taken his mask with him when he left Wycombe.

Robert jumped lightly off the ladder, joining his two colleagues in the narrow anteroom behind the ceremonial chamber. The air smelt cold and dank, with no lingering savour of exotic spices. Damp beaded the rough walls, seeping slowly downwards to the packed earth floor.

Miles regarded the small, rough-hewn chamber with palpable disappointment. 'Is this all?'

Not so much as a stray bead had been left to indicate the room's former function. The braziers and the beaded curtain had been tidied away, thriftily stored for use at the next orgy, along with the miscellany of monks' robes and the indicia of the elephant god. The only sign of human habitation were the torches in their metal brackets on the walls. Tommy had prudently lit one of the torches. The moonlight might provide adequate light above, but it did nothing for the subterranean regions below.

Robert flexed his shoulders, edgy with energy and anticipation. What more appropriate place to beard a dragon than in its cave? The entire scenario was directly out of one of Charlotte's storybooks, the stuff of myth and legend. He was fairly sure he had his lady's favour already, despite the reservations she had voiced on the boat, but it certainly couldn't hurt to emerge triumphant with a rescued king to place before her as trophy.

If the king was there.

He had to be, Robert assured himself. There was no other logical place. If the king wasn't being kept in Medmenham Abbey, that left only the caves and Medmenham's church, directly above. Of the two, the caves were by far the more defensible, composed as they were of a warren of tunnels and chambers. It was the ideal situation for a small force of men – or even one man – to ward off a would-be rescue committee.

'The main ceremonial chamber is next door,' Robert said in an undertone. 'I doubt the king would be kept there.'

Tommy released the torch from its brackets, hefting it high so that the flaring tip sent orange-red light guttering across the uneven surface of the walls. 'Where, then? You're the nearest we have to a map, Rob.'

Remembering his trek from the main entrance through the labyrinthine passageways, Robert was not filled with confidence.

Pretending to an assurance he was far from feeling, he took out his penknife and drew a small square in the dirt. 'This is where we are.'

The others followed suit, crouching beside him in the dirt, Tommy's torch illuminating their dirty and tired faces. The remnants of their formal evening clothes made an incongruous note to the scene, squatting in the dirt of the cave floor by the light of a single, sputtering torch.

Leading off the square, Robert drew a round shape, followed by two wavy lines. 'The main chamber is through this one. The ceremonial cavern is separated from the rest of the tunnels by a narrow river, which can only be crossed by boat. The boat carries two or, at most, three.'

Impatiently shaking his hair out of his eyes, Miles looked up from the drawing. 'And you believe the king lies on the other side of the river.'

'Almost certainly.' Robert drew another line, leading off from the river. A thick one, this time, to indicate a corridor. 'Across the River Styx, a series of small cells have been dug out of the tunnels. Most are secured by their own grilles and equipped with a bed and chamber pot.'

'When you say grilles,' asked Miles, 'do you mean with locks?'

Robert nodded.

'Well and truly cells then,' said Tommy soberly. 'The perfect place to store an unwilling guest.'

'My thought precisely. The only problem is finding the correct cell before someone else finds us.'

'We'd best get to it then, hadn't we?' said Tommy, and Robert was reminded of a dozen other instances in which they had ventured forth together to confront a mass of faceless adversaries, charging forward through the thick of powder smoke, shying away from the concatenation of cannons, running and firing, firing and running, horses shot out beneath them, men groaning and dying, adversaries faceless in the smog.

In comparison, this was a stroll in the park, an afternoon's tea party. But that didn't mean a stray bullet couldn't bring one of them down. All it would take would be one man, with the benefit of surprise and a quick trigger finger, one lucky strike, one fortunate ricochet. He had never worried himself about that sort of thing before. Battle was battle, and he knew that he could die as easily as the next man, that a sniper's rifle could kill just as effectively as a cavalry charge. It was all part of the job and there were no guarantees. He had simply been lucky so far.

But that had been before. How could he climb that ladder and explain to Lady Henrietta that her husband wasn't coming back? He wasn't particularly thrilled with the notion of having his lifeless body borne back to Girdings, either. He had other plans for his return, and they had nothing to do with mausoleums.

Robert spared a moment's gratitude that the women were safely above ground. It would be ten times worse having to worry about them as well. They might be cold in the deserted church, but at least they would be unmolested.

Robert staggered to his feet, jerkily wiping out the drawing with the sole of one shoe. 'I go first,' he said, 'since I know the way. Tommy, you take the rear. Dorrington—'

'Understood,' said Miles with a grin that suggested a mind happily free of funereal thoughts. 'I take the middle.'

'Once we pass the bronze doors to the river, I want total silence,' Robert said sternly. 'No talking, no whispering. We don't know how sound carries in these caves.'

'And we don't want to alert anyone to our presence,' agreed Tommy. 'It would be deuced unfortunate if they decided to do away with the evidence.'

It would be more than unfortunate. It would precipitate an immediate succession crisis. How was one to explain that the king had been kidnapped and murdered? The country would be in an uproar. And the Prince of Wales, with his dubious political allies, would be on the throne.

Robert grimaced. 'I don't think any of us have any interest in a Medmenham ministry.'

One by one, they ventured through the square-cut hole in the wall, lowering themselves from the altar to the ground. As Robert had suspected, the circular cavern was deserted, the great lamp hanging lightless from the arched roof. The bronze doors were shut.

With a finger to his lips to indicate silence, Robert put his shoulders to the door on the right-hand side, where Dionysus revelled with his maenads in a perpetual debauch. The door resisted slightly and then gave, moving open by inches onto total darkness.

The darkness was pregnant with the whisper of the water as it slapped and slithered against the banks, like a nest of serpents stretching. The silver chain chimed softly as the boat rocked in its moorings, like a spectral bell, tolling a mythical hero to his death. And through it all, Robert seemed to hear the hiss and whisper of drowned voices, batting against the banks, fighting the waves for release.

Kicking himself for supernatural fancy, Robert motioned peremptorily behind him for Tommy to bring the torch. It was a chancy thing, potentially signalling their presence to the enemy, but still less of a liability than plunging headfirst into the river. Into that chorus of drowned voices, a nasty voice in the back of his head provided, and he squished it.

It wasn't that he was afraid of the dark waters. It was simply common sense. If he recalled correctly, there were enough twists and bends in the tunnels that their light would only be visible to someone standing directly on the other bank. Or a creature within the water. It would be like Medmenham to stock his subterranean river with his own private sea serpent.

Silently, Tommy obeyed, circling Miles's broad form. The torchlight cast their shadows in relief along the bank and lent a reddish glow to the surface of the water, as though it burnt with subterranean fire. The boat had been chained to the near bank, creaking lightly in its moorings, the long pole braced against one side.

Robert listened. He listened hard, sorting out the slap and echo of the water, the natural noises of the subterranean system. It was too easy to imagine the sounds he sought, to turn the creak of the boat's timbers into the distorted echo of a man's voice or the slap of the water into the shuffle of boots in the tunnel beyond. The opposite bank gave way to a tunnel, narrow and slope-roofed, stretching upwards into unmitigated darkness. Once in the tunnels, there would be nowhere to hide, no cover from a wildly aimed bullet, save the very cells that might serve as bolt-holes for a waiting adversary.

Frowning, Robert stepped to the very edge of the water. His shadow stepped with him, a black blot stretching back across the far wall. There was something wrong. He only wished he could pinpoint what it was.

Miles waved one large arm to get his attention, jabbing in the direction of the boat, mimicking climbing in.

'By God, that's it,' Robert exclaimed, breaking his own vow of silence. 'Don't you see?'

'See what?' asked Miles cautiously.

'It's the boat,' Robert said, looking from one man to the

other. He was met by confusion on Miles's part and narrowed eyes on Tommy's. 'The boat is on the wrong side of the river.'

'I should think it's on the right side,' offered Miles, scrutinising the offending craft. 'If it were on the other side, we'd have to swim across.'

'Exactly,' said Robert. 'So how did our man get across?'

'Maybe he took the other entrance?' suggested Tommy. 'He might have come in through the front.'

'But the pipe was on this side,' Miles pointed out, looking perturbed. 'Right by the entrance.'

'Near the entrance,' Robert corrected, his lips feeling as though they had been frozen. He forced them to move. 'Near the entrance. Not at the entrance. What if we were wrong? What if your wife was right?'

'You mean—' began Tommy.

The torchlight burnt like hellfire against the cavern walls as Robert gave voice to the nightmare prospect. 'What if our man with the pipe was never in the caves?'

He didn't need to say more.

Without a word exchanged between them, the three men made an abrupt about-face, jostling towards the door. If the man with the pipe had never been in the caves, that meant he was above ground. In the church.

With Charlotte.

Chapter Twenty-Nine

'Lady Charlotte? If you will?'

Remembering the fate of the last man who had climbed that ladder, Charlotte clung tightly with both hands as she very slowly and painfully twisted her torso to look down below. She could see Henrietta pinned in the grasp of a man whose rough wool cap hid his face from Charlotte's view.

The man who had spoken, the one who had called her by name, obligingly stepped forward, into Charlotte's line of vision.

He wore a monk's habit, a rough brown robe of the sort the members of the Hellfire Club had been wearing, but Charlotte could see the tips of boots beneath rather than sandals. He had thrown his hood back, revealing close-cropped brown hair and a face that Charlotte might have considered handsome had its owner not been pointing a pistol at her.

'Won't you come down?' the Frenchman said lightly, as if he were asking her to stand up with him at Almack's rather than threatening her at gunpoint. 'I really shouldn't like to shoot you.'

'I shouldn't like to be shot,' Charlotte agreed, but she continued to cling to the ladder without moving. She wasn't particularly sure that down was a safe place to be. Unfortunately, up wasn't an option, either. He could undoubtedly shoot faster than she could climb.

'Now, Lady Charlotte,' said the monk, very, very patiently, and Charlotte reluctantly began to shimmy downwards, feeling her way down rung by rung. Henrietta had been wrong; it wasn't any harder going down than it had been going up, but Charlotte deliberately drew out the process, playing for time. If she dawdled long enough, there was a chance the men might finish in the tunnels and charge up to rescue them. Or they might stay down there, searching for nonexistent villains and exchanging witty quips. Charlotte suspected the latter. A more likely avenue of opportunity was Henrietta's discarded pistol. Where had she left it? Charlotte thought she remembered Henrietta setting it down by the base of the ladder, but her mind had been on other things at the time.

Twisting, shoulder level off the ground, she peered down at the Frenchman as though something had just occurred to her. Which it had. But it also made an excellent opportunity to try to look for the pistol.

Charlotte donned her daftest, vaguest expression – which, as her grandmother was fond of saying, was very daft indeed. 'How do you know my name?'

The Frenchman was neither impressed nor diverted. 'That would be telling.'

Charlotte widened her eyes at him in the way that had worked so well on the real Dr Simmons. 'I suppose it would be futile to ask who you are?'

'Very.' The Frenchman gestured with his pistol, but not before Charlotte thought she saw something metallic on the ground by the crumpled form of Wrothan's fallen guard. Charlotte gave silent thanks to St Lawrence, or whoever it was to whom Medmenham had dedicated the church. The curve of the man's body shielded the firearm from the Frenchman's view. 'Come along, Lady Charlotte, no dawdling.'

'I'm not very good with ladders,' said Charlotte disarmingly. 'I haven't a very broad acquaintance with them.'

'All the more reason not to prolong your acquaintance with this one,' said their captor pleasantly. 'Peter? Would you care to help Lady Charlotte along?'

It was decidedly unclear just what sort of help he intended. From the way Peter – Charlotte assumed he must be Peter, since he had sauntered forwards at the Frenchman's call – lifted his pistol, potting pigeons came to mind.

'No – no!' Charlotte flailed a foot behind her as she felt for the next rung down. It wasn't entirely an act. There was nothing like being aimed at to wreak havoc with one's sense of balance. 'That's quite all right. I can manage.'

Moving with more speed than grace, she deliberately floundered her way down the next few rungs. It was mostly deliberate, at any rate. She was feeling more than a little bit wobbly, and her skirt seemed to catch at her calves even more than usual. Just as a pair of hands reached out to lift her off the ladder, Charlotte contrived to fall sideways, bumping into Peter in the process. Peter stumbled gratifyingly, and Charlotte fell heavily to her knees by the side of the ladder. As Peter swayed and swore, Charlotte scooped the pistol up under her skirt, wedging it as best she could in her garter under pretence of floundering on the floor.

One could only flounder for so long; grabbing a hand, Peter yanked her unceremoniously to her feet, all but pulling her arm out of the socket in the process.

'I'm all right,' she said breathlessly, making a show of swaying dizzily. Her garter sagged but held, just barely supporting the weight of the metal. Charlotte clamped her knees together, trapping the barrel between her thighs. 'Really I am.'

'You are also,' said the Frenchman drily, 'blocking the ladder. Jack?'

Peter dragged her backwards while another of the Frenchman's henchmen made for the ladder, presumably in pursuit of the hidden king. Across the width of the ladder, Charlotte's eyes met Henrietta's. She let her eyes slide sideways, towards the ladder. In response, Henrietta lowered both eyelids in a discreet blink. That was one of the joys of over a decade of friendship: There was no need for words to communicate.

They were agreed. It would be much easier to let the Frenchman's men fetch the king down first and stage their rebellion after, while the Frenchman was preoccupied with the king. At least, Charlotte was fairly sure that that was what Henrietta's blink meant.

In the meantime, it was best to continue to be as daft as possible. Charlotte fluttered her lashes at the Frenchman, hoping he wouldn't notice that her knees were pressed together at a very odd angle. 'Shouldn't your men be Jacques and Pierre?' she asked. 'Rather than Jack and Peter?'

'I believe in supporting the local economy,' said the Frenchman blandly. 'It would be very inadvisable to travel with a foreign retinue. I am sure your brother would agree with me – Lady Henrietta.'

So he knew who Henrietta was, too. Charlotte had the greatest respect for the Frenchman's intelligence-gathering network. They were obviously immensely thorough.

Henrietta regarded him narrowly, as though staring long and hard enough might provide a clue to his identity. 'Do you know Richard?'

'So to speak.' The Frenchman had his eyes on the ladder, watching as his man climbed, steadily and far more speedily than Charlotte, up towards the painted scene on the ceiling, but Charlotte had no doubt that he was equally attuned to her and Henrietta.

'What do you want with the king?' Charlotte asked boldly.

If he was going to kill them, he would do it, anyway, so where was the harm in asking? Charlotte was nearly certain that he had no interest in killing them, unless circumstances somehow made their deaths absolutely imperative.

Robert would probably say that was taking her trusting nature too far, but Charlotte didn't think it was about being trusting. It was about the Frenchman not wanting to make more of a mess than he had to.

'I don't want your king particularly,' said the Frenchman with disarming frankness. 'But as you can see, events have forced my hand. I can't very well leave him here, can I?'

Charlotte felt that that was a rather disingenuous portrayal of the situation. 'But you drugged him,' she pointed out. 'Why, if not for this?'

With a Gallic shrug, the Frenchman dodged the question. 'The old man was half mad, anyway. He scarcely noticed the difference. All I did was . . . help him along a bit.'

'That,' said Charlotte sternly, or at least as sternly as she could with her arms clamped behind her back, 'is not an excuse.'

'Justice with her flaming sword,' murmured the Frenchman. 'How charming. If somewhat trite.'

'I prefer old-fashioned,' said Charlotte helpfully. 'It sounds better that way.'

On the very top of the ladder, his minion – Jack, if Charlotte remembered correctly – was beginning to descend with a man-size bundle draped over his back.

'Well done, Jack,' the Frenchman called. 'When you are finished, bring him out to the carriage.'

'Carriage?' said Charlotte, as Jack reached the midway point, carefully balancing his royal burden.

'I fear you will come to know it rather intimately,' said the Frenchman, and although he spoke matter-of-factly, there was something decidedly ominous in his words. 'I cannot leave you here.'

'Can't you?' faltered Charlotte.

'As much as I hate to disoblige a lady . . .' The Frenchman held up both hands in a stylised gesture of helplessness. 'You do pose something of an inconvenience, you realise.'

'What do you intend to do with us?' Henrietta asked darkly.

'Isn't the usual procedure to drop you in an oubliette pending ravishment?' He smiled blandly as Henrietta scowled at him. Henrietta had never enjoyed being made fun of. 'You really must resort to better reading material, Lady Henrietta. I am, I fear, flat out of oubliettes, and I have no desire to be pursued by your large and irate male relations vowing vengeance. I have,' he added tantalisingly, 'met them before. No. Once we have gone a sufficient distance from Wycombe, you will be left at a perfectly nice coaching inn to find your own way back to London. I will even pay for a private parlour.

We wouldn't want you mingling with the masses.'

'Then why take us along at all?' asked Henrietta grumpily.

'Because if I leave you here, you will be able to raise the alarm. It's really quite simple.' His air of superiority reminded Charlotte of Henrietta's older brother in one of his lecturing moods; it clearly struck Henrietta the same way. 'By the time your companions finish searching the grounds for you, we should be well out of the way.'

'There is a flaw in your reasoning somewhere,' insisted Henrietta.

'When you find it, do be good enough to let me know. Ah, Jack. Excellent.' The Frenchman's man presented the king to his master like a butler with a decanter of claret. The king was unconscious, unshaven, and strapped into a straight waistcoat. There was a distinctly unpleasant odour to him. Whatever other accommodations Wrothan might have made for his stay, he had never contemplated the incompatibility of a chamber pot and a straight waistcoat. The poor king. The degradation of it all made Charlotte's throat tight.

The Frenchman's nose twitched. 'This is going to be a very uncomfortable carriage ride,' he said resignedly.

'Couldn't we change him?' Charlotte suggested tentatively. 'We could wrap him in my cloak if there aren't any other clothes to be had.'

'Swaddled tenderly as a babe by your own lily white hands? I think not, Lady Charlotte.'

'It wouldn't take long,' Charlotte persisted as the man holding her muscled her over the threshold, out into the stinging night air. 'And it would make us all far more comfortable.'

'An excellent attempt, Lady Charlotte. But I refuse to oblige you by loitering here until the cavalry arrives. There will be plenty of time to tend to the king once we are under way.'

'Carriage rides make Lady Henrietta sick,' Charlotte blurted out.

Henrietta, who had never been sick in a carriage in her life, promptly blew out her cheeks in an attempt to look bilious. The Frenchman was not convinced.

'How very unfortunate for her,' said the Frenchman drily. 'Shall we?'

'Perhaps if you let her sit on the box?' Charlotte pleaded, submitting to being shuffled forwards by her captor. 'She is seldom as queasy in the open air.'

'And allow her to grapple with my coachman for the reins?' The Frenchman was bearing them inexorably away from church and mausoleum, away from the caves where their cavalry still hunted will-o'-the-wisps. At the end of the lane, Charlotte could see a carriage, a blur of unrelieved black. It was going to be a very tight fit with all of them in it, even assuming the Frenchman left his locally hired ruffians behind. 'Ingenious, but no. I suspect Lady Henrietta suffers from carriage sickness as much as I do.'

'How dreadful for you,' said Charlotte sympathetically.

'No, Lady Charlotte,' said the Frenchman. Although he sounded more amused than otherwise, there was a steely quality behind it that signalled that further discussion on the topic would not be well received.

'I suppose offering you money wouldn't work, either,' said Henrietta glumly.

'I am lamentably impervious to bribes.'

'And to odour, apparently,' retorted Henrietta.

'There are certain occupational hazards with which one must simply come to terms.'

'What is your occupation precisely?' demanded Henrietta.

'Right now? Seeing you into my carriage.'

Charlotte left them to their bickering. At least, Henrietta was bickering. The Frenchman was baiting. Whatever one chose to call it, it was keeping him nicely occupied. No one was paying the least bit of attention to her, including her own guard, who marched her along with the nonchalance of a groom with a particularly placid old mare. He was undoubtedly thinking about something else, like a warm fire or hot ale or whatever it was that ruffians thought about when they weren't being ruffianly. His grip had gone decidedly slack.

Knowing she only had one chance, Charlotte stomped down hard on his foot and drove an elbow into his stomach.

His boots were considerably harder than her heel. Surprise more than pain was her ally. In a reflex reaction, he loosed his hold on her wrists. Pulling away, Charlotte flung herself to the ground, rolling beneath his grasping hands. Above her, she could hear shouting and feet slipping on the wet grasses.

Charlotte kept rolling, clawing inelegantly at her skirts as she went, fumbling for the pistol snagged in her garter. Already sagging, the garter snapped, sending her stocking sagging down and releasing the pistol into her grasp. Scooting back on her behind, one arm braced behind her, Charlotte hefted the gun, angling it at the men rushing towards her. They abruptly stopped rushing. Pointing the gun first at one, then another, Charlotte levered herself slowly to her feet, never allowing the point of the pistol to drop, even though the muscles in her forearm and shoulder burnt at the strain. Her right stocking flopped around her ankle. It seemed like such a small annoyance under the circumstances, and such a very odd thing of which to be so aware.

There would be no pulling it up now, though. Charlotte picked her target, pointing her pistol in the direction of the man holding the king. 'Give me the king,' she said.

The Frenchman regarded her with something very like fraternal annoyance. 'Really, Lady Charlotte, must you? Put down the gun.'

'Put down the king,' Charlotte countered, keeping her gaze firmly on her target. 'Then I'll put down the gun.'

The man's eyes flickered to his master in silent question. He looked as though he would have liked nothing better than to drop his sovereign and run.

That, thought Charlotte giddily, was what you got when you hired help on the cheap.

She gentled her voice, speaking directly to the man with the king, as she might have to an animal in the gardens of Girdings. 'If you put down the king, you won't get hurt.'

'He won't get hurt, in any event.' The Frenchman's voice was as urbane as ever, but there was a tinge of annoyance under it. 'That gun isn't loaded.'

Charlotte drew herself up proudly. 'Would you be willing to wager a man's life on that?'

The Frenchman looked her up and down. He smiled with disarming humour. 'Frankly, yes.' He had a dimple in his left cheek. Who had ever heard of a spy with a dimple? Charlotte disapproved. 'If it is loaded – which I very much doubt – you wouldn't fire it. You would never risk hitting the king. Unless you are, much to my surprise, a crack shot, you run a very good chance of doing so.'

'I *was* raised in the country,' said Charlotte defiantly. He didn't need to know that her version of country pursuits had been sitting in the garden with a book.

Or perhaps he did know. It might be the way the gun was making her hands tremble, or the fact that she was holding it a full foot away from her body.

The Frenchman sighed. 'Put the gun down, Lady Charlotte, and come along like a good girl. Peter?'

That was the outer end of enough. Unfortunately, Charlotte didn't quite know what to do with a gun. She knew that there was something called priming that had to be accomplished before the weapon could be fired, and she believed it involved powder, but whether that powder was already there or needed to be added remained a mystery to her. And there was no time to find out.

Obedient to his master, Peter lunged for her arm. So Charlotte did the only thing she could do. She threw the gun at the Frenchman's head.

Her throw went wild, of course.

So did Charlotte's foot. The force of the motion sent her skidding on the wet grass, flinging her backwards into her would-be captor, who went sprawling backwards beneath her onto the ground, all tangled up with Charlotte's skirts. He broke the fall rather nicely.

Over the steady cursing of her unwilling human mattress, Charlotte could hear Robert's voice, shouting, 'There! That way! Follow the noise!'

Charlotte scrambled off her assailant, kicking him as he grabbed at her. In the confusion, Henrietta had also broken free of her captor. She dealt him a blow to his nose with the flat of her hand that sent him reeling backwards into the trunk of a tree.

Even in the dark, the Frenchman's distorted face was a glorious thing to behold. Ha! He had never expected that, had he? To be fair, neither had she. She had been aiming at the Frenchman's head. Instead, the gun had landed on his foot. Apparently, a falling gun could hurt rather a lot. Hopping on one foot, he was cursing far more inventively than the other men, in a selection of modern and classical languages.

Into the midst of it all charged Robert, Miles, and Lieutenant Fluellen. Nothing had ever sounded more welcome to Charlotte's ears than the thunder of feet as the cavalry charged down the hill, hooting and yelling and not really saying anything in particular but making a great deal of very martial-sounding noise. They were literally steaming in the cold night air, like a whole troupe of fire-breathing dragons, steam rising off their skin and their breath showing in ragged puffs. Two of the Frenchman's band broke and fled at the sight. At least, they tried to flee. Like a terrier on the scent, Miles set out in hot pursuit. Tommy dispatched Henrietta's staggering assailant with a swift punch that sent him reeling into a tree.

Robert charged towards Charlotte, breathing fire at the man who was trying, rather halfheartedly, to grab her arms. Charlotte suspected the Frenchman hadn't paid him terribly well. At the sight of Robert, he gave up altogether, breaking and running in the direction of the woods.

'The king!' Charlotte shouted, jumping and pointing. 'Robert, the king!'

He didn't need to be told twice. Neither did the man holding the king. Making a quick assessment of his options, he shoved the king at Robert. Robert's arms closed around the bundle in a reflex reaction.

'Take him! He's yours!' the man gabbled, and scrabbled off into the woods, following his fleeing colleagues.

'What in the—?' began Robert.

'Hired help,' explained Charlotte breathlessly. 'The real culprit is – oh, drat.'

While they were otherwise occupied, the Frenchman had made his own somewhat lopsided run for it, hitching and hopping his way towards his carriage at a surprisingly impressive speed for a man who appeared to have the use of only one foot. Charlotte wondered if she had broken his toe. With an arrogant wave, the Frenchman swung himself through the open door, snapping his fingers at his coachman. The coachman cracked the reins even before the door was fully closed. Charlotte could see the Frenchman's disembodied arm sticking out of the compartment, yanking the swaying door closed as the carriage lurched into movement.

Robert took two long strides forwards, remembered he was holding the king, and skittered to a halt, looking miffed. Miles dropped the man he was punching and gave chase, but it was too late; the horses were picking up speed.

As the carriage drew away, the Frenchman leant head and shoulders through the window. In the light of the carriage lamps, Charlotte could see the white of his teeth as he grinned at them, a rogue's grin, unrepentant and entirely infectious. Despite herself, Charlotte could feel herself grinning back. And why not? Even if he had escaped, they had won. They had the king.

'I wish you joy of your king!' he called through the window. His voice whistled back on the wind, rich with amusement. 'I never really wanted him, anyway.'

Charlotte couldn't be quite sure, but she thought he winked at them.

'Of all the cheek!' Henrietta exclaimed furiously. 'Next time, take the Prince of Wales!' she shouted, but the Frenchman was already out of range, the sound of his horses' hooves fading.

'Really, Hen,' remonstrated Miles, but his arm was tight around her shoulders as he said it and his voice was muffled from being buried in her hair.

The others all melted into insignificance as Robert approached Charlotte, bearing the king in his arms like Sir Walter Raleigh gifting Queen Elizabeth with foreign treasure.

'I brought you something,' he said, and there was something in his expression that hurt to view. 'Not quite a dragon's head, but . . .'

Charlotte dropped her eyes from the expression in his. It was safer to concentrate on the king, to ignore whatever else it was that Robert was offering along with the bundle in his arms. She was a coward, she knew. But what was cowardice but another term for prudence? What she didn't acknowledge couldn't hurt her. At least, not too much.

Evading the question, Charlotte dropped to her knees beside the king. 'Your Majesty?' she whispered, reaching out to the wasted figure in Robert's arms. She could be constant to her king, even if she couldn't trust Robert to be constant to her. 'Your Majesty?'

The rheumy eyes opened, trying pitifully to find a focus. His fingers tightened feebly around hers, like those of a child who hadn't yet quite learnt the use of his limbs. 'Emily?' he croaked.

Chapter Thirty

'Do come in, Lady Charlotte,' commanded the king.

Charlotte stood in the door of the queen's crimson dressing room, dazzled by far more than the double branches of candles that created patches of brilliance amid the late afternoon dusk.

It was a far cry from her last sight of the room, that very morning in the dark before dawn, when they had borne the unconscious king through the door. There had been flurry and excitement and torches flaming and the queen with her grey hair hanging all down her back and a robe flung hastily over her nightdress. Charlotte could still see the flashes of flame behind her eyes, the billowing white nightgowns, the pale, distorted faces of the princesses as their father was carried before them into the queen's chambers.

A mere twelve hours later, it all had the quality of a dream, everything coloured in shades of grey, faces blurry, voices muted. Standing behind their parents, the princesses were exquisitely gowned and coiffed, bearing no resemblance at all to the desperate, dishevelled creatures who had flocked about like the chorus of a Greek tragedy the night before.

The king was himself again; clean and shaven, he had traded his straight waistcoat for his scarlet coat with gold facings. The Order of the Garter once more glittered boldly on his breast. Beside him, diamonds glimmered in the queen's turban, on her twisted fingers, in the folds of her fichu. Charlotte's grandmother had ranged herself by the queen's side, claiming a prerogative that was not hers by right, and the jewels of Dovedale glared just as fiercely from her wrists and neck, as if in competition with the queen. But all of them faded into insignificance against the man who stood by her grandmother's right hand, lace at his wrists and throat, his hair gold as a Viking's treasure in the glare of the candles.

'Majesty.' Charlotte sank deep into a curtsy, wishing she had worn proper Court dress, feeling plain and drab and painfully aware that her hair hadn't been washed for two days. There had been no time to bathe when the royal summons came, only a scrabble to drag herself yawning from bed and into a dress, fuzzy-headed and stupid from sleeping in the middle of the day.

'Come in, come in.' The king gestured her imperiously forwards, and if his hand trembled, it was nothing worth being too worried about. 'You, as well,' he added, to her companions, as Miles and Henrietta made their obeisance behind her.

Robert must have received a like summons. She belatedly noticed that his friend, Lieutenant Fluellen, stood beside him. His regimentals were brighter than Robert's plum coat, his hair just as well brushed, his buttons and buckles polished to a royal sheen, but he still faded into insignificance next to his friend. When Robert was there, he tended to blot out other men, like the sun eclipsing the moon. Charlotte did not need an astrologer's chart to know that it was a planetary conjunction that boded ill for her heart.

Gesturing to Robert and Lieutenant Fluellen, the king had them fall in line with the others so that the five adventurers stood ranged before him, all in a row. Sandwiched between Miles and Lieutenant Fluellen, Charlotte couldn't see Robert at all. Masculine shoulders blocked her view to either side.

'We owe you a deep debt of gratitude,' began the king, the formality of his words a deep contrast with the relative informality of the setting.

It was a very odd sort of award ceremony, in the room in the Queen's House with only the royal daughters as witness. It was, Charlotte realised, as much a bribe for their silence as a gift for services rendered. It would be very embarrassing for the king should the truth ever come out. It would be more than embarrassing, in fact. Should the Prince of Wales ever get hold of the truth, he might use it to sow rumours that the king wasn't the king at all, but an actor, replacing the still kidnapped king. It might be untrue, but doubt could cause its own dangers. Detachedly, she appreciated the cleverness of the king's choice, rewarding and containing all at the same time.

There might be no fanfare, no public presentation of honours, but royal favour flowed like honey through the king's lips, as he promised a captain's commission for Lieutenant Fluellen, honorary posts as gentlemen of the bedchamber for Robert and Miles. He made them gifts of royal miniatures, enamel portraits of himself set into stickpins for the gentlemen, bracelets for the ladies.

Charlotte kept her head modestly lowered and concentrated

on the pattern of the floorboards. She could see the tips of Robert's shoes out of the corner of her eye. The polished black leather moved back and forth like the hooves of a horse at the starting gate, fidgeting with impatience.

'And now,' said the king, when the last stickpin had been fastened, the last honour bestowed, 'I understand my Lord of Dovedale craves a special boon.'

A rustle of interest quivered through the room as the king leant back in his chair, beaming benevolently at Robert. From her position in the middle of the line, Charlotte could only hear the swish of Robert's coat as he swept into a bow and catch a fleeting glimpse of gold as his head bent in obeisance to the king. That something was about to happen, Charlotte was quite sure – but what? Miles was as confused as she was, staring with frank interest, but the queen exuded patient kindness and the dowager burnt with a fierce and inexplicable triumph, incandescent as a Roman candle.

Robert's voice rang out clear and strong. 'With Your Majesties' pleasure, the boon I ask of you is the hand of Lady Charlotte Lansdowne.'

Charlotte's ears rang as though she had been holding her breath for too long underwater in the bath.

Tactfully – or by prearrangement – the others fell back. Charlotte found herself standing adrift and conspicuous in a sea of empty parquet as Robert smiled a victor's smile and extended his hand to her.

Behind their mother's throne, the princesses were all crying and whispering; the queen inclined her head at Charlotte in unspoken encouragement; and the king beamed with paternal pleasure as though he personally had arranged the match. As Charlotte stood there, frozen, Henrietta gave Charlotte a light push, propelling her forwards into the line of Robert's outstretched hand.

'A most economical outcome, eh, what?' chuckled the king. 'To reward you both in one gift. What say you, Lady Charlotte?'

Charlotte stared at Robert as though she had never seen him before. The delighted cries and whispers of the others clamoured at her ears like the caws of jackdaws; the jewels and smiles and candles all blurred together in nightmare shapes like carnival masks, too bright, too gaudy, too much. She watched expectation flicker to confusion on Robert's face as he held out his hand, more imperiously now.

She should take it, she knew. That was how the story was supposed to end. She was supposed to take his hand and then the bells would ring and the people would cheer and throughout the kingdom the very birds would fly into the air with rejoicing.

'Charlotte?' Robert wriggled his fingers.

Everyone was watching, waiting. Charlotte saw her grandmother's face harden in unspoken warning. She knew what she was expected to do, she who had always done everything that was expected of her. Until now.

Charlotte took a stumbling step back, bumping right into Henrietta, who let out a startled *oof*. The homely sound broke the spell, shattering the fairy tale into eggshell-fine slivers.

'No,' Charlotte croaked, never taking her eyes from Robert's face. 'With your pardon, Majesties, I – no.'

Her grandmother stalked forwards like a malevolent fairy, proving she could move swiftly enough when the spirit moved her. At the moment, that spirit was pure rage. 'No?' the dowager growled. '*No?*'

The king waved the dowager to silence. 'A lady wants some

wooing, what?' he said sympathetically, and his words had all the force of a royal command. 'Dovedale—'

Charlotte felt a hysterical urge to laugh well up in her throat. So she was to be the subject of a royally mandated wooing, was she? She wondered if court etiquette set certain time bounds to the activity. Was she meant to succumb after five minutes, or might one successfully resist for ten without exciting the king's anger?

His face carefully bland, Robert swept another bow. 'With pleasure, Your Majesty. Lady Charlotte?'

Rather than create another scene, Charlotte took the arm offered her. Robert's muscles told a different story than his mouth; beneath her fingers, his body was quivering with tension. Anger? Perhaps that, too. He had a right to it, having just been refused in front of not only his friends, but his monarch.

On the other hand, thought Charlotte rebelliously, he might have been spared that had he had the simple sense to ask her first instead of demanding her hand the way one might ask for a horse.

'Go, go,' said the king benevolently. He reached for the queen's hand, but she twitched her fingers away from him, moving restlessly to the far side of her chair. Shooting her mother a look of pure venom, Princess Sophia moved to stand by her father's shoulder.

Charlotte let herself be drawn through the door, through the black-and-gold-lacquered walls of the queen's breakfast room, into the closet beyond, a small and private room where they could speak without being overheard. Robert took care to shut the door, thwarting any potential eavesdroppers, before turning back to her.

In the tiny space, his presence was almost overwhelming.

Charlotte fought the urge to just lean against him and let all her weariness drain away into him. It would be so lovely just to sit, together.

'What is wrong?' he asked gently, touching her cheek with his gloved fingers as though he were handling something rare and infinitely precious.

Charlotte forced herself to look away, holding herself stiffly aloof until she felt his hand drop.

'Is it wooing you want?' he asked, bracing a hand on the wall behind her, the strong lines of his face arranged in an expression of concern. It was heady stuff, having all that attention concentrated on her. His blue eyes searched her face. 'If so, we can, er, woo.'

She was no longer a child to be placated with a bauble, no matter how desirable a bauble it was. And it was a desirable bauble, like a prism dangled in front of her, dancing with rainbow images of courtship. What would it be like to be really, truly courted by Robert?

Until he grew bored again, that was, and sought adventures elsewhere. There would be new quests to undertake, new prizes to be won. Like an old trophy, she would be hung up on the wall of Girdings, taken out from time to time to show off to guests.

Charlotte slid out from under his arm. 'It's not wooing I want,' she said.

'Then what *do* you want? I can't know if you don't tell me.' He sounded reasonable enough. But although the pose was right, his body angled towards her, she couldn't help but feel as though he weren't listening at all. He was already planning the post-betrothal feast, the congratulations of his peers, the return in state to Girdings. Where she would be just another piece of the tapestry, the lady riding at his side, passed like a parcel from king to suitor.

'Why did you ask for me?' she demanded. 'Why now? Why here?'

Robert blinked at her as though the question had never even occurred to him. 'Why?'

'Why?' Charlotte repeated firmly, unwilling to be put off.

'It seemed like the thing to do,' he joked, in an unfortunate attempt to lighten the mood. 'Hero rescues king, hero marries princess – isn't that the way these stories usually go? Even if you were really the one to rescue the king rather than me,' he added wryly. 'But I thought you would enjoy the romantic gesture. It seemed like something out of one of your books.'

Biting her lip, Charlotte looked away, knowing herself guilty as charged. He was right; it was something she would once have found dreadfully romantic. But now, she couldn't help but fear that underneath the gaudy fairy tale trappings loomed a gaping pit into which she was poised to tumble. What if all the grandeur and fanfare masked nothing more than an empty hole where honest affection ought to have been? Once the fairy tale was gone, what would be left?

'It's all very well for a book, but can't you see that this is different?' Charlotte said earnestly, scrabbling to put her misgivings into words. 'Stories end. Marriage is for life. You can't just leave when you decide you don't like the book anymore.'

Understanding spread across his face, and with it relief. Reaching for her shoulders, he drew her to arm's length, scrutinising her face. 'Is that what this is all about? I already told you—'

Pushing at his chest with both hands, Charlotte broke his

hold. 'And *I* already told *you*. Did you listen to anything I said last night?'

Robert looked slightly shifty, which Charlotte took as a no. 'I thought we had resolved all that.'

'Asking the king for my hand in marriage does not count as a resolution!'

'Isn't that what you wanted? Don't you want us to be married?'

So much that it hurt. Even now. Charlotte wondered if she were being a stiff-necked fool. A tempting little voice whispered that the means didn't matter so long as the end was right. But she had never agreed with Machiavelli in that. The means shaped the end. If she accepted Robert under such circumstances, always wondering, doubting the depth of his affection, it would warp whatever future they had.

'Not on these terms,' she said distinctly.

Robert was clearly reaching the limit of his patience. 'Not on these terms, or not ever? Be honest, Charlotte. No games. Is it the terms you don't want, or is it me?'

When she didn't answer, he prodded, 'Let's try this another way. Are there any terms you can name that I could fulfil to your satisfaction?'

Charlotte could only stare at him, in mute agony. What good were promises if she couldn't trust herself to trust him to keep them? The only term that mattered was as impossible as a unicorn – that he love her enough to never leave. No one could promise that truly. Even her parents had abandoned her for death.

'Right,' he said sharply. 'You don't need to say more.'

'That's not what I meant,' Charlotte said pleadingly. 'You said it best when you said that enchantments can't survive.

You can't make a fantasy real just by believing hard enough. I used to believe you could – but we never did find any unicorns together, did we?'

'And I suppose that's my fault for eating the filling out of all the tarts.' Robert raked a hand through his hair, dragging a ragged breath in through his teeth. 'Good God. Just listen to us. We're fighting about *unicorns*, for the love of God. We're both tired and overwrought. Tomorrow, once we've both got some rest—'

'I'll see it your way?'

A light flush mottled Robert's cheekbones, sign that her bolt had hit home.

'We can discuss this further,' he finished pointedly. He looked at her challengingly. 'Unless you don't want to.'

They might as well have been waiting twenty paces apart from each other across a duelling green, each waiting for the other to fire first. Charlotte wasn't quite sure how they had come to this, each poised to deliver to the other a mortal blow. It wasn't what she wanted; it wasn't what she wanted at all. She wanted to slide her arms around his neck and lift her face to his and let him kiss all her worries away and then prance happily home to Girdings in a carriage built for two. But the gulf between them was too wide to be compassed by a kiss.

Once on the duelling green, honour permitted no way out.

'Maybe that would be wise,' she heard herself saying.

Robert smiled a dangerous, tight-lipped smile. 'No point in sullying the bloodlines, is there?' he agreed, in a tone terrifying in its geniality. 'You go back to Girdings, and I go back to India. Everyone is where he belongs.'

'So you're running away again,' said Charlotte, in a voice

that shook. She hadn't realised how much she had hoped that he would fight for her – even if fighting for her meant fighting with her – until he didn't.

Robert twisted the handle of the door. Through the breakfast room lay the exit to the stairs, and the wider world beyond. Charlotte could see it, an endless series of shapes on a map, London giving way to England, to the ocean, to India.

'Not running away, Lady Charlotte,' he said, thrusting the door open as though what he really wanted was to kick it. 'Sent away.'

Across the way, Charlotte could have sworn she saw the door to the Crimson Drawing Room hastily shut, as though eavesdroppers were hastily ducking back out of the way.

'I didn't send you away,' called Charlotte softly from the doorway. 'It was you who chose to interpret it that way.'

But he was already past hearing.

Bonelessly, Charlotte slid down into a velvet-backed chair in the breakfast room. She felt like the survivor of a tempest, gazing out helplessly at the wrack of her world, all her worldly goods beaten into splinters around her. She was too exhausted to cry. That would come later, no doubt. It was, she thought, really quite impressive to have managed to destroy everything so completely so quickly. It was a positive triumph of destruction.

He wasn't supposed to have left.

Dropping her head into her hands, Charlotte found herself yearning, with a child's fervour, for Girdings. She wanted the sturdy stone walls and the quiet companionship of her books, where characters always said what they were supposed to and endings were always happy. A hero might storm off, but he always came back again; misunderstandings might occur, but they were always solved by Chapter Twenty-nine. She had been happy with her books and her daydreams, happy and protected and safe.

'Well?'

Charlotte lifted her head as an uneven thumping sound signalled the approach of her grandmother. Her drawn face and hollow eyes told their own story.

The dowager duchess's lips opened and closed in the sort of mute rage that summoned storm clouds and sank ships. She took refuge in a bout of soundless laughter. 'Handed to you on a platter,' she gasped, 'and still you manage to lose him! You have a rare talent. How did you do it? How do you make a proposal turn to dust?'

'We had a difference of opinion,' said Charlotte tightly, not meeting her grandmother's eyes.

'Opinion, is it?' The duchess exhibited her opinion of opinions with a hearty snort. 'A fine time for you to choose to develop opinions, after all these years! Opinions have no place in making a match. If we were to let measly little things like opinions interfere with betrothals, who would ever get married? Answer me that!'

Charlotte looked away. 'It was more than a little opinion,' she mumbled. The habit of obedience died hard.

The dowager paid no attention. She shook her cane to the heavens like a wizened Lady Macbeth calling on spirits. 'Do you think dukes just fall from trees? All my plans, all my efforts – all that money, bribing idiot roués to dance with you so Dovedale would think you had countenance. Sheep! Men are sheep! And I've never seen one yet that hasn't let himself be led to the shearing. But never before have I seen a shepherdess run away from the sheep!'

The metaphor didn't quite work, but Charlotte's mind was on other things. 'You paid people to dance with me?'

'Enough to keep your friends in fans and powder for a very long time,' said the dowager grimly, as if reexamining an imaginary ledger. 'And that's just the men! Medmenham alone cost me five thousand pounds, the gilded weasel. Not that he didn't earn it,' she admitted grudgingly. 'I always say you get what you pay for.'

'Medmenham did what?' Charlotte gaped at her grandmother.

The dowager rapped her stick impatiently against the uncarpeted floor. 'You heard me, gel! Or is your hearing going, as well as your wits? I got Medmenham to lend a hand bringing your duke to the parson's noose.'

Charlotte's head was ringing. Very slowly and very clearly she enunciated, 'You offered Sir Francis Medmenham Robert's money to get Robert to the altar.'

'It was for his own good,' said the dowager self-righteously. 'Until you had to go and botch it. He needed a Lansdowne of the true line. And you—'

Charlotte broke in before her grandmother could inform her what she needed. It was the first time she could remember ever interrupting her grandmother, but she was too rattled to marvel at it. 'Did it ever occur to you,' demanded Charlotte, 'that he might propose to me of his own accord?'

The dowager just looked at her.

'Of course,' Charlotte said shakily, her whole body beginning to tremble. 'Of course not. I should have known.'

'You should be thanking me, is what you should be doing,' said the dowager stridently. 'Did you think I would let the daughter of a duke marry anyone less than one?'

'What of love?' asked Charlotte incoherently.

Her grandmother leapt on her words like a gardener squashing a slug. 'Love has no place in a marital alliance, you ninny. Do you think I loved Dovedale? Most certainly not! That would have been common. Bourgeois, even. We had a perfectly satisfactory partnership. It was your fool of a father who had to ruin it all by running off and marrying—'

Charlotte went stiff with rage. 'Don't say it. Don't you dare say anything about my parents. They were *lovely*. And they loved me.'

'Lovely,' muttered the duchess. 'Love.' She made it sound like the rankest sort of refuse. 'Your mother ruined plans that were twenty years in the making, all for love. If your father had married the Belliston girl, we would have had a full quarter of Parliament in our pocket. Dovedale would have been greater than Marlborough, greater than Devonshire.'

'They were happy,' said Charlotte tightly, not trusting herself to say more. The rich black and gold walls of the queen's breakfast room seemed to press in on her, too rich, too lush, a visual symbol of the pomp and power for which her grandmother had been willing to barter her only child's happiness.

'Happy?' snorted the duchess. 'Happy? They're *dead!* Dead! And without an heir. All they left me was you.' And precious little I had to work with, her voice seemed to say.

Charlotte remembered that tiny graveyard in Surrey, a narrow plot behind the pleasant stone vicarage. She remembered the small, curved headstone with the raw Roman lettering that had marked her baby brother's grave. The heir. And behind it, like an echo, the larger stone that shaded her mother's final rest. It was her brother's birth that had taken her mother's life. But it hadn't been for the production of the heir. If he had lived, they would have loved him for what he was, for being a child and theirs, just as they had loved her, whether she was capable of inheriting Girdings or not.

'If you had married Dovedale as you ought,' her grandmother was saying, 'it would have put it all right. My great-grandson would have been next Duke of Dovedale. All you had to do was tell him yes.'

Charlotte's face felt as though it had been made of very fine porcelain that was starting to crack around the edges. Looking her grandmother straight in the eyes, she said very quietly, 'But that still wouldn't bring my father back.'

Caught mid-tirade, the dowager sucked in sharply, like the hiss of a snake against the lacquer walls.

Charlotte didn't need to see the crumpled flesh beneath her grandmother's eyes, the sag beneath her cheekbones, to know the shot had struck home.

She might have followed up her advantage, flung at her grandmother any of the stored-up slights of the past twelve years, but it didn't feel worth the argument. Nothing was. With Robert gone, any victory would be a Pyrrhic one.

It was all too much in too short a time, her grandmother's machinations, Robert's departure, the scene in front of the king, everything. All she wanted was to go home. Not to Loring House or to the room she had occupied on and off since her first Season at Dovedale House, but truly home, far away from London and Robert and the humiliation of knowing that a rake had been bought to pretend to court her – and that it had worked.

'I would like to return to Girdings,' Charlotte said woodenly.

The dowager turned abruptly towards the door, her stiff petticoats slithering across the polished floor. She held herself very straight, presenting Charlotte with a view of her elaborately arranged grey hair, pinched and powdered in the style of an earlier generation. There was no softness in her stance, no yielding. She was every inch a duchess and every inch alone.

'Do what you like,' she said brusquely, her back to Charlotte. 'You will, anyway.'

Chapter Thirty-One

Springtime at Girdings had always been one of Charlotte's favourite seasons. Not spring proper, but that period just before, when one awoke to find that the wind had softened, that the ground was soft and moist and dark, and that the still-bare tree branches bore tiny bobbles of buds that hadn't been there before.

At least, it had always been that way before.

It wasn't that Charlotte didn't try; she did. She took long walks through the winter-bare gardens and forced herself to take deep bracing breaths, telling herself all the while how utterly lovely it was. She read poetry aloud to herself, as though by declaiming the lines to the empty library she might catch her own attention. She plunged into her old books as though the fate of the kingdom depended on the reading of them, plowing methodically through favourites that had never failed to excite her imagination before.

It was no use. She had lost the key to that old enchanted land. The words on the page were simply that, nothing but print, flat and bare. The tournaments she had once attended, where richly caparisoned knights clashed for her favour, were closed to her, unidimensional pictures on pages that tore when she turned them too roughly. The heroes who had courted her, the villains who had menaced her in the Vauxhalls and Ranelaghs of half a century before had deserted her, and when she tried to make them speak, their plaster lips parroted platitudes in her own voice. Charlotte found herself dropping books unread by her bed, pacing lines in the flowered carpet that had never been there before and, on one particularly miserable midnight, dragging all the furniture away from the walls in an impulsive attempt at redecoration that inspired her grandmother to declare that she had gone mad and took three footmen to set it all right again.

It was, Charlotte realised, not nearly so satisfying as she had remembered carrying on a conversation all by herself.

As February dripped away into March, with dismal rains and chilling frosts, Charlotte was forced to admit that discretion might not always be the better part of valour. Maybe valour was the better part of valour. She had thought she was being so sensible, rejecting Robert – but what if she hadn't been sensible? What if she had just been scared?

Half a dozen times Charlotte took up her pen to write to him, but she foundered before she even completed the address. 'Somewhere in India' wasn't terribly much to go on. Penelope, on the other hand, was; Penelope, who was already halfway across an ocean. The prospect filled Charlotte with new energy. Once, her grandmother might have balked at the notion of allowing her to visit a friend a world away, but there were benefits to being in disgrace. Her grandmother had washed her hands of her. Noisily. Multiple times. And her grandmother adored Penelope.

At the very worst, in India, she might come face-to-face with Robert across a drawing room and encounter only indifference, proof that his affections were the ephemeral product of circumstance, like a mist that dissolved in the heat of the sun. At least she would have tried. At least she would know, rather than fidgeting and pining and wondering about might-have-beens.

On a misty morning in the middle of March, Charlotte tucked her writing desk under her arm and tromped out into the garden to compose a letter to Penelope. Little bits of damp clung like crystal beads to the yew hedges. The air was rich with the scent of damp, loamy earth and fresh-baked jam tart.

Charlotte crunched to a halt right before stepping into the jam tart. She had no idea what a jam tart was doing in the middle of the path. It wasn't even the right season for jam tarts. And yet there it was, unmistakably a tart and equally unmistakably filled with jam.

The tart had been placed smack in front of her favourite bench, right there on the ground. It couldn't have been there long or the birds would have been at it. As it was, a squirrel was already staring down a sparrow, each daring the other to make a run for it.

Who left a tart on the ground like that? That it had been deliberately left was quite clear. Across the top crust, someone had painted an arrow out of raspberry jam. The arrow pointed down the path, past an amused Venus, straight to another jam tart. With another arrow.

It was unicorn bait.

Charlotte felt a crazy hope beginning to swell in her chest that had nothing to do with the promise of spring or the scent of loam and everything to do with the bizarre incongruity of a tart in the middle of a garden path, the sort of tarts a teenage

Robert used to tease Cook into baking. They would lay them out just so, in a line to the edge of the woods, since Charlotte was firmly convinced that no unicorn could resist the lure of raspberry jam and that if they just waited long enough, one day they would see a shimmering silver steed nuzzling his way down the row of pastries, muzzle streaked with jam.

The only person who knew about the tarts was far away across the seas, on his way to India. Wasn't he? The only cause she had to believe it was his own departing salvo.

No. Charlotte shoved her mist-frizzed hair back behind her ears. The whole idea was too absurd.

But who else would lay a trail of tarts to catch a unicorn? Charlotte's fingers tingled with nervous excitement. To catch a unicorn – or a lady?

Depositing her writing desk on her bench, Charlotte followed the tarts. A third tart led down past the dry fountain; a fourth had been pecked but was still recognisable as leading towards the lake; and a fifth brought her across the ornamental bridge. By the third tart, Charlotte's stroll had turned to a trot; by the fourth, a run. By the time she reached the bridge, she was flying, her skirt lifted high over her ankles and her unkempt hair flapping like a banner behind her.

From the bridge, she could see a shadowy figure by the summer house, half reflected in the water. It was the form of a man, a tall man, in riding clothes, tossing bits of tart to the bad-tempered swans on the lake.

He looked like something out of a picture, out of a tapestry, out of her imagination. Goodness only knew, she had daydreamed him often enough, imagining his step in every squirrel scurrying across the gravel in the garden, every sparrow pecking at the windowpane.

Charlotte skidded to a stop a few feet away from him, lifting a hand to her chest as she struggled for air. He looked, at close range, astonishingly corporeal. Damp had darkened his hair and there was a splotch of raspberry jam on his buckskin breeches where a tart had tumbled wrong side down in the process of being painted.

'Good morning,' he said tentatively, swinging his hat from one hand, and Charlotte realised that he was as nervous as she was, that the whole panoply of pies was as much a shield as it was an apology.

'You didn't go to India,' she said wonderingly. 'You came back.'

Robert tried to look debonair, but he nearly squished the brim of his hat with the force of his grip. 'I heard the unicorn hunting was good this season.'

Charlotte wondered how many sleepless nights it had taken him to come up with that line. It sounded as though he had been rehearsing in front of his mirror. The thought made Charlotte's lips twist in a smile so fond, it hurt. But there was still one little question to be dealt with.

'And if there aren't any unicorns?' she asked, her heart in her eyes.

Robert didn't pretend he didn't know what she was talking about. 'I'm willing to take it on faith if you are,' he said seriously. He held out one gloved hand to her. There was a smear of jam on the palm. 'Are you?'

They had stood in just this tableau only a month ago, in the queen's chambers. Then, he had been poised and perfect, clothed in a king's ransom of lace and velvet with a real king beaming on to give his blessing. Now they were alone, save for the irritated swans who squawked and pecked their opinions from the shallows of the lake. No king, no queen, no courtiers. There was jam on his hand and goose droppings on his boots and the unmistakable spring odour of wet grass, new soil, and incontinent goose as he looked to her for her decision.

This time, it was a question, not a command. And Charlotte finally knew exactly what her answer would be.

'Yes, yes, yes!' she exclaimed, nearly incoherent with glad laughter, and launched herself across the space between them.

The swans were squawking and the squirrels were gibbering, and somehow a tart got squished against the back of her dress in the confusion, but her arms were around Robert's neck and his around her waist and they were both laughing and talking and kissing all at once and making so little sense that even the swans despaired of them and raised their tail feathers in derision.

'—love you,' he was saying, somewhat incoherently between kisses. It wasn't the polished poetry Charlotte used to dream of, but it was more than declaration enough for her.

'You came back!' she exulted, which seemed a perfectly sensible response at the time, and squeezed her arms so tightly around his neck that it was a wonder he wasn't strangled on the spot. 'You came back, you came back, you came back!'

Laughing, he tipped her back and kissed her thoroughly, until her head was spinning and the clouds wheeled overhead in a grey blur and the malcontented mumblings of the local animal life sounded like the cheering of a crowd of loyal subjects.

There was a bench by the side of the summer house and by unspoken accord, they wandered over to it together, collapsing onto the marble more by luck than design, since all their attention was entirely on each other.

'Why?' Robert asked, his eyes devouring her face as though she were his own personal jammy tart and he hadn't eaten for a fortnight. 'What made you change your mind?'

Charlotte looked at Robert. Not at the golden cousin she had adored in her childhood or the knight in shining armour she had imagined riding down the lane to Girdings on a cold Christmas Eve. Without even realising it, she had bidden both of them farewell long ago. The Robert she knew was equally charming, but it was a charm meant to keep people at bay rather than to draw them close; the long, mobile mouth that spoke gallantries so glibly closed tightly around personal confidences. This man was more brown than golden, marked body and soul by those eleven years of which Charlotte would never quite know the whole.

There were pockets of his soul she knew she would never quite know in their entirety, places he had been, demons he had borne, that were as alien to her as the carefully constructed fantasy world she had built for herself was to him.

But, for some reason, they understood each other. And she understood, without having to be told, just how much it had cost him to decide to come back.

'You came back,' she said. 'You could have stayed away, but you chose to come back.'

Robert made a wry face, as though contemplating the folly of his prior actions. 'As you so wisely pointed out, I had been running away long enough. It was time to come home.'

'Home to Girdings?' It was silly to feel jealous of a house, particularly one she loved so well.

'Home to you,' he said, framing her face in his hands. 'That's the only part that matters. We can stay at Girdings if you like, or set up house in London, or explore the Outer

Hebrides. I don't much care where so long as you are with me.'

'Girdings didn't feel like home anymore without you here,' Charlotte confessed. 'Not for all the books in the library. If you hadn't come back, I was going to go to India after you.'

Robert appeared inordinately tickled by the idea. 'Riding on an elephant?' he suggested.

'Sailing in a boat under the pretence of visiting Penelope,' Charlotte corrected. 'I did consider the elephant, but they seem rather large. And I'm not sure they can swim that far.'

Robert looked down at her thoughtfully. 'Since I spoilt your plan to follow me, what would you say to going away with me?'

'To India?' The Outer Hebrides also sounded interesting. As Robert had said, Charlotte didn't care much where they went, so long as they went together.

'We could visit your Penelope. And I'd like to show you where I lived. Parts of it, at least,' he corrected himself. 'There are rambling palaces with stonework fine as lace and hidden courtyards filled with flowers and temples grander than our cathedrals, with shrines to gods whose names I could never quite get right.'

'And festivals and elephants and princes wearing rubies as big as your fist?'

'All of that. I can show you India, and when we get back, I'll need you to show me how to get on at Girdings. You'll have to teach me how to be a duke.'

'I don't believe you'll find it that hard,' said Charlotte.

'Only because I have you as duchess. Someone very wise once told me that the trick of land management is to find a clever wife.'

Remembering the scene outside the queen's rooms, Charlotte made a face. 'Grandmama is going to be far too pleased. Did you know that she was scheming all this while to catch you for me?'

Robert blinked. 'I thought I was the blot on the family escutcheon.'

'Yes, but you're a ducal blot,' said Charlotte serenely, 'and that makes all the difference.'

'I didn't notice her flinging me at you,' protested Robert, once the ducal blot had firmly blotted the opprobrious words with kisses. 'Except for the seating at Twelfth Night.'

'Oh, no,' said Charlotte, eyes shining. In the joy of their reconciliation, the pain of it had leached away, leaving only amusement. 'She did you one better than that. She paid Sir Francis Medmenham to court me in the hopes of spurring your interest!'

Robert's brows drew together. 'No,' he said flatly. 'I can't believe—'

'Oh, yes,' said Charlotte, enjoying herself hugely. 'Five thousand pounds' worth of pretend flirting!'

'That interfering old harpy!'

'That does about sum it up,' Charlotte agreed, with a brisk nod.

'That interfering, *ineffectual* old harpy!' Robert choked out, sputtering so hard with laughter, he could hardly speak. 'If she hadn't set Medmenham on you, I would have declared myself far sooner! If it hadn't been so deuced awful, it would be funny. I was so concerned with keeping Medmenham *away* from you—'

'That you thought if you stayed away yourself, he would stay away, too?' Charlotte finished hopefully.

Robert nodded, making a mock-comical face.

Later, she might be indignant about the wasted time. Right now, she was too busy basking in the lovely, warm feeling of knowing that her grandmother's snares had nothing to do with Robert's feelings for her. Not that she had really thought they did, but it was nice to be told, just the same.

'It must be the first time I've ever seen one of Grandmama's schemes go so badly awry,' said Charlotte happily. 'We must be quite, quite sure to tell her. Eventually.'

'We can send her a letter from the ship. Once we're well out of range of her stick.' Looking thoroughly dazed, he shook his head. 'I still can't believe she *paid* Medmenham.'

'I'm sure he used the money to good effect,' Charlotte said cheerfully, 'paying for your orgies.'

'Not my orgies,' Robert was quick to say, tightening his hold on her waist. 'I count myself well rid of the whole lot of them.'

'What do you think will happen to Medmenham now?' asked Charlotte, curling comfortably into the curve of Robert's arm and tucking her feet up beneath her on the bench. 'Did the king punish him for his part in the king-napping?'

'No. There was nothing to prove that he had any involvement in the matter. And given his close relationship to the Prince of Wales, no one wanted to pursue the question.'

'I can see how that would be embarrassing for the king,' said Charlotte thoughtfully. 'It would be tantamount to admitting that his own son might have been plotting to depose him.'

'Let them plot all they like so long as they leave us in peace,' said Robert firmly. 'No more running around after the king in the middle of the night.'

'And you a Gentleman of the Bedchamber!' chided Charlotte.

Robert grinned a pirate's grin. 'His is not the bedchamber in which I have an interest,' he said.

Blushing a deep, pleased pink, Charlotte wiggled off his lap and held out a hand. 'Shall we?' she said breathlessly. 'If we ask the vicar nicely, he can start crying the banns this Sunday.'

Robert took her hand, twining their fingers together in a lover's knot. 'No special licence?' he teased. 'I thought they were all the rage.'

'I like this way better,' said Charlotte, as they strolled through the goose droppings to the little footbridge. As the sun slowly burnt through the mist, the air seemed infused with a celestial quality, a golden glaze that blessed the greening fields and the tangled brush of the home woods. 'Our banns, called in our church, for our tenants. It shows that we belong to them.'

Charlotte had spoken matter-of-factly, but something about her words seemed to strike Robert. 'It has a nice ring, doesn't it?' he said slowly. 'Belonging.'

Charlotte looked out from the footbridge, across the fields where their tenants would graze their sheep in summer, the tangled woods where their children would play, the formal gardens where their daughters would lay trails of tarts to hunt for unicorns. Along the paths lay the bird-pecked remains of the tarts Robert had set for her. It seemed terribly appropriate that the pies that he set out for her should nourish their squirrels and sparrows and swans, all the lovely living things that ran through their land.

And in that moment of magic, as the spring sun slipped through the clouds to dapple the lake with diamonds, Charlotte could have sworn she saw a silvery horn bending to explore the broken bits of jam tart where she and Robert had been sitting only moments before.

On an impulse, she waved.

'What is it?' asked Robert, his fingers twined securely through hers.

'Nothing,' said Charlotte, smiling up at him. 'Just a unicorn.'

Chapter Thirty-Two

In our modern age, we tell tales not of mythical beasts but of machines, those massive contraptions beloved by villains on *The Avengers*, replete with gratuitous knobs and bristling with levers, any one of which could send a deadly ray barrelling towards Earth via the moon and a few random planets. They're the griffins and unicorns of the twenty-first-century lexicon. We've all grown up on them. But I had never expected to see one.

I gawked into the dim interior of the ancient tower, straining against the rainy-day gloom. A huge shape loomed up against the side of the tower, stretching practically the length of the room, bristling with levers, spikes, wheels, and goodness only knew what other protuberances. A constellation of smaller machinery clustered around it, an arsenal of ominous equipment.

I was so absorbed that I never heard the sound of footsteps behind me until a tall form blotted out even such small grey light that the cloudy sky allowed.

'Eloise?' it said, in tones of great incredulity and not a little displeasure.

In my surprise, I lost my precarious hold on the door, which would have banged closed, whapping me soundly in the butt if Colin hadn't grabbed hold of it just in the nick of time.

'The door was unlocked,' I blurted out, sidling around to face him.

'That's not good,' he said, gesturing me out of the doorway. He frowned at the padlock. 'We keep this locked for a reason.'

'I can see why!' I said emphatically. One pull on one of those levers and Mars might be hurtling towards Earth.

'Most of those old mowers have gone rusty,' agreed Colin. 'It's automatic tetanus just from looking at them. And I wouldn't want a child trying to climb into that old harvester.'

'Mowers?' I repeated, craning to peer through the rapidly narrowing slice of door as he prudently closed it behind him. 'Lawn mowers?'

'Scythes, too,' said Colin, fiddling with the lock. 'Rusty and bent out of shape. The odd strimmer. There's even an old Victorian harvester back there. That's the big beast in the back.'

Victorian harvester, indeed! I wanted to scoff at it. But that lump on the side had looked awfully like a lawn mower, hadn't it?

'That's what that was? Garden equipment?'

'Among other rubbish.' Colin's attention was absorbed by the lock, in that classic man-with-tool way. He jiggled the curved bit in and out of the hole, trying to get the clasp to catch. 'There's a graveyard of old bicycles in the far corner where the garderobe used to be. We Selwicks never throw anything out. Ha!'

Colin tugged at the lock with a satisfied air. The fiddly

bit had given up the fight and decided to hold, securing the ancient stronghold of the Selwicks for another day.

'Isn't that dangerous?' I asked, thinking of that damning bit of paper beneath his desk. 'Not throwing things away?'

'I should think you would be pleased,' he said, trying the door one last time to satisfy himself that it had really closed. When I looked blank, he specified, 'Your research.'

'True,' I admitted. Without the Selwick pack-rat tendencies, I would have only the legend of the Pink Carnation to go on, with perhaps a frill of family stories to bolster the tale. But if the Selwicks held on to bits of paper, what else might they be holding on to? People did tend to follow in their parents' professions, for the simple reason that familiarity bred comfort – and connections. There was a reason my father, grandfather, and great-grandfather had all been lawyers. And that sort of tradition would be all the more important in a profession where there were no organised academies, no professional course of study.

Amy and Richard Selwick had started a spy school at this very same Selwick Hall. The spy school had initially been conceived of as a way of training outsiders, but it would have been just as natural for Amy and Richard to raise their children to play the same great game in the pursuit of which they had met. Goodness only knew, the middle and later nineteenth century hadn't lacked for opportunities for espionage.

What if it had continued on, on to this very day?

I looked at Colin as we walked in companionable silence away from the Tower, his hands stuck comfortably in the pockets of his Barbour jacket, his dark blond hair damped with wet, his Wellies comfortably smeared with mud and dead leaves. He looked every inch the English country gentleman,

492

straight out of an issue of *Country Life* – or Joan's magazine, *Manderley*. The thought of Joan brought to mind, with renewed clarity, her enigmatic words in the ladies' room of the Heavy Hart.

'Why do you not like to talk about what you do?' I asked, all in a rush. Blunt – but maybe blunt was what was needed.

Colin looked down at me in surprise. He maintained his casual pose, hands in the pockets, shoulders slightly forwards to accommodate my lesser height, but I didn't miss the glaze of wariness that settled over him.

'What d'you mean?' he asked, with studied ease.

'I found the piece of paper under your desk. About the gold souk – and the guns.'

Colin's eyes closed in an 'Oh, shit' expression. 'So you know.'

'Well, between the paper and all your books, I put two and two together. I heard Joan saying something in the ladies' room the other night,' I added, by way of explanation.

Colin's hazel eyes shifted sideways, towards me. 'I gather she wasn't complimentary.'

'No,' I said apologetically. 'But Sally defended you.'

Colin scuffed his already scuffed Wellies through the withered winter grass. 'I should have mentioned it to you before, but I don't usually like to talk to people about it.'

That was much better than 'Now that you've found out, I'll have to kill you,' or whatever the British equivalent of the witness protection program was. I didn't even know if the British had an equivalent of the witness protection program. I tried to envision myself trying to blend into Nowheresville-on-Thames under an assumed name and failed miserably.

'I can see why you don't like to tell people,' I said

understandingly. 'That would kind of jeopardise your position, wouldn't it? If people knew.'

'Jeopardise my position?'

'You know,' I said, waving my hands in the air. 'Give the game away. I mean, I always wondered how James Bond did his job when everyone knew who he was.'

'That's a good point, I suppose,' he said, in that way people have when you've just said something that's so off the mark, it might as well be in Sanskrit, but they like you, so they want to make something positive out of it so they can give you the credit you both know you don't deserve. 'And it would certainly be an interesting twist on the theme. But I think the reader should know who the main character is, even if the villains don't.'

Now it was my turn to look at him as though he were speaking Sanskrit. 'The reader?'

Colin shrugged self-deprecatingly. 'Potential readers, then. I'd like to think I'll have them eventually.'

Was he talking about his memoirs? 'I thought you didn't want to publicise what you do,' I said, in what I thought was a reasonable tone.

Colin smiled down at me, looking disconcertingly boyish for an international man of mystery. 'Well, I'll have to publicise it eventually, won't I? At least, if it all goes well.'

'Your mission, you mean?' I ventured.

Colin looked at me in confusion. 'My novel,' he said, as though that were self-evident. 'I suppose you could call it a mission, but I think of it more as a vocation.'

'Your *novel*?' The word tasted like a foreign object on my lips. 'But what about – oh! Then all those books – the travel guides . . .'

'All research. For my spy novel. But if you didn't know about the novel, then . . .' His face was a mirror of my own, bearing an identical expression of horrified comprehension as each of us realised just what the other had been talking about all this while.

I could feel my cheeks go a deep, painful red.

Colin rubbed two fingers against the bridge of his nose, as though trying to clear his head. 'So when you saw the books and the travel guides, you thought . . . you didn't really think' – he seemed to have trouble getting the words out – 'that I was a *spy*?'

'Only for about five minutes,' I muttered.

A snorting noise erupted from Colin's nostrils. It sounded like it couldn't decide whether it wanted to be laughter when it grew up.

'What was I supposed to think, with strange men getting murdered in the gold souk?' I demanded spiritedly. 'And there was Joan making cryptic comments in the ladies' room and you not wanting me to get too close to the family archives. You have to admit that it makes a *certain* amount of sense.'

'What did you think, that we had a spy empire?' choked Colin.

'Not an empire,' I said sulkily. It wasn't that ridiculous. OK, maybe it was. But it was his fault for being all strange and cagey about the family history. 'Maybe just a very small spy dukedom.'

The amusement faded from Colin's face as the implications sank in. 'You really believed it, didn't you? I hope you didn't think you were dating the Purple Gentian,' he said sharply.

'I don't see you in any knee breeches,' I retorted.

'I'm not my ancestors,' he warned me. 'I'm not some sort of – Errol Flynn on a rope.'

'You really didn't like that movie, did you?' I mumbled inconsequentially. 'I *know* that. I wouldn't want you to be one of your ancestors. If you were, you'd be dead.'

That one caught him up short for a moment. Folding his arms across his chest, he asked challengingly, 'Are you disappointed that I'm not the spy you thought I was?'

I scowled at him. 'Honestly?' Really, men could be such babies. 'I'm relieved. I wouldn't know the first thing to do with a spy. I was completely freaked out by the whole idea. Do you know the hours of sleep I lost because of that damn piece of paper under your desk?'

'Is that so?' He was still standing in the classic male pose of aggression, arms crossed, legs spread like Errol Flynn on the deck of a pirate ship, but I could see his elbows begin to relax, like cookie dough going soft at the edges in the oven.

Seeing my chance, I sailed into the offensive. 'And what's the deal with people calling you from Dubai at three in the morning?'

'Dubai? Oh.' Understanding dawned. He must have found just the missed calls when he woke up that morning, without having realised there had been predawn alarums. 'Did that wake you up?'

'What do you think, Sherlock?'

Looking harassed, Colin ran a hand roughly through his hair. 'That was a friend from university. He works in Dubai now. Great crunching numbers, but has some difficulties calculating time zones. I just visited him there,' he added unnecessarily. 'On a research trip. For the *book*,' he emphasised.

OK, I got it, I got it. As far as I was concerned, though, Mr Selwick still had some explaining to do.

'Why didn't you just tell me about the book?' I demanded.

'Instead of being all cloak and dagger about it?'

'What would you think of a grown man quitting his job to write a novel? It's a bloody cliché.' There was no mistaking the cri de coeur; the man was so full of angst, he resonated like a tuning fork.

My irritation washed away, subsumed in a tidal wave of intense protectiveness. I wanted to yell at all the other children in the play yard and make them play nicely with him. I could feel myself beginning to ooze sympathy like an underdone soufflé. 'It could have been worse,' I said bracingly. 'It could have been pig farming.'

'Pig farming?'

Oh, right. Colin hadn't been there for that spies/sties discussion. At least now I knew I hadn't been going crazy. Joan had said spies. She had simply meant fictional ones.

'At least writing is a nice, clean job,' I said, warming to my theme. 'And so nicely portable, too.'

'You don't think I'm crazy?' he asked guardedly.

'Only in a good way,' I assured him. 'Anything creative is probably a little crazy. But that's what makes it interesting. And if you have the wherewithal to do it, more power to you.'

'Thanks,' he muttered, shoving his hands in his pockets. 'I think.'

'No, really,' I said, more earnestly this time. 'I think it's splendid. And I want to hear all about it. But why didn't you tell me?' Rather than letting me jump to insane conclusions, I added silently. Fortunately, he chose not to bring up that bit.

Colin shrugged. 'It just seemed a stupid thing to do, leaving a good job to have a go at a novel. A pipe dream.'

'But it's your pipe dream. And if you actually do it, then it's not a pipe dream anymore, it's a career. Writing a spy thriller certainly makes as much sense as what I do,' I said encouragingly. 'It will probably sell a lot better.'

'If it sells at all,' he said.

'What made you decide to do it?' I asked curiously. 'That had to be a hard decision to make.'

'I'd always wanted to. It seemed so irresponsible, though. But then Dad died, and everything seemed' – he held out both hands palms up – 'different,' he finished flatly. 'Everything was different.'

I nodded furiously, keeping my mouth shut, trying to channel sympathy and understanding and encouragement without saying anything, even though, when it came down to it, I knew I couldn't really understand. I could only guess at what it must be like to lose a parent, and to lose a parent relatively young, in a lingering and unpleasant way. I'd never dealt with cancer close up, but it didn't seem a friendly way to go. At least not for the children and loved ones who were left behind.

'We used to watch James Bond movies together,' Colin said, in a voice so low as to be almost inaudible. 'He read everything. Follett, Fleming, le Carré, Forsyth, Deighton.' Some of the names were unfamiliar to me, but I recognised enough of them to guess that we were mostly talking spy thrillers. 'It was only at the end that he told me—'

I cocked my head, indicating interest.

Colin smiled wryly. ' – that he had been in intelligence himself, while he was in the service.'

'Service?' I asked in a very small voice.

'The army,' he translated for my American ears, specifying, 'Twenty-first Lancers.' I could hear the small boy's pride in his voice. 'So there's your spy for you. He was stationed in Germany, Hong Kong, Northern Ireland. And those are only the places he told me about.'

I didn't know what to say. Something about his tone suggested that he wouldn't welcome questions about his father. The entire topic was too, too fraught. I felt like I was playing 'red light, green light, one, two, three,' that child's game where you can only advance by increments when the other person's back is turned. Revelation had to sneak up on him; I couldn't force it. He would tell me what he wanted me to know in his own way, in his own time.

And then there was all that had been said by being unsaid. It made my heart wrench to think of what Colin must have gone through, seeing the centre wrenched out of his world. His change of career seemed in part a reaction to his own mortality, in part a tribute to his father. Either way, it went far deeper than mere fiction.

'I'd love to read what you've written,' I said finally, for lack of anything better to say.

It seemed to be the right thing. 'Thanks,' he said. The hint of a smile played around his lips. 'You know, I did think of writing about the Pink Carnation initially . . .'

'You didn't!' I made noises of exaggerated indignation. 'So that's why you wanted to be rid of me!'

The sound of my own voice made me wince. I was too loud, too strident, hamming it up to drum away the ghosts that seemed to be walking with us through the mist-ridden grounds, like natives clanging cymbals around a campfire to scare away the spirits.

'One of the reasons. There was Serena, too,' he said, and I knew he meant Serena's relationship with a man who had been dating her in hopes of access to their family archives. 'But I did initially think of writing a sort of quasi-history, starting with the Purple Gentian and ending with Dad.'

'I'm glad you didn't,' I said teasingly, sliding my arm through his. 'I'd hate to think of us being in competition. Not to mention that novels sell much better than histories.'

'Tell that to Joan,' he said dryly, but his arm tightened around mine.

'Why did you even bother to tell her?' I asked. Stupid of me, I know, but it bothered me that she had known before I had. She might be annoying, but she was quite attractive in her own way. And she had known Colin far longer. She had known his sister and his parents and the boy he had been before his father's death. It all made me feel a little bit insecure.

'I had hoped she might put me in touch with her agent,' he admitted. 'She wasn't too chuffed at the notion.'

'Won't she feel like an idiot when you're a best seller!' I declared loyally. Too loyally. I was like a one-woman brass band.

'Eloise?' I tilted my head up to find Colin looking at me understandingly. 'It's OK.'

He didn't have to explain what he meant. It was a little bit of everything: his father, the book, my silly assumptions, Joan. And it really was OK. We had, without my even realising it, overleaped an indefinable hurdle and landed safely on the other side. I was still getting used to the notion of Colin as novelist, but I found that I liked it. I certainly liked it better than the notion of Colin as spy. Of course, if I were a spy, trying to hide my secret identity from my girlfriend, isn't that just the sort of cover story I would come up with?

Oh, no. I wasn't letting myself go down that road again. Even if it might be a rather interesting road.

'I know,' I said. And then, rather nonsensically, 'I like you.'

Colin's eyes crinkled at the corners in that way I already knew so well. Funny how you can come to know someone's gestures, their mannerisms, so well, while knowing so little else about them at all. But I was learning.

'I like you, too,' he said. And then he grinned. 'But no more Errol Flynn.'

Everyone always does tell me that relationships require compromise. And if I wanted this to be a real one . . .

'OK,' I said. 'Tonight we'll watch Bond. Just for you. But tomorrow I get *The Scarlet Pimpernel*.'

'It's a deal,' said Colin.

Historical Note

In February of 1804, George III went mad. It wasn't the first time. The king had famously gone round the bend in 1788, precipitating both a crisis of government and the movie *The Madness of King George*. The formerly model monarch gave way to wild fits of lust, making lewd suggestions to ladies of the court, developing a fixation with the queen's ageing lady-in-waiting, Lady Pembroke, and, according to her own report, forcing his daughter-in-law Princess Caroline to leap over the back of a sofa to escape from his amorous advances (given Princess Caroline's relationship with the royal family and her level of personal hygiene, one has to take that claim with more than a few grains of salt).

I took many of the details of the king's illness in 1804 straight from the historical record. Like his other illnesses in 1788 and 1801, this one was heralded by rapid speech, agitation, and stomach pain. The king dismissed all of his pages and sundry Gentlemen of the Bedchamber. The Willis brothers, who had tended the king in his two previous illnesses, were flatly refused entrance, and a new doctor, Dr Simmons of St Luke's Hospital for Lunatics, was summoned. Upon Dr Simmons's arrival, he clapped the king into a straitjacket. The king was blistered, purged, and bled. An account of the king's treatments can be found in

Christopher Hibbert's *George III: A Personal History*. For those who wish to know more about treatment of the mentally ill in Georgian Britain generally, I recommend Jonathan Andrews' *Undertaker of the Mind: John Monro and Mad-Doctoring in Eighteenth-Century England*. For the behaviour of the queen and princesses during the king's crises, I relied heavily upon Flora Fraser's *Princesses: The Six Daughters of George III*. Fanny Burney, Charlotte's favourite author, kept a journal during the king's first illness, providing invaluable details about the king's appearance and behaviour. Charlotte's colloquy with the king in the library is heavily based upon Burney's accounts of her own conversations with the mad king.

There, however, reality ends and fiction takes over. Unlike the king's earlier illness, the queen was not forbidden the king's chamber in 1804. The Prince of Wales did throw his oar in, lobbying for a regency (Princess Sophia's irritated comment to Charlotte about her brother was taken from a letter she wrote to Theresa Villiers in 1804), but without any success. The French plot and the kidnapping are entirely my own invention. After treatment by Dr Simmons, the king recovered relatively rapidly and held on to his marbles until his final lapse into madness in 1810.

Would it have been possible for a spy to kidnap and replace the king? While it certainly didn't happen (at least, not that we know of), I don't believe it would have been outside the realms of possibility. Despite assassination attempts in 1786 and 1800, the king showed remarkably little concern for his personal safety. Burney's journals recount the king (while still sane) slipping off entirely alone, without any attendants, to visit friends in Kew, causing the anxious queen to come searching for him (as Burney reports, 'Yes,' [the king] cried, 'I ran here without speaking to anybody'). One of the most surprising facts I learnt in the course of researching *Crimson Rose* was that the king's bedchamber in Buckingham House opened directly into the Great Library. Public access to the library was provided through the binderies in the basement floor. The presence of pages and other members of the king's household would have ensured a certain modicum of security, but the sheer size of the king's household would have also made it relatively easy for interlopers to infiltrate unnoticed.

By 1804, the royal court was no longer the centre of political power and patronage it had once been (a fact that Charlotte's grandmother, reared in an earlier era, finds hard to grasp), but it was still an immense and complex entity that employed a plethora of people from all walks of life, from the Earl of Winchelsea, the King's Groom of the Stole, all the way down to the seamstresses and starchers who dealt with His Majesty's linen. For those interested in the workings of the royal household, I recommend the exhaustive report prepared by the Institute of Historical Research, *Office-Holders in Modern Britain (Volume 11): Court Officers, 1660 – 1837*, which lists every single office in the king's and queen's households as well as the individual holders of those offices (just in case you feel a burning need to know the name of every one of the queen's maids of honour). The chapter on the later Hanoverian court in Anne Somerset's *Ladies in Waiting* provides a more general overview of life in the queen's household, while Fanny Burney's journals present a detailed personal account of the odd mix of formality and informality that made up day-to-day life with Their Majesties.

Most of the action in the novel takes place in the Queen's House, now known as Buckingham Palace. Although St James's Palace was still the ceremonial centre of royal life, the setting for the king's formal levees on Wednesdays and Fridays and the Queen's Drawing Rooms on Thursdays and Sundays, the royal family preferred to live in Buckingham House, which the king had purchased for Queen Charlotte in 1762. For those of you who have noticed that the palace looks rather different, it was; the building was extensively remodelled in 1847. For the details of the palace's design and interior decoration in 1804, I am deeply indebted to Jane Roberts's *George III and Queen Charlotte: Patronage, Collecting and Court Taste*.

Like Buckingham House, Medmenham Abbey is a real location. In 1752, Sir Francis Dashwood founded the Order of the Friars of St Francis of Wycombe, known to posterity (although not to its members) as the Hellfire Club, providing inspiration for generations of libertines to come. Geoffrey Ashe's *The Hell-Fire Clubs: A History of Anti-Morality* provides a thoughtful and thorough account of both Sir Francis's club and those that preceded and followed it. As always, for the purposes of the story, I took some liberties with the record. I decided to place the Lotus Club's orgies in the caves, even though Ashe states that, contrary to popular legend, the group's revels probably took place inside the Abbey. Although the layout of the caves, including the River Styx, is much as I described, I added an anteroom to the back of the Banqueting Chamber and a ladder leading up to the mausoleum. Likewise, while the golden orb on top of the Church of St Lawrence was indeed hollow and designed to seat several guests, I moved it to the back of the church and made it accessible only by portable ladder.

As for the revels of the Order of the Lotus, they are very loosely based on the orgies of the Monks of Medmenham, combined with a few practices borrowed from a similar group that set up shop in Poona, in British India, in 1813. The

Asiatic trappings represent a hodgepodge of unrelated elements appropriated, willy-nilly, for their exotic flavour. (Neither Wrothan nor Medmenham was particularly concerned with cultural accuracy.) Despite the genuine setting, Sir Francis Medmenham was entirely a figment of my imagination; upon the death of Sir Francis Dashwood (by then, Baron Le Despenser), Medmenham Abbey and its grounds were inherited by Sir John Dashwood-King, not the fictional Sir Francis Medmenham.

Tempted to unmask more flowery spies?

Read on for further details of the
Pink Carnation series . . .

To order visit our website at
www.allisonandbusby.com
or call us on
020 7580 1080

The Secret History of the Pink Carnation

By LAUREN WILLIG

Nothing goes right for Eloise. The one day she wears her new suede boots, it rains cats and dogs. When the tube stops short, she's always the one thrown into some stranger's lap. Plus, she's had more than her share of misfortune in the way of love. In fact, after she realises romantic heroes are a thing of the past, she decides it's time for a fresh start.

Eloise is also determined to finish her dissertation on that dashing pair of spies, the Scarlet Pimpernel and the Purple Gentian. But what she discovers is something the finest historians have missed: the secret history of the Pink Carnation – the most elusive spy of all time. As she works to unmask this obscure spy, Eloise stumbles across answers to all kinds of questions. How did the Pink Carnation save England from Napoleon? What became of the Scarlet Pimpernel and the Purple Gentian? And will Eloise Kelly escape her bad luck and find a living, breathing hero of her own?

The Masque of the
Black Tulip

By LAUREN WILLIG

'If modern manhood had let me down, at least the past boasted
brighter specimens. To wit, the Scarlet Pimpernel,
the Purple Gentian and the Pink Carnation, that dashing trio
of spies who kept Napoleon in a froth of rage and the feminine
population of England in another sort of froth entirely.'

Modern-day student Eloise Kelly has achieved a great academic
coup by unmasking the elusive spy the Pink Carnation, who saved
England from Napoleon. But now she has a million questions
about the Carnation's deadly nemesis, the Black Tulip. And she's
pretty sure that her handsome on-again, off-again crush Colin
Selwick has the answers somewhere in his family's archives.
While searching through Lady Henrietta's old letters and diaries
from 1803, Eloise stumbles across an old codebook and discovers
something more exciting than she ever imagined: Henrietta and
her old friend Miles Dorrington were on the trail of the Black
Tulip and had every intention of stopping him in his endeavour to
kill the Pink Carnation. But what they didn't know was that while
they were trying to find the Tulip – and trying not to fall in love in
the process – the Black Tulip was watching them . . .

The Deception of the Emerald Ring

By LAUREN WILLIG

*'All in readiness. An unmarked carriage will be waiting for you
behind the house at midnight . . .'*

History student Eloise Kelly is in London looking for more
information on the activities of the infamous 19th century spy, the
Pink Carnation, while at the same time trying to keep her mind
off the fact that her mobile phone is not ringing and her would-be
romantic hero Colin Selwick is not calling.

Eloise is finally distracted from checking for messages every
five minutes by the discovery of a brief note, sandwiched amongst
the papers she's poring over in the British Library. Signed by Lord
Pinchingdale, it is all Eloise needs to delve back in time and unearth
the story of Letty Alsworthy and the Pink Carnation's espionage
activities on the Emerald Isle . . .

The Seduction of the Crimson Rose

By LAUREN WILLIG

⌘

Hoping to track down the true identity of the elusive French spy the Black Tulip, graduate student Eloise Kelly delves ever deeper into the archives at the British Library and the family papers of her boyfriend Colin Selwick, the modern-day descendant of her Napoleonic spy subjects. As she becomes ever more entwined with Colin, her research brings her closer to uncovering the Black Tulip's true identity.

Determined to secure another London season without assistance from her new brother-in-law, Mary Alsworthy accepts a secret assignment from Lord Vaughn on behalf of the Pink Carnation: to infiltrate the ranks of the dreaded French spy, the Black Tulip, before he and his master can stage their planned invasion of England. Every spy has a weakness, and for the Black Tulip that weakness is black-haired women – his 'petals' of the Tulip. A natural at the art of seduction, Mary easily catches the attention of the French spy, but Lord Vaughn never anticipates that his own heart will be caught as well. Fighting their growing attraction, impediments from their past, and, of course, the French, Mary and Vaughn find themselves lost in the shadows of a treacherous garden of lies.